AFTERTASTE

Lori Jean Phipps

ISBN-13: 978-1475212631
ISBN-10: 1475212631

Printed in the U. S. A.

Lori Jean Phipps
AFTERTASTE

In an all-night culinary quest and wine soiree embarked on the eve of Fourth of July, the correlation between food cravings and men are explored and devoured. Melody Rae Murphy convinces her friend Katarina (Kat) Ramirez to go on an emotional journey to commemorate her relationship fiascos while creating the ideal seafood entrée: salmon baked with mango and brie. Reliving her past she is left with a tart, greasy, spicy, bitter and salty aftertaste longing for something sweeter.

Knowing there are other "fish in the sea" and after reading an exorbitant amount of self-help books, Melody Rae feels prepared to take a fresh step toward change. The extent of her quandary is determinate on whether she is inherently capable of curbing her unhealthy cravings and altering her future to no longer attract a poor quality fish (a stale entrée), but rather a fancier cuisine (an elite main course), or destined to remain single and yo-yo diet in her relationships for eternity.

*Note: one hundred most beautiful words in the English language assimilated throughout the novel.
deshoda.com/words/100-most-beautiful-words-in-the-english-language/

Lori Jean Phipps

To Single Women Everywhere

If you are a woman who still believes true love exists, despite suffering deeply in past relationships, then this book is for you. I extend deep appreciation to my angelica mother, *Colleen Phipps*, and closest friends who have let me verbally throw up, in e-mails, and in person with endless analysis and self-interpretation. You have all been my therapists—*Gayle Elliott, Terry Schimke, Alicia Takacs, Elizabeth Porter, Danielle Perryman, Frances Alston, Kathy Orona, Marea Thompson, MariAnn Lucena, Carrol DeBusk* and *Likelee Snook*—thank you for your unwavering faith, love and support on my personal journey.

Contents

Lori Jean Phipps

Fish Bones

"My soul knew he was the right guy for me."

Are you kidding me? Come on! I mean, who actually verbalizes something like that? Seriously?! Fine, I know. Elitist women, who meander around town in a brand new, shiny, silver, convertible Porsche Carrera GT, wearing Louis Vuitton Evasion sunglasses and a six hundred dollar Lanvin-Palm silk scarf sipping a Starbucks coffee and driving leisurely along—just below the speed limit on a weekday—because they don't have to work for a living. Yeah, you know the ones. Of course, their soul knew he was the right guy. Their soul saw the money symbol reflection in his Louis Vuitton's. I sound so bitter. I'm not. I'm just jealous. I want to spend one thousand, two hundred dollars on a pair of sunglasses. No, I don't. Yes, I do. The sunglasses I own were purchased at a local gas station for less than ten dollars. Ridiculous as it may sound I love them—they totally make me look sexy—but that's not the point! I merely want the option to shop for sunglasses at a sunglass specialty store if I so desire.

Admittedly, I do have several girlfriends who are (cough) happily married. But no, they are not independently wealthy, or married to successful, rich gentlemen. Still, I don't know how many women can honestly say their soul knew, certainly not me. Do you ever wonder if after a certain amount of time it's too late? I do.

After having a myriad of relationships with an eclectic variety of men, I still do not know what *that* means: "my soul knew." My soul knew what? I mean, what does the soul feel like when it recognizes its true love counterpart anyway? And can I trust my "soul" to be capable of recognizing the right guy for me, seriously? Currently in my early forties and still single because I have not met any guy who I could say with complete certainty is the right guy for me. I believe I will always manage to have a scintilla of doubt. I am good at doubt—doubt comes natural to me. *Thanks dad.* I am convinced there is such a thing as a doubt gene. Though, I obtained a wealth of effervescent optimism from my fetching Patricia Clarkson-esque mother, Katherine Lee, I also received a heavy dose of pessimism from my adoring dad, Aaron, who despite being one of the most entertaining and personable people around (similar to NFL football quarterback Terry Bradshaw), has a pessimistic side, which of course, he merely considers to mean he's a realist. And this is why I would go into a relationship with extreme idealistic hope and then ultimately sabotage it by thinking too much. *Thanks again, dad.*

Certainly there were times in my past when I labored in thought with innocent eyes and naïve hope. *Maybe this guy is the perfect one for me?* But more time spent in the relationship would prove my apparent instincts were blatantly wrong. The more time invested, the more doubt would incur. I wholeheartedly believe ignorance is bliss. The fewer experiences I had and the less I knew about the reality of relationships, the more blind faith and optimism I incurred about my future.

Contrary to other women who have found that over time their love for their partner deepened, time did not make my heart grow fonder, quite the opposite. My heart didn't feel more secure over a longer duration of time spent in a relationship; it felt anxiety, and more than a little twinge. It became suspicious and wary, developing emotional heartburn.

Here's my problem: I think I have one. And I'm not even Jewish, and only slightly neurotic. In hindsight, I should have been Jewish. Life might have made more sense and been much simpler. I'd probably be married by now. Jewish men get me. I can't believe I've never dated a Jewish guy. *Aha!* Well there you go, a problem I can fix, I suppose. I will have to put more thought into such a prospective scenario, later.

First, I need to concentrate on becoming healthier—emotionally, physically and spiritually.

Here is my pattern: I get involved on an emotionally deep and thoroughly intense level rather quickly only to discover that the more I know about my partner, the more villainous and unattractive he becomes. Yes, I said villainous. This is not an exaggeration. I always seem to attract men with hidden, unusual, peculiar issues; dangerous, even.

I am resigned to accept my fate, assuming it is my destiny to have relationships with a variety of damaged and unhealthy types of men—helping them to heal in some facet or another—only to be left alone and shattered with deep emotional scars to prove it. Conceivably, it was my subconscious attempt to evolve into a more mature, well-rounded and well-seasoned character. *Ha!* At this point I think I have enough character to last me until the end of time, thank you very much. I did not know then what I know now. If I had known eating healthier was the solution, I could have saved myself a lot of heartache, not to mention time.

Before my recent breakthrough of discovering how my eating habits played such a huge role in the types of mates I attracted, I deduced it wasn't anything I had control over surmising it was my destiny to continually repeat the same lessons over and over again. Since I was the type of woman who needed a heap of tangible experiences before I'd listen to that small voice of reason looming in my head, it was not astonishing when I continued to repeatedly attract the same types of men.

For me that voice of reason (my brain) was not in charge. My brain, (although a logical, highly astute, brave soldier of the Army) was living in the neo-cortex—the barracks. My heart, (although a soft, yet, controlling commander of the platoon) was stationed in the aorta—the imperial office.

As we all know, the heart supplies blood and oxygen to the body allowing the brain to function properly. Therefore, nothing can be accomplished without approval from the heart, which explains why my heart ruled, at least for many, many years of my adult life, causing my relationship history to be so tumultuous. The commander (the heart) would ignore the soldier's (the brain's) inquiries with anxiety or resistance. For a long time my brain was a responsible, righteous soldier and did what the heart told it to. It wasn't until much later in life that the soldier felt privileged enough to interact with the commander and create some sort of balance. This is not to say that balance has totally been achieved, but at least the work in progress has begun to take form.

In younger years my heart was similar to a little five year old, innocently viewing the world through rose-colored glasses. My heart loved falling in love, with the idea of love, anyway. A pure intrinsic joy and pleasure comes from being loved. An obsessive, heart-pounding, euphoric thrill erupts when someone else feels that similar intense, magnetic-pole of attraction and connection, generating indescribably overwhelming feelings of contentment. Clearly this is why whenever involved in a romantic relationship, my heart ruled and won against my brain every single time.

I gather all these experiences were molding me into the person I wanted to become and without those escapades I would not have evolved into the person I am today, so in that regard I am thankful for them. I acknowledge how I needed every relationship encounter (good and bad) in order to reach a higher level of understanding of myself. Otherwise, I wouldn't have been ready for a meaningful and healthier experience…blah, blah, blah. *I get it. Fine!* But some people only require one, maybe two, relationships in their lifetime. Did I honestly have to endure so many?

It wasn't until after I began dating, in my late teenage years, that I had experiences which deeply scarred that blissfully innocent girl inside me. My childhood relationships didn't tarnish me, my adulthood ones did.

By age forty that little girl was no longer little, she was all grown up. And although now she wore contacts (most of the time), her glasses had scratched lenses and a slightly bent frame with clear scotch tape holding the nose-piece up. The little girl was not completely beyond repair. Obviously she is still here retaining a semblance of hope for what the future might bring.

Paradoxically, the periods in my life when I struggled financially and wasn't eating healthy were also the times when I wasn't in a hungry position to date anyone. For several years I wasn't hungry for anything lasting or of substance. I would seek a quick taste and then off to my next short-term relationship disaster. Eating well was not of primary concern, my education was. During those years I'd been living off of tuna fish, leftovers, greasy fast food, sweets and admittedly an exorbitant amount of top ramen, I was attracting men who were similar to the items I'd consumed; cheap, convenient and simple, requiring very little effort from me, which in retrospect was perfect for me at the time.

The correlation between my food cravings and the types of men I craved became transparent. When the successful efflorescence of my career manifested and I was eating healthy fresh foods and working out, I was attracting a higher quality man: the George Clooney type. When I was struggling and eating frugally, I was attracting unhealthy and shoddy, the lowest on the totem: the Charlie Sheen's of the world. *Sorry, Charlie.* It became evident that my food cravings were reflected in my relationships.

It's true; when I went through a phase of eating an ample amount of junk food, I dated a lot of garbage. No wonder I had been feeling sick to my stomach. I knew I needed to start craving a classier entrée when I found myself dating my brother's alcoholic, stoner friends. I inferred, since I could finally afford to spend more, I should expect more, and so I am.

In the past, supportive girlfriends would always comfort me after a break up by saying: "There are other fish in the sea." They were right. I decided to no longer eat day old leftovers, junk food, imitation crab and processed products. I was done with artificial. I wanted the real thing: the highest quality fish with no fish bones (red flags) popping up.

This book is an account of my relationship history and the importance of all the learning that took place after the heartache. Like many, I endured the pain of a repeatedly broken heart mingled with feelings of empathy, friendship, passion, love and commitment—and without red wine I may never have emotionally survived.

Welcome to my world.
Melody Rae

Chapter One

How do fish go into business? They start on a small scale!

Salmon Baked with Mango and Brie

Delicate salmon is topped with a wonderful combination of tangy mango and rich brie cheese. The best part is the brie bakes with the luxurious salmon.

July 3, 2011

Typical Daily Food Choices:
Kona coffee—black, no sugar
Quaker oatmeal w/raw honey, walnuts, pistachios, cranberries, blueberries & raisins
fresh broccoli, zucchini, orange bell pepper, acorn squash, sweet potatoes, brown rice & real unsalted butter
shrimp, cod, halibut, salmon
mixed greens, olives, artichoke, cilantro, avocados, sunflower seeds, cucumber, cherry tomatoes w/vinegar & olive oil dressing
feta cheese tortellini pasta w/pesto sauce
Trader Joe's soy chorizo
bottled water
green tea: Lipton
quality red wines: Clos du Bois or Rodney Strong

Kat's Cottage

Glass of Rodney Strong Old Vines Zinfandel 2000 in one hand, Marianne Williamson's self-help book *A Return to Love* in the other with the hit pop song *"Red, Red Wine"* by UB40 unobtrusively playing in the background, I floated aimlessly around my lagoon style swimming pool sitting in a Baja floating lounger wearing a luxurious ViX brick red one-piece swimsuit feeling at peace and relishing the warm eighty-

15

nine degree sun beating down on my face. I'd just finished reading an intense chapter on metaphysics and the last sentence was lingering in my mind: *"Our devotion then becomes our work, and our work becomes our devotion."*

That's it! I know what I need to do. I need to find my passion, my devotion, my niche. I set the book down on the walnut travertine tile ledge, rolled my shoulders, took a sip of wine and a deep breath followed by a moan. Immediately after reaching over to turn the volume up on the portable radio to hear the song *"Red, Red, Wine"* louder, it ended. Considering I had the station dialed to KBQB 92.7 FM it was not surprising another favorable song came on after. The song *"My Baby Loves Me Just the Way That I Am"* by Martina McBride came streaming through and I couldn't be happier. It's almost as if the station could read my mind and sense my moods. The station plays a tapestry of various styles of music that naturally uplift my spirit; every song a delicious surprise. *I love you BOB FM. If you were a man I'd marry you.*

Looking at the crystal clear water around me, I noticed the reflection of the pine trees on top of the water fluttering in the warm wind as if they were dancing to the country rhythm on the radio; even the trees were mesmerized by BOB.

I was unaware my head began to rock back and forth as I watched in amusement as the telephone pole reflection did what looked to be an interpretive dance. Supposedly, I needed a break from the quiet solitude because I began to sing along with the radio in my wretchedly out-of-tune, raspy voice capable of shattering glass, but, of course, to my own ears sounding identical to Martina. I stood and began to dance in the pool as if I was the star of my own movie. Luckily, I lived in the isolated, bucolic mountains of McCloud, California, in a remote location where the closest neighbor was at least a half-acre away, so I could safely assume I would have no interruptions or complaints to my off-key singing voice, which was good because I felt like belting the lyrics without being ostracized. Singing every word with deep emotional conviction brought me to a vehemently spiritually place. Unconditionally accepting and loving myself for who I am, just as I am, I belted out the corresponding final verse as I reached the top steps of the pool. The comparable words hit me like a ton of books. *Oh great! I'm an egotistical narcissist.* After reading too many self-help books I actually need help.

My black and white cocker spaniel dog, Oreo, and my tiny white Maltese dog, Marshmallow, who were my only critical audience, willingly stood from relaxed sleeping positions to applaud with a bark and a howl. In my experience, unlike humans, pets can always be counted on to be there for you. I giggled and sighed with bittersweet acceptance. Sadly, of the many relationships I've endured, not once had I felt loved just the way that I am. Regardless that I truly did love myself just the way that I am, maybe there should be a limit to how many self-help books a person is allowed to read. Perhaps, if you still need help after reading more than thirty self-help books, it might be time to seek professional help. *Stop it, Melody Rae. You're fine!* Fixating on only a purely supportive inner dialogue, I smiled, wrapped myself in a large, red, bohemian, chic cover-up (I hastily ordered from Bloomingdales online paying way more than it's worth), and while holding tightly to my wine glass doing best not to spill what little remained, gamboled toward the back porch.

Stumbling blithely up the porch steps, I did not realize until moments after that I had stepped casually, barefoot, half-naked and dripping wet over a veritable long and ample two-inch thick tiger snake which was moving steadily and horizontally along the crevice of the highest step. For a brief second I froze mid-stride, posing on one foot and constricting my abdomen with mouth wide open in an inaudible scream. No sound would come out; fear trumped my vocal chords. Fortunately, my arm felt empowered enough to grab the screen door and hurtle my body inside, slamming the log cabin style door behind me. Shaking with anguish, I took a deep breath.

"I'm okay...I'm okay...I'm okay," I repeated with clenched fists and squinted eyes.

My dad told me when I stubbornly elected to move up into the mountains that tiger snakes were commonly found in the country but were not considered harmful. *Must remember this.* That is, of course, not harmful unless unexpectedly stepped on or provoked. Shaking my head side-to-side a chill ran up my spine reliving the creepy snake sighting. A small high pitched squeal escaped my lungs as I rewrapped my overly-priced luxury robe around myself in a warm thankful to be alive embrace.

"Get over it," I said to myself with a self-berating attitude.

Entering the living room I noticed, next to the spicy Italian cookbook, the Shaun T. Hip-Hop Abs DVD was staring at me with condescension from the light oak glass coffee table. *N-o-o-o, not now! Jeez, enough with the guilt.* I grabbed the video case and took a hard look at Shaun T's sexy abs on the front cover wishing I had his self-discipline. Accepting that I don't, I tossed them into the adjacent study room onto my desk where I imagine they'll stay for eternity. The only thing I craved right then was to hear the Tone Loc song *"Wild Thing"* to motivate my body and spirit, indulge in a guilty pleasure of tomato basil and feta cheese tortellini pasta with rich pesto sauce, and drink more red wine. It's four-thirty in the afternoon. *I am NOT exercising!*

This triggered an epiphany. There was a time in my younger years when I was something of a *wild* thing. I recall my food cravings were as spicy as my male interests. For a period of time, Sriracha hot chili and Tabasco sweet and spicy pepper sauce complimented every fast food Mexican dish I ordered. No wonder the men I attracted then were savage types, elucidating why I had become uncharacteristically uninhibited and behaved with wild abandon.

I was convinced the choices I'd made in the past forty years with food and men had gone hand in hand. My eating patterns were identical to my relationship patterns; both were obsessions for me. Exhibit #A: naming both of my dogs after junk food. *Hello? This in itself says volumes about my mindset.* For the first time in my life I was craving equipoise rather than instant gratification. Incontestably, I needed to stop craving junk food or else be resigned to expect to attract junk into my life.

Feeling the necessity to write these thoughts down, I snatched a sticky note off the desk in the study. I'd always been a note-taker (eight years of college will do that to a person) and besides seeing something in writing helps me to follow through. I wrote:

PLEDGE TO SELF:
1) Take time to eat healthier—cook unusual, fascinating and enticingly rich flavorful meals with substance.
2) Replenish heart with flavonoids—drink heavy doses of green tea.
3) Find time to exercise—30 minutes <u>every day.</u>

I had to underline the words "every day." I know myself, if I skip one day, it's too easy to skip two days and then two becomes three and before long I fall into desuetude: no longer exercising at all. *All right, what next?* I pondered the idea of becoming healthier, visualizing what it would emotionally feel like and what type of guy I would want to attract. If I want the man I choose to spend time with affect me in the same way the food I eat does, essentially I want them to fill me up. In every past relationship I've done all the cooking (all the work), naturally filling them up. It was time for me to get something in return; a refreshing equal exchange.

Suspecting that eliminating junk food from the menu would remove the crap out of my life, I sighed with regret, convinced this would mean I had to give up my Fruit Stripe chewing gum habit as it was unhealthy and oddly similar to the men from my past—a short term fix which gave me a rush but never lasted long. I'd only been comfortable with the short-term experience because I lacked trust in my choices. I had a deep fear of choosing the wrong guy and ending up miserable, subconsciously hoping they would fail. Justifiably, the showman, non-committed fling type was unquestionably idyllic. However, dating a guy who is overly energetic, exciting and adventurous feels good at first, but so does the first bite of a Hostess Twinkie. The days of risking nemesis by devouring the golden sponge cake, where a sugary aftertaste generates a feeling of pure exhaustion and all I crave is a long nap, were over.

At the age of forty-four, I felt physically twenty-five, but emotionally sixty. No longer craving a "Twinkie" quick fix to my love life and willing and ready to not settle for cheap, disposable and artificial things lacking of substance, I set out to attract someone healthy. I dearly wanted to be left with the same feeling I receive from a healthy sip of quality red wine; peace and tranquility with a pleasant aftertaste.

I was finally willing to take the necessary time to develop a real and lasting, opposite-sex relationship in my life. Realizing, as in the creation of a good entrée via a good relationship, quality time is necessary and quintessential.

I grabbed another sticky note to add to the first:

4) No more quick meals on the go.
5) No more boxes of Kraft macaroni and cheese, canned tuna fish on white bread sandwiches, top ramen or Hostess Twinkies.

After applying the notes to the fridge where they can prevent me from grabbing something unwholesome, I stopped to consider the most delicious meal I would desire.

Walking to the corner edge of the kitchen counter, I snagged one of the several unopened cookbooks crammed behind the empty breadbox collecting dust. After blowing off years of accumulated lint, I sat to find something to satisfy my complex palate. The pages were saturated with deliriously enticing photos of savory seafood entrées and exquisitely delectable desserts. *O-o-o-o-o-oh, that's what I want!* Luxurious pan seared salmon with creamy avocado rémoulade sauce and a slice of rich New York cheesecake. I emphatically wanted a lasting flavor. I didn't always.

After all the rich inner contemplation over this new food philosophy of attraction theory I had the urge to call Kat, one of my therapy-friendly friends. Katarina Lee Ramirez is her full legal name, the one she was given at birth. Her parents are the only ones who refer to her as Katarina, however. When she was in kindergarten and a lissome little girl she thought her name was annoyingly lengthy and made her sound like a ballerina. Her parents deeply wanted her to become a ballerina, but she despised ballet; although her congenital lithe figure would have made her a prime candidate. I suppose shortening her name was in resistance to her parents. Ever since I met her, twelve years ago, she insisted she be called Kat. I don't profess to understand everything about my friends, although I do accept all aspects of their quirky natures, as they do mine. She confided in me the issue she had with her real birth name, saying I was one of the few who knew. Most of her friends think her actual legal first name is Kat.

Perplexing how simpatico Kat and I are, considering we come from complete opposite status levels and work in entirely different fields. Although I had an impoverished childhood, I managed to get an education and become a successful business owner of Petite Paws; a stylish pet grooming salon specializing in small breed (toy) dogs in Mount Shasta. And Kat, who was raised in upper-middle class suburbia, is a well-respected neurologist at Mercy Medical Center; a county hospital located in Redding. Both of us are caregiving, enabling type women who share a similar spiritual perspective on life, which categorically bonds us and ultimately what matters when it comes to friendship.

Precisely as I picked up my red Galaxy Android cellular smartphone about to dial Kat's number on speed dial, it dawned on me how superfluous it is that everything I own has to be red: my bathing suit, laptop computer, couch, bed spread, Jeep Cherokee, even my leather jacket—all red. It is a subconscious snap decision to choose red whenever I make a purchase, something I do without thinking. I mean, is it necessary I choose red for everything? No, but I do anyway.

I was anxious to hear Kat's reaction to my inspirational theory for change, predicting she would have some insight, which would aid me on this quest. I knew she'd be capable of comprehending my epiphanies and help me to further understand myself. We both agree that self-analysis is a healthy way to prevent repeating past mistakes. And Kat thrived on unusual self-realizations—the more bizarre, the more intrigued she was. She often said at the end of our conversations: "Call me if anything weird happens."

Weird to the both of us meant a good thing, something unique, inspiring and profound; worthy of a call. I was certain my awareness about food cravings and their connection to my relationships fit our weird category and warranted a call. I know she'd call me if she had a similar brain jolt. She loves discussing relationships and how the mind interprets the world, which isn't surprising considering she's a woman and a neurologist. For me this revelation was a bright fluorescent light bulb of hope inspiring insight into why my relationship choices have resulted in utter failure.

My thoughts were whirling faster than my fingers could press number five on speed dial. Kat picked up instantly. In retrospect, I should have waited to call until after I changed out of my bathing suit, but the bothersome dampness of my suit constricting my body and the passionate need to share my brilliant theory overruled practicality. And as a consequence of not owning a blue-tooth ear device for my cellphone, I had to twirl ridiculously about trying to maintain balance while avoiding dropping the phone.

You know you have a true friend when you feel comfortable enough to change your clothes while continuing a conversation on the phone, not an easy task. After I removed my ViX bathing suit, put on a white Fashion Bug bra and pulled up my red Joe Boxer cotton underwear and red spandex shorts, I was confronted with an obstacle. While attempting to slip on a white Danskin tank top over my head, my elbow went through the neck part of the tank top and I got tangled up, hopping clumsily backward and falling onto the bed. Although I did manage to keep the phone snug to my ear and not miss a beat in conversation.

After I shared my theory with Kat, her response was like a volcanic explosion of enthusiasm inspiring me even more.

"Holy f…udge!" she squealed, censoring herself (her daughter most likely nearby). "I was a total top ramen addict during my residency. It was just so cheap and convenient!"

"I know!" I yelped with delight.

"Time to start eating lobster."

"Exactly!"

We laughed simultaneously. For the both of us it was a numinous realization to know our personal relationship lives could change for the better simply by changing our eating habits.

First thing to do: find the optimum healthy fish entrée to emulate the characteristics of mister right. The following day was the Fourth of July, and since neither of us had to work we promptly devised a plan to engage in an all-night soiree at Kat's place (after her daughter is in bed asleep) to nurture ourselves with a well-deserved dinner and wine affair; convinced that satisfying our palates with a rich and heart healthy meal will diverge ourselves of our past poor-eating-habits and cleanse our souls to begin a new phase in our lives. Cooking while eating, drinking and gossiping is an excellent form of girl-therapy which incontrovertibly resolves past failed relationships. *Everyone knows this*. I have no doubt this fact is documented somewhere.

After our phone conversation ended, I went into the living room and picked up the remote control to change the music to The Coffee House radio station on Sirius XM to hear something acoustic to help me relax and focus. I was in the mood for a little John Mayor, but when I went to change the station I began channel surfing. When I came upon the Food Network, showing *Emeril Live* with Emeril John Lagasse, I was compelled to click on it. The episode had only been on for less than five minutes and what was he preparing?—a salmon recipe. *I know!* When I saw he was preparing a salmon baked with mango and brie entrée my mouth began to water. *It was a sign. It had to be.* Here I wanted to make a luxurious seafood entrée to replenish my palate and Emeril intuitively handed it to me. Not astounded the answer would come from Emeril as he was my favorite celebrity chef. Not only do I consider Emeril an outstanding chef, but I find him to

23

be an electrifying stage personality as well. Admittedly, I have a thing for Italian's.

Emeril described the salmon entrée as being full of substance, richness and luxury which made me feel it would be sublime for my situation. I imagined that digesting it would be a great way to attract those specific traits into my life. Naturally, I wanted substance, luxury and richness. *Who doesn't?*

I quickly called Kat again. And after describing how the salmon recipe is prepared I could tell by the way she gasped in excitement that her mouth was watering over the phone at the mere sound of the entrée, as mine had when I saw it prepared. This was the ideal seafood entrée to erase past troubles and summon a healthier future, I could sense it. We chatted a bit longer, continuing to share optimism over the new direction our lives will take, until Kat got interrupted by her six year old daughter, Brooklyn. At which time we agreed to continue the conversation later when I arrive at her house.

Since my mother is a gourmet chef, I called her to ask if she had the salmon baked with mango and brie recipe. She said she would find it and get back to me. Too anxious to wait I went online on the computer in the study and found the recipe within minutes, printed it out, and then folded it into my purse.

Encountering a few hours to kill before having to undergo the drive to the store to get all the ingredients to make the salmon entrée at Kat's place (a less than twenty minute drive away), I wanted to be productive. Before getting dressed into something nice, I decided to stay in my tank top and spandex shorts and proceeded on a mission to clean my house.

First, I wanted to throw out all leftovers and junk food. I opened the fridge and took out the pan containing macaroni and cheese from four days ago that I bought during a point of weakness when I relapsed and deviated from my healthy eating plan. Why I even saved it is questionable. Macaroni and cheese never tastes good reheated, besides entirely consisting of salt, fat and preservatives. Why did I just shove the whole pan into the refrigerator and not even transfer it to a Tupperware dish? *Who does that?* Me and most single people who live alone. When you have endured spinsterhood for a great length of time and rarely have visitors you honestly don't care. In fact, most general personal hygiene rules of proper etiquette go out the window; plucking eyebrows, shaving legs and using deodorizer become optional.

It was becoming cruelly apparent how my lack of concern for my own mental and physical well-being had played such a huge role in what men entered my life. Wanting to change my pattern, I proudly dumped the sticky old macaroni and cheese out the back door. My four unnamed wild outdoor cats, who I keep around merely as mouse destroyers, loved this. My little Maltese dog, Marshmallow, and my cocker spaniel dog, Oreo, naturally feeling left out, weren't too happy. So I gave them the uncovered plate of crusty rice and soy chorizo from a week ago, which I forgot about and found shoved way in the back behind the pickle jar and the moldy cottage cheese. The soy sausage was so hard, blackened and crumbly that Marshmallow gave a whimsical look with one ear slightly tilted and Oreo let out a pitiful whine. Even dogs question eating something that has a potentially bad aftertaste.

Deciding to make this refrigerator cleaning experience fun, I changed the channel from the Food Network to the old school rock radio station and turned the volume up as loud as it would go. It wasn't Tone Loc singing *"Wild Thing"* like I was hoping, but it was the classic song by Rick James *"Super Freak"* which is another favorite dance song of mine. This particular station always manages to pump me up and give me the proper motivation to get my body physically moving about, and so by the time I was done cleaning the fridge an hour had passed.

While washing my hands an idea came to me. I wanted to make a list of my serious ex-boyfriend's, to keep them in order when talking to Kat. There weren't many, only four. No wait, five. I retrieved a yellow-lined spiraled legal pad from the nightstand drawer where I keep stacks of notepads to write down my dreams at night. I love interpreting my wacky subconscious; one of many petty hobbies of mine.

Sitting at the kitchen table, I leisurely began to write down each guy's name along with their birth date. I have a fascination with birthdays. I have a book about the meaning of the day you were born along with a book about Chinese astrology and another one revolving around numerology. I'm into all kinds of spiritual and psychological self-analysis as I was raised by hippie parents; it's expected. I wanted to write something specifically unique about each guy, and after a few minutes of reflection a clever idea came to me. I decided to write down a song (easy), smell (simple) and food (fun) that generates a powerful memory of each one.

Before elaborating more detail to the list, I quickly glanced at the kitchen clock and panicked. *Darn it!* I didn't have much time before I had to leave. I also wanted to consider the similar qualities of seafood that each guy shared. *Jeez! Why do I always get creative near the time when I have to be somewhere?* The best ideas always come to me when I'm under pressure. I hurried and haphazardly completed the list.

I stuffed the legal pad into my brown Gucci, baggy style purse that I purchased at a local thrift store, and then after setting it on the bathroom counter changed out of my cleaning grubs into a summery outfit. Staring in the full length bedroom mirror, I admired my accessories. In particular, the variety of sterling silver and red, dangling, beaded, charm bracelets, one of which was inscribed with my initials—a talisman passed down from my great grandmother (Marta Rae Murphy) that I've worn since I was a little girl; and the four, thin, extra-long red necklaces with the oversized sterling silver loop earrings which complemented the long diaphanous blouse of shimmery red and white rayon tank top. Choosing to wear Ann Taylor white Capris and a silver anklet with low-heel, red flowered sandals, I felt as bright as I looked. Everything matched my fresh aura and sparkling view on life.

I sensed this new outlook would make me more attractive to others because I was not only thinking I was more attractive, inside I felt prettier. Although I know authentic beauty comes from within, feeling outwardly beautiful made me feel internally fabulous. I automatically wanted to share my enthusiasm for life and compliment others. It's fascinating how powerful our own personal thoughts are to our self-esteem. I learned about this from one of the thirty some self-help books I own and was elated the philosophy was engrained in my thought process lately. The belief that wearing the color red made me more attractive, in actuality, made me feel prettier. As long as I was wearing red, I felt more confident. But, what if the color red wasn't the best color on me, but it was simply my thinking it was that made me believe it to be true? *Oh, don't for a minute let doubt enter your thoughts, Melody Rae. Come on, you know better!*

Shaking off the negative vibe that was attempting to enter my consciousness I smiled and took a deep breath. *Red looks fabulous on me.* Although I am not a true ginger, since my hair is not a bright shade but rather more of an auburn tone, I can fairly say I am considered a redhead by most people's standards. And although wearing clothing with any shade of red is complimentary, candidly speaking, without makeup no color looks good on me. Let's be honest, here. My pale, freckled Irish skin is the true enemy. I've never seriously considered myself naturally beautiful. I simply give a lot of credit to my best friends, Maybelline and Cover Girl. I tell people: "It takes a lot of animal tested makeup to look this natural."

For me, makeup is essential in boosting my self-esteem. Now Kat, she's a different seed altogether. She rarely wears makeup. She doesn't need it. We are complete physical opposites. I'm a tall, five-foot-ten redhead with an Irish-Swedish decent—meaning I look best in winter colors. She's a petite, five-foot-one dark brunette with a Spanish-Japanese decent. No Irish whatsoever in her genes—meaning she looks sensational in summer colors. Kat requires little if any makeup. She's like a Castilian goddess. She is one of those pathetically, naturally gorgeous women. *Seriously!* She honestly looks good after throwing up. *I know, spare me.* After I toss my chips, the mascara dripping down from my swollen eyes and my beet red puffy cheeks combined with a sweaty hair mat stuck to the left side of my face and drool seeping out the side of my mouth usually scares my dogs into convulsions. Needless to say, I try not to vomit in public.

Despite Kat being thirteen years my junior, in many ways she's an old soul—partly due to having raised a child at such a young age forcing her to grow up fast. However, I find it incongruous how red is symbolic of power when Kat, the power oriented character that she is, never wears red. Though, she does sometimes wear pink which is essentially a lighter shade of red. But primarily she wears black, which of course, she looks phenomenal in with or without makeup. *Growl.* Black makes me look like a member of *The Addams Family.* Like Kat, the color black is dark and mysterious. Not me. I'm an open book with the pages flying about. Maybe Kat wearing pink is the pubescent stage of her power to come which will develop as she matures? When I was in my early thirties, like she is now, I wore a lot of pink. Interestingly enough, in my pink wearing days I had less life experiences and I was a lot lighter, too—physically and emotionally. The question then comes to mind. Does how much we learn from our past experiences determine how dark our color will be? What if we gravitate toward deeper, darker, richer colors as our inner depth evolves. *Is this why my mom loves to wear dark purple?* I need to not get side tracked by my own thoughts. When I do I tend to daydream and get nothing accomplished: story of my life.

I quickly scrunched my congenitally curly hair, reapplied a bright shade of red, Cover Girl Ever Red-dy 507, lipstick, powdered my face and headed out the door. Anxious to buy the book *The Secret Language of Relationships* written by Gary Goldschneider I stopped at Village Books, a quaint bookstore in Mount Shasta that is conveniently located on the way to Rays Food Place. My secretary told me the book delicately matches up the week surrounding the day a person is born with the week of another person concisely explaining how the two are compatible or incompatible. I knew it would be a splendid way for Kat and me to analyze my past relationships and help me to heal. I entered through the double doors of the New Age, spiritual and holistic bookstore and promptly escorted my way to the psychology/self-help section near the back. *Yay!* The book was available…and on sale! I think the bookstore clerk thought I was a nutcase when I squealed loudly with delirious excitement over discovering the book. After paying for the book, I kissed the cover, hugged it tight, and then rapidly walked to my jeep to venture on to the grocery store. If the clerk saw this, it probably convinced her I needed my head examined. *Doesn't she realize certain books have therapeutically life-saving properties?* I sensed this book would turn out to be my number one go-to for advice. Exhilarated, I drove toward Rays Food Place with a feeling of intense bliss.

Immediately after entering the parking lot of the market, I spotted an available parking space directly by the front entrance and quickly drove into it. I wasn't entirely bewildered by my luck because I felt this powerful and glowing aura surrounding me with light, hope, love and felicity. If I had recognized sooner how satisfyingly cleansing and galvanizing it would be to remove all the garbage from my life, I would have cleaned out my refrigerator a long time ago.

After closing the driver's side door of my jeep, I pressed the lock symbol on the remote-entry key fob and with eyes sparkling and head held high approached the store. Sitting next to the front entrance doors was an elderly gentleman near a table selling what appeared to be chocolate bars and holding a clipboard, which I instantly assumed was a petition to sign something I had no time to think about.

When his eyes caught mine he adjusted his shirt collar and sat up. "How are you?" he politely asked with a coquettish grin.

"Pretty good," I said smiling and bending over to snag a hand-held shopping basket.

"Pretty good?" he argued with his lips perched in a not-so-convinced expression. "I think you're doing better than pretty good, missy. First of all, you look amazing. You're wearing a knockout outfit and you have an incredible smile."

I blushed, caught off guard by this man's unexpected genuine declaration. "Well, ahem...I, uh," I stuttered. "I guess I am doing better than pretty good...then. Thank you."

Then he winked at me and smiled. I then lifted my shoulders and biting my bottom lip bashfully walked inside the automatic doors. He seemed like such a sweet elderly gentleman that I felt badly for not inquiring to what his petition was about, or buying a candy bar. *I will when I leave. Nice always wins people.* If the majority of politicians could understand this philosophy, we'd have a kinder world.

Minutes after walking down the frozen food aisle of the store a lady, who appeared to be in her mid-thirties, motioned to me as if she knew me.

"Wow!" she squealed. "I totally love all the red jewelry. That color looks sensational on you."

Are you serious? Two compliments from two complete strangers back to back? *Wow.* I guess my aura was shining. And although I was a bit startled to hear another bold statement from someone I didn't know, I put my hand to my chest and turned in her direction.

"Thank you. I LOVE red, I really do. Is it that obvious?"

"Yes. But that's a good thing. It's the perfect color on you...enjoy your day," she said grinning and then turning her cart down the next aisle.

I continued on with an even more confident stride. It didn't take long to grab the Land O' Lakes real butter, Ile de France brie cheese, Wild Alaskan salmon filets, Morgenster extra virgin olive oil and fresh mangoes. Mercifully, this salmon entrée didn't require too many ingredients, a lot of prep time, or too much extra work from me; equivalent to the type of man I would like to attract. The thought of a man taking care of me rather than the other way around made my lip twitch and brought a tear to my eye. I wiped it away with the back of my hand and took a deep breath. *You will have that one day, Melody Rae, you will.*

Standing in the liquor aisle, I reached the top shelf to grab a Merlot and a Cabernet from the Clos du Bois winery. After placing the wine awkwardly on top of the groceries I'd piled in the small carrying basket I looked up, and there he was. It was *him!* He was less than a couple yards from where I stood, kneeling down and holding a bottle of wine while reading the label. *Breathe, Melody Rae.* I couldn't believe my eyes. *Was it actually him?* It was! I thought I'd never see him again. The last time I saw him was four years ago. *What was he doing here?* I didn't think he would ever again resurface in my life. But I always thought that and, yet, he would. The symmetry of our past encounters remains a spiritual unknown for me. I do not know this man on any personal level, not even his name. However, I found myself running into him over the past twenty five years in the most unlikely places at the most obscure moments in my life. I'd predicted he would undoubtedly remain an eternal mystery. *Was the mystery going to end right now? Did I want it to?* To my knowledge he had always been married, yet, whenever we would see one another he would stare at me in this slightly provocative way. *Is he even real? Maybe he's my angel and no one can see him, but me?*

I have to tell Kat about this sighting. After I became close friends with Kat and disclosed the stories of this random guy showing up in my life she coined him the title *Mister S*, claiming the mysterious and serendipitous quality of his unpredictable appearances imply that he might be my soul mate.

I shook the urge to replay every moment I'd encountered this gentleman over the years and ignored the instinct to turn away and run. Instead, I chose to face the situation in the moment with gumption. After straightening my outfit, I fluffed my hair and then stood motionless looking in his direction to see if he would look up from his position. I couldn't feel my legs. I was numb. *What am I doing? I can't handle this right now.* I thought about turning around and sprinting to the checkstand. But, just as I turned and was about to concede with my instinct to run, out of the corner of my eye, I saw him stand and wave in my direction fanning his fingers in a slow "hello we know each other" manner. *Do we? Do we know each other? Do I want to know him?* My fingers began to tremble. *Can I trust him? Is he a detective?* Sweat began to drip from my brow. *Has he been following me all these years?*

Why? Okay, relax. Stop being paranoid, Melody Rae, you won't know anything unless you ask questions. Come on! You can do this. With a nervous half-smile attempting to ignore all the suspicions reeling in my brain, I turned toward him and methodically waved back.

Noticing him walk toward me, I neurotically began to arrange the two wine bottles a little better in the carrying basket. And then with my chin tucked into the side of my neck, I looked up with a squinty-eyed expression on my face and leaned to one side with questioning body language.

"I'm sorry, do I know you?" I winced.

"U-m-m-m, well, not exactly," he said while looking at me with a quizzical smile, "but you know my brother, Luca."

"I…do?" I stammered.

"Yes. Luca Marcello? He's tall with a dark complexion like me. He brings his dog, Cappuccino, to your grooming salon."

What in the world?! So it was him, in the parking lot of Petite Paws on that foggy day before Thanksgiving. It was *Mister S* sitting in the driver's seat of that white Ford pickup. I then began to wonder if he remembered seeing me over the years at all those unexpected times. Did he know it was me? The questions flooded my brain, but I was too flustered by his presence to think straight.

The wine bottles in the basket woke me from my dumbfounded daze when they started to tip over the edge. They would've hit the hard tile floor creating an embarrassingly loud clatter if *Mister S* hadn't rushed forward, grabbed the end of the handle and shoved the bottles down into the crate farther. That's when our arms touched. I could smell him…m-m-m. What was that scent? It was intoxicating, fresh and clean like bar soap. It brought me back in time to the Lake of the Woods campground in Oregon, where I spent my summers as a little girl. I've been burdened since childhood with a heightened sense of smell: hyperosmia—an increased olfactory acuity. Growing up (although I was never officially diagnosed) my brother's nicknamed me Scooby, implying my sense of smell was homologous to a dog's. Although *Mister S* most likely merely showered using a generic bar soap, the scent had a powerful effect on my equilibrium and I began to feel slightly inebriated by it.

"I'm so sorry. I'm a complete klutz," I said flustered, attempting to push the items even farther into the basket. "I spill things all the time…seriously!"

"Same here," he said grinning with those familiar heart-throbbing dimples.

Oh no! I recall every time I saw him, he would spill something. Does that mean he recognizes me? Feeling self-conscious, I began to scrunch my hair. Although an extensive amount of time had passed, he still strongly resembled Robert Downey, Jr., with those intense features that enveloped me the first time I saw him at the tender age of nineteen.

He seemed unaware of the serendipitous nature of us meeting and proceeded to give me unsolicited advice regarding the wines I'd placed in my basket, suggesting a few alternative brands. He sounded like a professional sommelier, saying words like nutty, fruity, fat, dirty, vanilla, cedar and acidic with a rich, long and complex aftertaste. Maybe he was as nervous as me? After thoroughly educating me about wine aromas, he started rambling about his dog, Faith—a cavalier King Charles spaniel—telling me about her latest foibles, while I stood there with a ludicrous grin on my face, giggling at everything he said. Although I was completely embarrassed by my own behavior, I was pleasantly surprised to discover Faith is Cappuccino's daughter.

After a long-winded testimony, he changed the subject and leaned forward brushing his hands across my bracelets. "You must like to jingle."

Astonished by his assertiveness, I pulled my hand back. "I do," I chuckled at my own proclivity for wearing jingling bracelets.

I suspected he was flirting with me, which made me even more overwrought. Then I remembered he's married. *Oh no! What would his wife think?* I felt flattered and guilty simultaneously, causing me to have difficulty being in the moment. I cut the small talk short by saying in a rather serious tone how I had to be somewhere, as if Kat's house was an urgent appointment I had to keep. But before walking away, I found the gumption to make a quick comment about his striking similarity to his brother.

"You know, I can tell that you are related to Luca. You two look remarkably similar. I mean, it's obvious you have his genes."

"No, I don't. These are mine," he smirked, looking down and tapping the leg of his jeans. "That is, unless he sold them to the Shasta Outlet Store in Anderson."

I couldn't resist chuckling aloud. "Very funny," I said, shaking my head in amusement while walking toward the checkstand.

Adoring his witty nature, I found myself in a quandary feeling physically attracted to a married man. Humor is a big turn on for me. *Focus, Melody Rae! Kat is going to flip out when you tell her you spoke to Mister S.*

I was shamefully relieved as I exited the store to find that the guy with the petition was no longer around because I was too rattled and wanted to leave the scene immediately. After sitting safely inside my jeep, closing the door and buckling the seat belt, it hit me. I forgot to ask him his name. *Dang! Why didn't you get his name?* All these years I'd wanted an actual name for *Mister S* and here the opportunity arose and I was too freaked out, side-tracked by my own conundrum and blinded by feelings of desire, to think to ask. Oh well, too late now—*Mea Culpa.*

I closed my eyes, took a long deep breath, exhaled and turned on the car radio to find a wave of pleasure come over me. The song I'd been craving to hear *"Wild Thing"* by Tone Loc was playing through the stereo speakers. *It was a sign!* All morning long the song *"Wild Thing"* had been on my mind. I turned up the volume. Vigorous chills shivered up my spine as I recalled the spiritual book *The Secret* where philosopher, Dr. John F. Demartini wrote: *"Whatever we think about and thank about we bring about."* I was becoming a true believer of this statement. I'd been feeling more grateful than ever and attracting all those things into my life that I wanted simply by feeling as if I had them already. I smiled intuitively aware of how blessed I am to have all that I do.

Before forging a sharp left up the long driveway toward Kat's classy, neat, meticulously manicured bungalow, I saw a luminous light in the distance. Driving closer, I noticed the curtains of her front kitchen window were surprisingly wide open. Whenever I visited her in the past—no matter what time of year—her place always looked subdued and closed off; not today. Was she feeling as optimistic about life changes as me? *I hope so.*

I parked my 1998 red Jeep Cherokee 4WD with its upholstery fabric interior next to her 2011 black BMW convertible with its leather interior. Although an image of selfish elitism might be a judgment some attribute to those who drive a vehicle like a BMW, you would never suspect this young lady earned her way without anyone helping her. She worked her way to the top via scholarships and grants, and is a devoted mother of a six year old daughter, who she raised by herself without a partner.

Kat is the least pretentious person I know and her single parenting skills prove she is one of the most altruistic people on the planet. Although she is rather materialistic and loves things of high quality, she doesn't judge others who don't care about that sort of thing. It's true, she is single and affluent now, but she wasn't always. Regardless of the countless relationships Kat has entertained, even when involved in a relationship she always appears markedly single. She has a healthy way of presenting herself to the world as open and available. Not only the choice of vehicle she drives is symbolic of that, but the way she dresses also sends a message to onlookers that she is free and acutely available. She always has men wanting her, after her, needing her and not willing to let her go. Though, primarily subconscious, I am pretty sure she enjoys this projection of herself. I would if I were her. I wish I was afflicted with such a dilemma.

On the surface onlookers would be amazed we connect at all, since our styles are polar opposite. My home elicits an authentic country feel with antiques and light oak furniture. An antiquated rotary phone, a primordial record player and passé VHS recorder inhabit my living room area and I use them regularly. *I know! I may be a dying breed.* My rustic red suede couch is adorned with an assortment of different sized pillows: solid red, navy blue, red plaid, beige and red checkered corduroy. Being raised by hippie parents most everything I own was acquired from a thrift store, including most of my clothing attire. Kat may have never seen the inside of a thrift store, but she can shop at Nordstrom's blindfolded.

Every piece of furniture and every article of Kat's clothing is trendy, classy and expensive. Her home is prodigiously modern. Other than the four oversized, fuzzy, pink pillows, which accent her opulent black leather couch, all her furniture is contemporary: black and white. She has a closet the size of an entire bedroom; at one time it was one. Those who know Kat are not astonished she converted the downstairs bedroom into a closet—a room that is three times the size of her kitchen—to accommodate her clothes shopping addiction, since shopping is her obsession. Her closet, conveniently located at the bottom of the stairwell adjacent the kitchen, aside from Brooklyn, is the center of her universe.

Kat has more purses than any woman I know. She has a purse for every mood, occasion and season. Though, the majority of them are black or white, they are all different sizes and beaded with colorful bling-bling. Her purses were the first thing that caught my attention when I arrived at her place. She was standing in the opening to her closet arranging them when I opened the door. Maybe she was equally inspired to organize her life and throw out all her garbage? *Wrong.* I don't know what I was thinking. Every purse she owns is well over one hundred and fifty dollars in value. There is no way on earth she would ever consider tossing any of them.

Before I could set down the groceries on her miniscule round kitchen table surrounded by three black genuine leather swivel bar stools, she pulled me over to show me the new purse rack she purchased online at Neiman Marcus. The rack fit across the entire wall and was mounted directly outside her enormous closet. Of course, the purse rack was black and white and ostensibly vogue. I expected nothing else; it had her name written all over it.

"How gorgeous! It is so you," I said, pivoting to set the bags on the kitchen table and then walking back to check it out closer.

While admiring the purse rack I assumed Kat was unpacking the items from the shopping bags, but as it turned out she was plainly searching for the red wine.

"Carpe diem," I exclaimed. "I was actually thinking the same thing, wine first!"

"Absolutely," Kat scoffed, rolling her eyes with a "duh" expression on her face.

She was the friend who gave me a card on my last birthday which said on the front: 'Do you know the calories in a glass of wine?" And inside the card it said: 'No, you don't…and that's why we're friends." When it came to wine, calories were an obsolete concern.

As Kat proceeded to set the corkscrew on the table and turned to retrieve two translucent blue oversized wine glasses from the kitchen cabinet, I remembered who I ran into at the market.

"Oh, Kat, guess what?!" I jumped up and squealed. "Guess who I saw at the grocery store?"

My overzealous reaction startled Kat, causing her to nearly drop the wine glasses.

"Sorry," I said, assisting her in slowly setting the wine glasses on the table.

Wide-eyed and puzzled Kat shook her head, knowing I wouldn't give her a chance to guess anyway.

"*Mister S*!"

"What? NO freakin w-a-a-ay?! Serious?"

"Y-e-e-es!"

"Get outta town?"

"I am NOT kidding."

"THAT is cr-a-a-azy!" Kat wailed with a stunned expression on her face. "I mean, when was the last time you saw him, anyway…like forever ago, right?"

"Uh, yea-h-h-h. But, okay, here's the thing. I'm freaking o-u-t!!! I mean, seriously freaking out because I actually talked to him. We exchanged witty banter. Well, he was the one asserting all the wit. I pretty much just stood there in shock," I exhaled in one long breath. "Can you just please pour me some wine now? I don't even think I can discuss this any further without some liquid courage."

"Wine pouring simulation in process," Kat said, leaping toward the wine and uncorking the bottle of Merlot.

As Kat poured the wine I began to relax. The visual image of the velvety red wine flowing into the glass like smooth silk soothed me. I imagine that, if I had better control of my internal mechanisms, I could get intoxicated simply by observing the wine being poured and then visualizing myself sipping it. And conceivably, if I could breathe in the scent of coffee grounds brewing to become energized, I would. I am sure that some people are truly capable of such spiritual feats, but I am not one of them. I snatched the wine glass out of Kat's hand as if I had been stranded in a desert for days and was dying of thirst. That first sip made me feel like I had left the desert and was high on a hill, lying right in the middle of a wine orchard surrounded by the smell of sweet berries mixed with the clean fresh taste of mountainous air. *Ah, nothing quite as heavenly as that first sip.* After a few more sips I inhaled deeply and let out a relaxing sigh, ready to disclose the story of the unexpected encounter with *Mister S*.

After divulging every detail of our serendipitous chance meeting, and spending some quality time dissecting the "meet cute", our expert deep analysis concluded that basically it meant nothing. I had no reason to think *Mister S* was flirting and for all I knew he was happily married. Common sense and rational thought extrapolated there was no reason our encounters were meant to be more than simple coincidence of nature. After our deep discussion I was inspired to share how I am at a time in my life where I refuse to chase any guy.

"If a guy wants me, then pursue me. I mean, isn't it the guy's job to be the pursuer, anyway? Jeez! Chivalry is certainly not dead in my book."

Thankfully, Kat was in agreement. We were both on the same page when it came to how a man should be the pursuer, but if you were to examine the charms dangling from the stems of our wine glasses it'd be apparent how different we were in other ways. Kat's charm was a shiny, pink and black striped high-heeled shoe made from glass, and mine was a glittery, red cowboy boot made from metal, appropriately noting our differences while celebrating our individuality at the same time.

Kat replaced the wine bottle she had opened with a diamond studded cork stopper, naturally. Kat is all about diamonds. Granted, it was a good plan to have a sip before beginning our chat session as a way to inspire our thoughts, but in truth we didn't need it. Whenever we convene the words inherently pour out of us uncensored rapidly bubbling over with ebullience like an erupting volcano. Although often interrupting one another and speaking simultaneously, we can hear every word the other is saying. Our socially-gifted, garrulous and multi-task conversational ability is something we pride ourselves in. *I wonder if we share this trait and have a strong connection because Kat's birthday is the third of March and mine is the third of December, making us both a numerology number three.* Undeniably, such thoughts emerge from the bohemian flower child in me.

The thought lingered as I stared at the suitably glittery, red cowboy boot charm dangling from the glass she handed me. I smiled and shook my head in amusement. Red is so me. I also collect a plethora of boot paraphernalia: frames, book-ends, candle holders and key chains, all shaped like boots. I have more than thirty pairs of boots in my closet, all styles, though, mostly western. Three are brown, one is white (don't know when I'll ever wear those, but had to have them) and the rest are all various shades of, wait for it...red, of course.

Lori Jean Phipps

Chapter Two

What did the mummy sardine say to her children when they saw a submarine? Don't worry it's only a tin of people.

Sardine

Simplicity is the key with sardines. Enjoy the rich flavor of the fish with little more than salt, lemon and a little olive oil. The meat is sustainable, enormously flavorful and good for you. Sardines can be enjoyed grilled, pickled, filleted, baked or smoked. They go well with full-flavored sauces—spicy, citrusy salsas also work well.

"The best way to a fisherman's heart is through his fly."

~Author Unknown

****

We both plunged into gab mode, talking simultaneously about the deeply parallel imbrications of our first serious relationship which we were comparing to top ramen. Kat's first boyfriend, Anthony, and my first boyfriend, Shay, were similar to one another in that they were both frugal and spineless.

"Top ramen is for those who are cheap," Kat shrugged with hands palm up and lips merging into a sly grin.

"Exactly, the noodle itself is spineless, soft and weightless. It has no strength without the seasoning packet. I mean, alone, it is weak," I affirmed and then toasted my glass in the air. "Here's to no more top ramen."

"Hasta la vista top ramen," Kat saluted.

****

January 1984

Typical Daily Food Choices:
Pop-Tart & Folgers medium roast coffee w/heavy cream
Coca Cola
barbecue potato chips
Hostess Twinkies or gummy bears
top ramen w/ginger
tuna & sardines

Gay Shay

In 1984, top ramen packets were not surreptitiously stashed behind the cans of Star Kist tuna, Chicken of the Sea sardines and Kraft macaroni and cheese on the bottom shelf in my parent's kitchen, they were in clear view on the top. At the pristine age of eighteen, I had moved out on my own into a claustrophobic, diminutive one bedroom apartment in the big city. And for the first two years, top ramen smothered every shelf and cabinet in my meager kitchen.

Growing up economically challenged, I learned early on to make due with having considerably less than others and to be grateful for what I did have. My parents were poverty-stricken during the majority of my childhood, therefore I was a broke teenager. Despite taking delight in eating, my priority was not food. On the account of not having a whole lot of extra time on my hands, I would thaw a bag of frozen vegetables, toss into a saucepan, stir-fry with olive oil, pour over top ramen noodles and then add a can of Chicken of the Sea sardines or tuna fish for the health benefits of protein, B-12 and omega-3 fatty acids. The fish added flavor to my bland stir fry and became part of my daily regimen because it was convenient to freeze the leftover top ramen noodle stir-fry ensemble to reheat later, and simple to open a can. It didn't necessarily have the freshest smell, and sometimes a not so pleasant aftertaste, but it was something that required little preparation and I was all about that.

Before meeting Shay, I'd converted to a lacto-ovo vegetarian—a vegetarian diet which includes dairy products and eggs with one exception; an additional allowance of seafood. Since my mom was a chef and my dad was an avid fisherman, I was educated about the health benefits of seafood and learned to appreciate the taste of various fish.

I didn't consider seafood to be in the same category as animal flesh. In my naiveté, I thought as long as I was not eating any animal I considered a pet (a living creature that you could literally pet) then I was a vegetarian. Fish are not exactly in the petting category.

I was on a new journey celebrating "my version" of vegetarianism and determined to get protein from somewhere other than what I personally deemed off-limits. Off-limit category; poultry: domesticated fowl and animal products such as turkey, chicken, ducks, geese and guinea fowl, cows, pigs, etc., and other than fish, any living organism characterized by voluntary movement and the ability to ingest complex organic substances such as plants and other animals. These were animals I considered friends: pets. Being a tremendous animal lover, how could I eat a pet? And, after learning how meat was processed in a high school science class I no longer had the urge to eat any type of animal product ever again. Lamentably, I did not get educated on what alternative meat options for protein I had. Fish was all I knew, which brings me to my first boyfriend, the sour and reticent fish, Shay Smith.

When I met Shay Smith, a quiet and fair skinned English boy originally from London, I was sixteen and a sophomore in high school. Although we didn't have many similar tastes in food, we did share a love for top ramen: the variety pack. Once we were deeply involved top ramen became "our thing." And in addition to Shay's favorite spice "ginger", my nightly ritual continued. I would throw in the wok a packet of top ramen with a bag of frozen vegetables, spice it up with sliced ginger root and then mix in my choice of canned seafood.

In the beginning, I found Shay's demure presence attractive, like a wounded puppy dog. Only later did I discover that all dogs, even those with a friendly appearance can still potentially bite. Shay's demeanor (his inner core personality) was basic, odd, sensitive, effeminate and secretive, like a **slimy sardine: unusual, simple with a strong flavor, but ultimately slimy.**

I was an innocently naïve, animated, exuberant and verbose teenager while Shay was an excruciatingly bashful, pitifully insecure and caustic boy. But through the lenses of my rose-colored glasses, he came across as a charming and modest boy with a tender and fragile heart. My personality exhibited a modicum of the unusual. Having an obsession with Captain and Tennille, Star Trek and Jim Henson's Muppets didn't particularly place me in the popular crowd in high school. Also being a huge thrift store shopper from a young age, I took delight in creating my own style from an arrangement of patterned clothing that didn't necessarily match. I went through a phase of wearing French beret's, colorful scarves, Star Trek insignia bracelets and corduroy vests with "Animal" Muppet T-shirts over knee-length patterned skirts complimented by polka-dot leggings and cowboy or military jungle boots. Admittedly, I wanted to be a Vulcan and date Spock (Leonard Nimoy)—my hero.

I found Shay's mysterious demeanor a complete and radical turn on. Physically, I liked the way his unruly, dusty brown hair flung forward covering most of the left side of his face. His aloof temperament while being titillating and alluring was also somewhat discomforting. His diffident personality made me inclined to think he was hiding something, but I wasn't sure what. Did he have a deeply disturbed nature underneath that calm exterior, an inner self-hatred, a neurotic insecurity, a vengeful spirit combined with a set of unrealistic fears? I wondered. Intrigued enough to want to know what made him tic powered me toward him.

As I grew to know him and then fall in love with him (the idea of him anyway), I became curiously suspicious of his motives and began to view him differently. Instead of finding his unruly hair a turn on, I'd look at him and his face would meld before my eyes into a British version of the

"Unabomber", Ted Kaczynski. Strange, how love can turn sour over time. It took a lot of years for me to become cognizant of the fact that not all introverted people were built with nobleness and purity, like I'd presumed.

As my feelings for Shay changed, it made me question whether I should have listened to my dad more closely growing up. Whenever a news story came out on television describing a community shocked to find the most demure boy in town was, in fact, a serial killer, child molester, or rapist, my dad would always say: "Never trust the quiet ones, Melody Rae."

Granted, to presume all timid human beings are secretive and untrustworthy would be judgmental and unfair. But in the case of Shay, my dad's presumption was accurate. As Shay's personality unfolded like the layers of an onion being peeled, burning my eyes and affecting the external surface of my body like skin cancer, my eyes could no longer see things the same. But, beneath the layers of scarring, my heart remained fully intact, even if later held together by duct tape. Thankfully, this unveiling of his true self occurred over a long period of time sparing my emotional core from any permanent damage.

Due to the fact that at the time we met I was seeking a challenge, someone to test my confidence and inner strength, I was more than willing to do all the work; to stir in the butter and mix together my rich flavor with his unusual tartness, all the while hoping he was the missing ingredient. Once I added my own ingredients (one moiety Melody to one moiety Shay)—my buttermilk flour batter to his sardine can—he appeared as if he was a whole individual: a whole sardine.

And when he behaved as if he had genuine qualities that were identical to mine, he became more attractive, naturally: I liked me. But, sadly, the traits he mimicked after we were dating weren't his own. He had managed to create an illusion of richness and depth when all that existed inside was this thin, separated, identity-less self, which made me realize why I had been so miserable. I had spent our entire relationship

45

waiting for him to change, or for me to change, or for us to change; for anything to change.

It made sense why the first guy I attracted was meek, awkward and sheltered, growing up feeling the same way inside. The reason I was shy and awkward came from being sheltered. My dad made sure he knew where I was at all times, up until I could legally move out of the house at age eighteen.

Me and my six older brothers were all born and raised in the scenic Jackson County hills of Oregon in the quaint town of Ashland, with the comfortable population size of a little over fourteen thousand. I was content and happy experiencing an idyllic childhood, until, in the winter of 1983, my parents decided to uproot us all to Portland, a city three hours away. And at the age of sixteen, it felt like we moved to a different country. I had no interest in ever living in a big city. With an overwhelming population size of over three hundred thousand, my eyes fogged over and my brain did somersaults. I reluctantly accepted this change, although I logically understood we had no choice except to move because my dad, Aaron Murphy, Sr., was permanently laid off from his job working for the forest service. He was guaranteed employment in the construction industry in Portland, since the city was expanding, and my mom, Katherine Lee Murphy, ended up getting a job too good to refuse, making moving inevitable.

Most people refer to my dad (the gentle giant) as "Big Guy", and not merely because he has a huge heart and is gifted with a deep booming voice, but he's also six-foot-five and weighs close to three hundred pounds. Half-Irish and half-Swedish with the physical appearance of Brad Garrett, the attitude of Terry Bradshaw and humor of George Carlin, he's a true character. Everyone loves my dad because when he talks to you he has a way of making you feel like a long lost friend.

Other than in height, many say I closely resemble Isla Fisher, and although we certainly have somewhat similar facial features, my hair is more identical to that of Bernadette

Peters—the curls reign. I get my height and cynicism from my dad, but my spunk and curly red hair come from my mom, who is a five-foot-six, full-blooded Irish, curly redhead. My mom, Katherine Lee, with the physical appearance of Patricia Clarkson, humor of Betty White and intelligence of Katie Couric is a firecracker. She had been working part time as a cook at Southern Oregon University since I can remember, and to be offered a high paying position as a food service production manager and instructor at Western Culinary Institute was something she couldn't turn down. It still seemed unfair. My worse fear was happening, we were moving and I had no control over it.

Every one of my six older brothers; Aaron, Jr., Gerard, Cormac, Shane, Adam and Brian had already graduated high school. Four of them were living on their own going to colleges in other states, so naturally they were not as affected by this move as I was. I was angry about having to leave a place where everybody knew my name—where I had an established identity—and transfer in the middle of the school year to try to find my place in a new town.

My two closest friends, Lillian Bennett and Carlene Richards and I were finally attending high school together, an experience we had anxiously awaited for nine long years. I had known Lillian and Carlene since the first grade. We connected in Mr. Libbit's orchestra class at Lincoln Elementary School when our shared sense of humor bonded us instantly.

It was the first day of Orchestra class and we were sitting at our desks in the back row enduring a boring lecture about music theory when the instructor went off on a tangent. None of us were listening, too distracted by the teacher's unusual characteristics. He had a similar resemblance to the weasel looking, although highly talented actor, Steve Buscemi. With a pathetic hair comb-over, massive buggy eyes and a wide puffy-lipped smile, he slightly resembled a frog.

When he began sharing a personal story about how he was teased as a young child for his last name and then oddly enough began comparing himself to Ludwig Beethoven, Carlene became amused.

47

She raised her hand. "Did other people bully Beethoven for his first name, Ludwig?" she asked politely.

"I'm not sure. Good question, Carlene," he declared, seemingly proud of her for asking.

"Thank you, Mr. Ribbit," Carlene asserted, smiling then sitting, unaware she had inadvertently mispronounced his name with an R instead of an L, unintentionally parodying his froglike appearance.

When she realized what she'd done she looked over at Lillian and I, who were staring at her with our hands over our mouths trying not to giggle. When the moment got the best of us, the laughing fit ensued and the three of us developed the giggles so fiercely we all turned bright red in the face, after which we became united friends.

"Stop it, I'm gonna pee!" Lillian shrilled.

The feet stomping fits combined with our chortling and gurgling noises eventually caught the attention of the teacher, interrupting the music lesson.

Mr. Libbit asked us to leave the classroom and sit in the hallway. He handed each of us a yellow spiraled notebook pad of paper and ordered we write: "I promise not to refer to Mr. Libbit as Mr. Ribbit" one hundred times, which inspired more giggling. From that moment on the three of us were inseparable, cemented by the bond of a homogeneous funny-bone.

We started calling ourselves "The Three Musketeer's" because there were three of us and we were mutually obsessed with the 3 Musketeer's chocolate candy bar, thus becoming our trademark. We would eat them as often as we could and then save all the wrappers, including the candy bar wrappers from the candy our friends ate, along with the mini wrappers of the candy collected from our annual Halloween stash. By the time we entered high school, you could imagine (between the three of us) how many shoe-boxes full of candy bar wrappers we'd accumulated. Last time we counted we had two thousand, four hundred and thirty-three wrappers.

The three of us grew to become as tight as sisters and many people thought we were, although none of us looked remotely alike. With my fair skin and freckled complexion, tall lanky frame and long, thick, curly red hair, Carlene's creamy tan complexion, petite curvy figure and shoulder length, wavy blond hair and Lillian's deep bronze complexion, average height and long, straight, wispy dark brown hair, we were an odd, albeit uniquely diverse, threesome.

Within a month after high school started, we knew who we did and didn't like. Proceeding to select who we would marry, what we would name our children, where we would live, what parks and schools our children would attend, and what local pizza parlor we would meet at every Friday afternoon: Vinnie's Pizza Parlor, of course. Vinnie's Pizza joint won hands down because it had a fireplace, the best video games in the arcade and a terrific selection of country music on the jukebox. We didn't consider that in adulthood video games would probably not be a significant priority.

Entering through the doors of Ashland High School each morning, we would meet at our lockers, jump and squeal, sharing our latest celebrity crush, usually hopped up on orange Crush soda and Frito-Lay Cheetos; breakfast of champions. We were gung-ho freshman and drunk with power, envisioning ourselves playing the lead roles from the movie *Grease*. I enacted the role of Frenchy, of course. I had the red hair and the spunk. Lillian portrayed Sandy because she was the most demure with the prettiest singing voice and Carlene executed Betty Rizzo because she was the most boisterous and fearless of us all. It was frequent for us to dance down the hallway on our way to class, arm-in-arm, executing cross-over leg routine's and singing the late 1950's Dion and The Belmont's *"Runaround Sue"* or the *Laverne and Shirley* theme song by Cyndi Grecco *"Making Our Dreams Come True"* from the 1970's sitcom, chanting: "Schlemiel! Schlimazel! Hasenpfeffer Incorporated!" High school was going to be the best time of our lives, we could taste it.

Then, without warning, life threw a curve ball. It felt like I'd swung the bat and missed, striking out with no chance of running a home run, let alone to first base. Lillian and Carlene managed to make a home run and live out "our" high school dream while I was left to meet all new people in a monstrous foreign city hours away.

Once established in Portland, Oregon, I was determined to reinvent my identity. Although petrified with guilt about doing so, being a lone third Musketeer without her two partners to join her in a weekly ritual of chocolate bar gluttony. Every time I saw a 3 Musketeer candy bar, the pit of my stomach tied up in knots and loneliness enveloped me.

Fortunately, a light at the end of tunnel materialized in late January of 1984. It was a chilly thirty-six degrees, a curiously cold and humid winter's day, when my mother dropped me off in front of Grant High School; an old, decrepit three story brick building whose structure resembled a state penitentiary.

Walking up the endless steps with the sensation that the doors of life were opening me up to a new world, a new life and a new experience, you'd think it would have manifested an exhilarating high, but instead I felt like I was entering what the building mirrored: a prison. *Can I go back to my old life now?* Roaming the halls alone, I felt lost, as if I didn't belong. There were three floors to this overwhelmingly gigantic school and I was late to my first period class. When I finally found the courage to ask the custodian he brought me to the side of the building, opened the double doors, and pointed across a football size field toward a humongous concert hall. *Oh great!* The orchestra class was located in a completely separate building and I was already late.

Breathing unevenly and shaking my head as it started to rain, I trudged nervously along what seemed like a limitless cement pathway aligned with a chain-link fence and surrounded by an infinite field of wet grass. With the hood of my jacket on, keeping my face hid from the wind and rain hoping no one would see me, I could feel the tears welling up inside. Noticing the time on my wristwatch, I began jogging. The massive handbag of school belongings hoisted over my left shoulder banged continuously against the left side of my body, intermittently clanking with the chain-link fence while the violin held tight in my right hand rapped repeatedly against my right leg. There I was arriving late to my first period class at a brand new school, alone and feeling like an outsider, could it get any worse?

Eleven minutes late with my coat drenched from the rain and sweat trickling down my back from jogging half way to class, I practically fell over when I reached the entrance doors to the music hall. After taking a deep breath, I opened the large doors and began walking down the long corridor. I flung off my hood and fluffed the front and back of my long, red hair. I could tell from the texture that it had curled up frizzing into a hideous Phyllis Diller ensemble, something it does in unforgiving rainy weather with high humidity. *Just lovely!* I then found the correct double door entrance to the music class. Before I could talk myself out of it, I walked in.

Immediately inside the classroom, I set down the brown violin case covered entirely with an array of funky stickers I'd collected since the first grade. And then I adjusted my brown and red plaid handbag at the shoulder, loosened my red and white striped scarf wrapped around my neck, and examined the room. I didn't see the instructor straightaway. It was a small class size of maybe twenty students and it felt like all forty eyes were on me. From the susurrus sounds and pointing, I suspected they were ridiculing my clothes. *Is my outfit all that unusual?* I suppose the brown thrift store army jacket, hand-me-down Justin roper boots and polka-dot leggings I wore under a knee-length, red, plaid, country style dress contrasted with the acceptable norm. I gathered not only were all eyes on me because I arrived eleven minutes late, but also because I was the only student not wearing black or gray. I felt like I was entering a classroom in New York City; the majority of students were wearing black trench coats, even the girls.

In ungainly fashion, I climbed over two rows of bleacher seats to an empty row and then shuffled myself toward the center and sat. I located the instructor, who was standing behind a glass doorway in what I inferred was a tiny soundproof piano room. Although I couldn't hear the conversation, he looked to be having an altercation with a student who was holding a backpack and forming threatening

51

disciplinary gestures. I was curious as to whether it was drug related. I heard big cities are filled with drugs and gang problems. Sudden panic set in. *Oh no! Could the kid have a gun? I miss Ashland. I don't fit in. I want go home. Mommy!*

Then a conservative looking older woman entered the classroom distracting my neurosis. She walked into the room where the instructor stood, shut the door behind her, hugged the teacher and then the boy. And then the male instructor and this woman kissed. *What?!* Although it appeared to be nothing but a family dispute, my gossip hungry ears were on high alert. Although I was still interested in knowing the details behind this story, I was much less concerned now, suspecting drugs, guns and explosives were not involved. I was simply thankful the teacher was too preoccupied with his own personal dilemma to notice my late arrival to class.

After scanning the classroom of peers a particular boy caught my eye, in view of the fact that he was the only student wearing brown. His trench coat was dark brown, which accented well with the wrinkled, beige, plaid, button-up shirt he had untucked over what appeared to be old man khaki slacks. He had Elvis Costello glasses dangling from his shirt pocket, a chestnut tie loosely strung around his neck collar while a tan and white checkered scarf adorned his trench, and a hazel Fedora hat with a paisley band covered his forehead. His peculiarly passé and antiquated style resembled someone from the fifties, like a character in a courtroom on the set of *Perry Mason*.

He had his head down and shoulders slumped over with one eye staring at me. As soon as our eyes met, he nervously glanced away as if he didn't want to draw any attention to himself. He seemed unbearably uncomfortable in his own skin as he gracelessly fidgeted in his seat, which strangely enough made me feel secure.

I decided to take the initiative to change seats and introduce myself to this mysterious boy in the Fedora hat. I clumsily picked up my belongings and darted in his direction with bounce and confidence, stepping down over the bleacher seats until I reached his row. I set down the handbag and violin case to the right of me and then sat to the left, directly beside him. I was so proud of myself for having the moxie to approach this guy I knew nothing about. Something about being in a new city (where nobody knew me) gave me the cojones to be a more forthright and outgoing person. There was also something about this boy's inferiority which made me feel more assertive. Maybe his supreme reticence made me feel empowered. I was deriving great pleasure at feeling secure and being in control.

"Hi, my name's Melody Rae!" I belted with my right hand outstretched to shake his, forcing him to confront his insecurity.

But instead of shaking my hand, he nodded his head and mumbled under his breath, almost inaudibly, although a melodic English lilt was clearly detectable. "Um…uh…hiya, mate, Shay Smith…all right?" *Oh, now that was sexy.*

After an innocuous exchange of few words, where I did most of the talking, we both seemed to feel at ease in one another's company. Following that first day in Orchestra class, Shay bonded to me like a broken table leg to epoxy resin; ostensibly unable to stand without me. Like a lonely puppy dog, he would follow me everywhere. Due to my enabling handicap I enjoyed doing all the communication, assuming I was teaching by modeling and that subsequently my confidence would rub off and encourage him to grow more buoyant, phlegmatic and self-assured. Being less feminine and more gregarious than the average female, more than likely due to growing up with six older brothers, toughened me in unexplained ways while at the same time fostered in me a naiveté to whether a guy liked me or not. I would treat guys the same way I treated everyone. I didn't flirt, or even know how to. I couldn't have possibly speculated that Shay would be my first boyfriend, or furthermore that he would turn out to be gay.

To clarify how naïve I was: when I met Shay's best friend, Patrick, a flamboyantly open homosexual, and witnessed obvious flirtatious behavior toward him from Shay, I didn't presume for a minute that he could conceivably be gay. It never entered my thoughts. *Why would it?* I grew up with the philosophy that everyone should be accepted as they are and not be compartmentalized into categories. It's ridiculous to think a person should be considered identical to another simply because they hang out together. Well, unless they were born on the same day at the exact same time, naturally. *My hippie, astrological philosophy weighing in.*

Shay was a mild-mannered, sixteen year old virgin, who not only came from a similarly large family as mine, astonishingly happened to have a birthday during the same month as me. After recently expanding my knowledge of sun sign astrology, notwithstanding the fact that he was a Capricorn and not a Sagittarius and born at the end of the month (twenty-third of December) while I was born near the beginning (third of December), I was convinced it meant something. Naturally, being raised by hippie parents, a curious intrigue into the spiritual and metaphysical world was inherently expected of me.

Throughout our inordinately long courtship—a two year platonic friendship—Shay never indicated verbally or physically any sort of carnal interest in me giving me no reason to think he was in any way attracted to me, but I was hopeful. I assumed because he was bashful and timorous that he needed a girl to be the instigator. *Wrong!* He needed a boy to be the instigator.

I'm not blaming Shay. I'm blaming myself for not paying attention to the flagrant signs along the way. I believe Shay was in denial and not ready to accept he was gay any more than I did, at least not in the beginning. We both wanted to keep out blinders on. In truth, there were little hiccups during our relationship that were hints of Shay's sexual orientation. Like the time that he dressed up like a woman for Halloween, and then wouldn't take the nylons off for days claiming they were comfortable. *Why did I overlook that?*

I was in denial, too. I preferred to believe my life was simple and traditional, something I needed to conjecture. I know part of me needed to presume my life was conventional, typical and common, due to the fact that I deeply wanted to fit in with the in-crowd, or what was considered by society to be acceptable. So, when peculiar situations arose in my interactions with Shay, I discounted them and became a skilled expert at ignoring the elephant in the room.

The first time I encountered a fish bone (red flag) and caught myself developing the ability to sugarcoat the absurd, was when we collaborated with a group of my artsy theatre major friends and his intellectual nerdy friends at Patrick's parent's house while they were traveling around Europe for the umpteenth time. We had known each other for about a year and a half, but weren't an official couple, yet.

Patrick's parents were both university History professors who seemed to eternally be on sabbatical. They had no knowledge that while they were off gallivanting in some foreign country, their son was off inviting an eclectic arrangement of friends for all-night shindigs in their home. I am certain they wouldn't approve.

Coincidentally, Shay related more to my friends and I fused more with his. I admired his chess team playing, English majoring friends because they were more logical, focused, driven and responsible, like I was at that time. And my unconventional, abstract, theatre major friends shared his similar perspective on sexual orientation and considered his quirkiness to be unique.

He would have fit perfectly amongst my theatre class friends, if he hadn't been too insecure to join the drama department. At the metropolitan high school I attended, the majority of the thespians were stereotypically, flamboyantly gay or bi-sexual and most were into experimentations of all types of altered states of consciousness: pot, drugs and alcohol. In fact, I was one of only eleven others in a class of thirty-five, who was sober, anti-drug, a heterosexual and a virgin. In drama class, your peers become intimately close as you spend an extensive amount of time together outside of class working on projects (plays): editing scripts, stage design, costume tailoring, makeup composition, music presentation, etc. I found all my artistic, multifaceted thespian classmates to be quite delightful and we grew to become like family. You will never be bored among a crowd of theatre actors. It's as if you are thrown in a room filled with Saturday Night Live cast members; laughter becomes contagious as everyone scrambles to upstage the other. I particular liked Patrick, because not only did he have a certain je ne sais quoi, he was upfront and honest. He never hid who he was or pretended to be someone he's not, like Shay did. The particular evening when we all "played house" at Patrick's residence revealed how uninhibited the theatre students actually were.

Patrick was meandering about like a waiter, winding through the living room, upstairs and downstairs, outside and back into the kitchen while serving everyone an unfamiliar concoction he'd created from his parent's well-stocked bar. It was a cocktail consisting of a variety of fruit juices mixed with club soda and a combination of hard liquors. I didn't drink, but almost everyone else did, although they were all under age. Opting for a Coca Cola, I snatched a can from the fridge, walked downstairs through the pool room and out the French patio doors which led to a sunken hot tub embedded into a massively long wooden veranda that extended the length of the house, but was devoid of railings. Despite acting as if we were grown adults it was obvious we were still at school on the playground, divided into our segregated and stereotypical cliques: hipsters, stoners, hippies, thespians, intellectuals and nerd/techies.

The affluent, progressive and fashion-forward independent thinkers (hipsters) were gathered on the couch looking at the latest magazines while the Goth dressed, coffee addicted theatre crew (thespians) were playing pool and smoking Kretek clove cigarettes. Shay was hanging out in that group. Inexplicably, he always had his left hand on the back of his hip, positioning all his weight onto his right hip when he smoked; similar to a hooker stance. I thought it oddly effeminate, but chose to overlook it like I did with anything I found weirdly outré about him.

The nonconformist students with an interest in art and metaphysics (hippies and stoners) were outside huddled by a tree on the side of the house staring at what appeared to be nothing, while the cerebral, analytical philosophers of the group (intellectuals) and the scholarly, computer geniuses (nerd/techies) were on the far side of the porch in a deep political conversation. Connecting on similar interests with this group, I joined them in a debate about the current presidential candidate. I wondered if this segregation of types would last throughout our lifetimes. In subtle ways, I think it does.

The revealing and somewhat unsettling fish bone moment occurred sometime after midnight. After the crowd thinned out and in need of a few minutes of solitude, I decided to walk out onto the veranda into the darkness alone. I sat on the edge of the porch dangling my feet and staring into the vast nothingness ahead, attempting to imagine what the stoners were fascinated by earlier. The dense fog was almost as eerie as the anomalous silence, although I could slightly hear a low murmurous sound; either the wind sifting through the trees in the barely visible olive orchard way off in the distance, or sentient creatures under the porch—I preferred to think the former. *What a great scene for a horror movie.* My body stiffened, all of a sudden feeling too isolated. Thankfully, my anxiety was alleviated when I could hear the faint pleasant sound of the classic Bob Marley and The Wailers reggae tune *"Three Little Birds"* radiating from the nearby bedroom window. Although music is my drug of choice, eventually its effects wore off. Looking down, I couldn't see my feet, the nebulous fog covering them like soft blankets of dust clouds floating up to the bottom of my ankles.

I began to feel tremendously vulnerable and decided to stand and walk to where there was a vacant wooden Adirondack patio chair closer to the house and farther from the edge. Once I sat, my chess possessed pals, Dwight and Eric, came out the French doors and sat on the porch deck near me. We ended up in a deep conversation discussing the ambiguous core of the audacious and surrealistic elements of Woody Allen's movie *The Purple Rose of Cairo.*

In the middle of offering my personal interpretation of the movie, we were unexpectedly interrupted by Shay, Patrick and two open lesbian theatre classmates as they came out the patio doors and strutted by us wearing nothing except their skin—completely nude—an obvious declaration savored of immodesty. Then stepping down into the sunken hot tub at the end of the long veranda, they began whispering to each other while intermittently glancing over at the three of us. How ridiculous for them to act like *we* were doing anything out of the ordinary when *they* were the ones naked, not us. Shay then began embarrassingly laughing and glancing periodically over at Dwight and Eric while leaning in and caressing Patrick on his shoulder in a manner similar to what a girl might do when flirting: huge fish bone. *Wake up, Melody Rae!*

If I had paid more attention and had been less naïve, I would have probably conjectured Shay was gay right then and never pursued him further. Dwight and Eric assumed that he was. But consequently, I was falling for this odd-duck and certainly didn't want to believe he was gay and be left without hope to one day become his certifiable girlfriend. I rationalized his behavior to be analogous of a healthy open bohemian free-spirited youth, and there was something quite alluring in that notion. Although I was secretly suspicious and therefore preoccupied by what I was witnessing in the hot tub, I made a concerted effort to be as discreet as possible in the presence of Dwight and Eric trying not to let on how distracted I was. While simultaneously staring at both of them and nodding my head, I tuned out their voices striving to hear the dialogue between Shay and his indecorous naked partners. But all I ended up hearing was the sound of spa jets swirling about their bare-naked bodies in places I didn't want to visualize. The image couldn't be avoided, my mind went there anyhow. *Ugh.*

After that uncomfortable evening I never questioned Shay about his behavior, preferring to repress my feelings rather than address them, and our interactions resumed as before. Until one day I made a physical attempt at kissing him, to which he surprisingly reciprocated and we became that annoying high school couple with the dual nickname: Melshay, which eventually morphed into Milkshake. We generally hung out within a group, typifying the fact we never spent much alone time together. It was equivalent to having a close opposite-sex buddy who never threatens your independence. We could be ourselves in every respect seeing that we were more like girlfriends. There were several propitious benefits to dating a closeted gay: Freedom, trust and independence; I wasn't suffocated by an intense commitment or consumed by feelings of jealousy, and I could continue on my own separate path without the restricted feeling of a confining relationship. However there was also a major disadvantage to dating a closeted gay: lack of sexual rapport. Throughout the entire four years we knew each other we had minimal intercourse, and none of which was slightly memorable because they were virtually devoid of passion.

Almost three years after dating Shay and one month after graduating high school, I left Oregon to move (by myself) to California to attend City College of San Francisco. My brother Brian, who was three years my senior, allowed me to crash on his couch until I found a place of my own. He was living in Berkeley attending the university as an English major. I enrolled in CCSF as a science major with a minor in business with the aspiration of transferring to a university to achieve a graduate degree and eventually own a pet grooming salon.

Prior to moving, I terminated my innocent liaison with Shay, explicating in detail how I felt the long distance relationship wasn't healthy. With a farewell nod and kiss on the cheek he gave the impression he concurred, so I presumed the break up was mutual. Dissolving this association eliminated a huge emotional burden and a weight was lifted off my shoulders. I could breathe again…until I couldn't.

Less than six months after I had found an apartment in San Francisco, he literally showed up on my porch, on his knees, (in tears) despondent and begging me to let him stay. I felt sorry for him. After discovering that he had caught a ride from an uncle, who was headed down South and had no return transportation, how could I reasonably turn him away?

Despite believing that Shay simply wanted to get out of Oregon and wasn't remotely interested in rekindling what we had any more than I was, before we knew it we had lived together for almost a year. He had regressed back into his role as a poor-me victim and I reverted back into the role of savior: a role I play all too well—and misery ensued.

And, though, I appreciated Shay's reverence to step outside on the balcony to smoke the Kretek clove cigarettes he was deeply dependent on, as I didn't approve of smoking inside the apartment, the pungent scent transferred inside remaining on him and his clothing for hours after. Of course, he had an entire spiel claiming there were studies proving how this particular type of cigarette was the "healthy" kind. *Is there seriously such a thing as a "healthy" cigarette?* This was simply an example of one of many things we disagreed on. He seemed to take great delectation in disagreements in general as he was pejorative and litigious by nature, always finding a reason to belittle my opinion or argue his point of view—something I didn't know about him until we lived together.

During the time I was cohabitating with Shay, times were hard. I had an inconsequential amount of money as I was only working part time, and although financial-aid allotted me some currency since I was a full time college student, it wasn't enough for two people to survive on. Therefore, I had to procure a way to be inventive in the kitchen by creating strange concoctions with whatever items I found abandon in the cupboards, mainly; tuna-fish, top ramen and sardines. Some of the ingredients I combined were never meant to go together, like Country Barn cornflakes, Star-Kist tuna and Kraft macaroni and cheese. I consistently felt either sluggish and low or anxious and agitated. Partly due to what I was eating and partly due to the strong premonition I was involved with the wrong person for me. I deeply desired to be single and live alone. I was miserable and dragged down by Shay's constant negative attitude and disregard for my feelings. We were both uneasy around one another and living together was progressing into a grueling and agonizing experience for us both.

A blessing in disguise materialized when Shay began hanging out regularly each night with an older, openly gay gentleman named Lou, who he met while working as an "extra" in a low budget formula type B-movie. Lou was a short, pudgy, bald and scruffy bearded misogynist whose derogatory personality resembled a boorish and arrogant, virulent rodent. Whenever I was in the vicinity of his presence, he would say something degrading about women under his breath and then resume picking his teeth with a noticeably worn toothpick. But Shay was smitten and couldn't say enough nice things about him. Interestingly, he worshiped him similarly to how he had worshipped Patrick.

As time passed I began feeling resentful, since we were theoretically together and he was physically living at my place. Here I was financially and emotionally supporting him while he struggled to make it big as an actor. *Oh please!* He never even liked the theatre, although he did connect to theatre people. He seemed adrift, struggling to invent himself, lost about who he was and what he wanted. I conjectured he simply wanted to be an actor because it was what I had wanted to be. It was *my* dream in high school (not his) and all I talked about for years, until realistically accepting it was too big of a long shot. Besides, the reality was that I didn't honestly enjoy playing the role of other people; I preferred to play myself instead.

What was more harrowing was Shay couldn't act. After he would get these small parts in local stage productions, I would run his lines with him and he would enact them with large exaggerative gestures, and unnatural facial expressions. *Are you kidding me?* I believed he had limited skill because he had no range, always playing the exact same character; a poorly represented 1960's Gomer Pyle style of performance. Goofy is terrific with the right script, but doesn't work with every role. Not only did he regularly forget the few lines he did have, he often broke character. The times when he did remember the lines that he had agonizingly rehearsed, he'd spew them with phony delivery and display gawky body posture. It was purely nauseating. Worse, after witnessing him seriously blow it on stage, I felt obligated to say that I thought he did fine because he had this inflatable image of himself; completely incapable of constructive criticism. Though, his performances were insufferable, I couldn't deny him his dream, or excuse me, *my* dream.

It was several months after he spent time as a crew member before he began doing work purely as an "extra" in the film industry; not exactly a stable or financially lucrative vocation. But somehow he would come through with rent the day it was due. Sweating profusely and running in the door in a panic to hand me an envelope of cash, which I know he didn't earn simply by being an "extra." However, I didn't question where the money came from because I gravely needed it and was worried that without it I'd be living on the streets of San Francisco panhandling at The Fisherman's Wharf having to utilize my minimalistic method acting skills—not quite the future I had in mind for myself.

Then things escalated into a whirling vortex of strange, making my head dizzy. Shay began staying over at Lou's place on a regular basis, calling me late to say how it would be ridiculous for him to take a taxi to the other side of town when he simply had to turn around and head back in a few hours. In relation to our apartment in San Francisco, Lou lived on the complete opposite end of the city, making it logically understandable why it would be easier and cheaper to crash at Lou's than get a taxi back to our place. But when one night turned into almost every night, I started to develop suspicions about what was going on.

Shay claimed he was helping Lou on a palimpsest screenplay they were rewriting in hopes to get read by some hot new producer. It became abundantly clear when any questions I asked Shay in regards to this supposedly brilliant screenplay were evasively repudiated, no detail about the title of the script or what (if any) producers were interested. His responses were serpentine and entirely vague giving his story little validity.

For the first time since I'd met Shay sincere doubts about his integrity began to surface regarding his sexual orientation. What was he doing all night with Lou, anyway, playing games? I certainly didn't think they were playing scrabble or monopoly, although maybe a torrid version of pok*er*...or poke*him*. I began having disturbing visions of them wrestling about and climbing on top of each other making googly eyes at one another. These visions would make my stomach churn. I sensed I was dating a fraud, someone pretending to be someone he wasn't. It felt dreadfully like betrayal. I honestly wished that things had ended between us in high school, like they were supposed to. Why can't he be honest and be the one to end things for good this time? Why do I have to, once again, be the bad guy? I don't think I could reject him again. I no longer had the emotional tools to leave him without feeling guilty, as if I was abandoning him.

Fortunately, it wasn't long before an incident brought clarity giving me the strength to accept reality and the ability to allow things to unfold naturally. I met up with Shay and Lou at The Hard Rock Café and happen to catch them acting rather mesmerized with one another. When I first walked in, they had their arms intimately wrapped around each other engaged in what appeared to be an intimate conversation. As I walked toward them the look in Shay's eyes became furtive and they behaved suspiciously contrite, instantly dropping their hands to their sides.

Ignoring my cynical thoughts, I put on my "happy face" knowing manufacturing negative assumptions would only stir the inner fire inside me. I knew it was better to feel zealous than suspicious if I wanted to achieve a desirable outcome. I had no yearning to rock an already turbulent boat. But an hour later, after exiting the restroom and walking down the hallway back toward the table where the three of us had been sitting, my conjecture proved to be true; what I witnessed made it indisputable that I had good reason to feel equivocal.

In a close embrace, sitting side by side in the booth, Shay and Lou both had their arms resting behind each other. And then, after scanning the room apprehensively assumedly looking for me, Shay turned and faced Lou and then they leaned forward and gently pressed their lips together. *What in the world?! Did they just kiss? Oh my...they did! I can't breathe. I need to get out of here.*

Not wanting to accept the reality of what I had just witnessed, my body became tremulous as I looked down and shuffled through my purse looking for some imaginary item to distract me from the moment. I kept rattling through my purse as I approached the table, and continued to do so while looking down as I slowly slid into the booth next to Shay.

Taking a moment to glance upward, I noticed Shay had a dubious expression on his face. But, instead of looking directly at me, he turned and took a sip of his light beer, and then smiled. Unhinged by his tyrannical happiness, I returned to nervously ramble through my purse.

Lou then took his time sliding his arm down to his side, seemingly wanting to be caught being deceptive. "Looking for something?" he catechized in his typically glib manner.

"Uh, yea-h-h-h, I lost something…but I'm not sure I ever had it," I mumbled without looking up pondering the profundity of what I'd said.

Lou looked at Shay then back at me. "Pardon?" he asked befuddled.

"Never mind, I found it," I rescinded while pulling out my red lipstick case to avoid an interrogation of my painful thoughts. I felt like I was drowning and I wasn't sure if I wanted to come up for air. *Can I just be a mermaid and live under the water forever in denial? Pl-e-e-ease?!*

"She can't live without her lipstick," Shay quipped in a disingenuous tone feigning interest while taking another sip of beer. *Okay, now there's some real acting. See how well you play a condescending, deceitful prick? Why can't you do that on stage, Shay? Afraid you might have to dig deeper and expose your real self?—of course. You're much better at faking who you are, anyway.*

I was horrified by my own feelings of anger which boiled in my stomach like a volatile tornado. I stared at my wine glass, too stupefied to say anything. I was steaming inside and about to explode. Knowing that I wouldn't be able to control my emotions much longer, I excused myself to leave. I fabricated a story about having to retire early claiming that a client at the grooming salon needed me to come in before office hours; and would ingratiate me by paying double. They both seemed enormously relieved that I was leaving.

As soon as I exited the doors of the Hard Rock Café, I bolted down the sidewalk with tears streaming down my face and running at top speed all the way to the Powell Street Station to take the BART (Bay Area Rapid Transit) train home. I felt cold and unambiguous like I was in a black and white silent movie surrounded by no color or sound, as I ran speedily from one block to the next stricken with the bold reality of truth. I don't even remember getting on the BART train, or walking to my apartment.

Although internally I felt emotionally shattered, after a long hot bubble bath my physical body found the ability to continue as if nothing had happened. I wondered if this was karmic retribution from high school when I willingly allowed our mutual friend, Miles Bocelli, to kiss me while leading Shay to believe I was solely interested in him. I needed to gain a healthy perspective and console myself. *No, Melody Rae! You can't punish yourself. You were not even an item with Shay then. Shay is living with you, now. You are irrefutably together. He should be the one to end things before moving on.*

Regaining my center, I was able to robotically go through the physical motions of everyday life while silently waiting for Shay to let me go. For nearly a week, I was able to behave like the naïve and loving girlfriend I'd consistently been. Then the deep gnawing pain of feeling as if I was living with a total stranger began to gnaw at my gut giving me sharp stabbing stomach distress until I could no longer discard the truth. I began to question what else Shay hasn't told me. I could no longer deny how witnessing Shay's display of betrayal (his slimy "sardine-like" kiss with someone who wasn't me) broke my heart. I knew I had to do the right thing, for myself, and be the one to end things with him, again. Although deep down, I knew the reality was that the end had already come years earlier.

I took a personal day off work, spending the entire morning packing up Shay's belongings. When he came home after doing his long hard day's work as an "extra" (wannabe celebrity)—hanging out with B-rated actors, doing nothing but watching others act for eight straight hours—and saw his suitcases and boxes of personal belongings packed and sitting by the front door, he simply nodded. And then, nonchalantly, he snubbed out his Kretek clove cigarette in his comedy-tragedy theater mask shaped ashtray that was sitting on the kitchen counter, coughed into his closed fist and sighed, as if he was relieved to no longer have to dissemble his real motives from me.

But rather than mention "the kiss" I simply apologized for being a poor communicator. And then after a lengthy, gushy monologue listing all his positive qualities, I told him where I felt we were as a couple, expressing how grateful it was to have known him and how we had learned all we needed from each other, adding how it seemed time to move on in order to grow as individuals. After he expressed mutual feelings to dissolve the relationship, he unexpectedly cried and then held me tight. I was convinced he only cried out of guilt because he knew what a "slimy sardine" he had been for not ending it sooner.

As predicted, we parted amicably without a nefarious confrontation fraught with outrageous accusations or anger; which made sense considering our relationship never ignited much intensity of emotion. It was clear that we both felt a huge sense of relief to no longer be trapped in a frigid, lackluster relationship. And as expected, after Shay left the apartment, I never heard from him again. Although I'll never forget the day he vanished from my life because it was two days before Valentine's Day, the twelfth of February, 1988.

Why do countless breakups occur right before Valentine's Day? After pondering this question and taking the initiative to ask the Google internet web browser, I discovered the reason. It appears that the romantic holiday puts a lot of pressure on people to examine their relationship status, and if the relationship seems doomed to fail, most want to be single to explore a new option. Although it does seem unusually cruel timing, in our case it wasn't. I was glad to be a free woman and not have to fake it with a guy who prefers men to women.

It was disconcerting that Shay could never admit to being gay. For quite some time after our break up I'd have episodes of resentment materialize when I replayed how long I had lived in an empty relationship with someone who evidently was intimately involved with someone else; and then I would feel ill and get a bad aftertaste in my mouth. Why didn't he just man up and tell me the truth when things with Lou heated up, thereby setting me free? Why did I have to take responsibility for the death of the relationship and be the one with the fortitude to end it, when he was the unfaithful one? He was the one with the secret! I didn't have a problem with Shay's sexual orientation, but I did have an issue with him not being honest when he was indubitably discombobulated. Why didn't he tell me he was confused about what he wanted? Why didn't I ask? Good question. Although I wasn't unfaithful, I had to take responsibility for allowing myself to stay as long as I did in a relationship with a disconnected, emotionless and taciturn partner. Regardless of how things ended, it was a lesson for me to communicate better in my next relationship.

A few months after our relationship disintegrated various clients from Paw Parazzi's pet grooming salon, who knew Shay, enlightened me by sharing how they heard through the grapevine that he had moved to the East coast with a guy roommate of short stature possessing a scruffy beard. I naturally suspected it was the infamous Lou, satisfyingly closing the door to that chapter of my life.

Finally able to move forward, I bought several new self-help books and began to do some serious inner homework. I examined my past and realized how peculiar it was that I had kept all my male friends, who I consider "typical men", at a distance. The entire time I was dating and then cohabitating with Shay I had not made myself accessible to a relationship which could potentially manifest into something real or serious. But now I felt ready and anticipated a growth opportunity. I wanted to date a guy who was definitely a "guy." The manly type of guy with hair on the chest—physically and metaphorically.

The type of guy who would fit this category would possess the character of someone humorous and slightly womanizing, homogeneous to Tim "the tool man" Taylor (Tim Allen) from *Home Improvement*—with his adorable signature gorilla grunts "*Ough, Ough, Ough*"—combined with the physical appearance and simple mindedness of Hayden Fox (Craig T. Nelson) from *Coach*; the more Neanderthal, the more attractive. I was ready to reject any guy with any effeminate characteristics whatsoever. *Back off metrosexual males!*

Less than four months after Shay and I departed, my life officially began to transform launching a recurrent element of peculiar serendipity. I received a promotion to full time assistant at Paw Parazzi's salon, which was a considerable blessing because I was seriously struggling to pay bills now that I no longer had Shay paying his portion of rent. Still not making ends meet, I took a second job; a part time shift as a clerk working at the San Francisco Cinemark Theater on the weekends. And this invariably led to my first siting of the legendary and mysterious, *Mister S*.

I was scheduled to work the late shift for the midnight screening of *The Rocky Horror Picture Show* when he walked in and my world turned upside down. I perceived the encounter as a sign that other men could be attracted to me. I was relieved Shay would not be the only one. And, to this day, the memory still sends a tintinnabulation of rippling shivers up my spine.

I was twenty-one and single for the first time in four years, which was exciting, but made me feel a little vulnerable to the opposite sex—no longer able to use the "I have a boyfriend" excuse. It was late on a Saturday evening and I was the only clerk at the Theater. The manager was downstairs working on the daily books and had left me to cover the counter, alone. I was assailable and exposed, but excited to be independent. It was approaching the midnight hour for the showing of *The Rocky Horror Picture Show* when this tall and dark brown haired gentleman with gorgeous bronze skin, who shared a curiously strong resemblance to Robert Downey, Jr., approached the counter.

He was twenty-nine years old. No, I'm not psychic. I knew this because I was required to check everyone's driver's license for age identification before allowing admission to the late show. The minimum age for entrance was eighteen. I mentally noted his height, too: six-foot-four. But I berated myself for not taking enough time to locate the month he was born, in order to do some astrology checking later. He was in line with a petite and attractive lady with long, straight, dark brown hair, who I assumed was his girlfriend (or wife), because when she saw him smile at me she gave me the evil eye, clutched tightly to his hand and led him through the theater doors, causing him to spill some of his popcorn and part of his soda. I thought I saw a large diamond ring on her wedding ring finger, but I could have been mistaken.

Whether married or not, it was apparent they were involved. He let go of her hand to pick up the lid and straw which flew off his soda as she marched ahead. And then after standing, he looked back at me smiling apologetically. I waved with both hands as if to say: "Don't worry about it." Then our eyes locked for a brief second and I became statuesque lost in his penetrating gaze as the room stood still. He had dimples, a smile which made my heart skip a beat and dark brown eyes that were deep and earnest. There was something intimately comforting in them, something which made my belly do somersaults and my heart leap to the front of my chest and pound rapidly.

And then his woman came back out the open double doors and pulled him into the theater as my face turned bright red and I caught a strong whiff of his smell sending tingles down my backside. He had this curiously strong and freshly intoxicating scent which mysteriously provoked familiar memories of showering in a campground as a little girl. Then I was abruptly interrupted from my reverie by an irritated customer at the end of the counter, who was coughing exaggeratedly with provocation, anxiously waiting to purchase a ticket. Although I wasn't remotely bothered, my thoughts adrift in a lovesick daydream with a smile permanently planted on my face.

A short time later, as I was enthusiastically cleaning the counter and organizing the concession stand merchandise, *Mister S's* woman exited the theater doors marching ahead while he followed with his head down like an injured puppy dog. Later, standing at the back of the theater with my broom sweeper waiting for the denouement, I developed all sorts of conjecture as to why they left the risqué show early, but all I cared to concentrate on was how mesmerizing his eyes were.

Fortunately, I didn't allow my escapist thoughts to take over. I had no time to be sidetracked with an obsession, especially over someone I didn't even know. I was not anxious to be anyone's girlfriend, anyway. Being tied down in a relationship seemed so restrictive. I decided to thoroughly enjoy being single and concentrate primarily on my studies.

In order to avoid obsessing over a guy I barely knew, I did some girl therapy; discussing my opposite-sex friendships with my female friends to understand myself better. In the past, I had maintained healthy, purely platonic friendships with men who were unusually benevolent, trustworthy and responsible and who were not at all gay, but who I was also not attracted to; with the exception of Miles Bocelli.

Miles was the guy I felt guilty for kissing while starting a relationship with Shay. My school girl crush on Shay couldn't compare to my wild infatuation for Miles. Miles was the opposite of Shay. He could make my heart go wildly bump-bump simply by looking in my direction. His endearing dimples had an eerily similar resemblance to *Mister S.* And his intensely overpowering eyes seared right through me while his deliciously kissable smile made my insides do cartwheels tormenting my soul; an amorous crush which lasted all throughout high school—a secret kept hidden from everyone, including Miles.

I met Miles shortly after Shay and I started hanging out together. Although Shay and I weren't officially boyfriend and girlfriend or even physically involved on any level, I felt unquestionably committed to him. Miles and I had honors English and theatre class together and worked on projects which would often last all night: studying, researching, writing, and watching films. We mostly discussed the elisions and distortions in movies, theatre productions, musical lyrics and literature. Whenever we hung out, we'd talk nonstop; I looked forward to our time together with ebullience. He exposed me to Bobby Darin, Arlo Guthrie, David Bromberg and Rickie Lee Jones, liberating me into appreciating a variety of musical genres. Whenever we had a break in studying, he'd give me a dance lesson. He taught me clever techniques on how to perform old fashioned swing, mambo and tango with passion and style.

One particular evening I'll never forget: Fourth of July, 1984. Feeling excessively patriotic at age sixteen, I strapped a U.S. flag bandana around my wrist and wore a red, white and blue checkered vest with a brick red, strapless, knee-length dress with frills along the bottom, blue tights covered with stars and red cowboy boots. Miles, along with a group of our theatre class peers, met out at Rubino's sandwich shop in downtown Portland for a group picture and celebratory toast commemorating Independence Day.

At dusk, I was supposed to join Shay and Patrick a block up the hill on the corner in front of Giovanni's Wine Bistro to enjoy the fireworks over the city. Shay was helping Patrick work with his dad on some house project in order to borrow his parent's 1957 Cadillac convertible for the evening.

Once it was getting late I excused myself to leave. Miles stood and offered to walk to the corner and wait with me claiming he wanted to be sure I was safe. I was taken by his old fashioned charm. Of course, I wanted him to walk with me. I privately wished Miles would pursue me, although I didn't know how I would end things with Shay if he did. Next door to the wine bar was Freddie's jazz club which exhibited large windows with open shutters, and as we were walking past Miles grabbed my hand preventing me from walking farther.

"Listen," he cooed, smiling with those kiss-me-now dimples which drove me wild.

The jazzy song *"Danny's All-Star Joint"* by Rickie Lee Jones was sifting pleasantly through the open windows. I looked at Miles with a wide smile, elated by the symmetry of our situation, telepathically suggesting we do what we both were simultaneously thinking. Our minds and hearts in sync, he pulled me in tight and swirled me around in a traditional old swing style move we had practiced many times before when breaking the monotony of our often tedious projects, and we tangoed like true lovebirds. Both of us beaming with enthusiasm while winking at one another and rocking with the beat eliciting an undeniable venereal chemistry as if we were celebrities performing on *Dancing with the Stars*. At age sixteen, I felt more alive in that moment than ever before.

Intriguing how different people bring out varying aspects of our psyches. Miles always brought out the performer in me, as I did in him. I giggled delightfully as Miles twirled me around while singing along with the lyrics. In and out we twisted around each other rocking back and forth in flawless rhythm. I continued to follow his exceptional lead, snapping my fingers at the right time while allowing him to dip me periodically. The music increased as the patrons crowded in the doorway growing in size like intrusive paparazzi. Near the end of the song, it appeared every customer was gawking through the open windows; the cynosure of all eyes there. Once the song ended the crowd whistled and started clapping wildly at our performance which aroused Miles' stage persona to respond. And he did, by pulling me aside and kissing me right there and then in front of an entire audience of strangers. He kissed me...on the lips! Time stood still. I was afraid to speak, not wanting the moment to end.

I was so completely captivated and under Miles' spell lingering in a daze from his unexpectedly hot and sweetly hypnotic kiss that I almost forgot we had an audience, until I heard the cheers. I turned to face the jazz club and curtsied to appease the hollering spectators. Then Miles gently took my hand and waltzed me to the end of the corner sidewalk where we sat on the curb leaning up against one another, laughing deliriously and flirtatiously. I kept shaking my head as if to say: "We shouldn't have kissed." Although I enjoyed it more than words could muster. Miles was unaware this was only the second time that I'd been kissed by a boy. I'd hoped it wasn't noticeable.

My official "first kiss" was only a year earlier with Zeek Cohen, a friend of my brother Cormac's. Everyone called him ZeekDaGeek because he was genius level studious: a physics enthusiast, a calculus team leader, chess team competitor, a fanatic "Dungeon and Dragons" player and a voracious reader. Coincidentally, these were my favorite things about him, although I didn't entirely relate. The "kiss" happened at my childhood home in Ashland during a slumber party when we played spin-the-bottle. Although I bragged about "the kiss" to Lillian and Carlene with exaggerative juicy details, to be honest, our lips barely touched. However, I did have a secret four year crush on Zeek and so for me it was memorable. Three years my senior, he was headed off to Cambridge, Massachusetts to attend (not surprisingly) Harvard on a full-ride scholarship. Subsequently, he met a girl in one of his college classes, who was similarly geeky, and they married at a private country club, near the Susquehanna River, in her hometown of Pennsylvania. It goes without saying that besides being a one-sided dalliance, the guy was unquestionably out of my league.

Miles' kiss was not remotely in the same category as Zeek's. It was bold, juicy, sensual, penetrating, lingering and warm. As the fireworks began to erupt high above our heads, my heart erupted with desire yearning for Miles to kiss me again. As if he could read my mind, he leaned back onto the sidewalk and goaded me to lie down next to him. Looking up in the sky at the exceptionally bright colors and listening to the crackling pops and thunderous sounds, I was blissfully and overwhelmingly happier than I'd ever been. *I am exactly where I want to be.* Exploding fireworks high above tall city buildings was a new experience for me generating a tear to trickle down my cheek. The connection I had to Miles was anomalous while simultaneous intoxicating. The idea of growing up and becoming a woman was frightening and titillating. I wanted this moment of hope for an unforeseeable and galvanizing future full of adventure to last forever.

Before I was able to allow my incurable fantasy full rein and hold Miles in my arms and kiss him with the unparalleled vigor and passion stirring deep in my soul, Shay and Patrick drove up in his father's 1957 Cadillac convertible to pick me up and head to a parking spot a few blocks away where we had planned to watch the fireworks continue. I hesitantly waved adieu to Miles wondering if he could tell by my facial expression how I dreaded leaving him. *Can't you tell that I am utterly crazy about you?* Although I wanted Miles to know how I felt about him, I hoped my feelings were hidden from Shay. I couldn't possibly hurt him. I discovered after many relationship debacles and several self-help books, incessant worrying about how men feel was one of my biggest personality flaws, causing me the most inner turmoil. I would do things time and time again, not for me, but for them. Consequently, this enabling quality of mine made me a prime target for attracting selfish men.

Although the natural chemistry between me and Miles seemed undeniable, I knew it needed to be kept in check out of respect for Shay. I was mysteriously devoted to Shay even before we were an item. I believe it was because he was timid which made me feel in control; a feeling I needed then. I wasn't at all in control of my feelings for Miles. He had the potential to break my heart, which seriously petrified me. From my perspective, Miles and I connected physically, emotionally and mentally as if we had known one another all our lives. But because I had no clue about how he truly felt about me, I held my emotional cards close to my chest. I worried my feelings for Miles would destroy Shay. And since I felt sorry for him, I repressed my true feelings. I suspected Shay was too vulnerable and would be totally crushed if I were to walk away from what we were beginning to build together. I didn't want to be responsible for his heartache. Shay was outwardly less evolved issuing me more power, while Miles was ostensibly more evolved fostering the illusory belief I wasn't good enough for him. I couldn't see him dating little ol' me. I saw him dating someone popular, more affluent and much prettier. Miles came from money and had friends in the popular crowd at school which intimidated me. Although he did ask me to marry him once, I'm certain he wasn't serious.

The entirely informal proposal took place only a few days after our dance debut, on the downtown city sidewalk out in front of Freddie's on that momentous Independence Day. Hours into writing a play together for a class project and after performing our characters lines from a script we'd co-written, he pivoted toward me, and then just stared.

"We're simpatico…marry me?" he pleaded with puppy dog eyes.

I gasped and then felt my heart skip a beat. "There's no one else I'd rather marry," I declared with unusual sincerity, lost in his smile.

I felt our bodies melt together. The moment was overwhelming, as we gazed longingly into one another's eyes. But then reality set in, and I came back down to earth and playfully punched him on the arm.

To avoid addressing my feelings, I anxiously obtained a pen and quickly added those lines to our script. "Perfect ending! Good ad lib, Miles," I trilled, pleased with our project while worried he could tell I harbored genuine romantic feelings for him.

I panicked for a minute when I thought he was about to lean in and kiss me. To avoid a Fourth of July replay, which had the potential to lead to something more that I feared unable to control, I shifted my head to the right and hugged him.

I often worried Shay could tell how I felt about Miles, as if he could see the insatiable desire commingled with a vestigial flicker of guilt in my eyes whenever his name was brought up. Despite the fact Shay and I hadn't even kissed, yet, and weren't officially a couple, everyone at school thought of us as an "item."

Tragically reminiscent of the evanescence of my first crush Zeek Cohen, nothing transpired between Miles and me. Once settled in San Francisco I received a call from Jeri, a theatre classmate inviting me to a going away party for our drama instructor Hilary, who had fallen in love and was

moving back east, and getting married. Hilary was like a mom
to us all. In theatre, you get closer to your peers and the
instructor than you do in most classes because you spend so
much time sharing personally intimate stories with one
another; in and outside of class. Jeri asked me if I had heard
from Miles lately. And when I confided that I hadn't, she
informed me how she heard he'd met a woman named
Melanie (a European fashion model), reportedly online,
married her and subsequently moved to Paris. I was
(selfishly) forlorn, but not surprised. I predicted he would
find love early on in life. He was a hopeless romantic who
thrived on partnership.

Despite the concealed romance with Miles Bocelli being
ephemeral, I still think about him from time to time and
wonder how he's doing because he was frankly the one and
only unrequited love of my life.

Although Miles was not the only good guy, platonic male
friend I nurtured, he was the only one I was overwhelmingly
physically, mentally and emotionally attracted to. I fostered
several male friendships with decent guys, who had steady
jobs and who were respectful of women, considerate, selfless,
giving and mature. However, these guys also happened to be
passive and weak-minded. I had no interest in dating any of
them as I coveted no physical attraction or natural
connection to any of them; they all felt more like brothers to
me. Inexplicably, all these men ended up dating women who
were opposite of them: needy, poor-me victim, controlling,
pushy types. *Go figure.*

Convinced I would be eternally single, I started going out
late dancing and eating poorly, once again. Leaving the
nightclubs in the wee hours of the morning, I'd pull into a
Carl's Jr., drive-thru and order a quick, unhealthy meal: a
regular coke, French fries and a ninety-nine cent spicy
chicken sandwich (hold the chicken). I was still a vegetarian,
but I loved the bread, sauce and fries which unfailingly came
with the order.

On the rare occasion I ate at home, for dinner I would
cook the most fattening, cheesy veggie tacos or burritos with

tons of beans, rice and salsa and eat two large helpings. I concluded, since I was incapable of being a controlling, needy female, I'd never land me a sensitive, genuine, responsible type of man. Assumedly, I was meant to be with the opposite of me; a one-dimensional, superficial, selfish, insensitive, secretive, insecure male. It was disturbing to think that this might be the only type of guy that would invariably work for me.

And as destiny would have it, shortly after my dive into a world of greasy fast food bingeing oblivion, I met the oleaginous and artificial fish, Tony (Big Boy) Salinas.

Chapter Three

What do you get if you cross a math teacher with a crab? Snappy answers.

Soft Shell Crab

The meat of the blue crab, which is found along the Atlantic and Gulf Coasts, has a rich, sweet, succulent and buttery flavor. Soft shells offer a crunchy texture, since the shell is edible. Enjoy soft shell crabs deep-fried, sautéed or grilled.

****

"You know, Melody Rae, to be brutally honest, considering how many relationships you've had, you should be grateful you never developed any serious long term emotional issues requiring a professional therapist," Kat orated, and then quickly stood from her stool to grab a paper towel off the counter to wipe up the wine spill caused when I gagged in reaction to her comment.

"Well, first of all, YOU are my therapist," I cackled. "And, secondly, I totally have been afflicted with emotional issues! True, I didn't feel completely damaged until after Kyle, but after Shay, Tony, Willie and Peter, while in many ways I grew stronger, I also became spiritually injured. It's not that I'm bitter. I'm not. But my adult experiences with men have definitely left me with a bitter aftertaste."

Kat nodded.

"In fact," I pondered, looking down, "I've thought a lot about this. You know me. That's what I do. I overthink e v e r y t h i n g—that *is* my therapy! Well that, and getting feedback from you—my official therapist."

Kat beamed.

I floundered through my large saggy purse on the floor beside me until locating the small legal pad that I'd stashed in the interior side pocket. "I devised a way to metamorphose my past trauma into a healing process. I figured that if I wrote down all the main triggers that kept me stuck in the past, I'd be freed."

"Like how every time you see an old, faded, white Ford pickup you're reminded of Willie and then become obsessed with him all over again?" Kat interjected.

"I totally do, don't I? But no, that's not the type of trigger I mean. I put more emphasis on triggers that stir up negative feelings. Seeing Willie's truck brings up the good times I had with him, not the bad. He sure had the power to make me weak in the knees. And by the way, thanks for bringing that up, Kat," I said, scowling and unfolding the list with fervor.

"Sorry," Kat giggled, amused with how rattled I still get over Willie.

I rolled my eyes. "Okay. Listen to this. Besides attributing a type of fish to each guy, I decided to address three senses: smell, hear and taste because these three senses trigger my past memories. I assume it's probably the same for you. I know that my past surfaces whenever I smell a specific scent, or hear a specific song, or taste a particular food. These senses elicit my emotional, spiritual, physical and mental memory. Do you think that's true for you, too, Kat?" I asked with sincerity.

"Totally!" squealed Kat. "Every time I smell vanilla, I'm right back at the beach house with Troy. He would outline the hot tub with vanilla scented candles, light vanilla incense in the bathroom and even put vanilla bath salts in my bath water. The man was a bit too fond of that smell. So, yeah, I sort of avoid vanilla scented anything now."

"Oh, see! You totally understand. I knew you would! So, here's the thing, if I am going to get on the healthy bandwagon, I need to tackle these distinct triggers that have left me with a bad aftertaste, so I can recognize them and not allow them to interfere in my potential for a healthy future. I wrote down every ex-boyfriend's fishy nature and then categorically what smell, music, and food elicit bad memories of each," I resounded, bubbling over with enthusiasm as if I was unleashing the creative tiger within. I felt an immense sense of accomplishment at discovering an innovative way to heal my soul.

I took a deep breath and then referring to my list, I continued, "Like after dating the slimy sardine, Shay, I could no longer smell Kretek Clove cigarettes, or hear the song '*Lola*' by The Kinks, or taste ginger without having a tart and deceptive aftertaste."

ginger root

"Aha!" Kat exclaimed and then sighed, slowly leaning back and clasping her hands behind her head. "All right, I get it. Now that's clever...crafty, actually. I like it," she said, and then nodded, picked up her wine glass and swirled it around in a contemplative state seemingly soaking in my theory.

"You get it! I mean, it's incontestable. Shay smoked Kretek Cloves and we were incessantly eating top ramen like it was going out of style; adding ginger to stir fry was like a ritual with us...Oh!" I clapped my hands tittering while looking down at my notes, "you're gonna get a kick out of the deeper reason for the song '*Lola*' because...well, I mean...you know that I found him dressing up in my clothes, right?" I queried with clenched teeth waiting for Kat to have another "aha" moment.

"Are you kidding me? Get out of town!" Kat shrilled, and then guffawed practically spitting out her wine. "Are you really serious? No, I don't remember you telling me that."

"I'm totally serious! Get this...I caught him wearing my strapless red heels with my white Marilyn Monroe style dress. The one that I wore for a role I once performed as a fifties high school student in an acting class skit. The song '*Lola*' instantly triggers the memory of catching him standing there in my closet. Where he still is, I suppose," I snickered, "considering he never left the closet."

We both chuckled simultaneously.

"I think it's ingenious that you created a list, seriously!" Kat proclaimed with an amused expression on her face and her left hand out frozen in stop mode. "But don't read the rest.

After we hash out the troubling aspects of each relationship, I might wanna see if I can guess some of the triggers."

"Cool! Yes. That would be great. Thanks, Kat!" I marveled with both hands clenched in fists of delight.

Kat grinned.

Then I remembered *The Secret Language of Relationships* book I had in my jeep. "Oh, guess what? I forgot to tell you. I finally bought that relationship book I told you about. It's in my jeep. I bought it earlier today. I thought it would be helpful in seeing why all my relationships haven't worked out—well, and yours, too. It combines each sign and explains why you connect with certain personalities and not with others," I proclaimed.

"Awesome…go get it! Let's check it out."

"I'm on it!" I yelped, fishing the keys out of my purse and jamming out the front door.

When I returned to the kitchen a few minutes later Kat wasn't there. I sat and decided to scan the relationship chart in the front pages anxiously searching for the paragraph combining the week of Shay with me. And after reading our compatibility, I let out an audible moan astounded by the details of verisimilitude. I was affected on many levels, as it was disturbingly accurate and thus enlightening. I wish I had knowledge of this book years ago; perchance, I could have prevented debilitating experiences. Was I about to discover that every relationship I endured was inevitably doomed? In spite of spiritually knowing that I needed to have every relationship I did in order to become as self-aware as I am, I questioned whether the pain was necessary.

Kat bounded down the stairs returning to the kitchen where I was sitting. Presumably, she had been checking on her daughter. She touched the book, procured her wine glass, sat and insisted I read the highlights aloud. After I presented her with a "sample" relationship combination, she claimed it would be simplest, for now, to only read the title of our combination, list of weaknesses and what we are best at as a couple. Feeling mutually agreeable, we toasted our wine glasses.

"Good plan," I reasoned.

Then turning toward me, Kat grilled, "All right, so what does it say about your combination with Shay?"

"Fine," I said, taking a slow deep breath. "The title for our combination, the twenty-third of December with the third of December is: the resolve to prevail. Weaknesses: undermining, overconfident, unhealthy. Best at: sibling."

"Whoa! That is spot-on, for sure. You two stayed together way longer than you should have which was unhealthy. And, I mean, from what I understand, Shay was arrogant and you both consistently undermined one other, albeit unknowingly. And I can see how you treated each other like brother and sister. Wow, that's crazy how accurate that book is…so weird."

"I know…too weird," I said, shaking my head and putting both hands over my mouth, inhaling despairingly and then exhaling slowly. Wine was desperately needed at this point. The reality that I needed this therapy more than I realized hit me like a rock.

While I poured myself some more wine and took a few sips, Kat seized the book off the table and quickly looked up her combination with Troy and thereafter her combination with Steven. Once we started reminiscing about our similar relationship foibles and unpacking the grocery bags time flew by. When I finally took a moment to glance at the hall clock above Kat's stairwell, I noticed that an hour had passed since I walked in the door.

By this time, we were both talking at warp speed and to anyone listening in, we undoubtedly sounded like two simultaneous radio stations competing for reception. It makes sense why onlookers listening in on our conversation always appear astounded. Often commenting how baffling it was to witness two people articulate with such speed, while simultaneously laughing and listening to the other, and somehow finding time to breathe.

Realizing my purse was still sitting at my feet and needing a moment to stretch, I decided to hang it up and at least make use of Kat's new purse rack. Although the simple brown Gucci, baggy style purse added nothing special to her panoply. Kat was a true purse pimp, possessing every size, style and brand in every imaginable color. And she was generous enough to allow her friends to borrow them whenever going out. I sat back down staring at her purse "whore" collection envisioning them as purse prostitutes wearing heavy makeup, fishnet stockings and stilettos. I giggled aloud, amused by my unorthodox vision.

"You know," Kat said, interrupting my improper stream of consciousness, "as your newly appointed *honorary* therapist, I would say, aside from the smell, sound and taste that will forever haunt you, your experience with Shay gave you the tools to sense when a guy is lying to you. You can be deemed the official queen of understanding slimy, sardine-like behavior. I mean, you've never dated another gay guy with his demeanor, right?"

I nodded while tittering and snorting intermittently. "Okay, okay, okay. I suppose I can agree with that interpretation," I replied, "but I was still quite inexperienced when I met Tony. Shay was my only relationship experience before him. So, while I may have been the expert queen of closeted gay men, superficiality was totally foreign to me. You know what I mean? And Tony was noncommittal and uninvolved which didn't seem unusual to me because that's how Shay was. I thought separateness was intimacy."

"So, was that the serious deal breaker with Tony, that he was a commitment-phobic?" Kat postulated.

"Um, n-o-o-o! There is w-a-a-ay more to it than that!" I whined argumentatively while shaking my head. *But was there?*

"What were you eating?" Kat demanded.

"Well, now that is a good question. When the theater unexpectedly closed, I was left with only working at Paw Parazzi's. And despite being a full time assistant, my salary barely paid the bills. And, since I was still attending college there was little money left over for groceries, so I was eating an excess of top ramen. And, since Tony was a movie fanatic and had friends in the industry that procured us tickets for free, we went to the movies an excessive amount of time where I consumed a ton of popcorn loaded with that artificial oily movie theater butter. You know, when I worked at that movie theater before I met Tony, I struggled to read the label on a huge tub of it once. Did you know there is no recognizable ingredient in that stuff? Seriously! And there's no actual butter in it at all!"

"Gross," Kat gurgled.

"Oh, and at home I'd often have a bowl of ratatouille with a handful of soup and oyster crackers. They're cheap. Of course, Tony, who loved to cook, put extra garlic powder on everything, mostly spaghetti noodles which he prepared *all* the time. After dating him I never wanted noodles with garlic marinara ever again."

"So, you ate a lot of greasy, cheap, artificial products?"

"Exactly!" I cried.

"That does sound like Tony."

"HA! You are so right!" I admitted while scrunching and pulling at the sides of my hair as I reflected back. "Boy, if I knew then what I know now."

"Then you would never have any rich experiences. The best adventures in life are the ones with risk involved. C'mon, Melody Rae, *you* know that! How else would you learn anything?"

"Spoken from the queen of risk…Miss bungee jumping, skydiving, tough mudder, thrill seeker."

"O-o-o-o-o-oh, I like that. I need a bumper sticker with that on it!" Kat squealed.

"Next birthday gift," I promised, tilting my wine glass and giving a nod.

"All right, so how did you meet Tony? Although you've told me a little bit about him, you'll have to remind me what he was like."

"Sure," I said, and then proceeded to tell Kat the sordid details of my unhealthy relationship with mister "Big Boy."

****

August 1988

Typical Daily Food Choices:
Folgers medium roast coffee w/heavy cream
Coca Cola or 7Up
movie theater buttered popcorn
Twinkies
top ramen
spaghetti noodles, thick marinara sauce w/extra garlic
bland soup & oyster crackers
sourdough baguette w/margarine
cheap red or white wine, generally from a box

Phony Tony

 T ony (Big Boy) Salinas was an unusually sexy dark-haired, five-foot-ten, full-blooded Hispanic guy. Although inherently born in Mexico, when he was less than a year old his parents divorced and his mother obtained full custody, and uprooted him to San Diego, California. He never learned to speak his native tongue, English becoming his first rather than second language. Growing up in a beach town, he became a sensational surfer and subsequently a certified instructor, making him even more alluring to the female species. Needless to say, before we met he dated more than a few attractive women.

Contrary to my first impression of Tony, he turned out to not only be a slippery fish, but homogeneous to a crab with no spine, like a **wishy-washy soft shell crab: sweet and sensitive on the outside while hiding his real true deeper feelings and crabby nature under his tender pliable shell.**

We met at a time in my life when I was financially struggling to make ends meet. I was enjoying the tranquility of living alone for a solid six months residing on the second floor in the same one bedroom apartment I had cohabitated with Shay. The three story apartment complex had a gated underground garage, which after living in the area for a while I was able to decode was a warning sign. If a building has to lock up your car, most likely it is not a safe neighborhood. *Hello!* Several neighbors shared stories with me of having their cars broken into. I didn't believe the neighborhood was terribly seedy until I had to park on the street a couple of times. I had a used, compact, faded, red, 1973 Datsun pickup truck (that my dad bought me as a graduation gift) and both times that I parked on the street, which I was forced to do because some stranger parked in my designated garage space, it was broken into. The first incident occurred when I accidentally left the doors unlocked. The thieves removed my insurance information, left the sun visors askew and removed the belongings from inside the glove box, which I found on the dashboard and scattered about the front seat. The second incident, the front passenger window was shattered and my cassette tape case was unzipped. When I peered inside the case, only the Captain and Tennille, Carol King, John Cougar, Rod Stewart and ACDC tapes were stolen, all the country tapes were left intact; meaning that we can assume one thing, the criminal wasn't a hillbilly.

Besides feeling more vulnerable living alone than with a roommate, and although in comparison to other apartment dwellings in the city, it was an affordable complex, I was finding it considerably difficult on my paltry salary to afford the lease while continuing to fund my education at the City College of San Francisco. The fall semester was about to begin and the cost for books and college tuition increased by almost thirty percent; and to make matters worse, at the beginning of the new calendar year, my rent was scheduled to be raised one hundred dollars per month.

I began to realize how much I previously depended on what I thought was a measly rent portion from Shay. I was considering moving to a studio apartment within the same complex, which had recently become vacant on the first floor, because I didn't want to be forced to get a roommate. I was a royal loner and not comfortable living with anyone that

I didn't know well. Especially not keen on the idea of living with a total stranger.

Before doing anything too drastic, I revised my personal bills, eliminating my food budget first, which forced me to endure a period of having to rely solely on my parents to help me out with food expenses; ineluctably humbling me further as I was stubborn and highly independent. But the last thing I wanted to resort to doing was move back home. *Never!* I would rather live on the streets of Berkeley as a panhandler.

Every few months, my parents would drive all the way from Portland to deliver food care packages and spend time with me. But I think they visited mostly to enjoy the city experience. The Broadway style live stage productions and the multifarious variety of restaurants captivated them both. After my mother read in the popular Food and Wine magazine a palpable review from a renowned chef, claiming Berkeley was the birthplace of California cuisine, she was especially interested in a sojourn to the area. And my father was especially fond of the art scene. Though, they saw the American illusionists *Penn and Teller* at the Phoenix Theater on two different occasions, since magic and comedy with an intelligent bent is their type of entertainment, Steve Silver's *Beach Blanket Babylon* (the pop culture pastiche) at Club Fugazi is one of their favorite productions, because of their shared love for current events with political satirical humor.

In view of the fact that my mother was the Food Service Production Manager at Western Culinary Institute in Portland, she was fortunate enough to have full access to a variety of foods. And owing to the fact that she received a considerable discount on bulk items, the care packages were colossal. Ordering from Sysco Food Distributor's, which offered things like Birdseye French cut green beans, Duchess baked potatoes and Phillip's crab cakes (although frozen), I was able to eat a better quality food than I did when dating Shay. However, as most people know, anything heated then frozen and reheated again doesn't taste quite as fresh.

Coincidentally, Tony, similar to a Sysco product, was more together than Shay as he possessed higher standards; coming from a family with ethics and money. Therefore, I can confidently say he was a fancier entrée than Shay, but nevertheless, he was still, like Shay, processed, leaving me with a bad aftertaste.

I was at the local Punch Line comedy club every Friday and Saturday night. My co-workers (dog lovers like me) would join me in taking the BART train to Berkeley for happy hour at Larry Blake's; a blues club where live music was a regular occurrence. I enjoyed the culturally diverse, eclectic, artistic, New Age, Greenwich Village style atmosphere espoused in downtown Berkeley because it attracted a high level of intelligent, unique, obscure people. My brother Brian, who lived in Berkeley and was currently attending the University of California, Berkeley, enjoyed the artsy downtown atmosphere too, and would often join us.

The entire Bay Area offered a wide range of things to do and the diversity of quaint bijou restaurants in the city and surrounding areas was stupendous. However, the average forty minute wait to get in one (merely to be seated) tested my patience. I adored the museums and the unique comedy clubs, but because the traffic was unbearable, I became unbearable. Living in San Francisco with the hustle and bustle and culture of the surrounding communities was enjoyable for a couple of years, but then I became overwhelmingly frustrated with the congestion, feeling claustrophobic, like I couldn't breathe. I began missing the small town of Ashland where I grew up and longed for days of staring at the sky from the white snowy rooftop of my childhood home on a serene winter's day, overlooking soft snow covered trees and listening to the whistling sound of the wind.

After numerous social outings, hanging out with friends and never meeting anyone I liked, I began to feel blasé. And then during a break at work, when I happen to come across a Rogue Community College pamphlet in the lobby, I began seriously considering transferring my credits and returning to Ashland, Oregon. And I probably would have, had I not met Tony.

After my promotion at Paw Parazzi's, I was given the awesome responsibility of having to interview new employees. I was scheduled to interview three people and choose one for a janitorial/assistant position, to do light clean up and help handle the bigger dogs.

Coincidentally, the night prior to the day I met Tony, I experienced an abnormally vivid dream about myself meeting a tall, dark-haired, clean-cut, handsome guy with a sturdy build at a downtown coffee shop. In the dream I am wearing a long, silky, red dress, sitting alone at a small round wooden corner table of a remote coffee shop in Berkeley and I am drinking a café au lait topped with cinnamon and whipped cream. In walks this tall, dark-haired jock wearing white Adidas tennis shoes, 501 Levi jeans with a navy blue windbreaker. I catch a glimpse of the Nike symbol on the back of his jacket when he approaches the counter. And then he turns around to face me, does a double-take and smiles exposing the most adorable Mario Lopez dimples. After ordering, he walks over to my table and without asking has the audacity to sit. Then he slides a bagel with cream cheese and lox over to me, leans back and cradling his latte stares at me with a phlegmatic look in his eyes. I was appalled by his arrogant behavior while simultaneously excited by his presence.

I look at him puzzled. "Seriously? You're not even going to ask me what *I* want?" I query while nervously circling the top ridge of my hot coffee mug with my index finger.

"I know what you want," he responds with an air of hubris self-entitlement. "Me."

I awkwardly chuckle and then wake up. I wasn't quite sure what the dream meant, but I liked how I felt after; infused with hope from the transparent interest of a charming gentleman who seemed sincerely into me.

I didn't put much thought into the dream as a premonition of anything to come because I wasn't into the athletic "jock" type of guy. I could however see myself meeting a guy in a coffee shop, or in one of my animal science classes, or in Montana where I would occasionally attend a workshop for the National Dog Groomers Association of America. I suppose it was because I relish my personal space that I never imagined meeting a guy at work.

But that thought flew out the window when Tony walked into the lobby of Paw Parazzi's pet grooming salon, to apply for the janitorial/assistant position, and I took one look at him. I completely lost my balance splattering a full mug of hot Folgers coffee all over my long, white blazer. He was tall, dark-haired with a sturdy build and had an adorable Mario Lopez dimpled smile; mirroring the identical physical characteristics and demeanor of the guy I'd dreamt about. The moment was indescribable, there were no words. I was instantly attracted to his appearance; except for the pink Polo shirt that I found somewhat off-putting, since I unfairly attach pink to femininity because of my past with Shay, who had an affinity for the color pink wearing it regularly. I was working diligently to avoid any guy who had any traits which did not fit a purely masculine model. I decided to overlook this minor detail, as I am logically aware pink is plainly a color not a label of sexual orientation.

This pink Polo wearing Mario Lopez twin approached the front counter I was standing behind with imperturbable poise. Wearing a ridiculously sly half-smile, white Adidas tennis shoes, a hemp style necklace and pink Polo shirt (with the collar up) tucked neatly into his light Levi 501 jeans it was as if he leaped out of my dream. *Am I psychic?* My grandmother Marta was presumably psychic. The one time she flew to the States from Ireland to visit us in Ashland, she confided in me how she would have dreams (more like nightmares) about relatives having accidents before they happen. Supposedly, she would dream the same exact dream three nights in a row and then it would come true. Her gift frightened her so much, she rarely shared her premonitions. I was only twelve when she revealed her psychic ability to me. But because my grandmother was considered by the family to be divorced from reality, I didn't put much stock in the validity of her stories. Even if I did believe she was psychic and thought I may have inherited her gift, my dream was in a totally different category. I only had the dream once and it wasn't negative. *Or was it? And could I have dreamt this other nights before and not remembered doing so?*

There I was, embarrassingly stretching for a paper towel to wipe up the coffee I had spilled all over my white coat, as this clean-cut gentleman reaches over the counter to shake my hand.

"Hi. I'm Big Boy," he said, then coughed. "Sorry…a nickname. My legal name is Tony. Tony Salinas. I have a ten o'clock interview."

Shaking his right hand with mine while holding a paper towel in my left to wipe the coffee spill off my coat, I noticed his nails were neatly manicured. I suspected he was the overly meticulous metro-male type, but since his presence was so unassuming I gathered he might also be fun. His acute resemblance to the guy I visualized about in my dream, the night before, caused me to overlook rational logic. I practically leapt toward him offering him the job, a uniform, a dinner date, and my body to use however he wished.

Auspiciously more professional on the exterior, I didn't let my inner crazy concupiscence do any talking. Inviting him to sit in the back office, I conducted the interview in a rather mature and stoic fashion. All he witnessed was a reserved, demure and tightly wound business woman. I sat with my legs crossed and clipboard on lap, asking basic routine questions, writing notes, nodding my head and tapping a pen on the clipboard while my internal thoughts raced with all sorts of lurid and nefarious images. *Stop staring at his lips, Melody Rae!*

My inner "nut-job" visualized ripping off that awful pink Polo shirt from his hard body and exposing his manly hairy chest, tearing off that hippie hemp necklace with my teeth, and allowing my lips to kiss those adorable dimples. I imagined licking droplets of trickling champagne off his belly while caressing his delicious six pack abs. Thankfully he couldn't read my mind and reveal this delirious fantasy. His conservative and rather serious attitude came out when he noticed I was emotionally somewhere else.

"Are you okay?" he asked.

I instantly snapped back into reality, blinked my eyes and straightened out my posture, which I imagined looked like a poodle in heat. I smiled, chuckling inside at my risqué wandering mind. Obviously he was hired. He could have been illiterate with no English skills and no experience ever working with dogs. In fact, he could have hated dogs and I would have still hired him. He was my "dream" guy, I had to hire him; he was going to be my new obsession.

Things took some time to evolve. I was finding it difficult to fuel my Tony fixation, because during the first week at work we never had a convenient opportunity to talk. I was either grooming a different dog in another room, or counseling a couple who had overprotective issues with their dog, which in some ways is no different than a parent with their child. Separation anxiety is always created by the adult. If the dog owner feels secure, trusting and comfortable, so will the dog. Never a moment for Tony and me to be alone in a room meant little possibility for flirting. I was about to give up on thinking mister pink Polo and I would ever become an item, until one night when we coincidentally ran into one another out at a Bay Area pub.

It was a Saturday night when my purely platonic male friend Bradley invited me out. He was also a science major at City College of San Francisco, and practically in every one of my classes. He professed it was for me to get my mind off of my studies, but I think it was more to get his mind off of his. Working full time and going to school full time, like Bradley, I rarely found time to relax. Needing a reprieve from my grueling schedule, I agreed to go. I considered Bradley a pretty boy because it would take him an hour and forty-five minutes to get ready to go anywhere, no joke. *What guy does this?*

Growing up with six bona fide, primitive, male-oriented brothers, who considered the urinal anywhere outdoors and hunting as natural of a routine as brushing teeth, a metro-male (metrosexual) was foreign to me. I never knew what one was, until Bradley. He was one of several purely platonic nice guy friends I had, which I'm inclined to attract into my life. I think that I find it easier to connect with guys rather than girls because I grew up with boys. As a young girl and the *only* girl, I'd lose the vote on whether to watch *Brady Bunch* or *Star Trek*. In order to survive in a household exploding with testosterone, I had to learn to enjoy male-dominated programming.

Although my platonic metro-male friends were empirically attractive, I wasn't physically attracted to any of them. Besides having no physical chemistry there is something abnormal and unorthodox about dating a guy, who not only takes longer to shower and get dressed than I do, but is more sensitive, better prepared, and greater at planning things. It makes me feel as if I must be an insensitive flake with poor hygiene, hence, the reason why my friendship with Bradley never materialized into anything more. Admittedly, at this juncture in my life, I was more comfortable to date someone who was less perfect than I, not the other way around.

Bradley invited me to join our mutual college friend Vivian out at Harry's Pub in Walnut Creek—a town across the bay—for chips and margarita's. They had live blues music playing across the pub's veranda overlooking the creek. Blues music is a style that typically caters to the soul of someone down on their luck, and since I was in financial hell, the lyrics were relatable.

My hair reaching almost down to the small of my back was its longest length ever. And I weighed roughly one hundred and forty to one hundred and forty-five pounds, depending on how many times I binged on Coca Cola and Twinkies that week. And due to my atypical height, I appeared thinner than I officially was. People were always amazed when I told them how much I weighed, implying I should weigh less. The general response was: "What? You're lying! You look less than one hundred and twenty pounds." Which, naturally, I took as a complement, but it did raise the question as to why I would lie that I was heavier? Wouldn't claiming I weighed less than I actually did be the more logical way to go?

There I was blessed with having a great hair day, no frizz, lots of curl and fluff on the back and top, which is what you strived for in the eighties—the bigger the hair the more "hip" you were. And dressed appropriately for the era wearing large loop earrings, a conglomerate of pink and sterling silver, Madonna style bracelets, brown leather fingerless gloves and a long, pink, rayon dress from The Limited with a long, brown, silk vest which I wore with two-inch, high-heeled brown leather boots that matched a stylish leather purse from Nordstrom's.

Preferring to drive myself, in order to have the option to leave whenever I choose, I told Bradley I'd meet everyone at the pub. Walking past what resembled Habachy style large windows of the lounge, I saw Bradley waving to me from inside. My excessive wafture in return showed how starved I was for social interaction. After my overzealous waving, I briskly soldiered on to the entrance. The room was crowded with a young twenty-something, suburban, middle-class business clientele. I didn't feel like I belonged necessarily, but I was excited to be out of the apartment and surrounded by fashionably pretty people. The live blues band, The Brewzers, was playing *"Gimme Some Lovin'."* I recalled hearing the same song before performed by The Blues Brothers. *Was this song indicative of how I'd been feeling? Was I that starved for affection?*— probably.

Little did I know my temperature (like the lyrics) was about to rise. I walked in the direction of Bradley and Vivian. They were facing one another and sitting on window-back wood barstools at a round, Boraam style table. The closer I approached, the louder the music resonated.

Feeling like a star in my own movie, I began pointing and snapping toward Bradley while dancing up to the table moving to the rhythm of the band…until I spotted Tony and my heart sank. Sitting two tables away near the wall in a booth was the pink T-shirt wearing, dimple-smiling hot thing. *Damn! Why am I so ill-at-ease when we work together?* Embarrassed by my uninhibited dancing, I stopped and quickly scooted onto the bar stool next to Bradley hiding my face away from the direction of Tony's table. I almost gasped out loud. Instead, I motioned to Vivian and Bradley to lean in and whispered why I was feeling so uneasy. And then, after I vehemently asserted them not to, they both instantly turned and glanced in Tony's direction. *Jeez!*

I bowed my head in my hands. "Thanks guys. No. That wasn't at *all* obvious," I uttered sardonically.

They both acquiesced halfheartedly claiming they wouldn't peek again.

Bradley encouraged, "He's a good-looking guy, Melody Rae. You should go over there. I'd do him."

"Bradley, you're incorrigible!" I wailed, hitting him playfully on the arm.

"You know I'm not gay. I'm just sayin' I can see why girls would find him attractive."

"Oh, I know. And your opinion does matter. I just feel totally overwrought seeing him outside of work, you know? A-a-ah, I can't believe he's here!" I wailed, shaking my hands fervently to release the tension. Although I was trembling inside, I was also feeling aroused and giddy.

Vivian turned to me with raised eyebrows. "What is up with the pink shirt? He isn't gay, is he?"

"No. But, I know…right? Embarrassingly, I thought the same thing, which is a completely gender biased stereotype. Pink is a totally acceptable color for straight men to wear."

"Absolutely! It's totally fine for a guy to wear pink," Bradley conceded. "He's probably just a metro-male. There are a lot in the Bay Area."

"Rod Stewart lives to wear pink!" Vivian reasoned.

"My point exactly," said Bradley.

However, pink or no pink, I didn't feel in my comfort zone seeing Tony outside of work. When the waitress came over, Bradley ordered us three mojito's. While Vivian and Bradley perused the menus, I decided to sneak a peek at Tony's table. It didn't appear as if he was on a date since he was sitting in a booth with three other guys. I was relieved he didn't catch me ogling in his direction. My face felt flush and I hoped nobody noticed. *Stay in control, Melody Rae.* The place was getting louder, busier and more crowded. I took a sip of my cocktail and glanced around at all the people.

As I lifted my menu to scan for a cheap appetizer, I felt a tap on my right shoulder. I turned my head to feel Tony's face dangerously close to mine. He was calm and collected, and with impetuous articulation he introduced himself to my friends before even acknowledging me. I must have glowered like a tall neon lamp with my pink dress and red face. *We matched! Holy cow! How embarrassing.* I didn't hear the live blues music, or what anyone said after Tony approached our table, including myself. I was in gaga land over this manicured man in a pink T-shirt.

What ensued from that day forward was a lot of social group outings. The four of us single friends; Vivian, Bradley, Tony and I became genuinely close, hanging out every weekend, religiously. We would frequent the live comedy shows all over the Bay Area, eating out habitually at a variety of au courant restaurants, going out late dancing at chic nightclubs and attending popular du jour theatre productions whenever possible. We were behaving as if we were characters on *Seinfeld*; a group of friends who hang out regularly without being romantically involved. But that didn't last long. I couldn't keep my desirability for Tony a secret from him much longer, and he couldn't resist being worshipped. According to astrology, I have one flaw: I idolize my mate. *No kidding.* The problem is that I haven't necessarily idolized the right guy for me. I was hoping I was on the right track this time.

Regardless that it took almost five months for me and Tony to become an official item, I thought he displayed an interest in me early on. But, in retrospect, it was more an interest in me being interested in him. Even when we were purely aloof friends, he always had his hand on my shoulder, or was leaning in to say something flirtatious. He would time and time again stay after his shift at Paw Parazzi's salon to offer to take me to dinner, or unexpectedly show up at Peet's Coffee and Tea, which I frequented daily before class, always offering to buy me a coffee.

What I didn't know then, but learned much later on, is that guys do this when in pursuit; they relish the chase. It's the chase that motivates them to make a fool of themselves. By having to prove to you that they are worthy of your love, they receive an adrenaline rush. Men like a job and want to work to earn you. They don't want you to come too easy. I love that stage of a relationship. *Why can't it always be like that?* Unfortunately, once a guy has you, the beginning stage completely ends.

When I decided to accept Tony's advances I'd convinced myself, aside from his affinity to wearing the shade of pink, he possessed the signs of not only a heterosexual male, but also a man who was apparently *into* me. This was refreshing and exactly what I needed at the time.

Tony could charm a serpent and was an innately humorous guy which appealed to me. I was a sucker for comedians and putty in the hands of any guy who could genuinely make me laugh, and he could. Who doesn't like a witty, entertaining, jocular guy? They were my weakness. Since we were both live stand-up comedy enthusiasts, sharing a fanaticism for humor was all we needed to feel connected.

However, it seemed the universe was still testing me. I wasn't sure why and didn't get the significance. When Tony and I were fresh in our relationship and we attended our first comedy show, guess who was there?—*Mister S.* Finally, I get on with my life in a real way and I see *Mister S?* I found the timing rather perplexing. *Why, now?*

It was Saturday, the second of December, 1988. I was still twenty-one, but I would be turning twenty-two the next day: Sunday at 12:05 a.m. And Tony and I were attending The Punch Line comedy club for a pre-birthday celebration.

When I spotted *Mister S* it caused me to reevaluate my feelings toward Tony. I didn't catch sight of his woman this time, but it didn't mean she wasn't lurching nearby ready to pounce. *Mister S* was sitting with an assemblage of guy friends at a table in the upper mezzanine. Tony and I had just sat on the left side near the stage, at one of the front row small square tables, when *Mister S* and I caught eyes. As I turned my head to scope the coterie of comedy enthusiasts before sitting, before the lights went down and moments before the announcer entered the stage, I saw him. And then, less than a minute after our eyes met, he spilled his drink all over the table and onto the lap of one of his friends sitting near him. At which time everyone in the audience heard someone yell: "Dude!" The waitress approached his table. He looked chagrin, rapidly scrambling to wipe up the mess with a cloth napkin. I sat and took a deep breath. I couldn't believe it was him, again! Why did I have to see this guy? What did it mean? I couldn't see any patron's in the mezzanine once the lights went down for the show, but immediately after the headliner's monologue concluded and the lights went up, I glanced around looking for him, and even went so far as to case the parking lot as we exited. But there was no sign of him. Tony displayed no concern for my neurotic behavior. Although not entirely unexpected, he rarely paid all that much attention to me.

Weirdly, it was part of Tony's appeal that he didn't pay much attention. The positive angle is that I never felt pressured to talk about "the relationship." It just flowed because we kept things light, which was how I liked things to be. But grievously, our romantic intimacy was a bit dry and infrequent. Although it was better than any corporeal act with Shay, because with Shay we merely engaged in doing everything except the actual carnal act: prolonged foreplay. I never liked the time spent on foreplay to begin with, and after Shay I disliked it even more. I pretty much believe there is no need for physical foreplay. Some emotional foreplay (flirtatious words are essential), but take too long caressing and kissing and you've lost my interest. *Let's do it, already!*

Although we were enrolled in different colleges with divergent majors, we were both in college and could relate to a tight schedule, making us seem more compatible than we actually were. I attended City College of San Francisco (an unpretentious community college) while he attended University of California, Berkeley (an intimidating university).

Tony was working on achieving his Bachelor of Arts in Business Administration while I was hoping to be able to afford to stay long enough at City College of San Francisco to get an Associate of Science degree, and eventually, like Tony, pursue a Bachelor of Arts in Business Administration at a higher institution, if I could ever manage the finances. Since Shay had never demonstrated an interest in higher education, it was refreshing to be able to have intelligent and sometimes even challenging conversations with someone I was dating.

I convinced myself Tony was unerringly what I needed. I was grateful he didn't want more than simply "dating" because I wasn't ready to discuss more. I had my whole entire life ahead of me. We never talked about a future together, purely enjoying the here and now. What I didn't know was that Tony was only seeking someone gullible enough to temporarily take care of him and financially put him through graduate school. And I did: sacrificial enabler at your service. I had a problem of being easily manipulated into feeling bad for others and would give too much of myself without hesitation. The poor-me victims of the world (like Shay) gravitated toward me like mosquitos to a kerosene lamp, drawn in by my bright light and doing whatever they could to smother me. I thought I was protecting myself with Tony by creating a non-contractual verbal agreement that he would economically support me after he graduated. I should have predicted this wouldn't proceed as planned.

Inexplicably, one year later, merely days before my life with Tony would evolve, I saw *Mister S* again. *Was I seeing this guy to tell me something? What?* I had the unsavory notion that I was not supposed to continue dating Tony. Was this because I wanted out of every relationship I dove into, or was it because I felt inept as the one part equation of a couple and only felt whole when I was single and available? I wasn't sure. This third sighting was overpowering, but it didn't quite answer those stirring questions.

It was a chilly evening and Tony and I were standing in a long line on a steep hill waiting to get into the sought after popular North Beach Pizza Parlor in San Francisco, our Friday night ritual. We had two weekly rituals: Friday night: North Beach Pizza for authentic Italian pizza. Saturday: a matinee at The Century Theater, always ordering the large popcorn, extra butter.

The strong smell of fresh garlic wafting in the air was heaven. I heard the margarita special with basil and tomatoes was, to quote my co-worker Leslie: "To die for." And tonight that sounded worth tasting. The waitresses were frequently walking up and down Telegraph Hill to the corner of Grant Avenue serving wine to the patient habitués waiting in line to get in—how apropos. This was the coolest, most contemporary thing I'd ever seen a business do. *Thank you, North Beach!*

Precisely as Tony and I reached the top of the hill and were at the door entrance, I saw *Mister S.* Of all the places in the world to be and of all the times to show up in my life, I didn't understand, why now? I saw him sitting in the restaurant near an open window facing Grant Avenue. He was not alone. He was with a different lady than the last one I saw on his arm. Maybe he wasn't married before? Well, I was convinced he was now. She was a petite and demure looking woman with bronze skin and thick, straight, shoulder-length, black hair, and noticeably pregnant.

As Tony and I walked legitimately closer to the entrance door, I was able to acquire a slightly better view. I assumed by their hand-holding body language that they were in fact together. I finessed a fictitious story about seeing someone from work in order to lean over Tony and get a better visual. Despite feeling slightly emotionally disturbed on some level by our coincidental encounters, I was curious as to why I kept seeing this mysterious gentleman. *Does he know me? How?* As I proceeded in a maladroit manner to lean forward, I was able to see he had a wedding ring on. Then, leaning a little too far forward, I tripped over a small crack in the sidewalk, loss my balance and bumped the couple in front of me, nearly spilling my glass of wine. The lady I fell into gasped loudly enough to cause others to look. I apologized profusely. She was grateful I didn't spill any wine on her precious outfit, and I was, too. I was perplexed as to how my minor trip aroused gawking from the other customers considering the raucous clambering of the dishes in the open kitchen floor plan of the parlor was deafening.

After my fortissimo and ignominious "bull in a China shop" entrance into the parlor, *Mister S* and I caught eyes briefly as he began to assist his wife out of her chair. He looked as bewildered as I felt. He flustered with his wife's jacket which in turn knocked down a glass on the table. Luckily, it was mostly empty and didn't break. I turned away humiliated for him. Seems every time we see one another something spills. He left the restaurant with his wife, only glancing back once. I caught him shake his head and smile. That's when it dawned on me that we were both in this mystery together.

The rest of the evening was uneventful. I sat eating my unbelievably delicious tomato and basil drenched margarita special pizza while daydreaming about *Mister S* saving me from a lukewarm life with Tony while half-listening to Tony drone on and on about himself and his personal accomplishments.

Three years later, I was unreservedly financially supporting Tony and still half-listening to him talk endlessly about himself. Although Tony and I felt more like roommates than lovers, I began to think differently and want more of a commitment from a relationship. I don't think I necessarily wanted a commitment from Tony, but I knew I craved more stability with a partner. After all the time we'd spent together, he never mentioned marriage, or even said he loved me. I began to feel like I was being taken advantage of. I started to question my choices—fish bones were popping up everywhere.

In spite of feeling suffocated, I didn't think there was a justifiable way out. Tony was nice to me and never did anything to intentionally hurt me. And, in my opinion, this gave me no good reason to abandon him. As an ingénue, I still believed he would support me through graduate school after he graduated himself. Unable to conceive why he would make a promise he didn't intend to keep, I took his word as truth and had faith that he wouldn't let me down.

After achieving an Associate of Science degree in Animal Science, instead of continuing my education and transferring to a state or university to achieve a Bachelor of Arts in Business Administration degree, like I'd dreamed of doing, I did the most unconscionable thing. I chose to put my education on hold to support Tony, so he could transfer into the graduate program at University of California, Berkeley and focus on achieving his master's degree. I began working long hours at the grooming salon to make ends meet. Once we agreed to extend the deal until he achieves his Master of Business Administration degree, believing I would get the same in return, I conceded. I desperately wanted the opportunity to earn a master's degree and felt this would be the only financial way to do so.

Oblivious to the fact that I was denying my own future for some guy who couldn't even muster the words "I love you", I persevered ahead utterly in denial. *This is only temporary, Melody Rae. Once Tony graduates with his master's it will be your turn to complete your education while he supports you.* Brought up spiritually to have unwavering faith in the humanity of others, I was clueless this decision to blindly financially support Tony would create an emotional minefield within my soul.

At the time "Tony's Plan" sounded reasonable, considering I didn't have the financial means to get a higher degree without his support. However, I learned a hard lesson when it came my turn to be in his shoes and have the roles reversed. Almost immediately after Tony graduated, with his master's degree from UC Berkeley, he claimed that he temporarily needed to move into his mother's house in San Diego to pay off his debts. *What in the world?!* It baffles me how the man accumulated any debt at all, considering I was the one primarily paying all our bills; he only had to contribute a portion of rent. Lesson learned: people will use you, if you let them.

Taking a share of the responsibility in the fallout of our relationship, I admit that I also had the door half-open the entire time—I wasn't full committed, either. We never talked about anything too real or too serious; nothing to rock a boat that could possibly generate depth. Honestly, neither of us wanted to get too close. I wanted my soft shell crab to keep wearing his shell, so I could be kept at a distance and not have to reveal too much, or risk too much. And Tony didn't require any more time, or intimacy than I was willing to give, which is primarily why it lasted as long as it did.

Shortly after Tony moved out, although I had achieved my Associate of Science degree, I was barely making ends meet and now had an enormous credit card debt, primarily from supporting Tony for all those years. Since I couldn't afford to stay in college and transfer to a different institution and get a higher degree, or even continue to pay rent, I had to temporarily stay at my parent's house to resolve my own debts and reexamine my future plans. Obviously, this plan was not part of "the plan."

During the time I was away at college in San Francisco, my parents had decided to move from Oregon to California. My mother received a job offer in Portland at Rivers Restaurant, a fancy establishment located on a beautiful riparian. It was a top chef position which allowed her to get back in the kitchen where she felt more alive. She discovered that she preferred cooking over managing and teaching. My dad found employment posthaste because he always found work promptly. Besides being mister "talk my way into getting whatever I want", he's six-foot-five in stature. Not that people felt intimidated into hiring him, but his presence made an indelible impression which invariably attracted people. Besides standing out physically, he always spoke with eloquence and was an exceptional entertainer. Since his forte was talking, I wasn't astonished when he obtained employment as a radio DJ host at Q97, the local country station. Since neither of my parents will ever believe in the conventional idea of retiring, this was the closest to retirement they will get. My mother was doing what she loved; cooking and getting paid handsomely for it. My dad was working a four hour work day and getting paid to talk. They were living their dream.

Surprisingly, despite the fact that he moved out to live with his mother, Tony claimed he didn't want things to end between us. On the day he moved out, he said: "In no way, shape, or form does moving in with my mother to pay off my bills affect our relationship." *Whuh?! Of course it does.* When those words escaped his mouth, I literally felt my eyes begin to roll and was concerned they may roll entirely into the back of my head, causing permanent blindness. Does he seriously believe using cheap platitudes makes him sound intelligent? *It doesn't.* He implied that once settled in San Diego he would find us an apartment. *Us?* He never even asked if I was interested in moving there, or questioned the uncomfortable fact that I had no alternative in the meantime except to move back into my parent's house.

It was only after moving back home and being at a great distance from Tony that I was able to distinctly identify the fish bones in my relationship with him. How come I couldn't see them when I was involved with him? I suppose, because often it's difficult to see something objectively when it's right in front of you. The first pivotal fish bone with Tony was the time his friends, who also attended the same university he did, gave us special reserved seating tickets to a UC Berkeley vs. UC Stanford football game.

Before leaving the apartment, Tony put on his Cal Berkeley sweatshirt to support his friends and the team, while I put on my favorite thick red sweatshirt, as it was a chilly fall outdoor game. Tony, astonishingly, commented how much he liked the sweatshirt I was wearing. I was stupefied since it was rare he ever complimented me about anything. Once we arrived at the game we grabbed a couple of canned sodas and then found our seats; which were unexpectedly located in the middle of a crowd of already seated sports fans. I thought it peculiar that so many people were sitting in our section when there was a conglomerate of available seats elsewhere in the stadium, more appealing seats that were much closer to the sidelines. But, since I knew little about the nature of football game seating, I remained quiet.

Soon, after the Berkeley football team entered the field, two guys ran up in front of our bleacher section holding microphones. They started chanting, their voices booming through the massive speakers propped next to them. Everyone sitting near us stood. Tony and I felt compelled to stand as well. We tried to keep up with the chants as best we could, but we were unfamiliar with what appeared to be well rehearsed cheers. *How come everyone knows these cheers except us?*

It wasn't until after I caught up with the rhythm and started dancing and clapping along with the group that I became suspicious. And once the coterie started chanting: "Take off that RED shirt! Take off that RED shirt! Take off that RED shirt!" it dawned on me what was happening. Not only were we sitting in the UC Berkeley cheering section—(the freakin' cheering section)—but *I* was the one everyone was chanting about. *I know, right?*

It was inconceivable, like a corny Disney afterschool special, everything went in slow motion. All I saw were people pointing at me and chanting so loudly they could be heard throughout the arena.

"Take off that RED shirt! Take off that RED shirt! Take off that RED shirt!"

They were talking about ME! Tony did not inform me that red was the color of the opposing team, Stanford! If he had, I would have worn the UC Berkeley school colors: blue and gold, instead of the Stanford: cardinal; red. I wasn't rebellious by nature and feared confrontation merely wanting to fit in, and here I was persona non grata in front of an entire stadium of college students. I was mortified. Tony simply shrugged. His banal response to my humiliation was a ginormous fish bone.

Glaring at Tony, I yelled, "There is no way in hell I am taking off this sweatshirt!"

Luckily, a guy from several bleacher rows above us tossed me a blue sweatshirt to wear over my red one, showing more sensitivity than my own boyfriend. I thanked him copiously when I promptly returned it to him at the end of the game.

Another memory of Tony's lack of a commitment to me was how, whenever we went to the movie theater, he would completely ignore me; clearly a fish bone which was there all along. I felt invisible. Although we were not the type to hold hands, especially in the movie theater, still, I expected our matinee movie outings to at least *feel* like a date. Tony always insisted we get a large order of popcorn with extra butter. At least I had popcorn as my friend, even if I was the one paying for it. I paid for everything, I expected to. I signed up for the "caretaker role" when I chose to date Tony.

Much later in life, I did learn that a lot of pleasurable fun can happen in a movie theater between two adults without anyone's knowledge. But Tony and I did not have a highly sexual relationship, so something intimate would never have been considered. We were that awkward stiff couple eating popcorn and staring straight ahead ignoring each other.

It was mystifying how Tony always managed to find strangers to instantly befriend. He'd transform into a charming and verbally alive social butterfly around someone who knew nothing about him, and then behave closed off and uptight around me. I surmised it was because he couldn't fool me, since I knew him so well and saw right through the phony Tony façade he was projecting.

One time at the movie theater, his superficial crab nature surfaced when he complimented this woman's dress-suit in front of me and then proceeded to engage in a heated debate with her husband about politics. I didn't even know he was political. *He isn't.* Not only does he neglect to introduce me, but he ends up standing between the two of them while I end up standing directly behind him (hidden), feeling completely invisible. Most of the time I would justify his behavior: Maybe he isn't aware he's ignoring me? Maybe he's so in the moment, he doesn't realize that he forgot about me standing there? I mean, he isn't doing it intentionally? Is he? He wouldn't! *He would.* While I was making ridiculous allowances and compromises: paying for the movie tickets, the popcorn and the sodas, and walking alone (far behind him)—only to have the door to the movie theater almost hit me in the face—he was walking ahead and engaging deeply in conversations with strangers. In fact, he'd already sat with this particular couple inside the theater without me. I had to search for him in the dark. Not only did I have to live with the knowledge that Tony didn't support me in front of a football field of fans, but I always had to be prepared to be alienated on other occasions. Welcome to the world of the wishy-washy soft shell crab.

Another substantial fish bone moment transpired the night we met up with Vivian and Bradley in Berkeley at Larry Blake's; the blues bar we frequented. Telling a story about a recent dog grooming disaster with my head and arms flailing about, talking with large dramatic gestures, as I tend to do, my hair catches on fire from a burning candle on the table. I was abashed, but tried to play it off like it was no big deal. It was educating to learn the smell of hair burning is almost as putrid as the smell of expired milk left outside for a week in the summer heat—maybe worse. Vivian helped crunch out the flames on the ends of my hair with a cloth napkin from the table. In spite of the horrific embarrassment, I laughed and then made a sardonic remark about my own clumsiness. Vivian and Bradley consoled me with a group hug. Tony laughed, like a serious laugh *at*-you not *with*-you kind of laugh. Then he left the table where we were all sitting and headed toward the bar, sat and started up a new conversation with complete strangers, pretending he didn't know me. Who does that to their girlfriend? *Tony.*

Oh, and another gargantuan fish bone that I copiously ignored was when Tony scored tickets from a friend in the film industry allowing us to take part as audience members on *The Barbara Bee Show* in the Los Angeles area. We were both elated to attend the taping of a new daytime talk show which had received high praise. The daytime talk show was known to discuss a conglomerate of issues from relationships and marital strife to weight problems. What daytime talk show doesn't?

We drove from San Francisco to Los Angeles on interstate-five during the time when the famous sensationalistic avant-garde artist Christo Vladimirov Javacheff had an exhibition displaying his large four hundred and eighty pound yellow umbrellas across the mountainous range extending for miles along the freeway. It was quite a lavish spectacle and certainly worth taking pictures of, which we did.

Tony drove as I took pictures of the umbrellas out the car window while we listened to the OJ Simpson trial on the WOLB am radio station. The trial was entertaining while pivotal in defining Tony, who was a certified social media freak, intensely fascinated by current news events. Whenever I was driving, he'd make me pull over the car whenever he saw a car crash or witnessed a fire or natural disaster of any sort—chaos mesmerized him. I found it troubling how Tony had to be as close to the action of a horrific scene as possible. And, unfortunately, I was subjected to witness this side of him frequently, because we were dating during a time when there happened to be a lot of news worthy tragic events in and around the San Francisco Bay Area. He even went so far as to create a video document of the two biggest disasters in the Bay Area; recording serious footage of the seventeenth of October, 1989, Loma Prieta, six point nine earthquake that devastated the Bay Area and the huge Oakland Firestorm that burned the southeastern Berkeley hills that started on the twentieth of October, 1991, and destroyed over three thousand homes. He and his friends would gather around and watch these tapes as if they were light entertainment. I should have recognized this as one of the ways in which we were too different, but I was blinded by my full face scuba mask and couldn't see the fish bones protruding through the seabed.

When we arrived in Los Angeles, at the studio entrance to *The Barbara Bee Show* to sign in as audience members, Tony was awestruck by everyone who worked there. He was a groupie to anyone in showbiz treating them as if they were invincible. I never understood that. I didn't feel being lucky and/or having an excessive amount of money necessarily makes someone extremely intelligent, or even talented. But Tony disagreed. We weren't informed of the topic for the show until Barbara came out on stage to announce it at the exact moment it aired live.

And when Barbara came out on stage and posed to the audience the question: "Can men and women just be friends?" I growled. *Oh great! Another issue Tony and I totally disagree on.* Of course, Tony rushed to speak anxiously raising his hand like a star-struck fan and yelping, "O-o-h, O-o-h, O-o-h," like Arnold Horshack—class clown of the Sweathogs from the 1970's sitcom *Welcome Back, Kotter*—his right hand stiff as a board. He wanted any opportunity to be in the limelight; any possibility of being seen on camera. Thankfully, Barbara called on him, otherwise I would've had to deal with his yelping and jumping up repeatedly throughout the show which was embarrassing enough to have to witness once.

When Barbara finally called on him he responded in his characteristically phony and ludicrous stagy persona, leaning his head back and scratching the imaginary stubble under his chin with the top of his right hand attempting to appear tough, like a member of the mob. "Uh, yeah…I would have to say… *(don't say it)* …in no way, shape, or form *(my vision just blurred)* would I disagree," he said, winking and pointing directly at the camera. And if that didn't discomfit me enough, he added, "Men and women can totally just be friends." *What? On whose planet…Tony's?!*

He always wanted to sound smarter than he was. Due to the fact he tried too hard, he came across as the opposite. He didn't need my approval, or even ask my opinion, nothing new. All he needed was the adoration of strangers to make him happy. I wasn't a stranger, so my admiration never made him happy. All the way home in the car, I kept thinking how farcical he sounded.

If I had allowed any one of my single heterosexual male platonic friends to think there was a chance sexually, they all would have taken it. The only reason I had male friends who were platonic, was because I chose not to allow them to become physical. However, it's very difficult to hang out for long periods of time at great lengths (especially one on one) with the opposite sex without one of the partners being interested in something more physical. The exception to this rule is when there's an obstacle, such as one of the partners being totally not attracted to the other, gay or unavailable; married or involved with someone else. *The Barbara Bee Show* was discussing this very topic, but Tony couldn't analyze it at any more depth, he had to keep it simple, like him.

It was obvious we were on different sides of the fence and the fence was too tall to climb over and neither of us wanted to attempt it. Neither of us wanted to risk getting closer, so we stayed on our opposite sides tending to our own grass. One quiet evening at home, later that week, we wound up watching the movie *When Harry Met Sally* and sitting apart on separate sides of the couch sharing an invisible icy wall between us. I didn't realize until that moment that a wall had been there throughout our entire relationship, and it wasn't a flimsy wall either, it was made out of brick and strung with barbed wire. I nodded during the movie where Billy Crystal's character (Harry) says: "No man can be friends with a woman that he finds attractive. He always wants to have sex with her." *See Tony, men and women can't be purely platonic friends without a barrier.* But Tony couldn't hear me through all that brick.

As expected, he stuck to his philosophy and I stuck to mine. He had a couple of friends who were women, who I guarantee you he wanted to sleep with. But, naturally, he didn't want me to think he did. I thought it profound timing that it was only days after we watched *When Harry Met Sally* when he voiced how he had to move back home and live with his mother to pay off his debts.

Although our emotional relationship had ended a long time before this, it was about the same time my love for the area ended. My breaking point was when the Loma Prieta earthquake on the seventeenth of October, 1989, shook the bay along the San Andreas Fault. It was the first time I had felt an earthquake, and it didn't only shake my physical body, it shook my entire sense of self. I wanted to move and get the hell out of the city right then and there. The quake only lasted ten to fifteen seconds, but it felt like a lifetime as my past flashed before my eyes. *Is this how I am going to die?* The quake was so devastating for me that I remember specific details, such as how it measured six point nine on the magnitude scale, killed sixty-three people and injured around three thousand or more. It emotionally shook me up so dramatically and disturbingly that afterward I became exponentially more anxious to get out of the area.

Tony and I reacting so differently to an earthquake was one of the pertinent reasons why we started to ravel and drift apart. Though, we never discussed why things weren't working or even acknowledged that they weren't. How things finally ended between us exemplified how gravely distant and uninvolved we were with one another. I started dabbling in reading Marianne Williamson books near the end of our relationship. This is when I became super seriously interested in spiritual and self-help books. I was frustrated that I couldn't communicate well and wanted to feel something when I was feeling nothing. In one of her books she said something which hit home, delineating my relationship with Tony so profoundly that tears came to my eyes as I read it. She said: "A person can live with someone and not be involved with them at all." And finally, anticlimactic, simple and with few words, symbolic of our dynamic, our relationship ceased.

But before the final curtain call, Tony was calling regularly from his mother's house in San Diego to my parent's house in Redding. It appeared as if he was calling out of obligation, his voice having an irritably anxious sound to it suggesting he wanted desperately to get off the phone moments after he called. I finally found the courage to mention how I didn't understand why he was still calling me when he'd chosen to live with his mom and made no plans that included me in his future.

When he had no response to that, I said, "C'mon Tony. Seriously, in the five years that we've dated you never even told me that you loved me. Not even once."

"Well…uh…ahem…I…I…love you," he mumbled, then laughed and coughed.

"I don't want you to feel *obligated* to say that," I said, then sighed. "Things shouldn't be like this. It's not fair to either of us. You know, you don't have to call me anymore…I mean, if you don't want to."

"Okay," he responded with frigid detachment and then hung up the phone. *Whoa!* Yeah, can you believe it? He downright hung up the phone without even saying bye. And, not surprisingly, I never heard from the man again.

Although I found it to be a heartless and callous end to a five year relationship, I felt Tony was perfect for me at that time in my life. He provided me with what I could handle. He was light in nature, simple, funny and entertaining. However, would I ever allow myself to solely support a man again? No. I learned that lesson.

After things dissolved, I realized that I wanted more out of my next relationship than roommate material. I wanted what had been lacking in both of my previous relationships. I wanted to connect more physically with someone, since I'd not done that with Tony or Shay. I was seeking a physical, sexual obsession. I wanted an intense and powerful opposite-sex attraction. And that's when I inadvertently met the piquant and licentious fish, William Bradshaw.

Chapter Four

*Why is a swordfish's nose 11 inches long? If it were 12 inches long it would be a foot!

Swordfish

A terrific fish to eat, swordfish is moist and flavorful with a slightly sweet taste. They have a firm, meaty texture and are rich and juicy.

****

"So what sort of damage to your little girl did Tony provoke?" asked Kat in a curious tone.

"Well, let's see what I wrote down," I said, grabbing the legal pad. "Ah yes, of course, after the wishy-washy soft shell crab, Tony, I could no longer smell garlic, or hear the song *'You Don't Even Know Who I Am'* by Patty Loveless, or taste movie theater buttered popcorn. Oh my goodness, you don't understand how true this is. I mean, we lived at the movie theater and whenever we watched a movie at home we ate popcorn. Just recalling how much popcorn we consumed leaves me with a greasy and artificial aftertaste."

movie theater buttered popcorn

I shook my head remembering the Tony years. "We also ate Italian food regularly: spaghetti noodles topped with extra garlicky marinara sauce served with Caesar salad practically every dang day. Not that I believe in vampires, werewolves or devils. I don't! But we never had to worry about them invading our house because it was doused in garlic," I said chuckling. "I remember how, after Tony would go for a run, his sweat would have a pungent garlicky smell. The memory of that smell makes me cringe, even now. I want to vomit just thinking about it…ewe."

115

Kat cringed and I shivered.

"Okay, now, the song I selected for Tony seriously brings up a lot of issues for me. It's totally the perfect song to describe us and honestly makes me cry whenever I hear it. I mean, the title *'You Don't Even Know Who I Am'* says volumes, don't you think? He didn't know me, Kat. Not the real me anyway," I said, feeling woebegone.

Kat titled her head to the side. "Well, you didn't show him the real you."

"And vice versa," I added agreeably. "I don't solely blame him. We both were responsible for keeping things autonomous. Regardless, I could never be involved in a relationship with someone so disconnected ever again."

"Wow, yeah, that's sad. If I had known you then, I would've never let you stay with someone so emotionally detached," Kat retorted.

"Oh, I know you wouldn't. But then of course, if I hadn't dated Tony all those years, I wouldn't have craved someone with more depth and passion. I needed Tony to instill in me the desire to want more for myself. Maybe I should be thanking him?"

"A toast to Tony," Kat simpered, and then poured the last remnants of wine from our first bottle.

"Cheers," I said grinning while Kat shook her head and then toasted her wine glass to mine.

"Oh, you have to read the combination from that book, that secret book, um, that, um, relationship book...whatever it's called."

"Oh yeah!" I crowed, jumping up, grabbing the book and ecstatically flipping through the pages. "The correct title is *The Secret Language of Relationships* as you can see," I stated, showing Kat the front of the book as if I were a model displaying a car.

She chortled.

After looking up the page number and scanning the words, I felt apprehensive. "The twenty-first of July with the third of December...Wait! I don't think I can read this out loud, the title is too scary."

"Just read it," Kat demanded.

"Okay, fine. The title: control through mind power."

"Whoa!"

"I told you."

"Yes you did. Now continue…I can take it."

"Of course, you can take it. You didn't date him," I sneered, shaking my head and placing my hand to my forehead.

"This process is about letting go, right? Maybe by reading it, you can accept it and put it behind you."

"Good point. Ok-a-a-ay. Fine. Here goes. Best at: friendship."

We both looked at each other and nodded in agreement.

I looked back at the page. "Weaknesses: repressed, obsessive, rigid."

"Whoa. Yeah, no kidding, Sherlock. Okay, that was totally right on. That was so how you were with him—eerie. Now, I'm gettin' creep-ed out. I'm so glad this is not about me."

I now had both of my hands covering my face and I wasn't sure to laugh or cry, so I did both. This prompted Kat to start giggling. And, once we both saw the other giggling we couldn't stop laughing.

"Why are we laughing?" I inquired while leaning on Kat's shoulder.

"I have no idea," Kat concurred, sitting up in a serious manner, which made us both laugh harder.

Once Kat's giggling induced coughing we couldn't stop. Once deep into a full blown giggle fit we both looked like we were about to pee our pants; standing, holding our stomachs in a tight embrace, bending over while using the stools to maintain stability. When our laughter escalated, Kat's six year old daughter, Brooklyn, peeked her head out through the banister of the stairway. We both stopped with a guilty "caught red-handed" expression on our faces, hand waving away our giggles. Then we both smiled at Brooklyn and slowly began to compose ourselves.

"I'm sorry sweetie, did we wake you?" asked Kat, still giggling. Then she stood. And proceeding to walk up the steps, she picked up Brooklyn while gently whispering kind words into her ear, and carried her back to bed where she belonged. I took this opportunity to use the bathroom and freshen up.

When I returned to the kitchen Kat had also returned and was retrieving her wine glass.

"What?! Is Brooklyn already back to sleep?" I asked in a surprising tone.

"Of course, just call me super mom."

And then Kat sat in a ready to get back to business manner.

"Um, I will…super mom."

We both smiled.

"Okay, this is too fun. I don't know if you realize this, but, by you rehashing your past relationships, you're in fact helping me to understand my own."

"Oh nice, I worried I was being selfish."

"Tonight, you're allowed to be. Especially since that's usually my role and tomorrow I want it back."

"C'mon, I see the way you're a mom. You are not selfish at all."

"Oh, trust me, I'm very selfish. But this night is not about me. Let's continue. Which guy did you date after Tony?" asked Kat, sitting and crossing her legs in a professional therapist manner, ready to unravel my drama and shrink me.

"Willie."

"Serious? But didn't you meet him in Redding?"

"Yes. Actually, after Tony left me, or we left each other—depending on whose perception you take—I was forced to move back with my parents, who were living in Redding. That's about the time you and I met? I'd just enrolled at Shasta Community College for the spring semester to take a few night classes in business. I was twenty-six and had procured a job working at Bow Wow's grooming salon. I was the one that hired you as a receptionist, remember that?"

"Yes! I couldn't believe I got the job, honestly. I had no experience," Kat admitted.

"True, but I liked you immediately. And it's not merely about how much experience a person has. It's the substance of who they are inside that makes them something on this earth…and their sun sign. At least that's what I read somewhere," I said, fluttering my eyelashes.

Kat beamed. She knows astrology and spiritual self-help books are my bailiwick. And although she is quite catholic in her thinking, our beliefs somehow resonate.

"Well, honestly, when we connected instantly, I knew we could easily gossip and at the time that was all that was important. And, Kat, I know you didn't feel qualified, but neither did I! Seriously, this was the first time I got to be a manager. I had only been an assistant when I worked in San Francisco. I never had to manage an entire staff, until then. I suppose, I was ready for the challenge. Remember how I was only working part time hours? It didn't pay well, but I loved the job…probably because I only worked five hours a day. I remember I couldn't stop talking about how I was going to have my own salon someday. Do you remember me talking about that?"

"Do I remember that? How could I forget? When did you not talk about opening your own salon? I learned to just tune you out because it got really annoying. Well, after you met Willie, then *he* was all you talked about. You couldn't stop talking about him. He totally distracted you from your future plans. Wasn't he the one you had sex with in the bushes outside a public bar?"

"What? Seriously?! That's what stands out to you?"

"Sex always stands out to me…or *up* to me," Kat said with her index finger signaling upward.

"Stop it," I teased, slapping her hand. "Outta the gutter, missy. Oh boy, now the wine's r-e-e-eally doin' the talkin'."

As if a light bulb went off in Kat's head, she jumped. "Oh, that's what we need more of…," she said while pouring each of us more wine.

****

July 1993

Typical Daily Food Choices:
Folgers medium roast coffee w/heavy cream
Coca Cola
Hostess Twinkies or red hot cinnamon candies
spicy Chinese fast food with Sriracha hot chili sauce
spicy Mexican fast food with Tabasco pepper sauce
cheap red wine
Budweiser beer

Hillbilly Willie

William (Willie) James Bradshaw was an all American "good ol' boy" from Texas. He was a six-foot-two, baseball cap wearing, Budweiser truck driver, possessing a dark brown buzz cut and goatee, and gifted with a southern drawl. Although he talked like an outlaw, his facial features were innocently boyish. With a small Edward Norton shaped mouth and slanted Nicholas Cage eyes, he looked harmless. He was larger than life in more ways than one, particularly his size which was prominent in all the right places giving new meaning to the saying: "Everything is bigger in Texas." And as you can imagine, I had no complaints about those oh-just-so-right sized parts of his that made everything oh-just-so-right with my parts. In that area everything worked exceptionally well, all too well, he was blessed with a gift and he knew it.

Willie's accent and confident presence was as sexy as hell and together we were a ticking time bomb waiting to detonate; not exactly emotionally healthy. We brought out each other's obsessive sides. But, oh man, was he difficult to give up. It's difficult to walk away from something that feels so unbelievably physically good. To be totally honest, because I feared missing out on amazing sex, I stayed longer than I should have, choosing to ignore his obnoxious control issues and nauseating male ego. This made me wonder if I was, in essence, using him as much as he was using me—probably—

although I didn't see it that way at all, at the time, naturally. I was naïve and young-minded and swept up by the idea that he was my prince charming. I was old-fashioned and thought this alarmingly boyishly handsome and rustic Neanderthal type of guy was exactly the perfect type for me.

I presumed Willie was my Hayden (Craig T. Nelson) and I was his Christine (Shelley Fabares) from the sitcom *Coach*. He was all-guy which made me feel all-girl. I especially liked how he made me feel feminine. But, truthfully, I was less passive than Christine and a lot more creative and out-spoken, and well, more of a feminist. Thus, why would I be with someone like Hayden Fox? I wouldn't. But, at the time, I wanted to believe I was more like a Christine. I even began to dress like her.

Before Willie, I thought no one could possibly be more simplistic than Shay, or more superficial than Tony. I was wrong. Willie was proof a man can indeed reach the highest level of vanity that exists and be pathetically proud of it. Like many common men, Willie's brain was in his pants and he was proud of its size.

He was someone who sincerely desired my body and needed me on a purely physical level so intensely that it was hard to think and breathe in his presence. He was exactly what I wanted—an obsession. Infelicitously, I became more than a little bit infatuated, I became certifiably nuts.

It was easy to choose a fish to compare to Willie because his demeanor was so notably penetrating, stabbing and sharp, like a **juicy swordfish: moist and flavorful with a slightly sweet taste, yet, firm with a meaty texture, rich and juicy.** And like butter to swordfish, I softened his exterior and he added flavor to mine. We amalgamated quite well, physically anyway.

When I first met Willie it was obvious he was the type of guy to "use" women. But whenever I felt deep in my gut that he wasn't to be trusted, I assumed it was just a case of mild heartburn. Generally my body tells me when something isn't healthy. Willie was the opposite of healthy, but the intensity of his spirit was such an irresistible drug I couldn't refuse him. I enjoyed being swept away for the first time in my life.

He was an unfamiliar, unpredictable, out of control, zealous type of guy, and I liked it. I guess you could say I was desperately seeking a big Willie and I got one.

With his buzz cut, short hair and wearing a blue, tipped-up baseball cap, overalls and oversized construction boots, he fit the physical image I'd envisioned of the ideal guy for me. I was seeking a typical male and he fit the bill. Instantly attracted, I practically fainted when he approached and asked me to dance. All those feelings, from all those times in junior high when I felt like the nerdish, dorky, awkward and geeky girl, vanished entirely. I now felt like the hottest girl on campus.

Enrolled part time at Shasta Community College at the age of twenty-six made me the eternal student. Despite managing Bow Wow's grooming salon, I was only working part time which didn't feel like a career but rather a temporary job. I didn't necessarily feel qualified, or even have the financial means to open up my own salon at this point. Although I did have high hopes to one day do so. I knew what I wanted, but didn't quite know how I was going to get it. I was once again, in a state of limbo, financially struggling and eating cheap fast food and frozen leftovers.

After three months of living back with my parents, I needed my own space, so I moved into a studio apartment in Redding. But after living on my own for less than a month and still feeling humiliated over my failed relationship with Tony, I needed to get out and surround myself with people to help deal with the loss. And based on analysis by my peers, unwinding by drinking was deemed to be the best panacea.

It was a stormy and dreary Friday night; my favorite kind. Whenever it rained hard, I felt giddy and all geared up for a night out on the town. I believe I relished the rain simply because I grew up in Ashland and the Willamette Valley of Portland where the occurrence of torrential downpours are common. I loved every drop. The petrichor in the air and sound of rain droplets hitting the pavement when it first rains after a dry spell, brings about pleasant childhood memories of jumping in mud puddles and climbing the nearest mountain with my older brothers while it poured down hard onto the hoods of our Parka's. To this day, rain has the opposite effect on me than it has on many of my closest friends. Conversely, rain uplifts my mood and motivates me. Ergo, the gloomy and rainy evening inspired my feisty nature gearing me up for a wild night on the town.

It was not only an exciting and blustering stormy night, it was also one of those rare occasions when my oldest brother, Aaron, Jr., and his wife, Suzie, who lived near Redding in Red Bluff, were visiting my parents and astonishingly had a babysitter and were able to join me. We decided to celebrate my leaving Tony (or his leaving me, still wasn't sure who left who) and moving closer to family to start over. When Suzie and Aaron, Jr., arrived at my apartment to pick me up, Suzie gave me a celebratory gift congratulating me on managing on my own and achieving my degree. It was an authentic bottle of Obsession perfume; a fragrance encompassing the exact name of what I wanted to enter my world.

It wasn't long after we arrived at The Lemon Drop dance club that I noticed Willie. Suzie and I sat on these unusually high style bar stools at a long table that faced the tiny dance floor of this newly remodeled hipster populated bar while my brother escaped to order us a couple of drinks that were advertised as the best lemon drop martini's around. Clearly from the name of the bar, it was their drink specialty.

After telling Suzie how unusual it felt to be single after being in a relationship for five years, I noticed him. He was boldly staring at me from across the room. He wore a baseball cap with a Budweiser logo embroidered on the front with the hat tipped-up high on his forehead, which I thought looked adorably boyish. He was unusually tall, which I liked. Possibly because I was comfortable around tall men since my dad and brothers were all over six-foot-three. He wore a blue plaid shirt, jean overalls and oversized light brown construction boots. He was standing with his hands in his pockets leaning up against the side of the brick wall near the tables that aligned the front window and his eyes were clearly locked in my direction. I was so attracted to him that I couldn't look at him for long without having to turn away.

123

My first thought was that he looked much younger than me. At age twenty-six I found myself attracted to the younger guys who were in their early twenties, primarily because there was something I liked about the boyish look. My friends would always tease me when I talked about a cute guy I'd just met, questioning with tongue in cheek: "Was he twenty-two?" *Of course he was.* Before long I was labeled with the nickname "twenty-two." I wasn't *that* much older. Being that I was twenty-six, it was only a four year age difference. But when you are in your twenties, it feels like a big deal. I didn't think it mattered that much, but my friends certainly did. I believe that I subconsciously wanted them to be too young, so it wouldn't ultimately get too serious.

I could not concentrate on anything Suzie was saying because I was so distracted by this guy with all his attention on me. I flirted with a fantasy (as I often do), visualizing this tall, baseball cap wearing boy and I sitting side by side drinking Irish coffee's and fishing in a lake off the back wooden porch of an oak cabin in Colorado, until Suzie hit my arm catapulting me back into the real world.

"He looks too young!" she snipped. *Oh crap, she was on to me.*

I knew she was right, but why couldn't she let me savor the fantasy? I hadn't even reached the part of the dream where I catch a fish and he grabs me, kisses me with fervency and we playfully fall into the water giggling while tightly wrapped in each other's arms and spinning with a ripple of waves circling around us. *Wake up, Melody Rae!*

Moments later, just as my brother was about to hand me a cocktail, the too-young-for-me hot thing from the brick wall wearing his tipped-up, blue baseball cap, overalls and oversized construction boots ambled toward me with an adorable hillbilly stride rocking from side to side. I don't know if it was because he was headed in my direction, or that I stood too fast, but I ended up dropping my drink and splashing it all over Suzie. *Ugh!*

As I was apologizing to Suzie and reaching in front of my brother to grab napkins from the center of the table to clean up the mess I'd made, mister hot stuff tapped my shoulder.

As I turned toward him and looked in his eyes, I could feel my heart palpitate.

He tipped his hat and in a good ol' boy polite manner with a cute southern drawl uttered, "Awful nice to meet ya, ma'am. Mah name's Willie…Dance?"

Inside my heart fluttered and I don't remember answering him. All I remember is being led into the center of an overly crowded dance floor surrounded by sweaty bodies who were dancing to blaring hardcore hip-hop music. I looked up and saw there were young girls dancing on top of the bar. *How did they get up there?* He smelled like he was doused in a pool of Polo Cologne, which I surprisingly found appealing. The smell reminded me of an old pool hall that I used to go to with my dad and his pals who were in a duck hunting club together. And although the fragrance was a bit too strong for my taste, on this guy it smelled delicious. The dingy pool hall that my dad would invite me to had a similar cologne scent. I wasn't sure if it emanated from the owner or from the duck club guys, but the smell brought back special memories of hanging out with my dad—funny how scents can do that.

I began to feel deliriously loopy when he kept attempting to stare into my eyes. I kept turning away, refusing to make eye contact because I didn't want to risk losing control. He was so damn cute and he was standing inches from me. Although our bodies were barely touching as we bump and grinded to the jarring beat, I could feel the sexual chemistry mounting. Whenever he would look to the side, I'd stare at his mouth with anticipation. The few times we did make eye contact, his sly boyish grin with that arresting rebellious look in his eyes, made me feel about sixteen. It was as if he was saying: "I can make you do things you never thought you would." I worried that he could. My face felt flush and I could feel my heart rapidly pounding. I gravely wanted him, feeling an impalpable, magnetic, moth-to-a-flame-like, animalistic attraction between us.

I wasn't precisely sure how many songs we danced to because one song blended into another leaving no opportunity to walk away, which would eventually be symbolic of our relationship dynamic. But, I certainly wasn't analyzing anything at that moment. All I could manage to do to deal with Willie's strong presence was figure out how to breathe. Not only was I feeling the effects from Willie's strong aroma, I was becoming inebriated by his sheer presence. I felt drunk, although I wasn't. I'd never in my life experienced a sensation like this before; my entire body felt warm and tingly while my heart fluttered with delightful giddiness rendering me completely off balance...and I liked it.

Then Willie leaned his face so intimately close to mine, I thought he might kiss me, which unnerved me, causing me to giggle uncomfortably. "Thank you," I obliged, and then turned and walked away from him to acquire a healthy perspective.

I rushed toward Suzie and my brother as if I had virtually escaped a jail sentence. My gut was warning me that I would end up feeling trapped, controlled and confined. I could feel the fish bone poking me, but ignored it. This brand new intoxicating feeling had me numb to pain and it was exhilarating, like choosing to go on a rollercoaster ride that goes upside down when you said you never would. I was out of my comfort zone, feeling cravings I never had before and staggeringly loving every minute of it. I wanted to try something new and Willie was so incredibly good-looking, smelled so good and looked at me in a way I'd never experienced before. I had to have him; my libido was in control, not me.

He had me at "dance" and I didn't care if I had to give up everything I was about. There was no logic to it—I wanted him to ad-nauseam. I was willingly headed for emotional prison and super thrilled my cellmate had a southern drawl, wore a baseball cap and was covered in blue jean overalls.

I slowly sat next to Suzie and my brother, attempting to hide the cat in heat aura radiating from body. They both had been snickering and pointing, watching me fall for a guy I knew nothing about, as it was visibly obvious how attracted I was to him.

I was puzzled by how quickly I was swept off my feet by a guy who merely danced with me. The loss of control I felt in his physical presence inebriated me into a drunken stupor. I wanted more of it and more of him; an obsessive feeling redolent of the perfume I wore. Although we danced a few more songs, no words were exchanged. When he would retreat back to his group of friends, I reconnected with Suzie and my brother. We made eyes at each other from across the room whenever possible throughout the entire evening. At one point, he had the bartender send me a drink. Once served I lifted my glass, looked in his direction, bit my lip slyly and mimed the words: "Thank you."

Near closing time, he approached me and placed his arm in front of me so I couldn't walk any farther, which made me giggle like a little school girl. My knees quivered and my heart fluttered when he leaned in and I could smell his intoxicating Polo cologne, and feel his breath envelop my neck.

"Yew gotta pe-yun thar, hot thang? Ah-ee'd shore like to call ya," he said while intensely staring into my eyes.

I quickly spun around, grabbed a napkin off the nearest table and scrambled for a pen in my purse. Suzie rolled her eyes as if I had completely lost my mind. When I handed him the napkin with my name and number on it, our hands touched and I could feel my body dissolve into butter. I could feel Suzie's glare judging me for being so forthright with a stranger, but I didn't care. I wanted him to touch me again.

With his prepossessing blue eyes, he stared deep into my soul and spoke in that adorable southern accent. "Darlin', ah be callin' yew."

His deep voice and sexy drawl took my breath away, transforming me into another world, and I responded with flirtatious enthusiasm. "I really hope so…you won't regret it," I pronounced using my voluptuous voice.

When Suzie heard me say that to him she slapped my arm—hard.

I winced and then chuckled.

Fortunately, I didn't have to spend money on a taxi because my brother was the designated driver. The smile that

127

was planted on my face remained there the entire trip back to my apartment and I heard nothing of the conversation between my brother and his wife. I was on such a high from meeting Willie that I couldn't sleep. As I lay there on top of my bed sheets staring at the ceiling, visualizing my future fantasies that were in the offing, I was the happiest I'd ever been.

The first call I received from Willie was the very next day, Saturday afternoon. I was sitting on the kitchen vinyl tile floor of my tiny abode and cleaning out the bottom drawers of the refrigerator when the wall phone rang. I had the antiquated kind of phone that hung on the wall with a long cord attached and I didn't want to stand up to answer it if it was a wrong number, so I waited to see if it would ring more than once.

After three rings I stood, peeled off the yellow rubber scrubbing gloves I had on, and answered the phone.

"Hello?"

"Hey kid."

"Uh-h-h, (giggle) who is this?"

"Ah caint believe yew forgot me? How many guys yew give your number to last night, missy?"

Embarrassed, I half-choked. "What?! None! I mean one…is this Willie?"

"Nope. Ah's Jack. Who's Willie?"

"Um…uh…,"

"Ah's teasin' yew. Yup, itch Willie."

"Don't do that to me," I whined.

He then broke into an abrasive laugh. "Listen darlin' if yer nice, I maheet let ya see mah truck."

"What?" *If I'm nice? That sounds conditional. I just met this guy. And why would I want to see his truck, anyway?*

"Hey, yew like pizza?"

"Who doesn't?"

"Yew make me layuf. Awrat, ah pick ya up your place next Friday night. Eight o'clock."

"O-h-k-a-a-ay," I answered unsurely, baffled by his forwardness.

128

"Cool. See ya then, kid."

"But you don't know where I live."

"Shore ah do," he declared in a sanctimonious tone and then hung up the phone.

My initial reaction was an exultant feeling of joy. I was thrilled this hot guy, who I lost sleep over, called me. Instantly, I wanted to call my mom and share the news that I had an actual date lined up; my first official date after things with Tony went south. But as I lifted the receiver to my ear, my mind began to replay our conversation and I started to feel a little uneasy, although I didn't quite know why.

I was giddy and shaking from excitement that Willie called me, but also feeling as if something was off. It may have been his arrogance that was bothering my sensibility. I wasn't used to a guy telling me when he was going to pick me up without even asking if I was available. I don't know. Something about the way he was "claiming me" made me feel kind of turned on while simultaneously insecure. *Focus on the positive, Melody Rae.* All right, I liked that he referred to me as "kid." That was cute. Although I wondered whether he did so because he thought I was kind of childish. Perhaps he calls everyone kid? I had all these questions reeling in my head. Why didn't he want to see me tonight? Why did he want to wait until next Friday, an entire week away? And I didn't like him acting as if he was doing me a favor by seeing me. *Why are you analyzing this to death, Melody Rae?*

Instead of sabotaging an opportunity for growth, I decided to relax and enjoy this new adventure I was heading on. Because I was so attracted to him and never had such powerful chemistry with any other guy before, I figured it had to mean something. He had all the ingredients of what I wanted in a mate.

After thoroughly cleaning the kitchen, I spent the entire day shopping for a new outfit for next Friday and daydreaming about Willie. I told my mother about how I had a date planned for Friday with a new guy. But I played it down, since I didn't know enough to make her feel sure about him. I didn't know enough myself, to feel sure about him. I rearranged the wording of our conversation so it sounded like he was more of a gentleman than he possibly was. I knew she would disapprove of the way he handled me on the phone and I wanted only positive energy about this new direction my life was taking.

Every day was consumed with daydreams about what my life would be like with Willie, and the week whizzed by more quickly than usual as I dined on the prospect of true love. I played out a myriad of scenarios as I organized something in the house every night after work, expecting him to visit someday and wanting to impress him. I reread a few excerpts that I highlighted from my self-help collection of books to stay centered, and even exercised. I never questioned it odd that he never called during the week, to at the very least confirm our date, assuming he was a typical guy. In spite of never having dated a typical male before, it is what I had asked the universe to deliver and so it's what I expected.

Friday finally arrived. Luckily, the last dog I groomed at the salon was a Maltese, who is trimmed bi-monthly and doesn't require as much preening like a dog that hasn't had a trim in months, so I was able to leave at a decent hour and even make it home in time to freshen up. I was relieved to have time to shampoo my hair in order to feel fresh and sparkly rather than drab. I poured myself a glass of cheap red wine that I'd bought at Safeway and then sat at the kitchen table with a Glamour magazine. Continually looking up and glancing at the clock about every ten minutes became tiring. It was seven-thirty, then seven-thirty-eight, then seven-fifty-one, then eight o'clock. He said eight o'clock, didn't he? How come he knew where I lived? Should I be worried? Should I call my brothers to keep them posted? What if he's a serial killer? *Stop it, Melody Rae!* At six minutes past eight, I took a deep breath and a sip of wine, and then stood to peek out the front window. And then the phone rang.

"Hello?" I answered, nonchalantly wiping down the kitchen counter as if I was preoccupied with a busy life and not expecting a call.

"Hey kid, tiz me."

Jeez, rather presumptuous. He says *me* as if he's the only guy I am seeing—even if it was true, still.

"Hi. S-o-o-o what's up?" I responded, gleefully.

"Well, ah know ah said ah-ee's gonna take ya'll to pizza, but sugar, ah caint… 'cuz the geese are flyin' and ah gotta go."

Whuh? The geese are what? I was completely lost. *What was he talking about? What geese?* Was the term "geese flying" a metaphor for not wanting to see me? I couldn't speak. I felt a lump in my throat building to a crescendo and worried if I said anything I'd cry.

"Hello, kid? Uhem…ya thar?"

"…yeah," I murmured in a barely audible voice, although the crack in it was discernible.

"Dagnabit. Yew ain't cryin' are ya?" Willie interrogated, sounding disgusted.

"No, no, no. I'm fine."

"Dadburnit! That dog won't hunt," Willie snapped. *Huh?*

My feelings felt an instant sting of pain. Although I had no idea what dog he was referring to, the agitation in his tone was apparent. I assumed he was upset at me for being too sensitive. When I was a little girl my dad would react the same way whenever I displayed my emotional side which would make me weep even more. I would end up crying because I was angry at myself for disappointing him by not having the wherewithal to control my feelings—I felt flawed. As my childhood past resurfaced, reminding me how my behavior disenchanted my father, I wanted desperately to get off the phone.

"Everything's fine. No problem. I gotta go."

"Ah ain't ever had a convasation with a woman like this," he said in a perturbed tone and then growled.

Now I felt worse, like he thought I was gauche and strange which hurt my feelings more.

"I'm sorry, I'm so sorry. We don't have to see each other again. I, uh, have to go…sorry."

"Hold your potato! Cah-alm down now, little missy. Listen. If ya say 'sorry' one more time, ahma gonna have to come over thar and kiss ya. 'Cuz ah like yew, awrat? Ah do. Call me crazy, but ah like ya an awful lot. Ah wanna see ya again. Ah

131

mean, ah have to. Yew wanna know what ahee spent my week doin'? Thinkin' 'bout yew."

"Really?" I muttered.

"Oh my gravy, yes! Aah reckon ahma on farh fer yew. I told all my friends about yew, ya know? While I was drivin' 'round in mah Budweiser truck, I was fixin' to stop by. I wanted to call ya every dang day. Ahee tryin' to play it cool, so ya know, yew wouldn't get turned off. Okay? I caint wait to see ya. Yew still wanna see me?"

Wow, this guy was bold and so sweet. His words soothed my heart and I felt better. No guy has ever been able to make me feel better so quickly. Although he was Neanderthal in his dialect, I sensed he inhabited a heart of gold like a benevolent, sweet, clumsy bear, and I fell for him right then.

"Yes…," I responded with diffidence, "of course I do."

"Awrat, listen, ahma call ya tomorey, k?"

"Okay. Thank you."

"Sweet dreams, kid."

This gentle giant found a way to make me feel weak, but feminine, and for some reason I liked it. He seemed to enjoy the power he had to cause me to feel smaller than him which, although somewhat stifling, also made me feel protected; little did I know at the time that this relationship dynamic would bring about the best and the worst in both of us.

Enervated from the call, I wanted to crawl under the covers, so I did. I removed my nice chic outfit and climbed into an oversized, red T-shirt emblazoned with the words "wine is life" on the front and slipped into bed pulling the covers over my head.

He called the next day, but that was the only other time we spoke on the phone. If cellular telephones with texting capabilities were available then, texting would have prevailed as our preferred mode of communication. Our relationship was anything but conventional. In the beginning, for the first two months, Willie would generally show up (without any notice) in his 1975 faded white, pickup truck and we would take a drive to the mountains, spending the evening with his guy pals: duck hunting, four-wheeling, or camping at the lake.

But after two months passed, doing any sort of activities as a couple dissipated. We would only meet up at downtown dive bars, or trendy dance clubs, with our friends. I would be out socializing with my friends and he would be with his, and we'd hook-up after two o'clock in the morning; either at my apartment, or at a house he shared with four other roommates. I never voiced a concern about our relationship dynamic, or ever expected anything more from him, and he never offered.

I was tormented by the arousing and thrilling adrenaline rush his presence ignited in me; he was a drug and I was addicted. But after six months had passed, I began to question whether our relationship was going anywhere. The sex was incredible, erotic, steamy, lustful and uninhibited, but all we did together was have sex. I wasn't complaining because I was having the most pleasurably and sexually fulfilling time of my life, but I was beginning to wonder if it meant anything.

Once, after a wild night of dancing out at a club, Willie found me with my friends, grabbed my hand and pulled me out the front door earlier than closing time, and he brought me to a semi-secluded place where I had a night I would never forget. Because our chemistry was undeniably strong and could be felt across a bar room of people, we'd play this cat and mouse game. First, spying one another in line to get into the pub and then across the dance floor and later at the bar ordering a drink. He would walk by me, delicately sniff my hair, breathe into my neck and then with a warm sigh he'd whisper "obsession" and then walk on. He knew I wore obsession perfume and relished how undeniably obsessed I was with him. And in turn, he consistently wore Polo cologne, knowing the scent aroused my senses, making my head dizzy with delight and my heart rapturous. Sometimes he would simply rub up against me so I could get a whiff of him, flirtatiously tap my bottom and then continue walking past me. Then looking back in my direction with his left hand holding a Budweiser and right hand in his pocket, he would tip his head up through the crowd of strangers, breathe in, and shake his head with a facial expression that implied he thought I was the hottest girl in the pub. He often told me this, too. He would say: "Kid, ya one smokin' hot thang. Hottest thar is. Yew could have any guy ya want."

Willie knew how to make me feel sexier than I've ever felt around any guy before. He rocked my world with his southern charm. How was I to know he was a serpent disguised as prince charming?

The night he pulled me out of the pub before closing, he was not a serpent, he was a tiger; an amorous and lascivious tiger. He pulled me down the street and then slid me past the side of a neighboring building next to a closed antique store, and behind a batch of bushes. The building faced a parking lot and although it was foggy there was a distant glow of dim gray light peering through the bushes from a corner street lamp. Consequently, anyone who was to walk along the sidewalk could see us, which would normally make me instantly self-conscious. Not tonight.

He pushed me up against the building with gruff but libidinous force and then began to moan while he undressed me evocatively with his eyes. His dominant left hand was caressing the left side of my body while his right hand was cupping the right side of my face. Kissing me passionately and ardent with full tongue, he nudged my right leg over with his left so that my leg was tucked under his, and then with his right leg, maneuvered my left leg up and over to swaddle his waist. Then grabbing my bent left leg, he kissed me on the inner side of my knee. *M-m-m.* He knows my weak spot. Now I wanted him so badly it was murky who was seducing who.

Feeling licentious, I became sexually aggressive for the first time. I didn't know I had it in me. The next fifteen minutes felt as if time was running in slow motion and I was playing a part in an erotic porno. We both managed to strip each other's clothing off until we were bare-naked. He then planted me up against the wall. I groaned and clutched his hard body while he gripped my head tight in the back as we played into one another's desires fueling our mutual hunger. Sensing my desire to feel emotional closeness, he slowly kisses my cheek and then pausing at my wet lips delicately kisses me with a sweet softness. And then tenderly kissing my neck, he inches down toward my chest as my heart pounds heavily in anticipation. All the while we are breathing and moaning in the same rhythm. Gliding his fingers through my hair and clutching my head in his hand, I grip him with both legs strapped around his waist as he holds me and we are kissing with intense, lustful and desirous fervor. I am melting into him and floating in ecstasy, lost in another world where we are blissfully alone.

We were both entwined in a perfect state of elation, until we heard an alarmingly loud screeching sound coming from a car peeling around the corner. At which time I gasp, drop to my feet and kneel down scrambling to garner my clothes. To my dismay, Willie starts howling with laughter. I was embarrassed and unnerved that he found my panic state hilarious. When the car turned into the parking lot near the bushes where we were, we both ducked down, Willie put his hand over my mouth, anticipating that I might scream. Although we were well hidden when the irrefutably inebriated fellow stepped out of his Mustang convertible and stumbled down the block away from us, I felt exposed becoming acutely aware we were both naked in public. Quickly covering my body and nervously giggling like a skittish school girl, I tossed Willie his clothes. He only put on his pants, while I hurried to get all articles of clothing on whether they were inside out or not. I insisted on completely clothing myself before exiting the bushes while Willie patiently waited on the sidewalk. I felt a tear trickle down my face. *Why are you crying after having hot sex, Melody Rae?* Did I think it was love? Yes, I did. Over the next month I would dine on this moment, replaying it over and over again in my head, smiling and feeling heavenly warmth all over my entire body.

Shortly after our publicly steamy sex in the bushes escapade, I was no longer okay with our distant relationship dynamic because I craved more of him, more often. I was no longer satisfied with just seeing him out socially with friends on the weekends hoping we might hook-up while never knowing for sure if we would, or when. Would I see him out

Friday night or Saturday night? I never knew. Sometimes I saw him both nights, sometimes not. Why didn't I ever ask questions? Why did he not call me, ever? Once my girlfriends at work started to inquire about the dynamic I had with Willie I started to question our situation. They thought it unusual that I knew so few personal things about him. And when they asked whether I was considered his girlfriend and I didn't have an answer, I suspected something wasn't right. They couldn't understand why I didn't feel comfortable asking him certain personal questions. I figured if he wanted to tell me anything, he would. I wanted to be unconditional and not pressure him. I liked how we had this understanding and didn't have to be typecast as boyfriend-girlfriend. It was exciting without the pressure of having to talk about serious stuff. It was nice. It was exactly what I wanted. And it worked…for a while.

It only became a serious issue when I realized we were never doing any sort of "couple" activities. And realizing how we never did anything in public together during the daytime started to bother me, making me question whether he respected me. Why didn't we go to the movies, or out to eat at a restaurant? We never did go out for pizza. We joined friends for a barbecue one time, but only stayed for an hour before heading out with our group of friends to hit the bar scene. It started to register that we were one another's midnight booty call, and that was it. Since I'd never been someone's booty call before, I didn't recognize the signs. Being an ingénue, I thought I was falling in love with Willie. When in truth I was falling in *lust* with him, not love. I was overwhelmed with a yearning infatuation and I couldn't see the truth in front of me. I wanted desperately to believe these intense feelings of avidity were healthy and meant I was truly in love.

Willie was adventurous and spontaneous which appealed to my basic needs. And I thought his wanting to have sex with me and being so undone by my physical body meant he undoubtedly liked me, or maybe even loved me.

But when things began to spiral out of control, I started to see a veritable pattern. It became apparent that it was not love, when the only time we were together both of us were heavily intoxicated. *Earth to Melody Rae!* Being overly inebriated, neither of us wanted to have any sort of deep, logical, enlightening, or even semi-educated conversations. Our encounters were all filled with heightened emotions and often libidinous physical exchanges. Which was a blast, but certainly not healthy. I learned having super passionately charged wild sex didn't mean we were dating. Although in my naiveté, I thought it did. I thought we were together. I realized that when I allowed him to call me up at any hour of the night, or stop by my house at two o'clock in the morning (any day) welcoming him with no questions asked that my emotions were out of control and I wasn't thinking rationally. I'd convinced myself that he had this magnetic power over my body and there was nothing I could do to pull away. Naturally, I could if I wanted to, but I simply didn't want to.

We mutually *physically* fell for each other hard; obviously not the main ingredient necessary for creating long lasting love. There was absolutely nothing healthy about our relationship. He wanted to control me and I wanted him to control me. Every time I closed my eyes, I craved him. *Massive fish bone.*

But before I achieved genuine clarity, I wasn't sure if I was feeling love or an illusion of love for what I thought we could be in the future were we to ever spend more time together in a domestic situation. I wondered were we to ever meet each other's parents, or do things that typical couples do; like go to dinner at a restaurant alone, or spend time around people who didn't know us, whether we might have something substantial. I ultimately decided not to question it. I was crazy about him and inundated with constant fantasies we would get married, and at the time I seriously needed those fantasies to exist. I wasn't ready to let them go. In fact, I had several dreams about our wedding day—which of course, I never told him about.

In every dream, I am wearing an unconventional, red wedding dress and walking down a grassy knoll toward a

Lori Jean Phipps

small outdoor gathering of people sitting in white chairs in a green woodsy setting. I suppose, in some ways, it resembled the backyard of the home I grew up in Ashland. Willie would be standing at the altar wearing his light blue jean overalls with his large, light brown construction boots and a Budweiser baseball cap, tipped-up on his forehead just how I liked it. The dream always ends with him looking at me, in that alarmingly hypnotic way he does, as if to say: "We get each other and we belong together." And then he kisses me and I wake up. It bothers me how I never get to hear myself say: "I do." It was a recurring and troubling dream because I never reached the "I do" part of the ceremony. I started to question whether maybe I wasn't supposed to say "I do" to Willie.

The dream subsided and things quickly soured when I discovered that Willie had been sleeping with my friend Bobbi, which more than woke me from my drunken stupor—I sobered up real fast after that. News of such ultimate betrayal unexpectedly brought out the crazy in me. I was beyond devastated, feeling violated and revengeful for the first time in my life. Feeling partly insane, my head swirled with unanswered questions: How could Bobbi do this to me? How could Willie do something like this? Didn't he know we were supposed to be together, forever? I didn't even know if I wanted that. I just wanted my dream to have a perfect ending and the search to be over. And here was the boy that fit the "image" of the guy I wanted to spend the rest of my life with. Well, the guy I wanted to spend the rest of my life having sex with, anyway.

I totally became undone when I first found out. At the supermarket when I ran into Sally (Bobbi's neighbor and a mutual friend), she confided in me that she saw Willie entering Bobbi's apartment late Saturday night and then exit early Sunday morning. It was one of the weekends that he had assured me he would be duck hunting. I'd met Bobbi only six months earlier through a group of friends, out playing pool one night. And although I hadn't known her long, it still hurt that she could do this to me. She knew I was

138

crazy about Willie. I even confessed to her one night how I saw us getting married one day. We only met out at dance clubs, so in reality, I didn't know her all that well, but it still hurt like hell to have someone claim to be your friend and then fornicate with your boyfriend.

After running into Sally at the store that Sunday and hearing the devastating news, I was wrought with so much anger and pain that I'd stopped by my parent's house in a panicked rage, slightly hyperventilating, and searching for solace. After a period of hugging my mom and dad and then bawling hysterically, I settled down, and explained what I'd heard from Sally. And then I did the most ridiculous thing and asked my dad if he would come with me to Bobbi's to confront her. *Confront her? Who am I? I don't confront people.*

Clearly I was not myself, and so unbelievably distraught that I had to know the truth no matter the cost to my self-esteem. But I knew I couldn't endure the pain without my dad along for comfort, support and protection. After several moments of pleading for my dad to go with me, he attempted to calm me down by rationalizing the situation with logical reasoning, striving to convince me to understand that nothing positive will result by confronting Bobbi. Of course, I was not hearing anything he said because I was too preoccupied with my own internal pain. I was like a vicious bobcat eyeing a large rat, panting excessively and exhilarated at the opportunity to catch my prey. While I was nervously wringing out my hands and nodding my head up and down, my mind was thinking about smashing my hard fist into her unscrupulous face. *I know!* I never had a violent thought like this in my life. Although I realistically knew that I couldn't literally follow through with hitting her, the idea of doing it gave me some relief.

My pragmatic and sagacious father who did not think anything positive would result from an imbroglio with Bobbi, decided to take me to her house anyway. I think he was worried about my driving in such an emotional and volatile state, and knew I was determined to go no matter what. It was obvious I wasn't thinking straight and his plan to rationalize the situation was failing. Accepting defeat, he gave up trying to persuade me otherwise, saying to my mother while shaking his head, "You can't rationalize the behavior of someone irrational."

Naturally, assuming he was referring to Bobbi, not me, I jumped in the cab of his truck ready to fight. Once my dad got situated in the driver's seat he inquired as to what my plan was when I arrive at Bobbi's apartment and she confirms the fact she slept with Willie. I don't know. Shoot her? Seriously?! No of course not. I had no plan. And I am not the confrontational type in any way, so why was I now suddenly confrontational? There was no rational explanation for my behavior whatsoever. I had completely flipped out and was temporarily and certifiably nuts. My turbulent, voracious appetite for Willie made my feelings for him intense, erratic, unhealthy and toxic: a recipe for disaster. I felt imbalanced and consumed with jealousy in a way I never had before.

When I arrived at Bobbi's apartment she acted like she normally did, ecstatic to see me and as friendly as ever. But all I could see was a nefarious and meretricious piece of trash, with every word coming out of her mouth sounding counterfeit.

She gave me a hug and complimented me on my outfit. "How come you always look so good?" she said in her superficial voice.

She had always been consistently adulatory, excessively fawning over my clothing attire. Coincidentally, months prior to this night, she started dressing like me. She would ask me where I bought my shirts, shorts and boots and then go out and buy the exact same outfit. It was bizarre, as if she had no identity. She was shorter than me by four inches, had long, straight, brown hair and a more curvy build—we couldn't even be mistaken for sisters. I was not suspicious to why she was trying so hard to emulate me, until now. Did she want to resemble me to attract Willie? I recalled her first reaction to meeting Willie months ago. It disturbed me then, but now even more so. When I first introduced them at a local bar, she shook his hand and started to giggle like me, in precisely the exact way I do. In fact, I remember her mimicking my mannerisms throughout the entire night. I thought she was simply *teasing* me, but now I realized that she was trying to *be* me.

Standing in front of Bobbi's apartment door, with my dad around the corner sitting in his 1979 classic, blue Ford pickup that he loves like another child, I decided to be straight forward and ignore her superficial attempts to manipulate me into feeling guilty by behaving with artificial niceties.

I asked her, point blank, whether she had slept with Willie. She didn't answer right away which I assumed to be a sign of guilt. Instead, she proceeded to act blameless, giving me this lengthy play-by-play excuse of how they accidently ran into each other outside The Lazy Lounge Chair after it closed. *How could you do this to me?* I was in so much pain, but said nothing. I couldn't move. Traumatized, my eyes glazed over as Bobbi continued to reveal the sordid details of how Willie returned to the bar after having breakfast with his pals and stopped her as she was walking to the parking lot. Reportedly, he wanted to talk to her without me around. And I thought I might faint, vomit or both when she declared Willie wanted her more than me. I didn't want to believe Willie would betray me like this. *Why would you want her and not me? She's just wearing my clothes, Willie. Don't be fooled. She's not me!*

As Bobbi kept talking, I replayed the events of the previous night. I remember her wanting to stay at the bar longer than I did, but I never suspected for a minute that this could be an opportunity for her to move in on my man. Willie and I even waved bye to Bobbi earlier, when we left the pub together. He kissed me before walking down the street with his guy friends to go have breakfast at the local Denny's, something he typically did without me. Not being invited was an understanding—it was "guy" time. Willie told me that he had plans to get up early to go duck hunting and couldn't make it to my apartment later. Being the "cool chick", I understood, as usual.

I don't know if it was because I had a blank look on my face or not, but Bobbi kept repeating how Willie followed her without her asking him to. She said that he approached her to thank her for being such a good friend to me. *What in the world?* I seriously wanted to barf. And then, supposedly, they started talking about me and how great I was. Barf, again. *Don't be so phony and just tell me the truth!*

Internally, I didn't feel the level of forbearance that I displayed on the outside, but I knew being restrained and holding my personal feelings in was the best course of action. Despite the fact that every formidable word coming out of Bobbi's mouth was hitting me so acutely hard on every instinctively primitive level, making me want to detonate, I remained calm. While she continued to expatiate in detail the colorful events of the evening, I held every thought to myself. *I think I'm gonna be sick.* She further admitted that they connected because they had a lot in common; claiming that originating from Texas and liking the same football team made them soul mates. *You've got to be kidding me.* At that moment when it became evident Bobbi didn't have strong moral clarity or courage, and her compass was clearly askew as was Willie's, I thanked her for her brazen honesty and without saying goodbye turned and walked away.

I wanted nothing to do with either of them. And although their fling only lasted two months, it destroyed any chance of Willie and me ever being together again, and naturally my friendship with Bobbi was obliterated. Three months after this egregious situation, Sally informed me that Bobbi moved back to Nebraska to live with her dad. *Thank goodness.*

After some time passed, in spite of the fact I was still relieved she left town, my perspective softened and any negative feelings dissipated and were replaced with indifference. I could no longer blame her or Willie. In truth, Bobbi wasn't intentionally trying to hurt me, or sabotage my life, she was simply being selfish. Although it was difficult to understand, since I would never do anything like this to a friend because I was raised with healthy moral courage (*Thanks mom and dad*), at least I could somewhat accept it. And with regards to Willie, understanding that he didn't consider us boyfriend and girlfriend, but merely hook-up buddies, he didn't believe he was violating any relationship code of conduct. In some ways this experience said more about my inability to communicate than anything else. From this I learned that I need to better communicate my feelings with men.

Unfortunately, because I didn't take Willie's betrayal as a personal attack on me, but rather a combination of his character flaws with my inept communication skills, my feelings for him remained unresolved. Although I wasn't altogether over him, I certainly wanted to be. Setting out on a journey to find someone completely opposite, I vowed to avoid anyone who had Willie's birthday, the nineteenth of June, 1969, hoping this would prevent me from ever being involved with a guy who was mendacious, pompous, overpowering and controlling. I knew I couldn't handle being hurt in the same way again. And I wasn't confident whether I inhabited the emotional tools to comprehensibly communicate well enough to prevent being manipulated again, either. Although I enjoyed being out of control for a short period of time, eventually it became petrifying. And in order to feel safe I needed to be back in control.

I can surely ascertain my eating habits played a role in attracting Willie. Since I'd been eating greasy fast food and drinking heavily, making me feel cheap and weak, it perpetuated my craving for easy and intoxicating: Willie. I began reading several new spiritual books and came across a great analogy for my crisis. Marianne Williamson says something to the effect that if you've been eating a lot of processed foods with artificial sugar instead of fruit that grapes won't taste sweet. But if you eliminate the unhealthy processed foods, your palate will change and grapes will taste sweet. From that I gathered, in essence, since I'd been eating a lot of garbage, I craved garbage." *Willie defining the garbage in this metaphor.*

I was concerned whether my palate could change? Could I crave someone healthier and less tempestuous? Could I meet someone who would make me feel the same level of fiery vigor while still allowing me to stay in balance, or was it Willie's controlling nature that brought about my deep desire? Being out-of-balance, although unhealthy, temporarily felt incredibly good. Similarly, foods that create an imbalance—high salt and sugary products—(although unhealthy) in the moment feel so good. Does that mean I can't have both passion and balance? *Why not?* What I really want is passion with stability. *Is that too much to ask?* I want to meet someone conservative, honest, predictable and healthy with whom I can experience wild passionate chemistry. An avid gardener and talented chef would be an added bonus. *Am I asking for too much, here? Does someone like that even exist?* I don't know. Obviously, I wasn't ready for the answer because I didn't end up meeting someone inhabiting those traits; not even in the ballpark. The next guy I met was someone distinctly similar to Willie. Although he didn't have a southern drawl, he was a six-foot-two, left-handed, Budweiser truck driver, who sported a goatee and had slanted Nicholas Cage eyes: the acidic and capricious fish, Peter Kelly—Willie's metaphorical twin.

Chapter Five

What game do fish like playing the most? Name that tuna!

Yellow Fin Tuna

Reaching up to 300 pounds, the yellow fin tuna is also called, Ahi. Yellow fin tuna has a mild, meaty flavor and can be served raw as sashimi and in sushi. When cooked, it is firm and moist, with large flakes.

****

Kat seemed a little tense. Maybe she had to pee, I'm not sure. But she looked at me with wide stabbing eyes of discontent as if to motion for me to get on with it, so I did.

"Okay!" I retorted, enthusiastically clapping my hands and grabbing the legal pad off the table. "After the juicy swordfish, Willie, I could no longer smell Polo cologne, or hear the song '*Why Don't We Get Drunk*' by Jimmy Buffett, or taste Budweiser beer without being left with a spicy and lustful aftertaste."

Budweiser

"Ha-ha-ha-ha," Kat cackled, slapping her leg.

I grinned while nodding my head.

Then, grabbing *The Secret Language of Relationships* book, I looked up the page number. "The title for our combination, the nineteenth of June with the third of December is: tried and true. Best at: family. Weaknesses: exhausting, oscillating, impermanent."

"Aye, yie, yie!" Kat snorted, shaking her head. "I seriously do not want to read any of *my* combinations. That is just too much, too real, too soon."

After taking a moment to process all that we had been discussing, Kat snatched the corkscrew and began to open our second bottle of wine. Then she poured us each a full glass.

I sighed.

Kat nodded her head empathetically and then toasting her wine glass toward mine, took a sip. We then mutually agreed that eating something after all the wine we had devoured was crucial. Precisely as I started the preparation for our salmon baked with mango and brie entrée, my cellphone whistled its Bobby McFerrin ringtone *"Don't Worry, Be Happy."* A song I selected because it made me feel instantly inspired whenever I heard it. The song sets the mood to expect things to be good; symbolic of my new philosophy about life. By choosing to be happy and not worry, I send the message out to the universe that everything will be fine; generating a mentally healthier and more attractive attitude, propelling healthier people toward me. My mission: to change my perspective on relationships in order to invite the right combination of a mate in my direction. I had faith that by preparing salmon baked with mango and brie, I was spiritually manifesting a future life of extravagance and abundance with an exceptional partner.

The Secret was one of the newest self-help books I'd recently sank my teeth into and the "laws of attraction" proved my theory: believing it's true, makes it true. You attract what you want by believing you have it already. Similarly, you attract what you eat. Since I believe what I eat determines how I feel, when I don't eat well, I don't think or feel healthy, and I certainly don't attract healthy. Eating healthy foods with substance and richness, I feel healthy, complete, whole and content. When I am feeling as if I have all I want and need, I am thereby attracting people of the same caliber. To bring about a healthy relationship, I have to genuinely believe and sincerely feel I have it already in my life in order for it to manifest; eating healthy brings about that feeling. Physiologically speaking, when a body feels good on the inside, it shines on the outside.

The phone continued to whistle *"Don't Worry Be Happy"* as I dug it out of my purse, which was still hanging on Kat's fashionable rack. I saw my mother was calling through, so I answered it. My mother is the closest person in my life and I am blessed to have such a healthy connection to her. She was calling while in the middle of a scrabble game with her sisters, which was as natural an occurrence as the hot morning cup of pure black Folgers coffee she must have to start each day.

She was calling to let me know that she had the recipe for the salmon baked with mango and brie entrée I called her about earlier in the afternoon after watching *Emeril Live*.

"Too late," I laughed, explaining how I was currently at Kat's house and had purchased all the essential ingredients earlier in the day. "I looked it up online—I couldn't wait. You know me! I'm totally impulsive when I'm motivated about something, but thank you anyway, I'll call you if we have any questions while cooking, okay?"

"All right dear. Well, have fun. And let me know how it turns out. I might want to make it myself."

"Oh, I will, absolutely! Okay, talk to you soon. Bye, mom. Love you."

"Love you, too. Bye, sweetie."

My saintly mother is always okay with everything—the epitome of someone who never sweats the small stuff. She has the remarkable ability to simply go with the flow of life, whether it is tragic, comical or intense. Her relaxed, calm and unconditionally loving nature is a rare quality which I deeply admire. It's a trait I naturally wish I'd inherited more of. Instead, I obtained a healthy dose of my dad's cynicism. But in many ways the combination of the two keeps me balanced. I can have extraordinarily fantasy rich ideas while remaining grounded in reality—most of the time.

We dived right into cooking with enthusiasm, talking over each other as usual. It was laughable how the loud rumbling sound of the laundry machine could barely be heard over our incessant girly jabber. We may have taken a break from

147

discussing stories from *my* past, but not from Kat's—it was her turn to ramble.

Kat is presently dating a highway patrol officer named Steven, and although she feels like she finally met her soul mate she's concerned about three issues: he only recently separated from his wife five months prior (*uh-oh*) and because of his job he's inured to violence (*yikes*), and he's almost twenty years her senior (*wow*). However, he's in outstanding shape—although he's approaching fifty, he doesn't look a day over forty. She showed me a picture of him and he resembles a younger, thinner Bruce Willis. We discussed how these issues will not matter if he's the right guy for her. And, since all of her close friends are at least ten years older than her, including me, it made sense that she would be compatible with an older guy as she was precocious by nature and mature beyond her years.

We began preparing the salmon as if we were choreographed surgeons. While Kat peeled and diced the mangoes and vented about her situation with Steven, I unwrapped the brie, and began to thinly slice it. Then I turned on the right front stove burner to the medium setting and preheated the oven to three hundred and fifty degrees while Kat handed me the skillet and I placed it on the stovetop. I began to pour the olive oil into the skillet while Kat placed the four salmon filets into the pan. In between dicing and slicing, either Kat or I would flip the salmon filets. When I was done slicing the brie cheese, Kat was done dicing the mangoes. By this time, the salmon was looking well marinated and the delicious aroma was permeating through the air, causing me to feel famished. We both then gently decorated the salmon filets with the thin brie cheese slices. Kat covered the skillet with a clear lid while I opened the oven and Kat placed the skillet on the middle rack. And then I closed the oven and set the timer for fifteen minutes. Promptly afterward, I placed the butter in a different skillet on the right front stove burner while Kat tossed in the diced mangoes.

While I poured us another glass of wine, Kat exited out the lovely French doors to the outdoor patio and set the table with pink placemats, glass plates and pink glittery handled forks. Naturally, Kat had forks that matched her plates. I fancied it, and wanted the red version. Once the butter melted I turned the stove temperature down to simmer the mangoes. When the timer buzzed, I promptly turned off the oven and retrieved the spatula while Kat removed the skillet from the oven and gently slid the salmon baked with brie onto each of our plates. Then Kat turned off the stove as I neatly topped each entrée with mangoes. Boy, when we get cooking, we get cooking. What a team we made. I wish I had this kind of symmetry with a guy.

Once Kat turned on her contemporary Pottery Barn lanterns, which surrounded the redwood deck, the patio was a spectacular sight straight out of a Nicholas Sparks movie. The assortment of beautifully lush green plants and luminous pink roses mixed with daisies and fresh white mums aligned her backyard fence like a mystical Balinese style garden, giving the impression you were on vacation at a resort hotel near a beach somewhere. I plopped down in one of the two black Adirondack chairs which were strategically placed on each side of a round glass patio table detained by a modernistic wrought iron frame. A glittery, translucent pink vase displaying a bouquet of pink and purple orchids, hydrangea, carnations and tulips was the centerpiece of the table.

Kat graciously admitted, "Steven gave those to me as a two month anniversary present." *He-e-e's a keeper.*

With fork in one hand and wine glass in the other taking one rich bite after another, I felt like Guy Fieri on an episode of *Diners, Drive-ins and Dives*. I attempted to express my opinion of the meal, the way he does, with exuberance and style.

"A funky kind of flavorful sweetness discovered here in Kat's little off the beaten path cottage; a messy and magical melt-in-your-mouth explosion for the senses—true love for the taste buds."

"Who are you?" Kat muddled, shaking her head while taking a bite.

"Guy Fieri!"

"Uh, don't give up your day job."

We both laughed.

"It's just so good, right?"

"Heaven," Kat groaned.

"Just the word I was looking for."

The taste was sensational, exquisite and pure bliss. With the first bite there came a deliciously creamy, rich and tangy flavor finishing with a smooth texture that melted in your mouth like a colossal dream you didn't want to wake up from followed by a delectable salty aftertaste. For a few minutes neither of us could speak, we were just moaning and savoring every bite.

"So tell me about Peter," Kat managed to gurgle after swallowing another healthy bite of salmon.

"Well…," I croaked, memories flickering like a strobe light before my eyes, "he was, in fact, the most difficult one for me to get over, a lot more painful than Kyle. He broke my heart Kat. He seriously broke it in half."

****

July 1998

Typical Daily Food Choices:
Folgers medium roast coffee w/heavy cream
grape soda
restaurant style tortilla chips w/hot Casa Lupe salsa
Hostess Twinkies or red hot cinnamon candies
spicy pepperoni hot-pocket
spicy fast food: Taco Bell, Burger King, Carl's Jr., with Sriracha hot chili sauce or Tabasco pepper sauce
cheap red wine
whiskey & Coca Cola

Cheater Peter

After my favorite uncle—a lucrative farmer from Ireland with a Ph.D., in philosophy—passed away from congestive heart failure, I was devastated and began to question the meaning of life. He would visit my family in the states, periodically (every three years or so), always managing to schedule one-on-one time with me. Whether it was a trip to the zoo, or a hike through the Siskiyou Mountains with our dogs, our bond was special. We shared a deep love for animals and a gift for gab, talking endlessly for hours. I felt our connection was rare. He was my idol. What I didn't know, until his passing, was that I was also his. This discovery changed my life miraculously. In his "will" he left me a personal note along with the sum of twenty thousand dollars:

My dearest Melody Rae,

I'm wanting you to do what you are good at, love. As Joseph Campbell said: "Follow your bliss." Think on it my dear. I never told you this (though I told your mum) you were my idol. We shared a true love for animals, we did. You were always needing them as much as they were needing you.

An Irish blessing for you, young lady: "May your pockets be heavy and your heart be light."

All my love—Cormac

His generosity overwhelmed me and his letter brought tears to my eyes. He also willed money to my parents and older brothers, but no one else received as sizable of an amount. Feeling truly honored and blessed, I knew right then

I was not only meant to open a grooming salon, but destined to.

A portion of my inheritance was used to purchase a bountiful amount of grooming equipment and supplies. And nearly the rest was used as a considerable down payment on a charming and classic Victorian cottage in downtown Mount Shasta, to serve as my new pet grooming salon. I was ecstatic as I began preparing for my new adventure. I named the grooming salon Petite Paws, advertising that I cater to smaller dog breeds: primarily toy dogs. If location says everything about a business succeeding then I chose the perfect town. With a selectively older and wealthy population, who happen to be exclusively small dog owners, I was a desirable commodity. Yorkshire Terrie, Poodle, Shih Tzu, Chihuahua, Pomeranian, Maltese, Havanese and Pug seem to be most popular in the region. Naturally, I accepted a variety of other dog breeds as well: Rat Terrier and Fox Terrier, Miniature Schnauzer, Beagle, Shetland Sheepdog, Llhasa Apso, French Bulldogs, Bichon Frise and various other dogs considered to be in the small dog category.

Some clients only want partial care: teeth, nails and tick and flea shampoo treatment, but most want their dog also trimmed regularly which is where I make my money. I don't do cats. And not merely due to the fact I'm highly allergic, which I undoubtedly am, but also because I'm not an ailurophile (cat-lover). Don't tell my clients, some would be offended by this oddity. My allergy to feline hair is all they need to know.

Carrying the belief that a dog is happiest in their own environment, my salon has a unique philosophy. I allow clients to send along a music CD—preferably, most often heard in the home—to play while their pet is being groomed. I also have a tapestry of music channels offered through Satellite that the consumer can request I play during their dog's appointment. I find it enjoyably refreshing to hear a variety of styles of music throughout the day. Once I had a client who brought in a Nylons CD; a five member band who sing classic fifties songs a cappella style, and it was notably satisfying to preen to.

Taking responsibility as a business owner, albeit empowering, was difficult in the beginning. If I or my receptionist misunderstood what a client wanted and I gave a dog a shave when they merely wanted a trim, for example, there was no one to blame but me. I could essentially lose a client if I wasn't fully rested, adaptable and welcoming. Luckily, all those years working in the grooming business and attending workshops helped prepare me to be professional while socially inviting. And, although occasionally I'll have absolutely no rapport with a client, I nearly always have a connection to their dog.

One time I made a huge mistake and paid for it, big time. After completing my two year dog grooming program and returning from a three day workshop with the N. D. G. A. A. (National Dog Groomers Association of America, Inc.) in Montana and receiving my national pet grooming certificate, I was feeling a bit cocky about my dog grooming talents, and my ego may have eclipsed the best of me.

Hastily scanning the chart created by my receptionist, I thought I'd read that the miniature poodle, Roscoe, was in for a continental clip; a clip where fluffy pompons are left around the ankles, the face, throat and part of the tail, while the feet and the upper half of the front legs are shaved. A request for a continental clip didn't surprise me, because it was summer time and considered a common cut for this style of poodle. In hindsight, I should have simply slowed down and double-checked with the receptionist, but fueled by my thoughts of superiority, I didn't. It should have seriously registered as a sign to slow down, when seconds before I started to trim the dog, it bit me. Although dogs try to bite me all the time, they usually aren't trying hard and rarely connect. This time the little rascal almost broke the skin on my left hand. Then, immediately after I began to trim his ears, I cut myself; although that's not all that out of the ordinary. Over the years I've cut myself more often than I can even remember and have the scars to prove it, but fortunately never so bad to require stitches. But, since I hadn't cut myself in a while, it took me by surprise.

Once I sweet talked Roscoe, and we reached a pleasantly mutual understanding, I was able to perform the continental clip. I was super excited for the practice as it was a style I had learned how to do well at the workshop, and until now had no opportunity to hone the skill. However, when I returned the dog to its owner and saw her horrified reaction, I was beyond deferential. She did not want a continental clip, she wanted a lamb clip: where the coat is cut short and even over the entire body. She didn't want the torso, or the legs shaved at all. She started to cry as she picked up her puppy. For a few minutes, she was inconsolable. I felt terrible. And of course, after apologizing I didn't charge her. It was solely my mistake; my receptionist had written down the correct clip. Obviously, I had glanced at the chart haphazardly instead of reading carefully. After losing that client, I vowed to personally speak directly to all clients and verbally confirm what they want before beginning any grooming whatsoever. It was a humbling experience and one I transparently needed.

While my career was taking off and I was genuinely clear about what I wanted professionally, my personal life remained in shambles. It was basically nonexistent. Since starting up my business was taking up most of my free time, I began neglecting my body and health, once again. I put my business first and my health second. After staying late at the salon, busily organizing, I'd be too tired to think about much else and would find myself quickly grabbing a vegetarian (meatless) rodeo burger at Burger King with a small order of fries. And this became a rather typical late night ritual. Thus, it was no wonder someone like Peter was drawn to me, my aura was depleted, hungry and confused.

I was extremely vague about what I wanted to attract into my personal life, because I was unclear about what I wanted on a personal level. I was sending mixed messages out to the universe, thereby receiving mixed results. I wouldn't be capable of recognizing a fish bone if it stabbed me in the face. As it so happens, I wasn't even aware I was suffering emotionally with unresolved feelings for Willie until I met the acidic and capricious fish, Peter Kelly.

After my business was in operation for seven months, I was able to afford to move out of my dreary apartment in Redding and rent a small house in Mount Shasta five miles from my salon. I had my friends Derek and Kat, and my mom and dad, Katherine and Aaron Sr., and two of my brothers Gerard and Aaron, Jr., who lived close enough, assist me in moving my furniture out of the moving van and into my lovely new residence.

Later in the day, my platonic friend Derek, who closely resembles Dr. Drew Pinsky, with his glasses and conservative look, invited us all to celebrate my thriving new business and new home by going out for drinks at JB's saloon; a small dive bar. Kat had to work, so she gave me a gift instead of joining us. It was an expensive bottle of Poison perfume. I loved the fragrance, but could never afford to purchase a bottle for myself. I dabbed some on before leaving the house, hoping it didn't have the same suggestive effect that Obsession had. I surely didn't need to attract poison into my life.

Most of the group showed up for a quick drink and then had to leave. Understandably, they were purely overcome by lassitude after moving furniture all day. But I was exhilarated that my career was finally on an uphill path, and having not been out in what seemed like forever, I fancied a chance to be social.

About an hour after family and friends left, Derek and I were the only patrons sitting at the bar. Surprisingly, there were only a handful of people in the entire establishment which seemed rather empty for a Saturday night.

"Wow. It totally thinned out in here," I declared disappointedly.

"Don't worry, it's early. Things usually pick up about eleven."

"That late? Jeez."

"Yep. Wanna shoot a game of pool to pass the time?"

"Sure. But I should warn you, I'm good."

"No way! Serious? You actually play pool?"

"Heck yeah, I play. I have six older brothers. Of course I play. I also play basketball, football, baseball and I bowl. Uh, yeah. Don't mess with an only girl raised with boys."

"I won't," Derek scoffed and then chuckled. "Well, cool then. Let's do it. And don't hold out on me, Melody Rae. I want to see your best moves, girl. You know, I'm gonna bring it."

"Fine, bring it!" I sassed while jutting my head side to side, wiggling my hips and sauntering over to the pool table.

Derek roared with laughter.

"Hey, would you mind if I called my friend Peter to join us? I told him I'd invite him out for a drink the next time I went out. Oh, and he enjoys pool, too. In fact, he brings his own cue stick. He's sort of a pool aficionado."

"Sounds like it. Yeah, I mean, absolutely, invite him. Why, not, the more the merrier, right?" I postulated cheerfully, while secretly wondering whether Derek was trying to set me up on a date. *Derek, you better not be trying to set me up on a date. That is the last thing I want right now and you should know that.*

After Derek called his friend Peter, using the payphone down the hall, he approached the bartender and procured us a game. Then he paid for our drinks and set up the pool table. After we played a few rounds of pool, I sat to take a sip of my cocktail. As I lifted my glass, an unusually tall guy wearing a tipped-up baseball cap charged into the pub and anxiously approached the bar counter. I was taken aback because he looked like Willie from behind, making my heart instantly do a backflip. *Oh crap. I'm not over him. He cheated on you, Melody Rae—with your friend! What is wrong with you? I can't breathe.*

"Hey," Derek said, tapping my shoulder and startling me out of my self-berating zone. "It's Peter. You're gonna like him. He's a character…and a charmer."

I smiled artificially. *Oh great, a charmer. Just what I need: another superficial smooth talker. Knock it off, Melody Rae! Derek is probably not even thinking of this as a set up. His friend Peter might even have a girlfriend, or be married. Just because your premonitions were accurate in the past doesn't mean anything. Relax, you are not psychic.*

Derek didn't know about any of my past relationships, and I didn't know about his. We didn't talk about that sort of stuff. He never saw me with a guy. For all I knew, he thought I was a lesbian. I relaxed my shoulders and took a deep breath.

Derek left my side and walked toward the bar counter, approaching the gentleman who just came into the pub wearing the tipped-up baseball cap. When the guy turned around, my mouth dropped open. I put my hand over my mouth, instantly self-conscious. His baseball cap had a Budweiser logo inscribed on it and he was holding a beer. *It's just a coincidence, Melody Rae, chill.*

I turned completely around and facing the tall table where my drink was, I took a sip. And then seizing my cue stick, I began abrasively coating the tip with chalk. When Derek tapped me on the shoulder, I knew I had to prepare myself emotionally, so I turned around cautiously.

"This is Peter," affirmed Derek.

And then Peter leaned forward to shake my hand with his left hand. *Oh no! Is he left-handed like Willie, too?*

"Hi, nice to meet you, I'm Melody Rae," I said coughing and tapping my chest with my right hand, with my left hand extended, until I noticed he switched sides and reached out his right hand, at which time I switched again before he could take the opportunity to switch back, and somehow we managed to shake hands, awkwardly. He had a strong handshake, and it was a bit unsettling.

"Peter James Kelly. I'm left-handed," Peter apologized with his face, and then proceeded to unstrap his cue stick secured in a case he had harnessed around his back.

"I gathered," I retorted nervously. *Crap! He is left-handed. And not only does he have the same middle name as Willie, but in examining his facial features, he also has those same slanted Nicholas Cage eyes and a goatee. Damn!* The Willie similarities were killing me. *Breathe, Melody Rae.* I had to do mental gymnastics, to redirect my thoughts in order to stay in control.

"You have three first names?" I asked teasingly.

"Threes a charm," Peter said, grinning in a way that would knock the average lady off her game.

Luckily, I wasn't average. I tried to center my attention on his hat, so I wouldn't look at his face and find him attractive. I became all business and turned around toward the pool table.

"Whose turn is it?" I commanded.

"I believe it was mine," Derek replied, "but Peter, you go ahead for me. We're playing eight ball, I'm solids. I'm gonna go to the bar and order us another round of drinks before it gets busy in here. Is everyone cool with the same?"

I nodded.

And without taking his eyes off of me, Peter also nodded.

I went directly to the pool table and began chalking my cue stick trying to avoid direct eye contact. Peter connected his stylish cue stick and took an impressive shot landing two solids in the right side pocket. I could feel his eyes on me while I shot the ball, which threw me off balance distracting me from playing as well as I normally would. I kept doing what I could to remain a considerable distance from him. The closer propinquity I was to his body, the more chemistry I felt. It was like a magnetic field was pulling me toward him. *Resist! This is not healthy for you. Ignore this energy, Melody Rae. You can do it.*

"Poison?" he asked, tilting his head up in a questioning pose.

"Excuse me?" I responded flustered.

"Your perfume? Is it Poison?"

How did he know that?

"Uh, yeah."

His eyes sparkled. "It's nice."

"Thank you," I stammered, exasperated by my own reeling thoughts. *Stop smelling me. Stop staring at me. Stop looking at me the way Willie used to. Stop making me feel this way.*

I tried to ignore him by walking in the opposite direction around the pool table and keeping my eyes solely on the table, but we kept crossing paths and I couldn't stop myself from looking over toward him at every opportunity.

"So, you keep staring at my hat? What's up with that?" he asked smiling brightly. *Uh-oh, he's on to me.*

I didn't want to answer him, so I studied the pool table as if I was concentrating on my next move.

"Are you a Bud drinker?" he continued, interrupting my strategic plan to ignore him.

"No w-a-a-ay!" I reacted, insulted.

"No w-a-a-ay!" Peter teased, mocking me. "Well, there goes that sale."

"What do you mean by that?"

"Peter drives truck for Budweiser," Derek chimed in, returning from the bar with our liquid courage. *Of course he does: extra tall, Budweiser truck driver, goatee and tipped-up baseball cap with a Budweiser logo, left-handed, same middle name. Uh-huh. Am I being punked? Is there a videotape rolling somewhere? This can't be for real. Is this seriously happening?* My body required a stronger drink. I should have asked Derek to make it a double.

While this was happening, I couldn't help question whether the universe was playing some sort of game with my soul. *But why? What am I to learn here?*

"He was probably hoping to sell you some beer on the side," Derek said, looking at me and then turning in Peter's direction. "Always lookin' to make a buck, aren't ya, Peter?"

"Jeez, Derek. You're making me sound like a slime-ball," Peter countered, shaking his head.

Derek laughed.

"I was just trying to impress a beautiful young redhead, who happens to be a sensational pool player," Peter articulated, oozing with natural charm and staring in my direction hard, and without blinking.

I smirked and rolled my eyes, because I could tell he was a player. He was trying to unravel me and I wasn't going to let him.

As I was concentrating on what move to make next, Peter leaned toward Derek, who was now sitting at a tall table directly across the pool table from where I stood. And then in a voice intentionally loud enough for me to hear, Peter bellowed, "Do you think she'll go out with me?!"

"No!" I answered adamantly while bent over perfecting my next shot.

"WOW! That was quick," Peter said laughing, sparked with fire in his eyes. The chase was on. I was resistant and that made him want me more. *Typical male.*

"What if I treated you to dinner and you didn't have to pay for a thing? I would pay for everything," Peter confessed, as if this was an incredibly generous offer I couldn't refuse.

"Uh, Hello?! You should always be the one who pays. You're the guy!" I pontificated.

"Hello?!" Peter mocked me, again. We were now taking turns shooting the ball and circling the pool table while having this combative debate about how a proper date should go. Derek sat, nodding with amusement enjoying our coquettish altercation. Anyone watching would be able to tell we were attracted to one another. But I refused to believe that, playing devil's advocate, by refuting every idea he had to convince me to go out with him.

"Come on. Just go out with me once and you'll see. I'm a good guy, I can assure you."

"No."

"So, there's absolutely no way I can convince you to go out with me?"

"Well…," I sassed assertively while staring into his eyes, desperately trying to think of a fail-safe answer which would furnish a way out of dating this guy. And before I could bridal my tongue the words foolishly left my lips.

"Not unless your birthday is June nineteenth, 1969."

I assumed that having him think I'm not over an ex-boyfriend was a brilliant way to turn him down without hurting his feelings. And I figured the likelihood that he would have the same birthday as Willie's was next to impossible.

Peter and Derek looked at each other with their mouth's hanging wide open as if they'd been struck by a thunderbolt of lightning. And then Peter tilted his head and looked at me as if he'd won a pyrrhic victory.

"It is," he insisted with a triumphant look in his eyes.

160

"N-o-o-o. Come on! Enough already…Seriously?! Yeah, right? Give me a break," I said dismissively while shaking my head not convinced.

"You want me to prove it?" he asked, reaching into his back pocket.

"What? You can prove it? Whatever," I shook my head. *This is NOT happening.*

"Uh, yeah."

"No. There is no way. C'mon! Get outta here," I said disdainfully, and then shuddered, worried he wasn't kidding.

"It is!" Derek confirmed, looking at me with an expression of astonishment.

Peter then took out his wallet from the back pocket of his Wrangler jeans, opened it up, pulled out his license and handed it to me with subtle confidence as if he'd won the lottery.

I abruptly seized the license and took a close look at the date. It clearly stated: the nineteenth of June, 1969. After which I gasped incredulously and dropped it on the table. Proceeding to tremble, I placed my hand over my mouth and shaking my head in disbelief, turned around and frenetically ran to the restroom.

Although it was a unisex restroom, fortunately it was a single stall so I could be alone. Once in there I locked the door and bent over, held my stomach and let out an audible whine. I wanted to cry. I unexpectedly missed Willie. *Why? Why? Why? I don't understand. Why am I being haunted by memories of Willie? Was it a sign that I am supposed to date this guy, or a sign that I need to ignore feelings of intense chemistry? I was so confused.*

I wanted to call Kat. She was the only one that knew of my history with Willie and would understand my agony. Although I knew Kat was working graveyard at the hospital and wouldn't be home until morning, I had to express my pain, it was killing me inside. I shuffled through my purse and found some change to make a call. I had to leave a message on Kat's home phone—I had to. It was either that, or I'd have to leave the pub right now, downright confusing Derek. I feared if I contained this information any longer, I would spontaneously combust. Luckily, the payphone was located in the hallway across from the restroom and out of view from the pool table area, so that Derek and Peter wouldn't see me calling anyone.

After leaving a message on Kat's answering machine, I could breathe again. Kat's mother, Deedee, who was babysitting Brooklyn, would be the only other person to hear it, and she was like one of us. Kat's mom was so cool. She was like a sempiternal giddy school girl who relished gossip.

After such emotionally disturbing news, I had to essentially put my acting skills to good use. High school drama class was going to pay off right now. I calmly approached Derek, who was sitting and taking a sip of his beer, while Peter was presently turned away near the pool table taking a corner pocket shot.

Derek looked at me with total puzzlement and consternation. "Are you okay?" he asked in his usual modus operandi—Dr. Drew manner.

"Yes, I'll explain later," I said adroitly, touching his shoulder, to let him know that now was not a good time to be candid. We understood each other with few words which I immensely appreciated right then.

Peter looked at me with one eyebrow up and a quirky smile on his lips, "How does next Friday night sound? Seven-thirty good for you?" *Jeez, he's relentless.*

"Fine," I responded disgruntledly, rolling my eyes and grinding my teeth. I was worn down and had no energy to battle anymore. Shortly thereafter, a group of Derek and Peter's mutual friends showed up at the bar, which was in my favor, as I was then introduced to a couple of ladies, Tessa and Gretchen, who were able to distract me with their own drama, saving me from having contact with Peter. Someone else's drama, other than my own, was a much needed respite.

After eleven o'clock, more people were shuffling through the front doors. I recall Derek saying that it would get packed after eleven. He wasn't kidding. By midnight there was little room to walk. *So, this is what people do in a small town?* I suppose, if I had stayed in my home town of Ashland, I'd be doing the same thing. There was something really comforting about knowing everyone in the town you lived in. It felt like everyone was family. I sincerely enjoyed meeting all these new people and genuinely liked most of them. I felt a real sense of belonging and the time miraculously flew by.

But when it began to approach one o'clock in the morning, my eyelids started to droop and I knew it was time for me to head home. I wasn't used to staying up so late since I opened my business. I had the bartender call a taxi for me. And after exchanging numbers and saying farewell to my new friends, I found Derek to say goodbye. We hugged and immediately afterward, I turned around and there was Peter…in my face.

"Where have you been all night?"

"Right here," I pronounced agitated. "And now I must go."

"Should I get your number from Derek?" he persevered.

"Uh, okay…yeah, I guess that'd be fine," I said with a forced smile. *Wow, I was not making it easy for this guy.* Too tired to care at this point, I began walking toward the front door.

"I'll call ya!" he yelled with his hand held high in the air.

I waved meekly, without turning around, as I exited the front door of the pub. Peter didn't offer to walk me outside to wait for a taxi with me. I could tell he wasn't the chivalrous type and I was glad. I didn't want to like him.

Peter may not have been chivalrous, but he was persistent, at least with women who act uninterested. He called me the very next day, Sunday evening. During our conversation, after explaining how I wasn't truly ready to date anyone, he said that he understood, but I sensed that he thought I was intentionally blowing him off.

Despite not going out on a date the following Friday, for the next four months, even as preoccupied with my career as I was, Peter found ways to get to know me. His method: unexpectedly showing up at every event Derek invited me to. The new friends, who I'd met at JB's saloon, would congregate together to have backyard barbecues at their homes, or meet up to Karaoke at The Tool Box (another popular dive bar in Mount Shasta), or gather up at Lake Shasta to go boating. And who would I always see there? Peter. Mount Shasta was a small community, so everyone knew everybody. And, like Derek, Peter grew up in the area and has known these people since elementary school.

I never saw Peter with a girl, but he certainly flirted with all of them. And, similar to Willie, he always had a drink in his hand. The difference was that Peter's drink of choice was not Budweiser beer it was Jack Daniel's whiskey. Yep, the hard stuff. A few times, I caught him sneaking a sip from a flask he'd retrieve from a hidden coat pocket. I thought Willie was a drinker, but this guy was a pro. I was naïve to the issues associated with someone who had a genetic predisposition to alcoholism and so nothing about Peter's behavior caused me concern. I assumed he only drank socially at parties. Besides, I was Irish, and typical of the stereotype, we were all big drinkers. Everyone in my family was a workaholic with a big party attitude. Most of my relatives knew when to drink and when not to and worked in high paying professions, only drinking on the weekends. Which I suppose, a few could be deemed to be functioning alcoholics, but I never labeled them as such. I knew nothing about the disease, until Peter. I didn't know that some people are completely incapable of controlling their liquor intake. I learned about this the hard way—witnessing it firsthand with Peter. But it took me a long time before I saw the signs of alcoholism. In the beginning, I was totally blind to it. I was too busy thinking about myself. My selfish mantra being: "No thank you. I'm not ready to date."

Peter eventually grew tired of hearing my resistance to his advances, officially throwing in the towel, telling Derek he didn't think I'd ever come around. I'd never been pursued so eagerly before, and despite that it was somewhat annoying, it was still flattering. I was concerned when I heard he was giving up on me and wouldn't be chasing me anymore. The conundrum was that I enjoyed "the chase" and was surprisingly beginning to fall for him.

He would drop by Petite Paws using a friend's dog to get an appointment just so he could talk to me: *cute*. Serve me drinks at barbecue events, like a waiter doting on me, making sure I always had a full glass: *adorable*. Make sure he was

164

selected on the same boat ride whenever we went on a group lake adventure: *sweet*. Stop by my house in his delivery truck to offer me a discount on beer and then ask if I was free for dinner: *gallant*. I didn't want to give him up. Gretchen, who had developed into a dear friend of mine and grew up with Peter, agreed that the chase for most men is a huge motivator, but then confided that Peter never *had* to chase a girl before.

"You know, Melody Rae, girls flock to Peter. He's charming, he's a character and he's funny. He was the most popular catch in high school. But he was a player and no one thought he'd ever be interested in just one girl…until now. This is the longest he's ever been single. I don't even think he's been hooking up with anyone, which is not typical of him at all."

"How do you know this?" I asked, puzzled.

"Trust me. I've known Peter a long time. But if you don't give him a chance soon, he will give up trying," she cautioned. And then, with a panicked expression of reassurance, she placed her hand on mine. "Now, don't worry about me. I am totally not interested in Peter. He's not at all my type. Actually, Derek's my type. I've had a crush on him since the third grade. But don't tell him!"

"Oh, I totally won't. But seriously…since the third grade?! That's a long time. Why aren't you together? I mean, he's a true sweetheart. He's such a good guy, and I can totally see you two together."

"Really?! Aw. Well, he's never pursued me and I just don't think he likes me in that way, you know?"

"Are you kidding me, girl? I can guarantee you that he likes you. He's always staring at you, like constantly. He's just not the assertive, pursuing type, that's all. It's not his style. He was raised with values to respect women. He's a gentleman. Besides, he probably doesn't even suspect you like him and that's why he hasn't asked you out. I mean, theoretically, it doesn't make sense why he and Peter are even friends. Listen, you need to ask him out. Seriously! That would work for him. He likes the girl to be in charge. Trust me."

"Really? You think so?"

"Yes! I know so."

"Okay, I will then!" Gretchen squealed. It was refreshing to see her so excited. She was one of my linear thinking friends with an unusually serious side, like Derek. Though, Gretchen is more assertive than Derek, both of them are responsible, observant, patient, objective, logical, respectful and mature introverts with moral integrity.

I guess all Gretchen needed was the green light from me, because after "our talk" she didn't wait long to go after Derek. She asked him out the very next day. And they eventually married, two years later. Naturally, she proposed. He's the kind of guy that needed a woman to be in charge; probably why he and I never had chemistry with one another. To feel romantic chemistry, we both need our partner to be the take charge personality type. *Funny how opposites indisputably do attract.*

And it was certainly true for me and Peter. Although having romantic chemistry isn't always a healthy attraction, it is easy to be deceived into believing it is. It wasn't until sometime after my adventure with Peter began that I was able to see the true Peter beneath his charming facade.

Peter's demeanor could best be described as having the quality of a **flaky yellow fin tuna: mild and meaty as he was easy-going, yet, intense when confronted and, firm and flaky, as was his stubbornness, and all too often indecisive and ambiguous nature.** He was evasive and rarely followed through on his promises or doing what he said he would. I suppose that was part of his charm. Although he was brassy and verbose, he was also entertaining and affable, which made his flakiness tolerable.

The adventure began at Petite Paws on a Tuesday at four o'clock in the afternoon. I remember distinctly how I indiscriminately clipped my left hand with scissors when doing a trim on a dark brown haired Shih Tzu named Midori. *Ouch, that hurt.* I had to leave my assistant in the room with the dog to grab an adhesive and gauze from the receptionist's first aid kit at her desk, because my order did not arrive as scheduled. I had forgotten to send in the supply order sheet the week before, due to being more distracted by my personal life than usual. Luckily, my lovely secretary, Lee, caught these issues and placed an order, although too late to matter at this moment in time. Since Lee was away from her desk, I scooted her chair over to retrieve the first aid kit from the cabinet above the front counter. Precisely as I set the kit on the counter top and heard the automatic front doorbell ding, I looked up into a scarce lobby and in walked Peter.

"Ah, yes, um, just the person I wanted to see," he stammered, nervously placing a severely wrinkled up map on the counter and boorishly flipping through it, completely unaware I was injured. Something about him was different. He was deferential and unpretentious. I never saw him uncomfortable before, it was endearing like a lost puppy dog.

"I know, I know. You want nothing to do with me. I accept that. I'm not here for me. I don't know if Gretchen told you, but a few of us go up every Fourth of July to a rodeo up at Green Valley. Well, this year it's on a Friday, so that's awesome. Anyway, um, Gretchen asked me to invite you…and bring you a map, so you can easily find where to go…um, that is if you decide to join us," he said, all the while looking down and smoothing out the map with his hands.

Amused by his gauche behavior, I smiled, and then applied the adhesive bandage and gauze to my superficial flesh wound.

"This is the easiest route to drive," he continued, clearing his throat and then pointing with his finger where he'd highlighted the road to Green Valley on the map.

Then he looked up at me with sparkly eyes, laughed uncomfortably and grinned, which I found staggeringly irresistible.

"Oh, okay…um, thank you," I said smiling while rubbing my injured hand. "I'm not sure if I can take a day off, though."

"I understand, sure. But just know, I promise I'll be a total gentleman…if you decide to go that is. I promise. I am just inviting you as a friend," he said with convincing eyes.

Something about Peter not pursuing me, and accepting defeat with a willingness to be my friend, attracted me more.

167

"I'll think about it," I said sweetly, charmed by his awkward diffidence.

He then lackadaisically attempted to fold the map, handed it to me in a wadded clump, tipped up his baseball cap to say bye and walked out of the salon. For the next two days, I pondered whether or not I should go. Kat helped me weigh the pros and cons of camping up at Green Valley with Peter within tent distance.

However, by Friday morning, I still wasn't sure. Since my relationship with Willie seemed resolved, I felt vulnerable with no excuse to prevent me from getting involved with Peter and this worried me. *Would I be susceptible to his charm? Did I want to be?* Camping can be such a private affair which made me leery as to whether it would be logically smart to go. *Why did I want to go? Did I like him in that way? Did I like him because he was similar to Willie, or did I like him because he was Peter?*

Taking into account the dichotomy of what Gretchen said about Peter being "into" me and Derek's viewpoint of how Peter had given up on me, I felt at odds and challenged wanting to do something to prolong the chase. And, although I wasn't sure if I was ready to be involved in a relationship, I couldn't imagine not seeing Peter again. I thought my feelings for Willie were obsessive, but they paled in comparison. The intensity of my attraction toward Peter was growing in a magnitude greater than a large earthquake. You think men sometimes only think with one part of their body? Women can be like that, too. I wasn't thinking with my brain, that's for sure—my libido was doing all the talking.

At three o'clock on Friday afternoon, a client unexpectedly cancelled her appointment, and I was still undecided. Walking in the front door of my unusually quiet house unpredictably early that Friday afternoon, painfully aware it was Fourth of July and I had absolutely no plans, I looked at my pathetic reflection in the mirror and thought: *why not?*

I loaded a tent, sleeping bag and a red Carhartt Jacket into the back of my jeep, first. Then I packed my Wrangler jeans, leggings, extra socks (for at night), makeup, first aid kit and one other outfit, into a durable, waterproof, nylon, red suitcase. I found it at a thrift store last year with the original tags shockingly still on it. I am always surprised by what people throw out.

After tossing the suitcase into the back seat, I started to have the same butterfly feelings in my stomach I had for Zeek Cohen, my secret four year adolescent crush and moreover first kiss. I contemplated whether my feelings for Peter were virtually indistinguishable from how I had felt about Zeek. *Did I only have a school girl crush on Peter, or was it more serious?*

Before stepping into the jeep and heading off on my adventure, I called Kat to vent more about my confusion. She suggested I relax and go with the flow. She also said that I had to vow to reveal every gushy detail when I returned. I promised. It was the least I could do, since at the time she had no guy prospects and wanted to vicariously live through me.

Finally approaching the Green Valley exit toward the rodeo campgrounds, I turned the steering wheel and sighed with relief. *I can't believe that I didn't get lost.* Peter's map was honestly helpful. But how did I expect to find my friends? No one knew I was going to show up, which actually made it all the more thrilling and invigorating to surprise everyone. *That is, if I can find them.* Supposedly, Gretchen, Derek, Tessa and her husband, Sean, headed to the campsite earlier in the week. I figured I would wander the campground until I saw one of their vehicles, or recognized someone, or someone recognized me. *Maybe someone will see my truck?* Everyone in Mount Shasta knew I drove a beat-up, 1986 blue Ford pickup that my dad bought me, when my Datsun pickup blew a head gasket the previous summer. And although it was not my color of choice, I was grateful to have a vehicle with no monthly car payment.

The entire understated campground was quite small. *Thank goodness.* I parked in what presumably was a public parking lot choosing to park first and meander around on foot rather than drive straight through to make my surprise appearance more astonishing. I stepped out of the truck with my

169

sunglasses on my head wearing white flip flops, a light jean miniskirt and a white tank top. I considered grabbing my light jean jacket sitting on the seat, until I felt the hot sun on my face and realized I didn't need it. It was hotter than I expected it to be in the mountains. It would never be this warm in the Oregonian Mountains. I breathed in the fresh clean warm mountainous air and began walking along the gravel road toward the campground, passing campsite after campsite seeing no sign of my friends. I started to worry whether maybe they indeed decided not to go camping, or in fact, left early. Maybe I should have called Gretchen before driving all the way out here? *What am I doing?*

Moments after my neurotic trepidation started to set in, and I seriously considered turning around and driving home, I heard a familiar voice: "Oh snap!" followed by a recognizable and contagious laugh.

Only Peter had a unique laugh like that. In the direction of the bellowing voice I saw the back of a tipped-up Budweiser hat. It was Peter. Grinning and tip-toeing over so as not to be heard, I slowly approached him from behind. As I crept up behind him, while gesturing to those who saw me in the group to be quiet, Peter started to get suspicious noticing everyone's sudden apprehension.

"What's goin' on? What are you guys lookin' at me like that for? Wus up? My fly undone?" he reacted perturbed, insecurely looking down at himself.

At which time, I swiftly nudged the back of his hat, causing it to fly forward off his head and hit the ground. He turned around with indignant eyes, until he saw it was me who was teasing him. He gave his loud signature laugh, spilling some of the whiskey from his red plastic cup. And then he seized me into a tight squeeze and kissed my cheek. Everyone started to laugh. I know if I was anyone else, he would have reacted royally pissed. His hat is as sacred to him as the whiskey in his cup.

"You came?" he said, looking at me with surprisingly emotionally filled eyes.

"Yep."

He smiled, tilted his head and stared at me with a look of reverence. "Did the map help?"

"Oh yeah, definitely…I needed it, thanks. It was a good map."

"Good. I'm glad."

I smiled.

And then Peter was abruptly snagged by Derek and Sean to engage in a game of horseshoes at the horseshoe pit in the center of the campground.

"Don't go anywhere. I'll see you soon," he said, pointing and delivering me a wink before waltzing away.

When Gretchen headed over to me I noticed a girl I'd never seen before, sitting amidst the group in one of the Coleman camping chairs, near the fire pit. She had becoming features, and in the light flickering from the crackling campfire her hair appeared blond gossamer, and was reasonably long. I was surprised to feel a twinge of jealousy sweep over me.

She looked over at me, checked me up and down with her eyes, whispered something to Derek, and then threw her hands up in the air.

"I'm outta here," she spewed, storming off down the road toward the rodeo grounds and away from the campsites.

"Who was that? Is she okay?" I asked Gretchen, who also heeded the girl's reaction.

"Oh yeah, totally, don't worry about her. We are so happy you made it. Yay!" she said, leaning in and hugging me. "She's an old friend of ours who grew up in Mount Shasta with us. I'm pretty sure she was hoping to hook-up with Peter later tonight. But she knows Peter is not gonna do that, now that you're here."

"What??? But I am NOT hooking-up with anyone! She and Peter can do whatever they want," I gasped. *I don't want to be thought of as a man stealer.*

"Oh honey, you don't get it, do you? Peter has it bad for you. I mean, big time. He immediately lost interest in her, when he saw you. You know, he's always asking about you when you're not around? He'll say, 'Where's the kid?' I don't know why he calls you that. I think it's because you're silly

171

and playful," Gretchen exhaled, in one long breath. *What?! He refers to me as "kid" just like Willie did?*

I began to scrunch my hair neurotically and shake my head with incertitude. "Are you kidding me? I need a drink...a really strong drink," I stammered, searching for a cup on the picnic table.

"Whiskey?" asked Gretchen.

"Ugh, no...well, maybe....NO...bad idea. Whiskey makes me excessively emotional, best if I stick to my usual. Did anyone bring wine?" I asked with bated breath.

Tessa stood and retrieved a box from the back of her truck. "I have a Franzia box of red wine, a Cabernet Sauvignon okay?"

"That'll totally work," I said while walking over to hug her.

After reciprocating my hug, she set the corrugated fiberboard boxed wine on the picnic table, filled up a clear plastic cup to the rim and handed it to me. I sat next to the other girls, who were sitting around the fire pit, with my cup of red wine and breathed in the crisp mountainous air, thankful to have a lovely group of friends who accepted me as I am. As it turned out, most of them set up camp on Tuesday. *Wow! I wish I could take that much time off.* Being a sole proprietor of a business, scheduling that much time off is nearly impossible.

As the boys returned to the campsite carrying their horseshoes, Gretchen filled me in on the rodeo events to convene on Saturday, and informed me about the famous glass six-pocket pool table at Lil' Jon's Spirits Lounge, where we were all supposedly walking to once it gets dark.

"They have billiards in this tiny town of...what...a population of one hundred and fifty?" I asked surprised.

Gretchen laughed. "One hundred and fifty-two."

I giggled. "I stand corrected."

Tessa chimed in, "Oh, it's so cool, Melody Rae. You have to join us."

"Of course, yes, totally...I want to!" I shrilled, and then shivered as an unexpectedly cool wind blew across my legs creating goose bumps. *I'm glad I threw jeans in my suitcase.* It wasn't nearly as cold as it would be in Oregon, but it was cold enough to wear pants.

"I should change into my jeans soon," I said, turning to Gretchen while rubbing my legs to warm them.

"Nah, just drink more," snickered Peter, sneaking up behind me.

"Ha-Ha," I sneered, then smiled.

As Peter passed by me, he ruffled my hair like a teenage boy would do to a girl he likes, and then headed to the other side of the fire pit where the boys were congregating. He sat in one of the camping chairs across from me and stared over in my direction with a penetrating look. I could feel his searing, fiery eyes on me. Thankfully, Tessa's husband, Sean, asked me to help set out the crudité and condiments for the burgers so I could avoid acknowledging Peter's intoxicating stare.

Sean prepared me an exquisite vegetarian burger which was succulent and mouthwatering: juicy, spicy, salty and sweet. It was scrumptiously out of this world. Since Tessa is a vegan, Sean has become well educated on cooking meatless meals and knows what ingredients amalgamate well together.

In truth, my overzealous reaction to the burger may have been somewhat aggrandized, as I have existed purely on fast food since I opened my grooming salon. Eating healthy, authentic handmade food was delectable and refreshing. Consequently, I couldn't help but groan and drool as I devoured Sean's intensely satisfyingly palatable veggie burger. The way I incessantly kept thanking him for making it, you would think I hadn't eaten for days. After eating the entire burger, I excused myself to set up my tent.

"Oh no you don't!" Derek interjected protectively, and then gestured to all the guys. "Come on boys, we've got a tent to assemble."

Derek then asked for my keys and where I parked, while Gretchen poured me another glass of boxed red wine. *I feel so blessed to have such a terrific friend as Derek.*

As the sun was going down, everyone began scrambling toward their tents to change into jeans in preparation for the walk to Lil' Jon's Spirits Lounge. Reportedly, it is walking distance from the campsite. I slipped on a fresh red tank top, threw on my red Carhartt leather jacket, blue Wrangler jeans and red Justin cowboy boots, which looked practically brand new as I rarely had an opportunity to wear them.

The glow of the full moon lit our way, as we headed in a group toward the top of a bridge that crossed a small creek. Once we reached the top Peter stopped walking and put his hands on my shoulders. Then he turned my body around, facing me in the direction of the campsites, and then enveloped me from behind in a tight embrace.

"What are you doing?" I said amusedly, while everyone else in the group kept on walking ahead.

"What am I doing? Well, I'll tell you. I'm protecting you," Peter smirked, and then (being a major science fiction fanatic) went into this ridiculous, although cleverly witty rant about how he would know how to keep me safe and find our way back in the dark later because he has super powers that can manipulate darkness, and extra-terrestrial senses which equip him with an internal GPS system. *Uh-huh, r-i-i-ight.* In spite of being charmed by his sui generis creative story, when it continued to parade on and on, sounding more like a chorus of whistling cockatiel's, I found myself only half-listening. My mind began to purely focus on the heat emanating from his body behind me, his strong arms wrapped around me and his warm cheek next to mine with the sweet smell of whiskey on his breath, and the soft touch of his hands over mine. I desperately wanted him to quit talking and kiss me already.

While Peter continued talking, completely unaware of his surroundings, I was awakened from my dreamy trance noticing off in the distance a gentleman who seemed strikingly familiar to me; although I couldn't quite figure out why. He was standing at a campsite, in front of a roaring fire pit, with his head down and holding a brown coffee mug next to a kid who was sitting in a navy blue camping chair adding a marshmallow to a walking stick. Then a woman came out of the camper trailer and he looked up toward her. And that's when I saw his profile and could tell who it was. It was him. It was *Mister S!* He was here in Green Valley, with his wife and son! *Holy cannoli!* I'm not sure what made him glance in my direction, but he did. First, I caught his eyes gazing in my direction, then his eyes caught mine and he recognized me.

He instantly spilled his mug of hot coffee all over his son's leg, causing him to stand briskly and yell, "D-a-a-ad!"

I gasped.

His wife immediately approached him and began reprimanding him for his carelessness.

It was at that point that Peter had finished his long idiosyncratic theory, spun me around, procured me seductively by the neck, and kissed me. The kiss was hard, yet, sensual and deliriously sweet, and it took my breath away.

He then took me by the hand and we walked toward Lil' John's. My heart fluttered while listening to him rant, mostly about himself, the entire four blocks there, as I became entwined and emotionally lost in a new adventure with Peter, bearing temporary amnesia about encountering *Mister S.*

The night was a pandemonium of events sprinkled with loud music, laughter, sexual chemistry, liquor and jealousy. Peter was possessive and had to know where I was at all times. But, after dating only inattentive distant men, I found his overprotective, clingy and proprietorial behavior flattering. It felt good to have someone so "into" me. It was a refreshing change. We had a terrific time playing pool on the trendy and popular glass billiard table with all its bling-bling. I guilelessly expected the entire pool table to be entirely made of glass for some reason, but it wasn't. The pockets, sides and legs were all glass and adorned with clear acrylic diamond garland, but the area on top where you shoot the ball wasn't. It was covered with the usual green woolen cloth. However, it was still impressively wild to watch the balls tumble down into the pockets, roll across the side of the table and converge at the opening. Although ostentatious and quite chichi, I still wanted to own one.

Although Peter appeared to need me consistently by his side, he never asked me questions, or tried to get to know much about me. It wasn't necessarily a concern at first because with Peter, like with Willie, we were usually inebriated. I learned the hard way that never having a sober moment to analyze "the relationship", or worry about whether it is or isn't working is a recipe for disaster. But I wasn't concerned at the time about where things were going. I was simply happy to have an attractive guy interested in me.

Instead of logically examining the relationship in a healthy way, I did what I naturally do at the beginning of every relationship: enable and idolize; placing Peter on a pedestal while neglecting my own needs, similarly to what I did with Willie, Tony and Shay.

To consummate our newfound relationship, Peter and I slept together in my tent that night. The experience was eerily similar to Willie. It was as if they were twins. *How can two people not related be so congruous? Was it because they were born on the same day?* Aside from the shape of their noses; their eyes, small mouth, short buzz cut hair and physical mannerisms were identical. It was impossible to ignore. I had to keep my eyes open, because if I closed them I would think I was with Willie. I was acutely conscious of every word I said, worrying I might slip up at any minute and say Willie's name.

Oddly enough, during the entire rest of the weekend, I never ran into *Mister S*. When my mind finally decided to replay out initial recognition of one another, I wondered whether he was as astounded as I. In spite of the puzzlement over seeing him, my attention was on Peter. And so I decided to chalk it up to pure coincidence. In the meantime, life continued.

The next few months felt like an illusion, a strange dream. My relationship with Peter was an ambivalent tornado, drifting up high and then floating along aimlessly collecting dust; a delicious, unbridled, passionate, fervent and whirling white cloud, frantically spinning with ferocity building into a volatile, calamitous cyclone of filth with nowhere to land.

After months into the relationship, it became clear how imbalanced and impure our union was. But before I could see the forest for the trees, I remained purely centered on my physical compatibility with Peter; floating aimlessly on an illusory love cloud. Peter knew how to put me on a pedestal. His adoration, compliments and flattery made me convinced that he thought I was the sexiest, most talented princess in the land. I believed every word he said, which is why I fell hard for him. I'd inadvertently mistaken our sexual rapport and vehement, fiery, salacious intimacy for love.

When in reality we had sex more often than we talked and, other than sex, rarely did anything alone as a couple. Always surrounded by his group of friends prevented us from getting to know each other more intimately. And when he started referring to me as "kid" on a regular basis, it discombobulated my senses exacerbating memories of Willie. I began to feel a powerful invisible source pulling me toward Peter. Maybe that force was Willie. Regardless of only witnessing Peter's personality around his friends, I began to inadvertently fall head over heels for him. Was I falling for the traits he had similar to Willie or his own? I didn't know.

Once my heart strings were pulled I could only see the good in Peter, remaining blind to the qualities he had that were unhealthy. The fact that things were always about him never concerned me. The signs were clear that he wasn't serious relationship material, but neither was I. And since I wasn't ready for anything serious, his living with two of his longtime high school friends, who were also truck drivers for Budweiser—making the only times we did see one another on the weekends—didn't distress me much. The occasions we spent together consisted mostly of playing board games, video games, or watching sci-fi movies with his roommates. Sometimes (not often) we would go out to the pub and have drinks and play pool. But in comparison to Willie, Peter and I did a great deal together. And considering my relationships with Shay and Tony had been so emotionally disconnected and physically sexless, I was grateful to have a partner with whom I shared phenomenal sexual chemistry.

Although I wasn't complaining, I started to feel like I was dating a teenager. And as time went by, I realized I wanted more. As a woman in my thirties, I no longer wanted just a fling. Despite never being satisfied with a day-to-day conventional relationship, like I had with Shay or Tony, (because they were dreary and lacked fire), I certainly didn't care to date a boy with no future goals whatsoever. And I didn't necessarily want to go out on painfully banal and monotonous dinner outings, either. I simply wanted to evolve with someone. I wanted someone to ask me what I would like to do and show interest in what I was about. Ideally, I wanted a mutual friendship with a guy who could also ignite my appetite for life.

Obviously my expectations were too high, thinking I could discover these traits in Peter. Nonetheless, there were some unquestionably positive sides to our union: he didn't ask anything of me and it wasn't hard work, or interfere in my professional life, and I liked that. However, there was undoubtedly a negative side: I didn't exactly feel like he was "into" me anymore, like I had felt in the beginning, during the pivotal chasing stage of the courtship. After the chase ended and he had me totally committed, he stopped working at keeping me interested. All I could assume was that this was the real Peter: a horny, inebriated teenager looking for an easy screw. *Was that me? Was I easy? Oh no!*

Feeling emotionally and physically unhealthy, I finally had to confront the issue, although I didn't know if I should. After spending too many sleepless nights eating tortilla chips with salsa as a main meal and boffing in Peter's cluttered bedroom, with his roommates in the next room; the smell of Jack Daniel's whiskey lingering in the air, along with the taste of Listerine on Peter's breath, started to make me feel ill. Although I did appreciate that in the morning wanting to kiss me without offensive breath odor, he'd swig a mouthful of Listerine antiseptic. However, despite the fact that I appreciated his respectfulness to not kiss me with day old whiskey breath and immensely enjoyed our sexual compatibility, I had to question whether this was where I wanted to be. *What am I doing?* I began to want to be more than his consolation prize after a hard day of driving truck. *Who am I? This isn't me. I'm not that girl who allows a guy to take advantage of her—am I?* Neglecting what matters to me most; self-respect, I compromised who I was, allowing myself to be swept away by his physical attractiveness and natural charm; like how he called me "kid", the way Willie used to do.

When I finally chose to discernibly see the truth, the fact our relationship dynamic was purely a sexual fling, I was compelled to take a stand. The fish bones were flying in every direction. He never considered asking me what I wanted to do and we never went to the lake for a picnic, or fishing together, or planned an adventure to the coast, or went to see a live comedy show at the casino—nothing. *Why not?* Doing anything ordinary, without his guy friends parading along, would have ensued a refreshing change.

Unfortunately, my attempts at taking a stand didn't proceed as effectively as planned. Worried at sounding like a nagging girlfriend, I chose to avoid asking him directly to invite me to do things without his roommates. Rather, after witnessing him down an entire bottle of Jack Daniel's whiskey one evening, I made a purely observational comment involving his liquor intake. *Big mistake.*

I gently touched the empty whiskey bottle. "Wow, you drank that entire bottle?"

His eyes narrowed. "Hey, I gave up drinking a lot for you. I used to drink a whole lot more," he said scornfully. Then stood, opened the cupboard and grabbed another bottle of Jack. "I'll drink however much I like, whenever I like and with whomever I like. I ain't gonna let no woman tell me what to do. Damn, woman, back off why don't ya?"

Stunned and frightened by his indignation, I walked out the door without saying goodbye. He didn't follow. He never snapped at me like that before. The self-effacing, awkward and geeky four-eyed little girl in me was petrified. I had no idea that he was drinking less because of me.

It became transparent after two weeks and no call that our ambiguous relationship plateaued. After which, Peter showed up at my work to inform me that he was given an ultimatum to either lose his employment, or continue driving Budweiser, under the provision that he relocate to Buffalo, New York. He confessed that it was time for him to move on and grow up.

And simple as that, it was over. Although I suspected the job relocation was an excuse to run away, I felt it was honestly to his advantage. He needed to be away from the town he grew up in, in order to mature. But I wondered whether he thought our relationship was ending because he was moving? In my mind our relationship ended because he chose liquor over me. However, I was in a quandary. I don't think he had the ability to slow down. And I didn't believe our relationship demise was based entirely on his liquor consumption? I mean, I was drinking around him, too. It was what we did together. I was left baffled. Especially since my feelings hadn't died. They remained as strong as ever. That is, until a week later when I stopped at the local Chevron gas station and ran into Marco, one of his long standing roommates.

Prefacing how he did not want to be a harbinger, Marco confided in me how no one is surprised by our break up because Peter is known to be a serious alcoholic and sex addict. *What?!* Marco assumed that I knew all about his reputation. *I didn't.* I was left beyond words, confounded. Supposedly, Peter had been cheating on me during the week with various promiscuous women from the local pubs in town. Going home with a different girl every night was apparently common. I felt so foolish. No wonder he never wanted to see me during the week. I felt like a complete idiot. Any residual feeling that we could possibly rekindle our relationship in the future was completely sabotaged.

I pledged to never get involved with an addict ever again. I wanted the next guy I meet to be mature and balanced, even if it meant boring. However, I learned that oftentimes the thing you concentrate on *not* wanting, because of all the thought put into it, is exactly what you do get? The universe doesn't hear what you *don't* want; it only hears what you are thinking about; positive or negative. Heavily determined to avoid an addict, I invariably attracted one; the briny and vitriolic fish, Kyle Spears.

Chapter Six

What's the difference between a catfish and a lawyer? One's a slimy scum-sucking bottom-dwelling scavenger; the other is a fish.

Catfish

A popular fish in Southern recipes, catfish comes to us from the Central United States, especially Mississippi. The firm, white meat of catfish is sturdier than most other white fish. Catfish has a delicate flavor and a small flake.

"Give a man a fish and he will eat for a day. Teach him how to fish and he will sit in a boat and drink beer all day."

~Author Unknown

****

Kat poured the last droplets of wine from the second bottle into my glass and then procured a 2004 Chateau Laforge Saint Emelion bottle of Merlot from her trendy black, wrought iron wall-mounted wine rack. After uncorking it, she poured a small taste into her glass.

Then she looked at me with a guilty and somewhat duplicitous expression. "My mom is taking Brooklyn to the waterpark tomorrow so that Steven and I can have an afternoon rendezvous, and I wanted to share this brand of wine with him...but I think we better test a bottle first. You know, to make sure it's of quality. I think we need one more glass of wine before coffee, anyway, don't you agree?"

"Uh, y-e-e-eah! Hello?!" I encouraged, boldly holding up my empty glass. Then, after Kat poured me a healthy portion, I leaned in to read the label on the bottle. "Where in the world did you find such an exorbitant French wine?"

"The Internet, I order all my wine online…I'm lazy. Besides, if you order in bulk, it's actually cheaper," she said emphatically, and then swirled the small sampling of wine in her glass, leaned her nose into it, took a deep sniff and a small sip which she first savored on her tongue.

I looked at her quizzically with one brow up.

She eyed me with an uppity expression. "This varietal has a dense and velvety texture. I'm getting a hint of coffee with a well-integrated new wood taste."

"I'm getting…drunk."

Kat burst out laughing.

"But seriously, Kat, how'd you know that? You sound like *Mister S.* Are you taking some wine-ology course I'm unaware of?"

Kat grabbed a napkin to wipe the spit off her face. "Ha-ha-ha…I sound educated, huh? No, I just recently started ordering the Wine Enthusiast magazine. Though, I do want to have my own vineyard someday, actually."

"Oh really, how very French of you," I said with my head held high and fluttering my tongue on my bottom lip accentuating the "F" in the word French. "You know, if you own a vineyard, you'll be seeing a lot more of me."

"Good, you can help me squash grapes. I read it takes approximately six to eight hundred grapes to make one bottle of wine."

"No way! Seriously?! That's nuts."

"I know! But how fun to be able to make your own wine, right?!" Kat shrieked and then paraded inside.

"Count me in!" I bellowed.

Kat opened her refrigerator, removing a small plate of rich New York style cheesecake and a container of fresh blueberries, retrieved two small plates along with two forks off the counter top, and set everything on the kitchen table.

She then peered out through the French doors. "Hey, wanna motivate inside? I don't know about you, but it's gettin' a bit chilly for me out there."

"All right," I said indifferently. Kat is known to get cold relatively easily. Me? I'm the complete opposite. I could have remained outside all night, especially after feeling well insulated from the wine and rather content and at peace from all the therapy. I stood, stacked our plates and utensils and slowly, after milling my way inside, set everything into the kitchen sink.

While Kat was pouring the fresh blueberries over our cheesecake slices, I rinsed the plates, forks, knives, spatula and pans, which were already soaking in soapy water in the sink, and then loaded everything into the dishwasher.

I was fairly salivating as I stared intently at the cheesecake. I couldn't believe I was still hungry after all we consumed, but I was. Unequivocally, there is always room for cheesecake.

After pouring water into the coffee pot, Kat pressed the on button and sat. Of course, she had pre-ground and measured the fresh coffee beans earlier and now only had to add water. Typical of Kat's character, as she has a tendency to be obsessive-compulsive. I suppose you have to be like that somewhat to be a neurologist, or at least a good one, which she undoubtedly is.

I then noticed the arrangement of empty wine bottles on the table. *I am so glad I don't have to work tomorrow. Sleeping in is going to be heaven.* Needless to say, I planned on crashing on Kat's couch for the night. Although both of us were a bit loopy, we felt toasty warm with a sense of well-being, rejoicing in the healing that had taken place.

Exhilarated on our mission to prove the theory of how food has played a role in attracting mates, we plummeted ahead. Flipping through the legal pad, I skipped ahead locating Kyle, the final relationship to tackle before making any strong conclusions. My body was tingling in anticipation, while my mind was racing with thoughts from my past. It was morally rewarding to retain a healthy perspective and discover the emotional tools to view things more clearly than before. I get why therapy works. I felt empowered to make conscious changes that would alter my future and no longer had fear of repeating past patterns—it was purely enlightening.

Kat stood. "All right, before we talk about Kyle, I have to check on Brooklyn. So, quick, give me the rundown on Peter. What did you write? Something about booze I imagine."

I suspected Kat had to pee; by the way she was standing in an anxious pose and snapping her fingers at me, like a frustrated New Yorker attempting to hail a cab. Empathetically, I turned to the appropriate page on the legal pad and rapidly read Peter's synopsis.

"Okay. After the flaky yellow fin tuna, Peter, I could no longer smell Listerine, or hear the song *'Alcohol'* by Brad Paisley, or taste Jack Daniel's whiskey without being left with a bitter and dishonest aftertaste. Sound about right?"

Jack Daniel's whiskey

"Oh, yeah, yeah, yeah, that totally fits. What else?" Kat snapped, wiggling back and forth like a toddler.

Instantly, I snatched *The Secret Language of Relationships* book, and then it registered that Willie and Peter had the same birthday.

"Oh, remember? Everything would be the same with Peter as Willie. They had the same birthday. So, yeah, it's all the same," I said, referring to where I wrote Willie's information on the legal pad. "Best at: family. Weaknesses: exhausting, oscillating, impermanent. Yep. They were identical, both born on the nineteenth of June, 1969."

"Holy Toledo, that's right! Stay away from Gemini's, girl."

"I plan to. Well, at least the ones born on the nineteenth of June. I can't stay away from all Gemini's. Come on! There's some awesome Gemini's out there!" I blurted, looking at Kat shuffling her legs. "Kat go pee already!" I insisted, with my hands in the air, waving in the direction of the bathroom.

Kat then darted to the bathroom, escaping down the hallway at leprechaun speed. I chose to take this opportunity to preen myself. Opening my purse, I retrieved my hair pick, compact, blush and lipstick. I powdered my face, revitalized my cheeks and lips, and neatened my curls with the hair pick.

After returning the maquillage to my purse, I went to the kitchen sink to wash my hands. I noticed on the counter, Kat had a new bottle of emollient: L'Occitane en Provence: Crème Mains Peaux Sèches: a dry skin hand-cream. I presumed it was more costly than the cheap Dollar Tree brand of warm vanilla that I have sitting on my nightstand at home, since the bottle was made in France and no bigger than my thumb. Oftentimes expensive things come in small packages. I was careful to squeeze only a tiny droplet, which not surprisingly was enough embrocation for both hands as it was (as expected) highly concentrated.

As I was conscientiously returning the pricey bottle to its exact spot, Kat scooted past me without a word and sprinted up the stairs, assumedly to check on her daughter. Picking up my near empty glass of red wine and leaning up against the banister of the stairway, I took a miniscule sip and drifted into deeper feelings of sadness about Peter. In the midst of replaying a bittersweet memory of us once happy together—Peter laughing at my clumsiness, as I spill my drink on the account I'm talking with my hands, and then staring at me in that altruistic, way misleading me to believe he was crazy in love—I was interrupted by Kat's entrance down the stairwell. She tapped my head knocking me into the present.

"Brooklyn's fast asleep," she edified, and then began to explain how ever since she left her ex-fiancé, Troy, and moved to this cottage, Brooklyn has had a difficult time sleeping.

I knew she was blaming herself for not being able to provide a stable father figure in Brooklyn's life. The relationship with Officer Steven was too recent for her to consider introducing Brooklyn, so she knows nothing about him, which we both agreed is best for now.

After detailing her situation, Kat took a deep breath and her eyes glossed over. Then she turned and walked down the hallway past the kitchen and out of sight, and then came back in with a laundry basket full of Brooklyn's clothes. She began sorting through them, separating the lights from the darks on a side table next to her retro stackable washer and dryer unit hid behind a pocket door. I have known Kat long enough to know "getting busy" was her way of not dealing with her feelings, or in fact precisely how she does deal with them. I've certainly resorted to physically busying myself as a way to quiet the mind and relax. Some people meditate, some people drink heavily, some people do drugs and some people get busy. Maybe I shouldn't have encouraged her to talk about her new situation with Steven. I was concerned she was feeling ambivalent about leaving Troy, and worrying whether it was in the best interest of her daughter.

Brooklyn was comforted by Troy reading her a bedtime story religiously every night. And I must say that one of the great things about Troy was his commitment to Brooklyn. However, their relationship was inauspicious, due to his overly vigilant role as a father figure, and predominantly inattentive role as a partner. Regardless, I would think that it would be a challenging task for any man to be a successful mate to a single mom, because there needs to be a balance of attention given to the child and the mother.

Listening to Kat's story made me feel grateful to have chosen a parental–free life and not have to deal with such a perplexing dilemma. However, I intensely admire any woman who chooses to be both a mother and career woman—true heroes, in my opinion.

"Do you want me to help you with that?" I asked Kat while reaching for the Tide laundry soap.

Kat put her head in her hands. "No…I'm sorry. I don't actually feel like doing laundry. It's just so difficult to watch Brooklyn miss Troy is all. I am so done with him and, yet, it's too soon to introduce Steven to her, you know? Not that that would fix anything. I just know she needs a male figure in her life to be grounded."

In empathy, I put my hand on Kat's shoulder.

Kat then sighed, shoved the laundry basket aside and walked toward the kitchen table. "I don't want to talk about me. Tell me about Kyle, I don't really remember him. I think I was busy with my own group of friends at the time, though, I do recall when I did see you, you seemed unhappier than I've ever known you to be."

I followed Kat to the table and sat while she filled our glasses to the rim with wine. "I was sad wasn't I? I didn't even know how unhappy I was, until after he left me. He knew we weren't meant to be together, before I did. You know, it's true what they say. When one person is unhappy, more than likely both people are unhappy and one person just hasn't realized it, yet. And, uh, that'd be me. I wanted so badly to believe I'd made the right choice. I mean, I married the guy. I didn't want to think I was a failure at commitment. Can you believe we met online?"

"N-o-o-o! Seriously? I don't remember that. Well, Melody Rae, that says volumes, don't you think? I think online dating can work out for some people, but it still seems like a huge risk."

"It was. The biggest risk I've ever taken…and not one I will ever take again."

****

August 2000

Typical Daily Food Choices:
Folgers medium roast coffee w/heavy cream
donut
Coca Cola or 7Up
barbecue potato chips
Snickers bar or Hostess Twinkie
Kraft macaroni & cheese
barbecue: (vegetarian) chicken, hamburgers, hotdogs, bacon, steak
cheap red wine
vodka & Squirt

Denial Kyle

Methodically clicking the arrow cursor down the page of my laptop viewing dozens of photos of eligible men on a popular and free Internet dating site, I scrutinized one unattractive older man after another. They were either bald, going bald, or wearing a hat to disguise their baldness. *Is an Internet dating site really the answer to finding a mate?* Believing that the Internet was the best option for me in finding a compatible partner ended up providing me with more character than I needed. If it's true that what doesn't kill you makes you stronger, then I should be able to lift a semi-trailer truck with one hand. I felt as if I was out of options and it was either meet someone online, or decide on living a life of celibacy, which I was seriously contemplating.

Once again I wasn't taking care of myself, or eating right at this time in my life. I was too busy with my career. Donut's and coffee were my regular breakfast ritual while Kraft macaroni and cheese my habitual dinner. Because I had little free time I did not put a copious amount of energy into considering what I was putting into my own body. Quick and cheap were all that mattered.

And then, once settled in my career I did the most unexpected thing and purchased a puppy; an endearing black and white cocker spaniel who I named Oreo. Although I had inconsequential personal free time I still wanted company, simply not the kind that required reciprocal conversation. And since only the highest quality dog food would I sanction, she, in fact, ate better than me. After all, owing to the fact that I wasn't having a child of my own, she was my baby.

Definitively, I had a pet, a career, and a home. And although it was only a rental I was no longer apartment restricted, and therefore patently ready to set out on an adventure to attract a stable partner. I knew I wanted one day to be married, and predicted my reputation as a business owner might potentially improve if I was married rather than single. Ultimately hoping my friends and relatives would then stop trying to fix me up with their melancholy, repugnant, unimaginative, lazy, dull-witted, obtuse loser friends. *They're not married for a reason, people!* Of course, I suppose the same could be said for me. Nevertheless, I hoped to be the exception to the rule. Now, these fix-up dates my friends would send me on, trust me, they were not the exception.

Soon after going on more than a dozen dates since Peter, I was able to safely ascertain every guy in the mountainous range of northern California, available in their mid-thirties, who had not been married, or involved in any serious relationship at one point in their life, had unresolvable and unusual personal issues. Perhaps, not unresolvable for everyone, but they were irrefutably and unequivocally unresolvable for me. I evidently didn't have the stamina or emotional tools to deal with the particular issues these men had. Admittedly, it wasn't purely the fault of my friends who had the best intention by introducing me to these lonely singletons. Some of these boys, guys, men, Neanderthal species, predators, convicts, criminals and aliens I met of my own volition while out dancing. *I know! Trust me, not a proud admission.*

One gentleman, a heavy smoker with a severe form of OCD (obsessive compulsive disorder) combined with schizoaffective disorder (a form of schizophrenia), openly admitted to having these disorders on our first date. Did he think these were admirable qualities? *Kudos for honesty, but why in the world would you tell me this on our first date? Jeez!* Another guy, who asserted to be five-foot-nine when he was clearly five-foot-one, revealed how he was an ex-convict and a transgender with sixteen indoor cats. *What?* Obviously, this guy had too many fish bones to overlook. *Get real, buddy!* Another gentleman lived in the basement of his parent's house and on our first date, in front of our waiter and gawking patrons, went on a rant about his anger toward his doctor, who told him he can no longer take the celecoxib drug for pain because of his allergy to sulphas as it has a sulphonamide moiety. And then to escalate my blood pressure further, he switches gears legitimizing how his Tourette's syndrome caused him to be a wrongly accused sex offender. *What in the world?* Needless to say, there was no second date with any of those men. Several other men, who I entertained, declared to be divorced when they were still married while living in their spouses' house. *What is wrong with people?*

When I ventured online, after having absolutely no luck meeting anyone in person considered relatively sane and discovered Kyle, the odds were in his favor. At least he appeared to have all his marbles, and wasn't a Gemini—the picture perfect profile of sanity. He was a Libra on the cusp of Scorpio; astrologically a perfect combination of air and water, which I predicted to be an ideal match for me.

I sincerely wanted to believe Kyle could be "the one." In hindsight, I had an excessive amount of hope, but not enough faith. I wanted to find a soul mate, but in my gut I didn't altogether think or feel it was possible. *Thanks again for that doubt gene you passed down to me, dad.* However, when Kyle Ray Spears's online profile spoke to me, I did what any naïve, vulnerable, lonely singleton in their mid-thirties would do. I threw caution to the wind and dived in head first with no net to catch me.

I was blind to the reality that Kyle was the epitome of the metro-male: delicate (a true mama's boy). Rather than being comparable to a prestige salmon, he was more similar to a **nocturnal catfish: firm, flaky, sturdy, nocturnal and prevalent in Mississippi.** Incidentally, Kyle was born in Jackson, Mississippi and had a firm sturdy build which eerily resembled a catfish, with his unusually round face and fuzzy mustache peculiarly similar to whiskers. And, coincidentally, he was similarly nocturnal; a night owl only sleeping during the day. He also had a strong southern accent, fair-skin and a sharp resemblance to the actor Jack Black. To which I unfairly projected onto him the assumption that he must possess the same humorous temperament which inevitably increased my attraction to him.

I reasoned that, since I was not instantly attracted to Kyle, I could maintain control, and after Peter I verily needed that to feel empowered. I was done with instant physical chemistry that would ultimately immobilize me, transforming me into a doormat. Possessing volatile physical chemistry with Willie and Peter only proved to be toxic to my sense of self.

I didn't discover Kyle until after browsing through hundreds of profiles on the Internet dating site. *I thought older men were supposed to get more distinguished and better looking as they age?* Apparently not, at least not the men I surveyed. I felt rather superficial deciding whether a guy had decent qualities based purely on his head-shot. I would scan over a facial silhouette and immediately think: *ewe, he's bald.* But why not judge a man by his head? Doesn't a person's portrait say volumes about their personality? I had too many illogical, stereotypical and judgmental opinions rattling through my head, which I knew wasn't fair, but I was overwhelmed with thousands of men's profiles considered via the Internet to be compatible with mine. I didn't know how else to eliminate profiles and narrow the playing field. I knew there were empirically sexy bald men in the world (Bruce Willis, Vin Diesel and Patrick Stewart, to name a few), but I needed to limit my options. I believe I had no alternative, except to delete the list below of egregious profiles from my matches, based on the following essential, albeit ridiculously nonsensical, preconceived notions:

Men with receding hair-line
  *insecure. Delete.
Men with red hair and receding hair-line
  *hot-tempered. Delete.
Men with frizzy androgenic alopecia hair
  *flaky. Delete.
Men who wear a hat to hide their baldness
  *evasive. Delete.

After that point, I was down to two hundred and fifty-three profiles left and most of them were nearly bald. Next delete strategy: eliminate addicts, short men (under six feet), those with tattoos, piercings, kinky interests, or mama-boys with metro-male traits.

Analogous to that of a forty year old man's hairline, I had receded. I'd receded down the stairs and was living in the basement, only climbing up to the third floor periodically to snag a few breadcrumbs. I wasn't thinking with a healthy third floor level mentality when I was reviewing dating sites, of course not. If I had been living on the third floor, I would not have logged on to the site at all. Obsessively, with the squeaky click of the mouse, I proceeded figuratively to that of a bona fide mouse seeking a durable piece of cheese searching for a fresh quality substance, preferably with no mold.

Click

H-m-m-m…maybe…nah, too many tattoos.

Click

Uh-h-h…nope, way too short.

Click

M-m-m-m…yes…wait. Piercings?! Where? Oh g-a-a-awd no.

Click

Sensitive, kind spirited, nice eyes…uh, wait. No. Too sensitive.

Click

Possible…sexy…uh, what? Who in the world drinks hard liquor for breakfast? And why would you advertise your alcoholism as a veritable strength? Strange. Buh-bye.

This searching went on literally for hours. I couldn't figure out why anyone would put in their subject line: Can *you* fill the emptiness in *my* heart? No, I can't. No one can. Why would anyone be drawn to someone who is empty to begin with? *Argh!* I was so frustrated and seconds away from deleting my own profile, when I came across Kyle Ray Spear's profile. Notwithstanding, he was ten years my junior, at least he had hair. He was twenty-five and I was thirty-five. I figured in ten years it wouldn't feel like such a big age difference. Naturally, I planned on us hitting it off and getting married.

When I first found out his name was Kyle Ray Spears I had a comforting thought. *What a normal sounding name.* But what is normal? Isn't normal highly subjective? Of course it is. The sound of his name had no bearing on the type of person he actually was, but I wanted to believe it did. I wanted to believe it meant he was moral, decent and astute. I further dissected his dating profile in detective style fashion. It said he never wanted children. Which I considered a bonus, since;

although I love children, I was not planning on having children of my own. I neglected to consider that a man not wanting children could be considered peculiar. In my open-minded capacity, I assumed he was in the not-so-typical category (like me), which made him more appealing. Perception is everything. And, in my perception, he was ideal.

He first contacted me via e-mail, sending a brief and to the point one sentence introduction:

Hi, I'm a youthful (only child) and an independently wealthy entrepreneur from Mississippi with a weakness for redheads...and you?   —Kyle Ray

To which I reciprocated a similarly forthright response:

Hi, I'm the youngest of six (only girl) and an independently impoverished dog groomer from Oregon with a weakness for red wine.   —Melody Rae

But his second e-mail was diametrically different, complex and descript, indicative of a short novel. It was a four page synopsis detailing his entire life. Of course, I was delighted, considering all the men I'd previously dated could barely communicate their feelings let alone write them down.

After dissecting the entire second e-mail, which took an interminable amount of time and three cups of strong coffee, I learned his parents are the ones who are affluent, not him. He's their only child, so, as one would expect, they lavish money on him. If he doesn't desire to work, he can choose not to. *Lucky.* In spite of finding his situation disturbingly elitist, I was relieved because my pattern had been to attract men who had no capital and wanted a free ride.

Kyle was refreshingly different and exactly the elixir I needed to break out of my single zone. Having an affinity for the outdoors, one of his hobbies involved renovation of a bungalow in McCloud—as a hobby! *I know!* I was more than impressed. I was living in an apartment in the city of Redding erstwhile and had never been to the remote mountainous range of McCloud. Although a few clients of mine who lived there, who regularly brought their small dogs to my grooming salon, enlightened me about the area; fueling my wish list of reasons to eventually move there. It's only a short ten-minute drive from Mount Shasta, and as I have an immense fondness for snow relishing country seclusion and even breathing better surrounded by tall pine trees, it's idyllic for someone like me.

I additionally learned from Kyle's verbose e-mails that he only lived in California for a year, which is most likely why his southern accent was so strong. He also wrote how he performs as a stand-up comic, is a skilled skier and an avid fly fisherman. *Busy guy.* It made sense why he would choose to sojourn the mountains of northern California as the creeks were designed for great fishing. He then proceeds to mention his recent acceptance into law school at UC Davis School of Law. *Are you freakin' kidding me?* It sounded too unbelievable. *Is this guy too good to be true, or seriously bipolar?* Despite his mental balance slightly in question, I nevertheless was willing to get to know him. I figured that a man with unlimited financial mobility could afford to dabble in whatever hobbies he liked. Time and money were of no concern for Kyle, which concerned me a little because a world free from pecuniary anxiety was foreign to me. I wasn't sure how we would connect, but I was willing to find out.

According to Kyle, his parents own a great deal of property all over the United States, yet, still maintain their homestead back in Jackson, Mississippi. However, due to traveling for a living, they are rarely home. He never explained how they became monumentally wealthy, and I never asked. Primarily because, whenever I mentioned his folks he would clam up, or change the subject. In spite of the fact that I found his omission of information peculiar, I was thrilled by the prospect of not having to monetarily take care of someone again. When he told me that he could live wherever he wanted to and chose California, it was music to my ears. For me, being anywhere far away from my family was a relationship deal breaker.

Kyle was different from me in many ways, but I welcomed opposing views, and it challenged me to be more open. He despised humidity and snow, but loved the sun and crowds. Therefore, New York was out and California was in. Most likely he would have settled in southern California near Los Angeles had the University of California, Davis, School of Law in northern California not accepted his application, but they did. And once accepted he conceded that Sacramento was a good central location to everything, anyway. At a moment's notice he could easily drive to San Francisco, or Napa Valley wine country, fly down south to hit the streets of Los Angeles, or San Diego, or drive east to Tahoe for the day.

He was renting a house in north Sacramento because he didn't believe in buying a home. He said home ownership was limiting, preferring to always be on the go. Although he did purchase a cabin in McCloud, claiming that it was a future investment not a homestead. He planned on doing major renovations and eventually flipping it to make some retirement cash. *Is he bipolar?* I questioned this quite frequently in the back of my mind when reading his e-mails, but once we met I completely forgot that thought ever crossed my mind. In person, although highly astute, he was mesmerizing, engaging, entertaining, witty, funny, exuberant, odd, unusual, versatile and talented. I forgot about me and melted into him losing myself completely. From our first meeting I was whisked away into a world of delusion and Melody Rae was nowhere to be found.

But before utterly wrapped up in Kyle's world, I had my logical and skeptical hard hat on. At first, after reading his loquacious e-mails, I became instinctively wary pondering them for hours. I remember feeling abnormally anxious and e-mailing Kat his profile to get a second opinion. I was worried about getting involved too deeply and too quickly. After my previous failed relationships, I didn't entirely trust my own instincts. But when Kat e-mailed back quickly with the response: "Go for it!" I did. I figured I could blame her later when the guy turned out to be a serial rapist.

Shortly after Kat's confirmation I logged back on to the dating site to send Kyle a response to his e-mail, but as soon as I accessed my account a new message abruptly dinged in my inbox. I could tell from the e-mail address that it was Kyle. *Wow.* He must be anxious to reach me considering he's sending a second message. But I wasn't ready to read another message from him. I hadn't even responded to the last one. I was somewhat flattered, but more flabbergasted than anything else. His persistence seemed awfully presumptuous as if we were already an established couple, which felt unnatural. Concerns began to flood my brain. *Do I seriously want to meet a guy this way?* I became discombobulated and torn. Instead of opening my inbox I distracted myself by closing the laptop computer and frantically cleaning my house.

Later in the evening, near midnight, I sat enjoying the languor and peace of relaxing on my couch with my laptop to one side and stack of books to the other. Thumbing leisurely through a book, searching for a virtuous quote for the annual summer letter that I send out to all clients whose dogs I've groomed, I came across a quote by Robert Anthony that profoundly affected me: "If you don't like the direction the river is flowing, don't jump in." *Oh boy. Do I like the direction? I'm not sure.*

Radiating from my laptop, in the midst of my reverie, emerged Mike Myers' arch-villain Dr. Evil voice: "You've got frickin' mail"—the idiosyncratic celebrity voice I chose for my AOL greeting inbox. I started laughing. I have configured my life to have a profusion of reason for laughter. And, if laughter is the best medicine, my elder years will be blissfully chipper, although I may end up living longer than I care to.

I seized the moment to glance at my unread e-mail inbox messages. The current title in the subject bar read: "Are you there?" It was, yet, another message from Kyle. I was considerably proud of myself for not responding earlier and hastily jumping at reading Kyle's other message when I wasn't ready. However, since this letter was sent to my AOL e-mail address rather than my dating site inbox (a totally different portal), revealing his overt anxiousness to reach me, I thought it was time to respond. And although I wasn't emotionally ready, I felt at least logically prepared to handle whatever he had to say. What I forgot to do was put on protective clothing and bullet proof armor. *Uh-oh.* The universe was sending me a luminous message and I was ignoring it completely. It was rather contradictory that mere moments before I'd read a quote about looking before leaping, and not jumping into the river unless I like the direction the river is flowing, and now found myself willing to jump right in regardless of the direction. And I did, head first against the current without much forethought. Isn't that always how it is? We are always being guided to do the right thing and, yet, most of us ignore the signs right in front of us. Unaware that I was headed in the complete opposite direction of happiness, I leaped toward Kyle with vigor and purpose.

The beginning of our courtship felt similar to hurdling into a pile of soft pillows made of marshmallows and Hershey kisses: sweet, soft and cozy. Kyle was exactly the potion I needed to get over Peter, who I had to accept was gone for good, although his essence still lingered inside me like a sunken ship. Accepting the reality that Peter wasn't the one for me was difficult. Remembering that he was an alcoholic and chose another life without me helped the healing process. Although sometimes the pain of the loss of what I thought we had would rise to the surface and scald me again in places so deep that I'd literally plunge forward, clutch my abdomen and weep.

During the early stage of our fledgling courtship, when my relationship with Kyle was flourishing via e-mail exchanges, the internal battle of losing Peter went on inside me. When overwhelmed I would garner a self-help book. Stepping away from my feelings and listening to logic I selected the book *He's Just Not That into You* by Greg Behrendt and Liz Tuccillo from the living room bookcase, and reread the excerpts that I'd highlighted. The specific passages feature segments which imply he was never "into" me, completely encapsulating my relationship with Peter and guiding me back to reality. The bottom line is that if Peter had been "into" me, he would still be with me. *Wake up, Melody Rae!*

These three components are Peter in a nutshell and help me keep perspective:

1) P.S. Don't spend your time on and give your heart to any guy who makes you wonder about *anything* related to his feelings for you.
2) The drunks I've dated were all spontaneous, funny, passionate, smart, creative, emotionally unavailable, unreliable, insensitive, dishonest and slightly abusive.
3) "Bad boys" are bad because they're troubled, as in having little self-respect, lots of pent-up anger, loads of self-loathing, complete lack of faith in any kind of loving relationship, but yes, really cool clothes and often a great car.

Due to the fact that Kyle entered my life before I resolved the issues which erupted as a result of dating an alcoholic, he became the distraction to my own healing process. And in turn, I became the savior to his loneliness. In actuality, we needed each other to redirect our personal lives.

Books were (and still are) my therapists, offering the medicine of knowledge I need in order to cope. According to the book *In the Meantime* by Iyanla Vanzant, I was in basement survival mode. If I interpreted the book correctly, people go back and forth on different floors of their emotional house. Understandably, living on the third floor is a healthier place than the basement and the attic is when you've reached a higher level of self-actualization, where you are no longer defensive and blaming others for the choices you've made. I've visited the attic, but hadn't stayed as long as I would have liked to. I knew I needed first to spend more time on the third floor, where I can master how to apply love to every situation.

But there I was stuck in the basement and searching for signs that Kyle that I could be compatible, so I could tell myself I'm still desirable and loveable. I needed to feel love from an external source. I was not centered, since real self-love does not come from outside of you. And as soon as I found myself regressing to the basement and feeling off-balance, Kyle entered my world.

Kyle's foot was always on the accelerator while mine was on the brakes. By his second e-mail he had already asked if I wanted to join him for coffee. *Yikes!* I remember every muscle in my body panicked. *Too soon!* I couldn't fathom how that would happen anyway? He lived in Sacramento. Was he going to drive all the way up to Mount Shasta—a good two and a half hour drive—for a coffee date? Was I expected to drive all the way to Sacramento to meet a stranger at a coffee house and then drive all the way back?

When I finally e-mailed him a response to his audacious e-mails, explaining precisely where I stood and my concerns and questions, I thought I would never hear back from him. But, surprisingly, I did. When he e-mailed in return, he was logical, rational, cordial, understanding and business-like; the lawyer in him emerged. And part of me was drawn to this controlled, analytical, discriminating, perceptive side, while part of me was a little intimidated.

Two weeks, seventeen e-mail exchanges and three phone conversations later, we mutually agreed to meet in Reno, Nevada. *I know! What the heck?* Well, the reason was quite simple, I felt safe there. After Peter and I parted ways, I'd been taking periodic weekend vacations to Reno to appreciate being single. I would attend the Catch a Rising Star comedy club inside the Silver Legacy casino to watch talented stand-up comics perform; not only because I was a huge stand-up comedy fan, but it was a secure, protected and guarded place. There are security guards everywhere you turn, so you can meander alone without being a target. Many people wander the casinos solo. My ritual was to rent a Jacuzzi room, light candles, drink wine and order room service. For me, Reno was a mini resort, exclusively catering to my mental health and well-being.

We planned to meet at six-thirty in the evening for drinks at Seraglio's blues café, which was conveniently located in visual proximity to the Catch a Rising Star comedy club. Kyle mentioned his relatives lived in the area and said that he would plan a trip to visit them, so I wouldn't feel obligated to show up if I changed my mind. He offered to buy both of our tickets to the comedy show and insisted on mailing mine to me. He assured me that I could back out anytime, no pressure. His considerate, fair, logical, protective character subdued my instinctively suspicious and untrusting side, which had escalated after my relationship with Peter. Kyle had everything covered and appeared to respect me enough not to push me to go faster than I wanted. He reassured me that if after we meet and I felt uncomfortable, he wouldn't attend the show; leaving me with the idiomatic expression: "no hard feelings." *Really?* Well, how could I refuse? He gave me no reason not to go with the flow and take the risk to meet him.

After arriving in Reno, Nevada, and before booking into the Silver Legacy hotel, I strolled through the main floor lobby, which leads past a strip mall of specialty shops: brunch cafes, coffee houses, cocktail lounges, sandwich deli's, an oyster bar, overpriced clothing boutiques, and stores full of knick-knack paraphernalia and touristy trinkets.

I was compelled to pause at the store window to one of the clothing boutiques when a lovely blouse caught my eye. I stared, favorably admiring a lime-green rayon button-up sleeveless shirt. It had a silk tank top that went underneath and came with a compact purse to match, which would accent well with the long, black, rayon pencil skirt I'd planned to wear on my date with Kyle. I desperately wanted it. But it was clearly out of my price range. It was nearly sixty dollars for the entire ensemble. But then I heard the blouse say: "Buy me." It may have even said: "Melody Rae."

After examining my wristwatch I deduced that I had just enough time to stop at the next available slot machine, on the way to the lobby desk, before checking in. Fortunately, there was an empty seat near a Wheel of Fortune slot machine (my favorite) positioned at the end of a row of machines, so I quickly sat. End spots have always been lucky for me. Sitting with unmitigated optimism, thinking, feeling and believing that lime blouse I saw in the window of the casino boutique was meant to be mine, I inserted the three quarter maximum limit and pulled the lever. *I am going to win enough money to buy that shirt.* And to no surprise, after one pull of the slot machine handle, I was sixty dollars richer and had done exactly as I expected to. I immediately cashed out and went directly to the boutique and purchased the purse and lime-green shirt with tank top ensemble, without even trying it on. I knew it would fit, it was meant for me.

After I went to the hotel lobby desk and checked in, I went up the elevator to the deluxe Jacuzzi suite that I'd reserved and unpacked my belongings. After freshening my makeup and hair, I changed into the sexy, silky, lime-green tank top with its breezy undershirt and purse to match and then slipped on the long, black, rayon pencil skirt with the slit up the left side, and buckled the two-inch black open-toed heels. Then, feeling sexy and courageous, I went downstairs prepared to meet Kyle.

In many ways, Reno is an adult Disneyland with its many amenities: free cocktails, reasonably priced seafood buffets, spectacular live music, sensational comedy shows, high-end celebrities, loose slot-machines. It caters to my every whim, making me feel invincible, as if anything is possible. The detailed architecture and high ceilings simulating the night sky, with stars and planets accurate to scale, were mesmerizing as I walked along the indoor boardwalk passing various bar entrances, clubs and restaurant venues, with their flickering bright lights and deafening music.

Peering in the window of the Rum Bullions Island Bar located near the top of the escalator which leads to the blues café and comedy club down on the casino floor, I ascertained it was a happening joint. Two pure white prodigious grand pianos faced one another on a center stage where two attractive gentlemen wearing pristine tailored white tailcoat tuxedos were playing expeditiously with exceptional rhythm singing Elton John's "*Crocodile Rock.*" Girls were surrounding them, dancing and screaming. The place was howling with whistles and buoyant laughter. I wanted to be a part of it. And, since I had a little time before meeting Kyle, I approached the entrance door and paid the two dollar cover charge. I was carded, which for anyone over the age of thirty is flattering.

Ordering a glass of house red wine and then dancing near the bar, while enjoying light flirtation with random people, was making me feel whimsical. My natural pheromones were in full swing and I was attracting men toward me like bees to honey. Taking a moment to glance at the clock behind the bar I observed it was six-twenty, which meant that I only had ten minutes to get downstairs to meet Kyle at the blues café. *Oh no!* I instantly felt my nerves and stomach flutter and throb. I questioned myself. *Was I planning on throwing myself into a relationship to avoid dealing with the pain of losing Peter? Probably.* I didn't know how else to handle the pain. I missed Peter. And although I realistically accepted we could never be involved again, because there's no way I could ever again be in a relationship with an alcoholic, sex addict...still...what if he ended up rehabilitated? *Stop it, Melody Rae! Peter will never choose you over booze...or sex with other women.* I concluded the only way for me to get over Peter was to dive head first into a deep involvement with someone else.

Directly after stepping off the bottom of the escalator and onto the casino floor, I saw Kyle: the "someone else." He saw me, too. But I felt nothing. I unequivocally had no physical chemistry with him whatsoever. However, despite not being instantly attracted, it didn't matter because I was simply seeking nice marriage material. He possessed a conservative appearance wearing a posh, dark blue Armani suit and tie and brandishing an exceedingly proper, benevolent and calm demeanor.

After we hugged, he asserted in a phlegmatic tone that he thought my appearance was stunning. I smiled. Then he put his hand to the small of my back and led me gently into Seraglio's blues café. My first thought was cynical. *Wow, this guy is stoic and robotic. Does he have any real emotion?* But when he

pulled out my chair and ordered us both a glass of
exorbitantly expensive red wine valuing over eight hundred
dollars, my mouth dropped open and I found it within myself
to look beyond his prosaic nature. I always wanted to be
treated like a felicitous elite woman of high status, although I
was slightly annoyed with myself for being so enamored by
him. Holding my wine glass delicately with my highfalutin
pinky finger sticking upward, I felt like an authentic princess.
For a moment I worried that when he discovers I'm generally
more often than not etiquette challenged, improperly
boisterous, embarrassingly vocal, a certifiable klutz and a
liberal, he might not be so smitten. But of course, I wasn't
going to spoil a good evening and fret about that tonight. I
was thoroughly reveling in being put on a pedestal and
delighted to be doted upon, and planned to relish every
minute of it. The dulcet tones of the folk singer possessing a
bluesy, sensual voice tenderly vibrating amidst the crowd the
lyrics to Melanie Safka's *"Brand New Key"* simply added to the
classy ambience. I clearly didn't belong, but I didn't care. I
allowed the lyrics to marinate with hope that we had what the
other needed, like the song implied.

Then Kyle proceeded to tell a rather pugnacious, fervid,
albeit informative explanation to his involvement in various
professions (hobbies), as if he were defending himself on trial
for taking pleasure in too many things in life. He had this
unusual timed maniacal laugh that erupted every time he
mentioned his parents. I wasn't sure if he was trying to be
funny, or attempting to hide a darker sinister side. I gleaned
from his harangue that his parents weren't too happy with his
lack of concentration on one career. I empathetically
reassured him, allocating how truly propitious it was he had
so many interests and talents, when many people can't find
even one thing to be passionate about. He nodded as if to
appease me and then continued on his rant. I had difficulty
focusing on his tirade because, although Kyle didn't notice,
during his speech the beautiful singer had left and a thin
untoward gentleman had approached the microphone with a
wrinkled piece of paper and began reading a strange

onomatopoeia poem about chattering teeth, tweeting birds, quacking ducks and buzzing bees.

It was apparent that Kyle wasn't aware of anything other than his own voice, clearly wanting to continue talking about his ski adventures and law classes at the university. But once he noticed the time above the bar he abruptly stood and in an enigmatic tone pronounced, "We'd better go. We don't want to miss the show."

In spite of finding Kyle's tone inappropriately indignant, I was relieved to leave and not have to falsely attempt to enjoy the peculiar amateur entertainment on stage. Although I found his indifferent tone questionable, I was beguiled by how he'd behaved so responsibly. I was used to being the one that kept time in a relationship, so it was refreshing he was the take-charge type; a nice change to relax and have someone else lead. Besides conveying his adoration for me, he also insinuated we had a unique connection, being that we both loved animals and were practical and ready for the marriage stage of our lives. It was quite adult from what I was used to. The fact that he paid for everything and put me on a pedestal captivated my heart, causing me to completely overlook his lack of jocularity. The man didn't seem to have much of a sense of humor, but he had a colossal amount of respect.

Once we were in front of the Catch a Rising Star comedy club and standing in line he checked his watch a second time. "Well, it's close to show time. I have to take a quick trip to the John. How about we just meet inside, sound good? Front row seats would be best. Save me a seat?"

"Uh, um, uh, ok-a-a-ay…sure," I stuttered.

Then he kissed me on the cheek and took off through the crowded casino. As he walked away, it registered how short he was. His dating profile stated he was five-foot-eleven. It was plainly obvious he was not above five-foot-nine, as I towered over him. Of course, I was wearing heels. But, still, he was assuredly not five-foot-eleven. Another baffling inconsistency in his online profile was where he claims to be old-fashioned. I would think, allowing your date to walk into a comedy club alone is the antithesis of old-fashioned. Of course, he was ten years my junior and times have changed. Most likely it was a fish bone I was, once again, sweeping under the rug. Though, I was naturally observant and analytical, I wanted to remain blind and consciously pushed away any thought interfering in my vision of perfection. I was overlooking many things, because this guy was the marrying type, and all I could see or hear were wedding bells. It was all that mattered in my mind at that point in time.

Approaching the entrance door, I handed the doorman my ticket and went inside the comedy club. I swiftly found a couple of open seats directly near the front center stage and sat. *Perfect.* At a small round table with my legs crossed, I anxiously waited for Kyle. When the waitress came over, feeling adventurous and ready for a big life change, I ordered a Tequila Sunrise. Then I replayed our conversation pinpointing his uncommon qualities that were refreshingly different, like his mustache, which I surprisingly fancied. Traditionally, I was more attracted to goatees, but something about his mustache was alluring, friendly: parental. It lessened the appearance of our age difference, making him look older rather than younger than me. His trustworthy demeanor, and the way he talked in a stoically parental tone, made me feel safe and protected. I luxuriated in the feeling I was in safe hands. He was subtle, confident, serious and mindful, which brought out the little girl in me. In many ways he encompassed the rich flavor of depth I craved. *Was he as mature as he came across, or was I projecting onto him what I wanted him to be?* Brushing my nagging doubt aside I contemplated the positive, choosing to have faith instead. I needed to.

I was beginning to adore this guy, and the idea that he could be perfect for me was making me feel bemused and woozy. My biggest concern was whether he had a sense of humor. Immediately after this thought came into consciousness, the lights in the comedy club went down and the announcer came out and introduced the headliner.

"And now for your funny bone give a warm welcome to the edgy man who can make even Larry David chuckle…Kyle Spears!!!"

What in the world? No way! It was Kyle! On stage! I stared for the next few minutes with an expression of incredulity. The man, with no apparent sense of humor, was talented enough of a stand-up comedian to have his own show? I was stupefied and beside myself with admiration. When Kyle first entered the stage, he was winking and pointing a finger-gun in my direction like a cheesy lounge singer. His entire comedy routine had a self-deprecating, poor-me victim, Woody Allen flavor, which was quite hilarious. Knowing Kyle was a celebrity (at least from my perspective) made my heart do a double flip.

It didn't take long after that for Kyle to cleverly sweep me off my feet. After six months of old-fashioned courtship; a rendezvous to Carmel Beach for a weekend with his parents, an escape to San Francisco to enjoy fancy cuisine and live theatre, several beach excursions and another adventure to Reno, and we were engaged. He proposed, at Seraglio's blues café where we met, with a chatoyant chrysoberyl and diamond trillion engagement ring that cost more than his Mercedes-Benz.

I kept insinuating how we didn't have to rush anything, but he prodded and pleaded, behaving as if he unreservedly had to be my husband, or he'd nearly explode. I didn't interpret his impetuousness as unhealthy; I merely assumed that he was in love with me. I was gleeful to be a part of his surreal world. That is, until we embarked on our honeymoon cruise— traveling from Los Angeles, California to Ensenada, Mexico—and he casually divulges an earlier history of drug abuse over key-lime margarita's and tortilla chips. Internally, my world spiraled out of control, and I wanted to run away as fast as I could, and as far as I could. But I was married and believed in abiding by the lifelong commitment I'd made. I didn't want to divorce; Murphy's don't divorce!

Looking back, things had a flavor of unsettling discreetness from the beginning. Our quaint wedding at one of his parents' estates in the sumptuous hills of Carmel Valley was alarmingly private—too private. His mom and dad were the only ones who were present from his side of the family. Of course, my parents, six brothers, their wives and kids were all there. I deemed it rather anomalous Kyle's mother and father were alienated from both sides of their families and didn't wish to invite any aunts or uncles, or grandparents even. *Why are they estranged from one another?* One of many questions I allowed to linger in my mind without choosing to debate.

I should have picked up on the subtle sign that I was headed for a huge debacle when the best man at our wedding was his dad. I thought it was an atypical choice, but discounted it as being anything disconcerting. I assumed he chose his dad because he didn't have any close friends, not realizing that he had no friends at all. He talked about college friends, but I never met any. Whenever I questioned him about them he'd get eerily silent, or cut me off as if I entered an off-limit forbidden zone. *How dare I ask personal questions!* Although deep down his secretiveness disturbed me, I sensed he had a volatile side which unnerved me making me respect his wishes and stop with the inquiries. A veritable coward, I didn't even say a word to my mother who I told everything to. I consistently kept looking the other way; overlooking all the fish bones. I wanted more than anything to believe someone could love me enough to marry me, and the self-effacing, awkward and geeky four-eyed little girl in me thought this was the only guy who ever would. Theoretically, the marriage was over before the rice hit the ground, but by the end of the honeymoon it was irrefutably doomed, although we were both in total denial about it.

The first time I had an unequivocal hunch that there might be a serious problem with my marriage was the moment we boarded a cruise ship. A honeymoon cruise we'd booked for a three day, two night adventure. After unpacking our belongings into the microscope sized cabin (no exaggeration), Kyle sat on the edge of the bed looking uncharacteristically sullen. *What is wrong with you?* We were on a cruise ship and he was brooding. *How come you're not jumping up and down with joy?*

Choosing to ignore my puzzlement over his colorless gaze, I went into the bathroom to change into the tropical attire purchased specifically for the cruise: a red sun visor which complemented a red and yellow flowered swimsuit with matching flip-flops, and a yellow wrap-around sarong. When I returned to the room, he was still sitting on the bed, except he had positioned his body away from me and was peering out the circular shaped porthole of the cabin. Since our cabin was located on the first level of the ship, the ocean floated along only inches below the bottom of the window. Looking out the window, the water was serene revealing a beautiful bluish color that rippled up and down with the gentle sway of the boat.

I looked at Kyle and spoke in my characteristically upbeat tone, hoping to break him out of his mood. "Wow! That's so gorgeous...I could totally live on a boat."

He said nothing.

Then I tried another method to awaken his senses. I plugged in the portable CD player that I had brought along and set it on the dresser—the only existing counter space—and pressed the play button. It was cued up to a naturally motivating song to start our adventure in sanguine fashion; The Kingsmen's tasty rock and roll sea shanty *"Louie Louie."*

I began to sing along, but before I could finish the second verse, Kyle, while remaining seated on the berth, pivoted and leaned over to the CD player and pressed the eject button. Everything in a conventional cruise ship cabin is in such close proximity there is barely room to breathe, so understandably, it was not surprising that Kyle could reach the CD player from the bed. But why was he being such a killjoy? Instead of behaving in typical fashion and being amused by my quirkiness, he simply curled up into a ball, leaned up against the wall and faced the small porthole. *Something is not right.* He was ordinarily charmed by my singing and silliness. Not this time. This time was different. Rather than putting on a happy face, his face remained deadpan. It was almost unnatural how his face wouldn't change—it was disturbingly expressionless. *Are you seasick; claustrophobic?* I was expecting classic Kyle (the ego-driven, big-talking showman) to lead me out the door and get this party started. But he sat transfixed and said nothing.

I stood there for a second unsure as to what to say. He's never behaved this way before, ever. His uncharacteristic insouciance was alarming. *Are you experiencing symptoms of cabin fever? But don't you have to be stuck in a small space with nothing to do for an extended period of time? Or did the term cabin fever first come about from someone who experienced an actual fever after being kept in such tight quarters?* Anxiety and distressing thoughts rambled about in my head as I started to feel myself overheat. I fluffed and fiddled with my hair waiting for Kyle to say something…anything.

After about six minutes of intolerable silence, I had to say something. "I'm sorry…I love you," I muttered quietly.

He looked at me with a despondent expression and spoke in a monotone voice. "I'm going to stay here, okay? I think I am gettin' seasick." Then he began to uneasily rock back and forth while holding his stomach. *Serious? We hadn't even left the dock.*

Then continuing without any real conviction or alter in his voice, he proceeded to explain why I should leave him in the cabin, claiming he wasn't mad. Although the pupils of his eyes were enlarged with an unfamiliar glossiness to them, making me question the validity of his words, his despairing mannerisms convinced me he sincerely wanted me to go have fun and leave him alone.

"I'm just tired. I wanna get some rest. Please go…please," he said with a look of ennui in his eyes.

I wasn't sure whether he cared if I stayed or left the cabin, but I didn't feel compelled to be near him, so I left him to wallow in his anti-social malaise while I did the opposite. And by doing so, I learned just how much pleasure a cruise could be. It was an exuberant shock wave of entertaining thrills; a euphoric melee of high jinks. After experiencing more fun without Kyle by my side, it dawned on me that I'd be happier single.

The truth of my marriage finally registered into reality—whenever Kyle was around his listless energy affected me in catastrophic ways; I was less optimistic and social, less me. While I unknowingly used all of my positive energy to make Kyle feel good, physically and emotionally, I depleted my own psyche. Although I had not witnessed Kyle's acutely temperamental, sour and mercurial side until now, I wasn't entirely astounded, as his demeanor always carried a pessimistic undertone.

During the time that I had spent alone on the cruise I was a social butterfly fluttering with a glowing spirit. I was me; me for the first time since I had met Kyle. Strangely, I didn't know that I had lost myself in the relationship until I found myself on the cruise.

Spending the majority of the time bathing in the shallow end of the pool, drinking Mai Tai's tickled with a cocktail umbrella and conversing with all sorts of interesting people, I was the happiest I'd been in a long, long while. I permitted myself to be adopted (metaphorically) by this clique of teachers from San Francisco; a mix of predominantly married couples with a few singletons whom I naturally gravitated toward and vice versa. They invited me to the most exclusively happening events on the cruise. It was pleasurable reminiscing about the comedy clubs and restaurants that I used to frequent during the time I was a legitimate city girl. With my newly appointed "cruise-family", I enjoyed singing Karaoke at the lounge, gambling at the casino, feasting at the midnight taco bar, dancing to live bands by the pool, sitting in the double Jacuzzi's and drinking margaritas at all hours.

The contests, comedy shows and live performances at dinner time were momentous, imbued with humor and talent—I was awe struck. Going on a cruise was an extraordinary "dream come true" experience, and an inspired part of me wanted to give up grooming dogs and work as a host on a cruise ship full time.

Surprisingly, my "cruise-family" didn't believe I had a husband, teasing me that he was a delusive imaginary spouse I'd dreamt up to appear attached; until they were bubbled out of the Jacuzzi (along with me) when he unexpectedly showed up at our exclusive late night hot tub conclave. In a desultory manner he introduced himself to my friends, stayed for less than ten-minutes, complained about being exhausted and headed back to the suite. Of course, like a dutiful wife, I slept next to him each night, or should I say morning. For a four hour stretch he remained under the covers while I rested on top. His body was out cold while he slept fairly outré, practically immobile, like a brown bear in hibernation. But, the next day, when Kyle abruptly announced that he wanted to join me once the boat anchored in Ensenada, Mexico, everything went down, except the ship.

"We need to talk," he insisted.

Inexplicably, he was still dressed in the same clothes that he wore when we initially boarded the ship. He never changed his clothes! His pants and shirt were all wrinkled, his hair was disheveled and his mustache was shaggy, but he didn't seem to care. It was unnatural to see him like this. I thought his hair looked better a little messy, but this was ridiculous. The Gene Wilder hair style didn't suit him, although it was nice to see him not so uptight about his appearance, since he was typically a neat freak. Unfortunately, however, a lackadaisical Kyle did not mean a happy Kyle.

Walking down the sidewalk in Ensenada, we arrived at an authentic Mexican restaurant where there was optional outdoor seating. Giggling in anticipation, I pulled him enthusiastically to the entrance. Kyle knew I had always wanted to try an authentic Mexican made key-lime margarita. Once we were seated and served our drinks the mariachi band, standing two tables back from ours near the wall of the veranda, began to play. I calmly dipped a large tortilla chip into a bowl of fresh salsa and took a juicy bite. But after the jalapeño spice hit my nasal passages activating my eyes to water, and after a failed attempt to subdue it with a generous gulp of the palatable margarita, I motioned frantically to the waitress to bring over a few bottled waters.

Kyle was looking down at his feet and fidgeting with his hands during my entire near-death-by-salsa episode. Then, as soon as I began to impatiently chug my water, he breathed in deeply and began to bloviate details of his past, every word spewing out on the table like a fountain of verbal venom. With a frozen shocked expression planted on my face, I sat paralyzed as I listened to him orate, unsure at exactly how to respond. It felt as if my simple life was falling apart and pooling into little crystals of quicksand below my feet and I was about to be swallowed up.

Initially, he divulged with delicate solicitude how he had been secretly smoking marijuana, periodically. Then, he proceeded to inform me how he had been officially diagnosed with severe clinical depression and bipolar in his early teens. The clincher: recently he had stopped taking his prescribed antidepressant and antipsychotic medications claiming that since I entered his life he didn't need the pills anymore; he felt happy. *It gets worse.* After expounding why he used to be a habitual whiskey drinker, he revealed how he was also a heroin addict. *Yes, I said heroin. I know!* He admitted to his parents expending an excessive amount of money toward his therapy. Come to find out that he had been in and out of rehabilitation programs since he was eighteen. I was silent and bemused. He justified not taking the Zoloft, Prozac and Risperdal nearly two months before the wedding because he "felt" better. *What in the world?!!! No wonder he's a basket case.*

In between hellacious and honest tears of emotional distress, he apologized promising to resume his medications once we returned to Mount Shasta. After Kyle's homily of repentance, I was unable to form words. I sat in shock with tears of fear and deceit trickling down my face. The folk music from the mariachi band sounding like it was miles away was replaced by a hollow humming vibration in my ear and the sky clouded over turning gray until we were no longer in public. I couldn't see anyone else around, except Kyle. Selfishly, I wanted to scream and run as fast as possible back to the ship and ask to be transferred to a separate cabin. The self-effacing, awkward and geeky four-eyed little girl in me wanted to call my mom. I felt invisible, frightened and alone. When the waitress approached I came back to reality. Knowing that if a stranger saw me and offered comfort I'd break down and sob hysterically I had to leave. To avoid attention I grabbed the napkins on the table and hid my face, snatched my purse off the dirty cement floor, and then

212

hurtled toward the restroom inside the bistro to collect myself.

Thankfully, it was a single stall restroom so I could privately cry. After I let the tears comparatively flow, I smacked my cheeks to prevent unraveling completely. Before returning to the table, I fluffed my curls with a hair pick and splashed cold water on my face. Then I wiped away the eyeliner streaks and powdered my cheeks, applied lipstick and put on my sunglasses. When I returned to our table, Kyle had already left and was standing outside the patio against the wall of the veranda, slumped to the side and scratching his head. I saw on the table that he'd left a large lagniappe for the waitress, almost certainly out of guilt for our tense and emotional intrusion at their fine establishment.

With arms crossed, I stepped toward Kyle and leaned in. "It's gonna be okay," I quivered while my body trembled. "I just need some time to take this all in...okay?"

He nodded.

I turned and began to stiffly walk back in the direction of the cruise ship. Kyle followed a few feet behind. I worried it was noticeable that I couldn't stop myself from shaking. *I can't believe this is happening to me.* Replaying everything Kyle said made it difficult to walk. I needed to focus my attention on something positive and clear my mind in order to make it back to the dock without falling to the ground. Each time I inhaled, my heart pulsated with an aching in the chest. I could physically feel my heart breaking. While walking, I tried to calm my nervous system to prevent further tears from streaming down my face by breathing in through my nose, holding my breath and then exhaling slowly. I was worried that my choppy breathing might give the impression I was hyperventilating. I needed to get my physical presence under control before I saw anyone from the ship, like my "cruise family." I couldn't possibly explain any of this right now.

Out the left corner of my eye, I could see Kyle a couple feet behind me. He was walking near the curb of the sidewalk with his head held way down. I slowly swiveled away, staring off to the right and away from him, continuing to do my best not to break down in tears.

Once back on the cruise ship I reverted into complete denial, a survival defense mechanism necessary to endure the trip back to California. Kyle incarcerated himself by choosing to remain cooped up in the cabin suite, while I found respite with my San Francisco "cruise family." Other than regarding the time and where the plane tickets were, no words between us were exchanged. Nothing was said on the plane trip to the Redding airport, or in the car ride home.

Once we returned home I plunged into researching information about heroin addiction and mental illness. I kept replaying Kyle's words of disclosure. Staggering how he had actually thought that being happy with me in his life cured his mental illness. How could he think his brain didn't still require medication? His mind was deceiving him. Thoroughly educating myself by reading NAMI (National Alliance for the Mentally Ill) newsletters and various online research articles regarding mental illness helped me to understand Kyle. Mental illness is a chemical imbalance in the brain. Depression, bipolar, borderline personality disorder, schizophrenia, etc., are brain disorders: a disease of the brain. And, apparently it's a common issue for those who have mental illness to stop taking their medications. What is misunderstood by many is that the drug is still in their system after they stop taking it—for a month or so—and that's why they think they're okay without their meds. Once they stop taking their antipsychotic medications and it is completely out of their system, the illness takes over. By this time their mind is too far out of touch with reality to believe that they have an illness anymore. Oftentimes, once an ill person resumes their medication it takes at least three weeks for the prescription to start working again. Luckily, for most of Kyle's life he's had a strong support structure; his parents, particularly his mother.

After we returned from the cruise, Kyle called his parents for help and they asked to speak to me. When we spoke, they confided how there are a string of addicts with mental illness in their genealogy—the reason for their distance—and that they had dealt with Kyle not taking his medications many times before. When they illuminated me about his general sleep patterns, of only sleeping during the day for short periods, it was most enlightening. Other than the cruise, where his depression took hold and he did nothing except sleep, Kyle typically never slept at night. I chalked it up to being a night owl and the eccentrically creative type.

I finally comprehended his parents need to be possessively dominant in his life. I honestly don't think he ever felt safe without them hovering, or somehow involved heavily in his existence. It was standard for him to call his mom every day, sometimes more than once. I understood why, now. He needed them to maintain his sobriety and personal sanity. In some respects his parents were not merely his guardians, but his therapists as well as prison guards—the sine qua non to his sobriety.

What I discovered via Kyle's ancestors and personal research about the nature of drug abuse, namely heroin addiction, made me feel less secure about my future with Kyle. I realized that I'm ill-equipped at being a patrol officer and don't have the tools to deal with the behavior of an addict. *I'm sorry, Kyle.* The lying, stealing, threats, violent and deviant, sociopathic behavior combined with deep, depressive episodes will destroy me. These issues already were killing me. Obviously, I proved to be inept at coping with his issues when on the cruise I chose to escape rather than remain in the cabin with him.

I felt inadequate and unqualified to deal with someone with his personal issues. I thought that maybe I could deal with his depression and occasional delusions, but his heroin addiction petrified me. After more forethought, I came to the understanding that it wasn't entirely his addiction, or his illness which was the serious issue with our marriage, it was "us." I didn't sincerely believe we earnestly loved each other, and I was using his mental illness as an excuse to find a solid way out. In all honesty, from the moment Kyle and I met, our love was surfaced. The closest I ever came to feeling "true love" in my life was with Peter. *Why did I marry a guy I didn't honestly love?* I suppose that I thought I was in love. And now, I was trapped in a marriage to a man who was an ex-heroin addict with a mental illness—not quite the man I thought I married.

Finally, I called my mom. I dialed her number during a break between appointments at Petite Paws, and revealed the details of the cruise fiasco and all my fears about my marriage to Kyle. Near the end of the call, I pleaded with her to understand my position.

"Mom, he didn't cheat on me and he wasn't abusive, so-o-o I don't feel like I have a very good reason to divorce him," I whined.

She was completely understanding and sympathetic. *I love my mom.* However, unbeknownst to me, I was on speaker phone the entire time and my dad was listening in.

He was about ready to pounce through the phone. "Melody Rae, he lied to you! That's enough grounds to get out. Maybe you can get an annulment?" he growled.

I imagined my dad pacing back and forth, wringing his hands in fight mode, furious that his little girl was suffering and wanting to protect her.

"I know he lied. You're right, I know! Thanks dad, I love you!" I bellowed.

Then I lowered my voice and requested my mom take me off speaker, so I could continue to vent uncensored. "Mom, it's not that easy. I kind of blame myself. I feel like (cough) maybe I should have seen this coming on and said something before, you know? I don't know. I just feel horrible. I mean, he needs professional help…and, and, I just don't know what to do."

My mom was unusually empathetic and comforted me with sweet words of supportive praise and love, and then we cried together on the phone and I felt much better. Later in the day my mom called me back. Despite my dad being anti-divorce, he uncovered the particulars about the cost of a divorce and said he would do all the paperwork for me. *I love my dad.* He explained how an annulment can't be filed unless one person had been plainly deceiving. For example; if Kyle was, in reality, a woman, but not until the wedding night did he tell me that he'd had a sex change. *Yikes!* The person has had to have lied to you, to that extent.

I thanked my parents for their support and said I would contact them if it came to that. I wasn't ready to make any changes and cringed at mentioning divorce to Kyle worried that might send him over the edge; I didn't think I could handle his violent side. I preferred things to resolve on their own. Ultimately, I wanted to deep-six what had happened between us; dusting everything under the carpet, because the reality of the situation was simply too much to bear.

For the next few months I went through the motions of life like a robot, assuming time itself would resolve everything. Most of the time Kyle was off engaged in one of his many hobbies, but when he was home I was present. I'd kiss him when he came in the door and cook him dinner, and then we'd sit in awkward silence. Me: reading at the kitchen table. Him: in front of the television.

Then things progressively worsened. I didn't know if he was neglecting to take his medications, or whether he was back to doing heroin, but something wasn't right. Although I had been reading at length about clinical depression, bipolar and heroin addiction (hoping to protect myself), I didn't quite know what specific "signs" to look for. But soon enough I didn't have to search for any, because the signs were blatantly in my face.

After returning from a fishing trip, on a serene Sunday afternoon, I sensed something was off-balance with Kyle. Rushing in the door in a manic state with his pupils constricted (miosis: symptomatic of heroin use) he asked me to sit and then lectured me about how we needed to buy a house...right then! He brazenly insisted we go house hunting all around Mount Shasta and Redding, so we did. I certainly didn't argue with him in that state of mind. We went on an absurd escapade, searching all over for a massively huge house. Why did we need to own an enormous home, anyway? I was perfectly comfortable with living in a home under two thousand square feet. More space meant more to clean. Although I am sure Kyle would hire a live in housekeeper as he grew up with that, I didn't feel comfortable with a stranger living in our home and he knew that. I don't know why we needed to do this now. I was content living in the house we were in. We had only recently moved in together, prior to our honeymoon. We hadn't even been married a year, and now he wanted to move again?

Before we married, after he had convinced me to give up my rental, he bought us the house we were currently residing in. It's in a nice neighborhood and close to my salon—I liked that. But, supposedly, it wasn't enough for Kyle because now he wanted something even bigger. I wondered if this was his mental illness talking, or his drug addiction. I was mystified. He suggested finishing the cabin he had been renovating in McCloud, and we move up there. It wasn't a gargantuan home by any means, but it was on two acres. Maybe he needed to be surrounded by trees and space, and feel more secluded? Now, that was something I certainly could relate to. I agreed, although I didn't understand the urgency. I felt like I was headed on a monumental roller coaster ride and was hoping it was the kind with minimal twists and turns that didn't go upside down.

Inexplicably, after putting a rush on the McCloud home, hiring tons of workers to complete the project, he began to act pugnacious; picking fights with me out of thin air. He would glare at me with incipient anger, and then storm out of the room leaving me puzzled. Then return repeatedly to beleaguer me about the remote control being lost, or the garbage not being taken out, or something insidious. His words were so filled with spite and anger that it brought me to tears. He knew I was not the confrontational type, but it was as if he was trying to get me to yell at him and cause an explosion between us. I wasn't a fighter. And so the more he screamed at me, the meeker I became. And the more I retracted into a quiet shell, the angrier he became. But then things finally came to a head. It was a little after five o'clock, on a Tuesday afternoon. I came home from Petite Paws and saw him standing in the doorway to the kitchen.

In an agitated voice, he said, "We need to talk." *Oh, how I can't stand those words. It's always an invitation to get hurt feelings.*

He then looked me hard in the face and said, "I'm not ready for this. I need to go. I'll be in Mississippi."

Before I could even say a word he picked up his suitcase and stormed out the front door, supposedly flying off to Mississippi to spend the week with his parents. He never called. When he returned late the following Sunday we sat at the kitchen table to finally talk. He had a much calmer and more settled demeanor about him.

"I'm sorry, but I was wrong. I'm not ready for marriage. You did nothing wrong. I'm just not ready. You're beautiful and wonderful, but I want a divorce."

With my hands in my face I began to sob. I felt like a failure. I pleaded for him to reconsider and seek a marriage counselor with me, but he wouldn't have any part of that conversation. It was evident he had made up his mind.

"I know it wasn't right to have you move out of your place and into this one and have no place to go, so you can either stay here for free and I can sign the home over to you, or I can give you the cabin in McCloud," he said, handing me a box of tissues off the kitchen counter and then crossing his arms.

Sniffling and distraught, shocked by what I was hearing, I grabbed another tissue. "What?"

Kyle then walked around to my side of the table and forced himself to give me a friendship hug from the side, and then patted me on the back like a brother might.

"I thought you enjoyed working on your cabin. I thought it was going to be a place for us to retire?" I uttered, blowing my nose and wiping my tears.

"I'm moving back to Mississippi. I can hire people to move your stuff out and into the cabin if you'd like."

Stunned, I simply nodded.

The next day after work when I drove up the driveway to my house, the once brightly lit home full of security and aspiration was now an empty shell of lost hope and crushed dreams. The house that once resembled that of a married couple looked now more like a home which had been vacant for years. I think it had always been vacant, void of anything deep or honest; an empty husk of abandon treasures. It was

219

completely soulless. All my belongings, clothes, furniture, and trinkets were gone. The only resemblance to the life we shared, as a married couple, was a fishing boat magnet on the refrigerator, which was now holding up a small piece of paper with a typed impersonal message from Kyle:

```
Mel,
Your things are at the cabin, which is now officially
yours. The signed legal documents for property
ownership of the home and the demesne of two acres
are sitting on the kitchen table. My lawyer will
write up the divorce papers and deliver them to you.
I'll pay for everything. Take Care.
K
```

What? Take care? That's it? That was his au revoir? It's seriously over? *I can't breathe. I think I'm gonna be sick. Is this seriously happening to me?* The fact that we were never anything more than business partners sunk in. I knew I should be feeling blessed, to at least have a home to live in, but I could barely process the reality of the situation—everything was still so fresh. I could only address the sharp stabbing sting of pain aching inside my heart from being left; the feeling that I wasn't worth staying married to. I felt a loss of dignity: abandoned, inadequate, embarrassed and ashamed, like a complete failure. As I leaned up against the barren kitchen wall and reread Kyle's letter, my legs began to feel heavy and numb. A penumbra of doom descended over me like a partial eclipse of my heart. I began to lose feeling in the entire lower region of my body and could feel myself begin to slowly slide down the wall, until I collapsed onto the floor into a little ball with my head cradled between my knees. And I sobbed like a little girl who lost her daddy.

The next thing I know, I'm sitting in my parent's living room hugging my mom. I don't remember driving there, except I do remember feeling guilty and blessed at the same time, mostly because I had a place to live and a vehicle to drive. I was driving the 1998 red Jeep Cherokee that Kyle bought for me as a wedding gift. *Yeah, a freakin' wedding gift!*

He paid for it, upfront in cash, like he did our home and everything else. All I gave him was a Rolex wristwatch, which sincerely hurt my pocketbook—I'm still paying it off. Pessimistic thoughts of how my life was doomed from the beginning flooded my brain. *The Cinderella deal is a myth. People from incredibly diverse status levels don't work out.*

Being able to dive into my daddy's arms and feel okay again, at least for a little while, eased my pain. We all had a healing evening. I achieved the support that I needed before driving to my new bungalow in McCloud to start my life as a single divorcee. My dad helped me to comprehend why Kyle did what he did. I had to understand in order to move forward.

He clarified how Kyle's behavior was typical of an addict. "They have to replace one addiction with another. You, my dear, were Kyle's replacement addiction—his narcotic."

I theorized that since heroin was not a choice any more for Kyle, I was his heroin. It now made sense why he had wanted to get married so quickly and then buy a different house so soon after; and how when he wasn't getting filled up enough he wanted a bigger house. It was as if he was trying to fill a void, or reach some kind of a high. But I suspected that nothing would ever be powerful enough to feed that source. It had been difficult to fathom Kyle's motives, but after a vast amount of research, therapy with my parents and watching a few Dr. Drew episodes, I felt a lot more knowledgeable and wasn't taking the divorce so personally.

It wasn't long after living in my quaint McCloud cabin that I began clubbing again, like I used to in my mid-twenties. Here I was in my mid-thirties and single, again. I felt too old to be partying, but I needed to escape from the feeling I was a failure as a wife. However, being married and divorced aged me tremendously, making me skittish to get close to a man. I was done with being a part of any profoundly serious relationship for a while, and indubitably didn't crave a partnership involving any sort of institutional commitment.

Since Kat was also single and of the same ideology, we ended up hanging out more than usual. And, after attending the Red Bluff Round-Up rodeo together, we became closer than ever. We planned to spend the day at the rodeo enjoying the eye candy, and then afterward attend the late night dance held in the large indoor arena. We ended up camping overnight in our vehicles. Wherever we ventured anywhere we always drove our own automobiles, basically so neither of us felt restricted to stay longer than we cared to; an agreement that worked well for two supremely independent women.

When we first arrived we parked our cars near the camping site area, and then walked through the stationary cars and campers in the direction of the rodeo bleachers. But we were stopped in our tracks by an unforeseeable and surreal vision that left us both wonderstruck. We encountered *Mister S*. I couldn't believe my eyes. He was set up with his RV at one of the campsites we happen to be sauntering by. After a double take of his profile in the distance, I knew it was him. I saw his son sitting next to him along with a couple of other gentlemen, all wearing white cowboy hats. I presumed his son to be thirteen by now.

When I realized it was him I squealed and nabbed Kat on the shoulder practically knocking her over, and then jumped behind the closest positioned car. Then I motioned for her to join me on the ground while I explained my inane behavior. She was ecstatic and delighted to finally get a peek at *Mister S*. His wife exited the trailer, and for the first time I was able to get a clear view of her. She was unostentatious and plain wearing no makeup or jewelry, but there was a delicate sweetness to her face. Their teenage son and two older men along with *Mister S* appeared to be playing a card game. He was holding cards in one hand and a red plastic cup in the other. I was unnerved, while elated for this opportunity. I'd wanted Kat to get a visual of this guy for almost a decade, since she was the one who created the theory there was some spiritual reason for our serendipitous encounters.

I anxiously awaited her reaction. "Well?" I queried.

She held her hand up in my face, taking time to get a good look, and then turned in my direction. "Dang, he's old."

I laughed and slapped her teasingly on the arm.

Kat is thirteen years my junior, so of course, to her he was old. We were fearful of being discovered, so we decided to vacate before we got caught staring. Kat stood first and then began to walk briskly toward the rodeo arena. The fortuity of the moment made me excitable like a doltish school girl. I wanted to take one last sneak peek at *Mister S* before following Kat. And, precisely as I turned to look in the direction of the campsite, our eyes met. He must have heard my nervous giggle. *Oh no! He saw me!* He dropped his cup (presumably of beer) warranting an instant reaction from the guys, who were boisterously livid he spilled all over their deck of cards. Before anyone else could see me I sprinted as fast as I could toward Kat. And then, she grabbed my hand and joined me in frenetically racing toward the rodeo grandstands like foolish teenagers. Once we found a hidden alcove under the bleachers we huddled together and couldn't stop laughing.

Although I never saw *Mister S* again during the rest of the rodeo, the evening was a shock wave of amusing flirtations, unrestrained laughter, amateur swing dancing and cheap beer. I lost sight of Kat, after witnessing her intertwined behind the bleacher seats in a rather heavy public display of affection with a rather handsome cowboy. And soon after, I danced with a guy named Randy who was charming and had an absolutely hilarious personality. I didn't get to know him all that well, but he was a delightfully animated dance partner, and kept me laughing all night long. I like those cowboys; they sure know how to treat a woman. That night I slept in the back seat of my 1998 red Jeep Cherokee, alone. And at the break of dawn, when the campsite was as quiet as a ghost town, I drove home.

It was a long while before I encountered *Mister S* again, in fact, several years later. I was thirty-nine and still single. It was the day before Thanksgiving and I had to get up early for work, and the alarm was blaring for the third time…bomp-bomp-bomp-bomp…forcing me to spout expletives. Instead of hitting the snooze button again, I turned off the alarm and sat up in bed. Shaking my head in disappointment at myself for waking up frustrated, I decided to do what I learned after recently reading the book *The Secret*. I planted my right foot onto the floor, saying: "Thank," followed by my left foot, saying: "You."

I realize having gratitude and being thankful is an essential part of living a halcyon, healthy and successfully fulfilling life. However, I also acknowledge that it is conscious work to pinpoint those things that are going well, when life seems overwhelming. While rushing through my morning routine I was profoundly aware that I needed to alter how I was thinking and feeling. First step: send ex-husband a thank you letter.

I was grateful for Kyle. The recession hit many, especially those of us with small businesses. I had fewer regular clients than ever and no waiting list. The only reason that I wasn't insolvent was because of Kyle. If he had not granted me his cabin to reside in, and gifted me with a jeep, I would be living destitute on the streets, or living in my parent's basement. *No thanks*. I knew I should be more grateful than I felt. I needed to do more meditating. I knew that if I ever planned on having another serious relationship in my life, I needed to climb the stairs to the metaphorical third floor. Thankfully, I was out of the basement which felt tremendous—I only lived there for a short while, during the first year, after my marriage crumbled into pieces. For the last few years, I've mostly resided on the second floor, which I believe is why I had a conglomerate of awful dating experiences. Once again, I wasn't completely centered on taking care of me. I wasn't eating well or exercising regularly. I made a pact with myself not to date anyone, until I was healthy and clear. If I could manage to do that, I presumed I'd attract someone similarly healthy.

After mailing the letter of gratitude to Kyle, I walked through the front doors of Petite Paws, feeling grateful for all the blessings in my life. I was especially thankful to be my own boss. After the loss of my marriage, my career was my saving grace; the emotional and spiritual glue holding me together. I made it to the salon only two minutes before my first client arrived. I was frazzled, but took one look at this cute sheer-white purebred Maltese and relaxed. Dogs are the one constant I can always count on to make me feel at peace. It was fun to primp and preen this little Maltese, who happened to be only six months old. He was unbelievably patient, allowing me to comb out all his matted hair. The lady who brought him in proclaimed that in their household they usually listened to golden oldies. *Yes!* I was stoked. Classic oldies are one of the most upbeat styles to trim to, and impossible not to dance to. I preened and trimmed this cute little pup to the tune of Aretha Franklin's *"Rescue Me"*, Sam Cooke's *"Twistin' the Night Away"*, Three Dog Night's *"Joy to the World"*, and The Rascals *"Good Lovin'"*, along with many other great dance hits. Singing along to the music, I danced and trimmed away, totally bonding with this sweet little Maltese named Mark. After the successful short hair trim the lady, who delivered him, revealed how the dog belonged to her mother who could no longer physically care for him and they needed to find him a home. I jumped up ecstatically.

"I want him! Seriously, I'll take care of him. I'm not kidding. I fell in love with him the moment I laid eyes on him. He's s-o-o-o adorable."

She instantly approved, sweetly giving me a gracious hug and saying how thrilled she was that a dog lover wanted to rescue him. Then she ran to her vehicle to retrieve the paperwork and his certified pedigree registration certificate. After the transfer I gave her a healthy donation and found my new best friend, who I renamed Marshmallow. With the nickname Marsh, a sound similar to Mark, I was hoping to make the transition easier on the little fellow. Resembling a marshmallow, he was as white as snow and as sweet as candy; I wanted to eat him up. And planned on taking him everywhere with me, ready to hone the label "certifiable crazy lady with dog in purse." I couldn't wait to bring him home to meet my faithful cocker spaniel, Oreo. I knew they would be best friends, Oreo gets along with everyone. Luckily, I maintained a pet-friendly room in the back of the salon where I could keep Marshmallow during trimming sessions.

All six of my older brothers, with their wives and kids, were already at my parents visiting for the Thanksgiving holiday.

Sadly, I was the only one who had to work the day before Thanksgiving. I was anxious to be home in time for the family poker game, scheduled to begin at six in the evening. I anticipated finishing my last trim before five, aiming at having enough time to change at my house and get over to my parents before dark.

I was with my last client at the grooming salon, trimming a friendly, elegant, little cavalier King Charles spaniel dog named Cappuccino, who preferred classical music. The violin crescendo in *"Bach's Brandenburg Concerto No. 5 in D major"* was powerfully invigorating. The sun was descending precisely as the song neared its end, and at the distinct moment that I completed the preening. I replaced the dog collar and leash onto Cappuccino, and setting her gently down on the tile floor walked toward the window.

Although the vertical window blinds were already open, I wanted a larger view, curious if it had started to rain as the weatherman predicted. All I could distinguish through the misty fog was a white, construction type pickup truck pulling into the parking lot. At brief glance it looked like *Mister S* in the driver's seat. But before I could get a hard look I was interrupted by my client Luca Marcello, who walked in the door to pick up his dog, Cappuccino. By the time I closed up the business and headed out the door, the white truck was gone, and I discounted the incident as being anything noteworthy.

The plan to focus on myself, and not date anyone until I was ready, felt like the healthiest decision I'd ever made in my entire life. I was getting healthier, physically as well as emotionally; change was imminent. I had ceased my injurious dating habits and unnatural eating practices—wholly relinquishing my Twinkie addiction—because I certainly didn't want the epilogue of my obituary to read: "After dating a myriad of Froot Loops, she died eating a Twinkie." I was becoming the self-actualized woman I always knew I could be. Attic, here I come.

Chapter Seven

What happens when you put Nutella on salmon? You get salmonella

King Salmon

If you are looking for a choice wild fish, look no further than the king salmon, which are the largest and top-of-the-line among Pacific salmon species. King salmon have a pronounced, buttery and rich flavor and can be enjoyed in a variety of ways.

"Good things come to those who bait."   *~Author Unknown*

****

Kat poured us each a hot mug of coffee, adding a splash of hazelnut cream. Toasting our mugs we both took a slow steamy sip, which tickled and warmed the insides going down.

It was approaching morning and Kat and I were both sitting on the living room floor, leaning up against the couch, with our coffee mugs nestled to our chests and the birthday book open on the coffee table with blankets and pillows strewn about the room. I was ready to head home and get some needed rest, but I had to first sum up my debacle with Kyle.

Looking directly at Kat I was about to get down to it when she interceded with her own train of thought. "Wait a minute. Was Kyle the last guy you dated? Have you seriously not had sex in almost seven years? Holy moly! You could be a nun."

I looked at Kat speechless, because of the dangling element of truth spewing from her mouth.

"I don't know how you could be celibate for so long? Lord knows, I couldn't."

I don't know if my reaction was due to being premenopausal, consuming such a large amount of wine, absence of sleep, or hearing my life played out like a pathetic Lifetime movie special (Hopeless Middle Age Woman Becomes a Nun), but my emotions went haywire, and once the tears began to flow I couldn't stop them.

"Aw, Melody R-a-a-ae! My bad, I am so sorry. I so didn't mean it. Damn my big mouth," wailed Kat, as she comforted me in a tight warm hug.

I straightened up, while Kat snagged the tissue box on the corner table behind her, and handed it to me.

I wiped my face, blew my nose and scrunched my hair composing myself. "No, no, no. It's not your fault. You were being honest. I know, that you know, it's not like I planned my life to turn out like this. I didn't choose to be sexless. In all honesty, I probably would settle for a guy who is interested in pure sex, I just don't attract that type. You want to know the type I attract? Needy control freaks who want to suffocate my time and then take all my money…seriously! I'm a total leach magnet."

Kat guffawed.

"Oh, and to top it off, they're usually suffering from some sort of peculiar malady…like schizophrenia," I sneered.

Kat reached for a pillow off the couch and threw it at my head and we both started laughing.

"But seriously Kat, the older I get the fewer choices I have."

She nodded in sympathy. "Well, now me? I *do* attract the horny bastards. I can give you some numbers if…,"

"NO!" I quickly retorted before she could finish her sentence.

Kat responded with a hard cackle. "Of course I was kidding, which you know. But on a serious note, Melody Rae, you will meet somebody…someday. Timing just hasn't been right. You're lovely, and it's never too late to meet Mister Wonderful."

I sighed and then clutching my mug with both hands, took a sip of coffee which had cooled considerably. "I know you're right. You're right...one day. But it's not a priority right now. So, can we just get back to where we were and end this madness?" I growled.

"Yes absolutely! Sum up Kyle. I'm ready. Bring it on," Kat exclaimed, while rubbing her hands together. Then shifting her body onto her knees, she did a mini drum roll on the edge of the coffee table.

With weary eyes and a half-smile I grunted and then yawned while sluggishly rummaging through the legal pad to find the last page of written documentation. I was relieved to be able to conclude our all-night wine fest. Although it had been rejuvenating and healing, I was utterly fatigued.

"Oh, that's right, after Kyle I had trouble choosing just one song. I had to write down two...our break up was that unsettling. But I selected the one that was most fitting. Ready?"

"Of course, read," Kat insisted pepping up and fluffing a pillow she had crumpled on her lap.

"The song that brings instant memories of the nocturnal catfish, Kyle, is *'I Can Get Off on You'* by Waylon Jennings and Willie Nelson. Little did I know that when he sang that song to me at our wedding, he was a recovering addict. The lyrics explicitly say *I can get off on you*, clearly suggesting I was his drug."

"Oh lord, ain't that the truth. Yeah, he really needed you. You know, it's one of my favorite songs...the lyrics are emotionally powerful," she quivered. Then clearing her throat, she sat up straight, adjusted her top and began to sing the analogous lyrics about weed, cocaine, pills and whiskey.

After her voice resonated around the room I choked up, and placed the back of my right hand to my lips, feeling a tear well up in my eye. I recalled Kyle singing those lyrics to me in front of my entire family on my wedding day. I can't believe how delusional I was, thinking I'd finally found the one. Hearing those chilling lyrics for the first time since the divorce was hair-raising and Kat's fruity, smoky voice propelled me to become overcome with emotion.

"I should have married you," I cooed, cocking my head to the side and leaning toward Kat.

Kat smiled and gave me a hug.

After shaking my head in disgust at myself for all the mistakes I'd made in the past, I retrieved the legal pad which had fallen off my lap and onto the floor beside me. "Since I felt like my marriage to Kyle took such a one hundred and eighty degree turn, I also wrote down *Lover, Lover* by Johnny Nash, but then decided that one wasn't as suitable (yawn). Maybe I'm too tired to think about it right now. Do you know any of the words to that song?" I asked.

Kat then melodically trilled, with sweet resonance, the bittersweet lyrics of a lover turning against you.

I shook my head in amazement. "Wow...just wow. How you can sound so utterly breathtaking, singing in perfect tune after drinking all night, is, is...unreal. Seriously, I don't get how you can do that. You're a prodigy. If I had your talent, I tell ya, I wouldn't be a dog groomer, that's for sure."

"Are you kidding me? That was terrible! My vocal chords are totally shot," she said with a bemused expression.

"W h a t e v e r," I said leisurely with my eyes glazing over while looking up at the ceiling and forming the letter "W" using both hands.

She laughed.

"You are a vocal goddess, Kat. Just accept it. Now, let's get back to Kyle. He was not only my last relationship, but probably the last one I'll ever have in my lifetime...ever!" I hollered vehemently and with my hands out to both sides.

"Oh stop! That is so not going to be true. You just haven't met the right guy," she argued.

I rolled my eyes. "Yeah, yeah, yeah...blah, blah, blah, I guess. Time will tell," I said, unconvinced. Then seeing Kat's aggressive and threatening parental look, I conceded. "Okay, okay, fine! All right, you're right. Now let's just get back to how Kyle destroyed my ability to love."

She slapped my knee. "Stop it!"

I chuckled, amused by my own snarky wit, and then reflected my eyes to the last page of the legal pad. "I think it might be somewhat obvious that after the nocturnal catfish, Kyle, I could no longer smell the beach without awful memories resurfacing. The salty ocean breeze brings me right back to that day the cruise ship docked in Ensenada and I got the shock of a lifetime."

Kat nodded, giving me an empathetic look.

Not wanting to replay that horrific game-changing moment with Kyle, I geared the topic back to our agenda. "Moving on…before I fall asleep. Okay, I can no longer taste Kraft 'thick and spicy' barbecue sauce. Seriously! I don't remember a meal where Kyle didn't add it. Whenever he cooked, he used barbecue sauce, no matter what he was grilling, year round, rain or shine. Seriously, he should've slept with his barbecue grill. They were way more compatible than we were. Do you think he used the sauce to mask the smell of the joints he was secretly smoking?"

Kat's lips perched and she nodded repetitiously.

"Ugh. Just thinking about that barbecue smell leaves me with a salty and…ahem…fraudulent aftertaste."

Kraft barbecue sauce

"Ah, well said, Melody Rae," Kat cheered, toasting her coffee mug to mine.

Immersing my nose deep into my coffee mug in contemplation, and then leaning back slightly to stare at the shallow pool of coffee grounds at the bottom of the mug, I deliberated. "Kyle was a manipulative mental termite, who daily ate away at my spirit, until there was nothing left but crumbled edges."

"Oh, you're not bitter," Kat said sardonically while raising her eyebrows and scratching her chin.

I smiled. "Bitterness aside, can we move on now? I'm so ready to crash. I can barely find the wherewithal to be civil."

"I hear ya. Yes, please continue. My eyelids feel like five pound bags of sand."

"Mine, too," I concurred, snatching *The Secret Language of Relationships* book off the coffee table and looking up the page number. "Okay, the nocturnal catfish, Kyle, and final guy to put behind me. Drum roll please."

Kat picked up on my cue and began to weakly drum roll on the edge of the coffee table.

"The title for our combination, the twenty-fourth of October with the third of December: capturing hearts. Best at: colleague. Weaknesses: competitive, unconcerned, projecting."

"H-m-m-m, I would say unconcerned and projecting, yes. But competitive?" Kat winced. "Well, maybe if he hadn't been such a pot head, he would've had more of a competitive edge. Best at colleague totally fits. You guys communicated like business partners. You didn't behave like a couple 'in love'. But you both did capture one another's hearts before you married, even if you were both in an illusion with one another, since you were both projecting onto the other what you thought the other wanted you to be."

"Touché," I said, surprised my issues with Kyle were so apparent.

"I must say, Melody Rae, I am proud of you. You have managed to safely avoid any long term mental illness by revisiting the mistakes you've made and divesting yourself of your past failures by letting go," Kat asserted, rewarding me with a hug.

I giggled, and then let out a sigh.

"All right, now I'm officially too tired to analyze or even understand what I just said, so…I must go to bed. You can let yourself out. But please lock the door on the inside before you close it…or you can stay. You are certainly welcome to crash on the couch."

"Oh, no, no, no," I said, standing slowly, feeling my middle-age knee joints crack. "Earlier I thought that I might do that, but I think I need my own bed. But, thank you."

"You know…," Kat said, standing, seizing the throw blanket off the floor and walking toward her bedroom, "it's interesting how none of these men had the title, 'best at love or marriage.' That means he's still out there."

I beamed and then had an obscure thought. "Wait," I blurted, feeling a sudden brain jolt and flipping through *The Secret Language of Relationships* book.

"What?"

"Ha-ha. I knew it!" I said in an affirming manner, shaking my head after reading a paragraph from the book. "I should have been a lesbian."

"Whuh? Why?"

"You won't believe it. Our title combination: Best at: marriage."

Kat seized the book out of my hand. "Are you freakin' kidding me? No way?!"

"Weird, huh?"

"The third of March with the third of December: Best at: marriage," Kat read aloud.

"Makes sense why we've been friends for so long," I stated.

Kat narrowed her eyes and made a funny expression. "Sorry honey, I don't swing that way."

"Ewe, me neither! I like men," I said assuredly.

Kat laughed. "So, after all the male anguish you've endured you're not going to pursue a life of celibacy?"

"What?! (cough) Yeah, right. I don't think so. I like sex too much. Besides, I believe, once again, that the next guy will be the right one for me. Obviously, every guy I dated was the right one for me at the right time for what I needed to learn. But in the past, I was always unclear about what I wanted. Now, I know exactly what I want. And I also have faith and believe that I seriously will meet the right one for me, who I'll grow old with for eternity. I can feel the type of love I want to experience as if I have it now and I will settle for nothing less than my soul mate. My soul will know it, when I meet him," I announced with assertion, smiling at Kat.

Kat put her thumb up supportively.

Then I looked up at the ceiling. "I am ready universe," I resounded with my hands up in the air.

"I believe you will meet him...if you haven't already."

I nodded and smiled, marveling at my bright future.

Kat then hugged me, turned and walked into her bedroom, crawled into bed and bundled herself under her pink billowy duvet comforter.

Once I retrieved my large birthday book and wrinkled legal pad off the table, I carefully headed down the stairwell, tugged my large purse off of Kat's classy rack, and schlepped toward the front door. After opening the door and turning the inside doorknob to lock it as Kat requested, I closed it behind me and shuffled to face a radiant and glistening early morning sunrise peeking over the mountain. It was a lovely soft orange and light yellow shade of serenity. I took a deep breath, breathing in the clean crisp mountainous air. Hearing dogs barking off in the distance elicited thoughts of my sweet pets, Oreo and Marshmallow, at home waiting for me, and I began to miss them.

Clumsily searching through my purse for my sunglasses, while sauntering wearily toward my jeep, I was concerned that I might fall; acutely aware my body was feeling the subsequent effects from the long evening of debauchery. After pressing the unlock symbol on my remote key fob, I tossed my belongings onto the passenger seat and scooted myself onto the front driver's seat. Then I shut the door, started the engine, and drove home in a half-asleep mechanical daze; my brain and body completely on autopilot. I couldn't recall driving at all, until I blinked and noticed the beautiful pine trees aligning the glorious countryside of McCloud. Fortunately, I instinctively knew the way and could probably drive the roads blindfolded having driven from Kat's house to mine numerous times.

Blessed, hopeful, thankful and emotionally content it seemed I was pounds lighter than the day before. I felt almost weightless, rejuvenated, clearheaded and jubilant as if I'd experienced a spiritual awakening. Stretching, I rolled my neck to the left and then all the way around and then inhaled and exhaled slowly. There it was all out in the open. *I did it.* I divested my soul out on a platter for the world to see. My tragically dysfunctional relationship history filled with insecurities and fear were served on a plate with a side of guilt, recalibrated and then removed from my physical body. I was released by sharing everything out in the open and replaying the pain to its fullest. I felt alive, renewed: reborn. I began to understand why people go to therapy. It's tremendously healing to tell your innermost painful memories to someone. Thank goodness Kat is a cheap therapist. A few bottles of wine and her time, and I felt able to move forward for maybe the first time in my entire life.

****

July 4, 2011

Typical Daily Food Choices:
Kona coffee—black, no sugar
Quaker oatmeal w/raw honey, walnuts, pistachios, cranberries, blueberries & raisins
fresh broccoli, zucchini, orange bell pepper, acorn squash, sweet potatoes, brown rice & real unsalted butter
shrimp, cod, halibut, salmon
mixed greens, olives, artichoke, cilantro, avocados, sunflower seeds, cucumber, cherry tomatoes w/vinegar & olive oil dressing
feta cheese tortellini pasta w/pesto sauce
Trader Joe's soy chorizo
bottled water
green tea: Lipton
quality red wines: Clos du Bois or Rodney Strong

McCloud Cabin

Returning home early, on the morning of the Fourth of July holiday, I immediately rushed to give Marshmallow and Oreo their Pedigree milk-bone dog treats, big squeezable hugs and nose kisses. After feeding them their Purina breakfast, I walked straight into the bedroom and collapsed on the bed from pure exhaustion and wine overdose, and slept until noon.

After being accosted awake by an affectionate cocker spaniel and an eager Maltese, I laid in bed embroiled in a zealous petting competition, staring at the ceiling, feeling grateful and deliriously at peace. Being utterly fatigued earlier, I hadn't taken the time to get under the covers, or hang up my purse, which I discovered was slumped at the end of the bed with its contents scattered about. I did however manage to pull the throw blanket over me which had been folded neatly at the bottom of the bed. I rolled onto my stomach and felt a hard lump beneath me. It was the notoriously wrinkled and well-read legal pad of my personal antiquity. I decided to reread the list of fish entrées I'd attributed to each guy I dated. I laughed out loud while reading, amused by the symmetry of truth to each one.

Shay—*the slimy sardine*
Tony—*the wishy-washy soft shell crab*
Willie—*the juicy swordfish*
Peter—*the flaky yellow fin tuna*
Kyle—*the nocturnal catfish*

The list made me skeptical as to whether there were any fish left. The yellow fin tuna, Peter, had been particularly painful to resolve. I had been disillusioned into thinking he was the "catch" for me. Facing the awful reality of our relationship scared me right out of the polluted water and onto dry land, leaving me with a bad aftertaste; a deadly catch with mercury poisoning. My heart took much longer to heal with him than with any other man. Only since I'd been consistently eating healthy did I no longer have a fishy aftertaste in my mouth, and could once again swallow without tuna flashbacks. And although this "eat a healthy diet to attract a healthy man theory" made me shake my head and giggle, I was still dedicated to proving it.

Continuing on a serious mission to prove my theory, I stood, showered, dressed and headed to the store. When I returned, I packed the refrigerator with a variety of fresh fruits and vegetables and stuffed the freezer with prawns, oysters, lobsters, and salmon. I knew I could handle the strong flavors and richness of these delicate and luxurious fishes. These were not merely ingredients I intensely craved, but nutrients my body required as well. It took me nearly twenty years to evolve into a physically healthy and emotional being. I progressed from eating cupboard processed packaged grub to frozen processed and leftover garbage to purely fresh food. I now felt as fresh and replenished as what I was putting in my body. Any food items that were even a day old were going to be thrown out. I wasn't going to allow easy-to-prepare foods to have even a tiny chance of surviving. Packaged foods loaded with preservatives, such as a box of Kraft macaroni and cheese with added tuna placed in a Tupperware container and stuffed at the bottom of the fridge were forbidden; officially banned. I wasn't going to live a long or halcyon life if I continued an unhealthy pattern. I surmised that by eating fresh foods only, I could savor each day and live a rich, full and better quality of life. And, since I've come to deeply believe we attract what we eat, I was going to eat quality to attract quality.

Marinating at my Shangri la bungalow, in the idyllic and utopian mountains of McCloud, an area referred to as a place of relaxation and spiritual healing, you would think I would have attracted my spiritual match by now. Since I had not, but predicted I would soon, I selected to manifest love into my life by taking some time to listen to the trees and do something out of the ordinary, and meditate.

Sitting outside on the patio in a red wooden Adirondack chair and meditating for the next hour with my eyes closed while quietly listening to the delicious sounds of nature was purely cleansing. I was moved by the beautiful and mellifluous melody of nature: birds chirping, squirrels rustling, wind whistling, dogs barking, tiny lizards scrimmaging, bees buzzing and then pure silence. I get it now. I get why meditation works and why doing nothing makes you something. You become more harmonious with the universe, more aware of your surroundings and your existence; able to see and feel more profoundly.

I desired solitude and looked forward to enjoying my Independence Day holiday alone to take care of me. I put on the classic Melanie vinyl *Gather Me* album on my antiquated record player, to hear the song *"Little Bit of Me"*, which always brings me to tears, making me feel more connected to everything around me. Then I uncorked a 1999 bottle of Dom Pérignon champagne, which I'd been saving especially for such an occasion. Honoring the Fourth of July holiday, I retrieved the red juicy strawberries and ripe blueberries from the freezer. After dropping two blueberries and one strawberry into a champagne flute, I leisurely poured the champagne. This was something my most etiquette savvy friend, Tessa, showed me how to do. She was the Martha Stewart of Mount Shasta, always creating, crafting, baking and designing—impressing others with her talent to create artistic masterpieces utilizing a variety of mediums. Recently dabbling in blown glass art, she designed an exquisite plate for me, which I currently have hanging in my kitchen. It delineates a breathtakingly gorgeous and abstract representation of small dogs, using glittery shades of red, teal and gold. I feel intense appreciation for my friendship with her every time I look at it.

Treasuring the blessings in my life, I slipped into a new Sabz swimsuit that I'd bought a week ago at the pricey Mirabelle's, a fashionable boutique in Mount Shasta: a red, white and blue striped beaded one-piece. Sitting on the ledge of my private steamy Jacuzzi, allowing my feet to dangle in the bubbling hot water, I relished the seclusion of my home with its lagoon style sunken pool surrounded by overgrown pine trees which align the backyard concealing a six-foot high redwood fence. Ironically, hidden from others and thoroughly alone, spiritually forging my connection to nature vitalizes me to feel less alone. Seclusion nurtures me to feel safe, accepted, loved, content and at peace. *What is wrong with me?* I confess I know. Growing up with six brothers and never having any real privacy generated a craving to be alone. But also, over time, I've learned how to love myself in an unselfish way. Alone, I can blast whatever music I choose and sing (out of tune) without bothering anyone, except for possibly the neighboring wild squirrels. I have long been my own biggest fan. I accept myself more than anyone else ever has. *Why do I need a mate, anyway?* I wanted to marinate in my own thoughts, sink deeper into my inner world and replay the conversation I had last night with Kat, so I did.

After some quality alone time and profound evaluation, I conceded that, although the solitude was revitalizing, I couldn't survive continuous solitary confinement; even a week without human interaction would make me nearly crazy. Unaffectedly, I desire to retreat into an inner sanctum periodically, but eventually, I necessitate sharing my thoughts and having physical contact with other human beings. And there are certain persons in my life who uplift my spirit, who I welcome to invade my personal space, and who I will give up my privacy for. My niece Mimi is one of those kindred spirits. She knows how to listen and provide reassurance while at the same time keeping to her own tune.

Mimi is my eldest brother's daughter. She turned twenty-one less than six months ago, but is beyond her years in maturity and self-awareness; most assuredly an old soul. She's an Aquarius born on the third of February, 1990, and considered numerology three, like me and Kat. We're all three's. All of us share a similar physical disposition and sanguine essence and are superiorly gifted at multi-tasking. Some might say we appear scatterbrained, since we are all over the map, but we know it's because we simply think faster than most; at least that's what we tell others.

My head lucid and tranquil, I began to sink my body down into the steaming tub feeling grateful for those like Mimi in my life, when my cellphone rang, shifting me back into the here and now. The Brook Benton and Dinah Washington *"Baby (You've Got What It Takes)"* ringtone that I exclusively set for Mimi prompted a smile. How serendipitous to have her call after thinking of her moments before. I was more than delighted to have her interrupt my solitude. I'd been anxious to hear from her and find out about how things were going with Kent, the recent love of her life.

Lifting my body out of the water, I scrambled to my feet, wrapped the large beach towel around my waist, snatched the phone off the patio table and swiped my finger across the screen to accept her call.

"How fortuitous, Mimi! I was just thinking about you!"

"I'm just down the road, less than a mile from your place. I'm gonna stop by, okay?"

"Serious? Yay! Of course it's okay. It's more than okay. You just made my day. Get over here, I've missed you!"

After we exchanged a few more brief words, I hung up the phone, flung the beach towel onto the nearest patio chair, slipped on a pair of white Old Navy flip-flops and wrapped a matching red, white and blue striped sarong around my waist. I sprinted into the living room to straighten the pillows and then scrambled into the kitchen, and quickly attempted to rinse the dishes piled in the sink. But before I had a chance to finish, I heard the tires of Mimi's white Mazda Miata turning up the gravel driveway. Her wealthy Uncle Bill, on her mother's side of the family, bought the sporty car for her as a graduation gift. I fluffed my frazzled, red hair in the living room mirror above the fireplace and then put a Bob Marley CD into the CD player, turning up the volume considerably and cueing it to play *"Three Little Birds."* As I exited through the back patio gate leading to the driveway to greet Mimi, she was reaching into the back seat and retrieving a designer beach bag. Approaching her, I grinned and began to sway and sing along with the Bob Marley lyrics.

She turned, half-smiled and shook her head in embarrassment when she saw me approaching and heard me crooning, mostly erroneous lyrics with obvious mondegreen, in my dreadfully off-key singing voice. "Don't worry...,"

"Uh, sure, whatever you say," she said in her characteristically sardonic tone."

After Mimi slammed the door to her cute Miata sports car, we hugged and walked back up the driveway toward the gate. She then proceeded to tell me about this guy (a new guy), not Kent, but rather someone she met a month ago named Kaden. She seems to always go for these guys whose names begin with the letter K. Her first adolescent crush was with a boy named Keith and her first official boyfriend was named Kirk. Apparently Kaden is more than simply a crush, but rather someone who she's crazily obsessed about. It seems he recently moved out of state and she's completely forlorn. As she put it: "Life is completely over and there is no hope or purpose." Oh heaven forbid. Life is so dramatic at age twenty-one. *Was I like that when I was her age? Oh, who am I kidding? Of course I was. In fact, it wasn't long ago when I felt similar naïve and obsessive, irrational cravings.*

After Mimi changed into her blue polka-dot bikini, we sat on the ledge of the spa reminiscing about past holidays with family, until things shifted into an intense conversation about our favorite topic: men. Mimi was indeed blessed with the best of the Irish genes. She possesses the physical features of a model: gorgeous and slender with long, straight, red hair which extends beyond her waist. It is not surprising she receives a tremendous amount of attention from men. She plays hard to get, so for men she's the long awaited prize at the bottom of the cereal box. If you agree with the campaign adage "men go cuckoo for Cocoa Puffs" they get even kookier for long hair.

"Do you know what song I selected for your ringtone on my phone?" I crowed, interrupting her ramble.

"No…uh-oh, wh-a-a-at?" she asked with reservation.

"It's perfect for you. Here, call me right now and you'll hear it," I said while picking up my phone and turning up the volume.

After she snagged her phone and pressed three on speed dial and heard the lyrics to the song *"Baby (You've Got What It Takes)"*, she squealed, "Oh, Mel, I love it! I r-e-e-eally like that song. The words are awesome. And that's so cool you think that about me. I guess I got what it takes."

"Yes, you, do."

Mimi laughed tapping my arm playfully and then resumed her story which unexpectedly led to an entirely different guy, a boy named Tyler. Someone she met in her college English class, who happens to be a friend of her most recent ex-boyfriend, Kent. *Oh boy.*

"Uh-oh! You can't go there…his name doesn't start with a K," I teased with both hands on my cheeks in playful shock.

We both started laughing.

Our giggling was then momentarily interrupted by a rumbling, pounding, rhythmic of sounds that we both heard escalating off in the distance. We looked at each other with eye-opening curiosity and then resumed laughing. When the pleasant drum-like booming sounds escalated even more, we presumed it was coming from the neighbor's house nearly an acre away which was not visible due to the tall fence and pine trees. And although I understood the house to be vacant, someone could have moved in without my knowledge, as all the homes in the area of McCloud were hidden in the trees, something I relished of the area.

The drumming then intensified, possessing a deeper echo, characteristic to that of the Afro-Cuban percussion sound of bongos, which I pleasantly enjoyed listening to perform on the streets of Berkeley in my early college days. With eyebrows raised and mouth's gaping in awe, we were in agreement that what we were hearing was spectacular.

I looked at Mimi, sparked with an idea. "Hey, Mimi, I don't know if they can hear us, but we should cheer and clap as loud as we can when they end the set. What do you think? I mean, they're really, really good…right?"

Mimi cheered in agreement, "Woo-hoo! Oh yeah, for sure. Let's do it!"

We continued talking and enjoying the pleasant drum beat serenade our evening until the music stopped. Then we both stood in the Jacuzzi, and in unison clapped and screamed embarrassingly loud, "Woo-oo-oo-oo-oo!"

Moments later, we could faintly hear guys laughing, although they had to be nearly an acre away. It's fascinating and bewildering how sound travels when surrounded by trees and mountains. I imagine, were we to have a barrier of buildings between us, we wouldn't be able to hear them at all and vice versa.

After our hollering cheers of delight, I handed Mimi her liquid courage of choice—a Sierra Nevada beer—as I cradled a half-full flute of Dom Pérignon. And then we both sunk deeper into the deliciously hot and steamy Jacuzzi, settling across from each other. I smiled and closed my eyes, to savor the moment, feeling deliriously content. But before my eyelids could relax, they were startled open by the sound of tires veering up my gravel driveway. I turned to peer out of the top lattice of the redwood fence and saw a black, Ford F-150 pickup truck adorned with a heavy duty truck rack with the words "DD Construction" written across the windshield. At first I was overcome with fear, imagining myself searching for the hidden loaded shotgun I didn't own. But paranoia vanished, replaced by giddiness and euphoria. Not sure if it was caused by the heat of the Jacuzzi, or a purely nervous excitement of the unexpected, but I started giggling. I couldn't see who was in the cab of the truck because their faces were shaded from the trees overhead and I could only see the back of the head of a guy who was sitting in the bed of the truck, seemingly on a high bench with his arms enveloping two large bongos.

The driver yelled, "Melody Rae!!!"

What?! He knows me?

I instantly stopped giggling and with a look of consternation eyed Mimi, who responded to my neurosis by stepping out of the tub, wrapping a towel around her waist, and holding a pool leaf net like a weapon.

Using mouthy articulation, I muttered to Mimi, "I don't know who it is?"

"Well, answer him anyway!" she said, sharply waving her hands toward me with insistence.

I cautiously exited the Jacuzzi and responded hesitantly, "Uh…yea-h-h-h???"

"Hey, it's Derek…Derek Dreesen!" the voice bellowed.

I stood paralyzed; stunned.

"Remember me, Peter Kelly's friend?"

What was he doing here? Derek had been one of my closest friends who I hadn't seen in ages. I was thrilled to see him, although questions flooded my brain. *How did he know where I live? And why did my past with Peter always have to resurface?*

I quickly slipped on my flip-flops, wrapping my sarong about my waist and walking toward the fence dripping wet and discombobulated, while Mimi assisted in opening the gate. Reuniting Derek with a monumental hug, I noticed he looked exactly the same as he did years ago; the man doesn't age. He was still in phenomenally robust shape; thin and perfectly muscularly cut as ever. Although he had a tiny amount of gray in the beard of his goatee, it made him look distinguished rather than old, adding to his appeal. It's too bad we never had physical chemistry, because not only was he a respectful, honest, loving and decent guy, he was empirically good-looking.

I love-tapped Derek's arm and asked him where his wife, Gretchen, was. He explained how she was out of town in Maryland visiting relatives. They had a stalwart and deeply loving (although unconventional) relationship that allowed a lot of freedom, which is why their dynamic appealed to me, and probably why it worked for Derek. We share a similar need for a lot of private alone time. He and Gretchen spend a lot of time apart, permitting them to miss each other, and in my opinion fueling the fire of love, thereby keeping it burning bright. Distance doesn't always make the heart fonder, sometimes it makes the heart wander, but not in their case; their love is extraordinarily strong.

"Do you wonder how I knew you lived here?" Derek asked.

"Yeah, how'd you know?" I replied.

"Well, sorry, Melody Rae, it's not a psychic phenomenon. I have to give credit to Gretchen. She knew you moved to McCloud because of the address on the return label of your Christmas card."

"Ah of course, Derek, always with a logical explanation," I said.

"But it's true!"

I nodded and then laughed.

"When she noticed that I had a new building contract on Cabernet Way, she suggested I find out where you live and pop in and say hi. But, you know, your house wasn't all that tough to spot. Your red jeep sort of gave you away. I kept thinking how I need to pop by sometime, but you know how that goes. Then I heard the both of you howling when we were playing just now, and figured that this would be a perfect time to visit."

I leaped forward hugging Derek again, tighter. "It is the perfect time. And I've seriously missed you!"

As I was hugging Derek I realized that I had not even introduced Mimi to him. Before doing so I pulled her in close to my side and gave a flattering speech about how much I adore her. Then this young, bronze complexioned, dark-haired kid, who looked about twenty-one, jumped from the bed of the truck and approached Mimi. He introduced himself as Giacomo, and then kissed her hand and then both cheeks. At which time her face flushed and she started awkwardly laughing, and began to fiddle with her hair how I do. *We're obviously related.*

As I hugged Mimi to cover up her embarrassment, out stepped the gentleman from the passenger side of the truck. And surely as I turned around Giacomo leaned toward him, pat him on the back, and introduced him.

"This is my dad," he boasted.

What in the world? Mister S?! No freakin' way!

Our eyes locked.

Utterly astonished that *Mister S* was at my house and in my driveway, when I opened my mouth to say hi absolutely nothing came out.

He shook his head. "Well, well, well, look who it is," he smirked.

"Do you two know each other?" asked Derek, looking bewildered.

Mister S put his hand to his chin. "Somethin' like that," he said with alarming intensity, and then flirtatiously stared into my eyes.

I had to look away.

"Well, we haven't formally met. I'm Zeek. Zeek Marcello," he said while nodding his head and reaching for my hand. *His name is Zeek? Like my adolescent crush. That is weird.*

Then he leaned forward to take my hand to kiss it. But before he could I immediately grabbed his hand in a firm grip, and began shaking it sternly to control my own nervous shaking. I worried the attraction I felt toward him was too obvious and would be noticeable.

He laughed. "A strong woman...I like that," he said calmly raising his brow, tilting his head and smiling earnestly.

It was unnerving. His son, Giacomo, was quite similar to him in that he also had short dark hair, a gorgeous bronze complexion, and dark brown eyes. They both exuded confidence and were undoubtedly people persons. While everyone shared small talk, I stared at Mimi to avoid coming undone.

Although he was strikingly handsome and smelled delicious, he was presumably married making me exceedingly trepidatious. His presence was overwhelming and the scent of him made me quiver. Recalling how ruffled I became when I first smelled him at the grocery store yesterday, I became jittery. And then, noticing he was not wearing a wedding ring, I shuddered.

Needing to collect myself, I invited everyone to my back patio for cocktails. As I led the way Zeek gently put his palm on the small of my back sending tiny shivers up and down my spine, and for a moment I forgot how to speak.

"You don't remember me?" he said, turning his face toward mine.

I looked back at him with puzzlement. I was tongue-tied for the first time in my life. I sped up walking slightly ahead of him so I didn't feel him, or smell him.

"Oh, that's right, Derek told me. You only speak dog language," he said chuckling.

I attempted to race ahead, but he caught up to me.

And in a benevolent manner he leaned in with his face inches from mine. "My dog's name is Faith, by the way. Ring a bell?"

I began giggling like a school girl and then stopped walking, composed myself, and turned to face him. "Yes, of course. You're Luca Marcello's brother. I ran into you at the grocery store yesterday. I remember smelling you…I mean…when I saw you, um…I…uh, well…," I coughed and began fluffing my curls, unraveled by my own Freudian slip.

"Y-e-e-es?" Zeek responded, in a deep voice with an enormous grin on his face, evidently amused by how flustered I was.

"You have a distinct smell is all, a good smell. I just can't place, um, the type of cologne it is, er, uh…or scent…is all," I said, while looking everywhere except into his dreamy eyes, as I continued to neurotically fluff my hair and fidget my weight from side to side.

Then I abruptly turned and briskly walked away from Zeek toward the outdoor patio near the Jacuzzi to retrieve my champagne flute, desperately needing a sip to calm my nerves.

I wasn't sure if I could handle being in this moment, being that it was unusually surreal. I attempted to busy myself by cleaning the champagne flutes at the outside bar, while Mimi assisted Giacomo with removing the bongos from the truck and carrying them onto the patio. Derek wandered into the living room and was unpretentiously snooping around, examining the makeshift operating system of my music equipment with its stereo speakers askew and wires tangled about, looking for a way to improve the sound quality I imagine. Obviously, his area of expertise, not mine. We always felt comfortable to enter one another's space, like brother and sister, with an unspoken welcoming permission to intrude.

As I began to pour everyone a glass of Champagne, Zeek walked toward me to transfer the glasses to the high standing table near the Jacuzzi.

Precisely as he went to garner a few glasses, he leaned in and in a whispering voice revealed his secret scent. "It's Kirk's Castile bar soap…if you must know."

"Serious???" I responded, my face flushed, still processing the fact *Mister S* was at my house.

He gave a perfunctory nod and smiled.

It made sense now why the scent provoked a familiar, safe, loving feeling. I used the same bar soap whenever camping with my family growing up. Not only was my nasal receptor responding to his presence, I could feel my entire body on blazing hot fire simmering inside and out as my knees began to buckle. *How can he have such a physically extreme effect on me when I know nothing about him?* The last time I remember feeling this weak in the knees with such desire was at age sixteen, for my high school crush Miles Bocelli. *Miles was Italian, too.*

Once everyone had a drink in hand and Mimi and I were able to sink back into the Jacuzzi, comforted by the bubbling hot security blanket of steamy water, I was able to feel more centered. I articulately murmured to Mimi how I'd quite the story to tell her later, but I don't think she heard me. She was too preoccupied with staring at Giacomo, who was staring back at her as intently; their eyes filled with naïve childlike hope.

Once Giacomo was able to break his infatuated gaze from Mimi, he procured his guiro instrument from the truck and joined Derek and Zeek, and the three of them played a formidable set of impressive rhythm, which sounded like Afro-Cuban percussion enchantment. And, from my point of view, it exhibited uninhibited sex appeal. I kept looking at Zeek with ardor, like a moonstruck roadie, as if he was some sort of celebrity. I would look away whenever I felt someone might notice I was staring with ogling sex-starved eyes.

After I complemented the three of them on their marvelously entertaining bongo performance they joined us by sitting on the edge of the hot tub, while Zeek expounded upon his life being raised with an Italian father and a Cuban mother. His mother's siblings all played the bongos, which is where he got his early exposure to the instrument, at the impressionable age of three, and eventually discovering it to be his passion as well as his meditation. He taught his son, Giacomo, soon after his wife died of lung cancer, as a way to help with the healing process. Mimi and I gasped when he shared the particulars, although he didn't take much time to reveal his feelings of loss, other than to say that he used music as a way to focus his energy and deal with the painful memories. I could see how drumming could therapeutically drown out pain, it's like transcendental acupuncture massaging the organs in your body by repairing tissue with a healing vibration. It made sense to me as my entire body felt tremendously relaxed after the set.

And then abruptly changing gears, Zeek went on a "soap box" ranting about his engrossing and adventurous life in the city and in the wine industry as a master wine sommelier sales rep-consultant, and single parent. Speaking with large gestures he was boisterous, comical, witty and expressive. We were all mesmerized and immensely charmed by his magnetic personality. He also illuminated how he and Derek connected musically six months ago, when he hired him to renovate his new abode. When Derek noticed Zeek's bongo set in the living room, he revealed how he'd been taking bongo lessons for the past five years and was looking for a partner to jam along with him. It was a moving and male-bonding moment for both of them, making them fast friends.

Derek interceded, "In fact, we are currently forming a bongo band and hoping to perform at the Labyrinthine Lodge. You know, it's that new hoity-toity restaurant that overlooks Lake Shasta. So we need as much practice as we can get."

Feeling more at ease after three glasses of champagne, I turned to Zeek. "Wait a minute. Your brother, Luca, is a chef at that restaurant isn't he?"

"Yes, in fact, he is."

"He'd always bring in flyers, advertising upcoming events that they offer, whenever he had an appointment set up to have his dog groomed at my salon. I love their logo!"

"Yeah, isn't that the coolest design? Well, they all know me pretty well there, too. I happen to deliver them the best wine in northern California, so I have a feeling I'll have no problem setting up a gig. It just so happens that they want us to perform right now. I just want to be sure we're ready, first."

"Uh, yeah…me, too," Derek said with trepidation in his voice.

Zeek laughed.

"I've always wanted to go there and check out their menu…s-o-o-o, let me know when you officially set a date to perform and I'll show up," I avowed, and then turned toward Mimi. "You want to go with me?"

But she didn't hear me. She was totally entrenched in a conversation with Giacomo, who was as enamored with her as she with him. You could tell that he wanted to eat her up; he was staring at her as if she was the cherry on his parfait. How sublime to witness the innocent sweet tooth of young love.

Zeek then turned around and, although he was solely facing in my direction, proceeded to invite us all to try a bottle of his wineries newest and best-selling Italian varietal red wine: Chianti Classico. Incidentally, he had a case of the Bravante red wine in the back of the truck which he had planned to offer Derek as a gift.

"I'll get you another case, Derek, I promise."

Derek smiled. "Not necessary. Seize the moment, I say. Wine is best shared in the company of others, anyway."

After our universal response was eagerly enthusiastic, Zeek ran to fetch the case of red wine from the truck. Once the box of Bravante wine was reclaimed and sitting at Zeek's feet on the patio he retrieved a bottle and gave a speech, claiming the exceptionally elegant noteworthy wine was an impeccably good year with intense aromas, inferring that this particular Chianti was his favorite varietal. After he ardently described the wine as being fresh and full-bodied with a feminine feel of silky tannins and floral aromatics, I felt tingly all over my body. We were all sold, even Mimi who is not typically a wine drinker. Who wouldn't want to taste something that sounded like it pleasured your erogenous zones?

I lifted myself out of the hot tub and flung on my long, red, white and blue, long-sleeve, semi-sheer cardigan and went into the kitchen to acquire wine glasses for us all. When I returned, Derek was away from the hot tub and sitting in one of the Adirondack chairs facing the Jacuzzi and Mimi was sitting up on the ledge of the hot tub with her feet in the water. Giacomo was sitting as close as he possibly could next to her with his hand on her leg, which he quickly removed when he saw me. Zeek had independently located the corkscrew from behind the outdoor bar and uncorked a couple bottles of wine. So I elected to assist him, by pouring each one of us a glass, hoping the slight trembling of my hands caused by the irresistible smell of him near me wouldn't give away my overwhelming attraction. I took my glass of wine and retreated to the Jacuzzi where I could dip back into the steamy bubbling water and hide my lustful appetite and save myself from obvious embarrassment.

After we all had a sip and expressed our utter delight in the phenomenal aftertaste of the Chianti Zeek disclosed more personal anecdotes from his life, which we all pleasurably anticipated since he was such an enchanting raconteur.

Discovering Zeek was originally from Italy made my heart flutter, although he didn't live in the country long. He was originally born in Rome, Italy, but only lived there until the age of five. His family uprooted him and his older brother, Luca, to Portland, Oregon, where his Italian dad, Giovanni, retained employment as a technical writer, and his Cuban mom, Mia, opened a wine bistro which both Luca and Zeek worked at. It is no wonder he's a sommelier after growing up in the wine industry. They had to move to America due to his father not finding decent work in Italy. Incidentally, in any metropolitan city in the United States his dad could get paid a considerable wage as an IT tech. His dad, Giovanni Marcello, is a brilliant technical writer who writes technical manuals, online help, users guides, project plans, test plans, system manuals—all those dull but quintessential guides for us layman. It's anti-social, laborious, exhausting, tedious work, but admirable. Fascinating how both of his sons chose work of a more social nature, although not entirely surprising since their mother was in the customer service industry with her wine bistro.

I was flummoxed, hearing how Zeek had lived in Portland about the same time I did. When I had my tragic upheaval to Portland at the age of sixteen, Zeek—who is eight and a half years my senior—was nearly twenty-five. At the age of sixteen, twenty-five seemed like a colossal age difference, but in midlife our age difference seems inconsequential.

Refreshingly, Zeek is an open book and willingly divulged his life story without much prompting. I learned a great deal about him, his family and his past. When he left Portland at the age of twenty-six, shortly after I moved there, he moved to San Francisco to hone his literary vintage skills by attending San Francisco Wine School and enrolling in the Court of Masters Sommelier program. After passing the rigorous series of exams he achieved the Advanced Sommelier Diploma and also met his wife; a waitress at Wolfgang Puck's, a fine dining establishment he and his classmates frequented. I was mystified when he revealed Wine and Spirits magazine named him "Best New Sommelier in America 1988." *Cool!* He also explained the reason he travels all over California is because he works as a Wine Sales Rep for Bravante Vineyards, located in the Napa Valley.

The story of his family was almost as engrossing. His brother, Luca, Zeek's one and only older brother, uprooted his lovely wife, Liberty, and their twin girls, Lori Rose and Lilla Rose, to Redding because he received a terrific job offer as head chef at the Labyrinthine Lodge. Their dad stayed in Portland for some time before moving to California. Although it wasn't until after his wife had died and he sold the bistro that he decided to move to Mount Shasta to retire. He had long wanted to be near his sons, since with Italians family is everything. When Zeek would visit his dad he found the area rather appealing. And after his wife passed away he decided being near family and the change of scenery and clean mountainous air would be a healthy respite for him and his son, and eventually sought to purchase a home.

In addition, I learned that Zeek purchased the house next door to mine nearly six months ago. It may seem peculiar why I don't know who my neighbors are, but in McCloud it's easy to live next door to someone and never meet them. Most lots are two to five acres in size and, due to the rolling hills and trees, most houses are not visible from the road. The house that Zeek now lives in had been vacant for the previous ten years. I heard through clients of mine who also live in McCloud that the family didn't want to sell because it had sentimental value to their grandfather who helped build it. But, according to Zeek, the grandfather died a year ago which altered their outlook and they decided it would be best for everyone, financially and emotionally, to dispose of the property.

Intriguingly, Zeek actually met Derek through his wife, Gretchen, as she ordered regularly from the Bravante winery. And when Zeek found out Gretchen's husband had his own construction business, he wanted to meet him and set up a barter of wine for construction materials. Derek was eager to assist, because it pleased his wife to get a discount on wine.

While Zeek was amusing us with his juicy past, Mimi and Giacomo escaped to the poolside. And whilst mostly hidden from all of us through the trees, I could partially see that they were engaged in heavy flirtatious petting mixed with some canoodling. And, although I was thoroughly enjoying Zeek's enthralling stories the night sky was appearing overhead, indicating time was fleeting, and I seriously needed to excuse myself to the bathroom before my bladder exploded. A chill enveloped me when I stood out of the warmth of the Jacuzzi, the crisp air much cooler than earlier. I swiftly towel dried myself and then snagged my semi-sheer cardigan while Derek and Zeek changed the topic to the latest score of the most recent Giants game. Thankfully, I had little interest in the game and wouldn't feel I was missing out on any hot conversation by leaving the scene. Before rushing to the bathroom I crossed through the living room, snatched the remote off the coffee table and inserted an eclectic CD that I'd burned titled "Uplift Me." It contains every song that empowers me with instantaneous euphoria. After clicking the remote to set the television to CD mode and turning up the volume so the music could be heard outside, I fled down the corridor to the main bathroom.

After powdering my face, reapplying lipstick and brushing my frazzled, red hair with a pick, I remembered that I wanted to locate my phone and call Kat. *Oh no! I left it in the kitchen.* If I was expeditious I anticipated I could seize it, without being

253

noticed through the screen door by Zeek or Derek. I didn't want to appear rude for calling someone while I had company. Skidding down the hallway and turning through the opening, I sped into the kitchen. Eyeing my cellphone lingering near the sink, I leapt forward and picked it up, and with my head down swiped my thumb to unlock the screen. But at the distinct moment I pivoted to retreat with full speed toward the bedroom, I physically collided head on into a six-foot-four, tall, sexy dark-haired Italian. As my phone went flying through the air, I slipped and was forced to clasp onto his arms. And that's when I felt the weight of my body pulled up into a tight embrace. I was embarrassed while at the same time aroused. I felt Zeek's hard body against mine and for an instant ached for him to kiss me.

But instead of letting on to what I was feeling I pushed him away, unskillfully fumbled with my cardigan making sure it was still on, and then clumsily responded. "I...I...uh, I'm so sorry."

"Nothing to be sorry for," he said, in his alluring husky voice, making my insides flutter.

I promptly began looking to see where my cellphone landed, attempting to remain in control. Fortunately, it landed on my soft, red floor rug and didn't break. I picked it up, closing the open keyboard and set it on the kitchen counter. Feeling completely ridiculous with Zeek standing in the kitchen, smirking with delight at my scatterbrain behavior, I nervously reached into the bottom drawer of the refrigerator where I store bottled waters and retrieved a couple. After I offered him one he revealed that it was precisely why he came inside in the first place.

Feeling rattled as well as dehydrated from all the wine I faced away from Zeek, uncapped the water and chugged almost half the bottle. After I turned around to witness Zeek doing the same thing we simultaneously let out an audible refreshed sound, making us both giggle at our timely mimicry. Once our laughter subsided he stopped and stared at me coquettishly, prompting me to fill the awkward silence with chatter. I knew my imperceptible hippie freak flag was flying when all I could think about was *The Secret Language of Relationships* book. I anxiously wanted to go search for written acknowledgment confirming our compatibility as healthy. Decades ago, when I glanced at Zeek's driver's license at the movie theater, I never had time to view the month he was born, only the year. The bohemian chic in me was dying to find out his sun sign and whether our affinity for one another was harmoniously written in the stars.

I didn't want to come across as a nutcase, so I leaned on the counter and preoccupied myself by stacking the mail into neat piles and presented the question in a clever and flattering manner. "S-o-o-o, can I ask you how old you are? I mean, you're in great shape. My guess would be...forty-three?"

"Funny girl, uh, not even close. I wish I was still in my forties. More like fifty-one," he clarified, shaking his head in amusement.

"Get out?! Well, you look...um, incredible. And you're still young. Fifty-one is a terrific age!" I said, smiling and busying myself by walking around past him toward the sink to grab a paper towel and wipe down the counter top.

He grinned while his eyes followed me, seemingly unaware my line of questioning was for astrological research.

I continued to wipe down the counter, lifting items and wiping under them. "So, when will you be turning fifty-two? Do you have a birthday soon? Wait! Is today your birthday?" I asked, stiffening my body with my right hand palm-up in his face as if I was psychic.

"You're a goof ball...I like it," he said with a twinkling in his eyes.

I blushed as he leaned in toward me.

"And no, my birthday is not today, little miss sassy pants. It's February tenth," he said, raising his eyebrows. *Did he just call me miss sassy pants?*

I couldn't think clearly, but my internal hippie chick did a mini somersault for successfully getting the information necessary to research whether we were simpatico. *Isn't it obvious you have something unique with Zeek? What is wrong with you,*

Melody Rae? Can't you feel it in your gut? You belong together! You don't need a book to confirm what you already know to be true.

I knew my instincts were right and I didn't need written proof, but I wanted it, nonetheless. I deeply wanted literary confirmation to affirm the authenticity of what I was feeling. Knowing Zeek was an Aquarius, similar to many friends and relatives who I have an instant connection to, was a testament in itself. I've always had an affinity toward Aquarius', although I've never dated one. I couldn't stand it any longer. I had to justify a retreat to the bathroom to glance at *The Secret Language of Relationships* book stacked on my magazine shelf. Thankfully, Zeek accepted the "having to pee" excuse to exit the room.

After I shut and locked the door to the bathroom I put the toilet seat lid down, sat and swiftly flipped to the page number of our combination. Blown away, I let out a partial squeal and then stopped, fearing I could be heard through the door. With my hand over my smiling mouth, I read. Best at: love. My heart fluttered as my stomach swirled in a parade of tumbles. Immediately anxious to text Kat, but knowing it was not the right time to do so, I inhaled and exhaled slowly to contain my overwhelming feeling of excitement. Then I read the title for our combination, the tenth of February with the third of December which read: forceful persuasion. Then I read the first line of the paragraph:

Because of their unusual natures and special requirements, these two may recognize each other as soul-mates.

My jaw dropped and my heart danced as a tear trickled down my cheek. I wiped the tear away and continued to read. The second line read:

Furthermore, they are both quite likely to have suffered more than their share of rejection and misunderstandings before meeting each other.

The veracity and understated nature of what I had read generated an audible laugh. And the realization that this guy was going to assuredly "get me" caused my eyes to glaze over bringing about more tears. I grabbed a tissue as I read a tiny bit more. The title for his week read: the week of acceptance. Our strengths as a couple read: sharing, soulful, risk-taking. Abruptly, I slammed the book closed. I couldn't take the time to read any longer, I had to get back in the kitchen. I can't let this guy get away. He was my soul mate.

I returned to the kitchen. *He's still here. Yay!* I did a little happy dance inside myself. He was standing and leaning back on the counter and smiling with arms folded in a confident but approachable manner, appearing as if he'd been waiting for me. And the music radiating from the speakers seemed to be reverberating louder than before.

"Did you turn up the volume?" I asked, motioning with my right index toward the digital player.

"Maybe," he said with his tongue in his cheek and a half-smile on his face.

I smiled.

And right then Eric Clapton's song *"Wonderful Tonight"* concluded and Rickie Lee Jones' *"Danny's All-Star Joint"* song came on setting the idyllic mood. I was feeling the same way I'd felt at age sixteen dancing on the street with Miles Bocelli. My heart was pounding out of my chest and telling my body to send in the paramedics because I was going into cardiac arrest. Of course, no need to call nine-one-one, my symptoms were not life threatening. Although the euphoric feeling was so overpowering, I imagined myself floating upward.

"Whoa," Zeek lamented, rubbing his strong jawline and looking off to the side as if thinking back in time.

"What?" I asked amusedly.

"This song…Rickie Lee Jones...brings me back."

"Me too," I said, as my face blushed recalling the past.

But feeling more at ease with the music booming, I lifted myself up onto the kitchen counter top and scooted near where he was leaning against the counter. I'd completely forgotten about Derek, Mimi and Giacomo, who were still outside. Appreciating a man who enjoys the same type of music, I tilted my head from side to side with the rhythm, quiet and melodically reciting the lyrics. Zeek began to sing along with me. Side by side, we sang in unison as our voices vibrated together, making me want him more. I wanted him to turn and kiss me.

Thankfully, the less memory provoking Taylor Swift song *"22"* came on next, because I had to break the carnal tension as it was too much for me. "So, what memory does the Rickie Lee Jones song stir up for you?" I asked inquisitively while shivering inside with tingly butterflies.

"Oh, well, actually, it's a pretty cool story," Zeek simpered and then stood back from the counter and turned to face me. "The first time I heard that song I was in downtown Portland having a drink at Freddie's, this little jazz club next door to my mother's wine bistro…um…I want to say circa 1984. It was the Fourth of July and my brother and I were sitting near an open window which faced the street, right? And…," he said, and then chuckled.

I gripped the counter stunned by the words coming out of his mouth. *Is this for real? Uh-uh, no way!*

"These two young teenagers are walking by and they stop and then start, like ballroom style dancing, right there on the sidewalk in front of the bar. Totally, serious! I will never forget it. The young kids were singing along to this song *'Danny's All-Star Joint'* and performing what looked to be a well-rehearsed routine. The bartender even turned up the volume to the song while everyone in the pub gathered around the front windows hollering and applauding. It was really somethin'. I remember the young girl had gorgeous, thick, long, curly red hair, kinda like yours; it caught my eye. She seemed like a real firecracker layered from head to toe in patriotic attire. She even wore these star speckled tights," Zeek said, and then laughed.

I sat with my hand over my mouth in shock unable to form any words. Before he could say anymore, I slid off the counter and retreated into the living room.

"Where are you going?" he crowed.

I swiftly obtained a photo album from the cedar chest in the living room, near where my dogs were snoozing, and then sat on the couch and began flipping through the pages. Zeek followed me into the room, looking at me with puzzlement. Still unable to speak or face him, I continued to flip through the pages while motioning with my left hand for him to sit near me. He did.

"What?" he asked, bewildered by my behavior.

After locating the group picture of me and my theatre classmates taken in 1984, on the Fourth of July at Rubino's sandwich shop, I sat the album on Zeek's lap, and with my index finger pointed to me in the photograph.

I breathed in. "That was me," I said, placing my hands in a prayer position to my face, awaiting his response.

"What?" Zeek said, shaking his head in disbelief.

Overwhelmed by this coincidence, I began to giggle and chortle. "Crazy, huh?"

"Are you kidding me? What? No way!"

I nodded.

Zeek rubbed his chin, looked at me and then back at the photo, held it closer to his face and then shook his head. "I've never been a huge believer in signs, but I'm starting to think this is one."

I continued to nod with my hand covering my mouth.

"Well, you know, that isn't the only other time our bodies have crossed paths?"

"What?" I snapped, shocked by his boldness.

"Well, let me see if I can refresh your memory," he said beaming and shifting toward me on the couch.

In reaction to his forwardness, I leaned back, lifting my left leg to my chest, clasping my hands around my knee and holding myself in a comforting embrace. *Did he remember the other times we've seen one another over the years?*

He looked at me with guile. "I seem to recall a comely young lady wearing a cashier name tag at a midnight showing of *The Rocky Horror Picture Show*, whose physical beauty actually caused me to spill my popcorn and soda. Ring a bell?"

I winced with one eyebrow raised. *He remembers me?*

"I also remember a lovely young thing sitting at a front row table in a comedy club breaking my concentration, causing me to spill my drink all over my buddy. Sound familiar?"

Biting my right thumb, I shrunk farther into the couch stunned by his accurate memory recall.

"Oh, I also seem to remember a gorgeous lady that I spotted across the parlor of North Beach Pizza in the city, who caused me to stumble over my wife's jacket and spill her glass," Zeek spewed while leaning closer to me.

At this point, I had both legs nestled to my chest with a pillow held close to my left side as a barrier. *I can't believe Mister S is in my house and remembers all those times we encountered one another over the years.* I was beyond perplexed.

Zeek leaned farther toward me on the couch and began to caress my leg while continuing to share his memories. "Of course, I can't forget camping up at Green Valley and seeing a beautiful young lady on a bridge, who took me so completely off guard that I spilled my hot coffee all over my son," he grimaced.

My hands were covering my face, as I let out an aching laugh.

"Oh, and of course, I remember a vivacious young lady at the Red Bluff rodeo who startled me into dropping my drink cup, which then spilled all over my friends playing cards. Uh-huh, yeah, that made me real popular. And I can't forget the time that I drove my brother, Luca, to pick up his dog at Petite Paws the day before Thanksgiving, only to be seduced by a gorgeous dog groomer peeking her head out the window, which caused me to knock over the hot cup of coffee into my lap," he sneered playfully.

I giggled amused, charmed and mystified.

"Do you realize that every single time I've seen you over the years, I've spilt my drink? Don't you think that says something?"

"Yeah…you have a drinking problem," I snickered.

"No. I don't have a drinking problem, little miss sassy pants...I have a Melody Rae problem. And she is the only elixir I need," he said, pulling me toward him.

Feeling his sweet breath on my cheek and smelling his refreshingly clean Castile bar soap scent while gazing into his warm dark brown honest eyes, I felt closer to him than I have with anyone in my life. I desperately yearned for him to kiss me.

Then he caressed my face with the back of his hand and looked deep into my eyes. "I'm sorry it took me this long to figure out that I was being sent a sign, and that you were my destiny."

Then he held me close and kissed me longingly, seductively and passionately with a burning intensity. I felt like we were floating on a billowy cloud high up in the sky.

I was blissfully lost in the most sensual, amorous, tender, libidinous and steamy kiss that I've ever experienced in my entire life, until vibrating through the speakers the song *"I Can See Clearly Now"* by Johnny Nash came streaming through. We both stopped kissing. And by the way in which we were staring at each other, it was clear we were thinking the same thing; the lyrics reflected our synchronicity.

"Things are finally clear," he proclaimed.

"It's no longer raining," I said while looking at him with an emotional sparkle in my eye.

"This is *our* song."

I was nodding and smiling while he closed his eyes with an expression of unbelievable joy on his face.

And then he lifted me off the couch and twirled me around guiding my body down into a full embrace. And once the song ended we could hear the faint sounds of firecrackers bursting outside in the distance. Glancing over at the clock above the plush-cushioned inglenook, where I desired to sit and snuggle with Zeek later on, I noticed the late hour. It was daunting how fugacious time can be, and I wished that I could freeze this ineffable moment.

"Let's go!" Zeek encouraged, breaking me from my trance, grabbing my hand and pulling me out to the patio. Both dogs followed us outside to where Mimi, Giacomo and Derek were already sprawled out on lawn chairs and covered in blankets on the opposite side of the pool. I ran back inside to snag a couple more throw blankets and some bottled waters, while Zeek obtained a corkscrew, a bottle of wine and two glasses, and then shoved two lawn chairs together for us.

When I returned, and sat next to him, he handed me a taste of wine and clinked my glass. "Here's to seeing clearly now."

I grinned. "Here's to serendipitous encounters, um, magical timing…and the pleasant aftertaste of Chianti."

"Well said."

Then we gently kissed and he placed his warm hand on top of mine and we sat back to watch the fireworks commence. I felt on top of the world. Looking out across the night sky I could see the fireworks sparkle in the distance. They were being set off from an open field five minutes away where the community gathers for an annual Fourth of July Picnic celebration. Although the fireworks weren't directly over our heads they felt mystical, as I marveled at being surrounded by love in the warmth of my own backyard.

After the powerful culmination of the fireworks display, Zeek and I shared our hair-raising, transcendent and unnerving serendipitous encounters over the years with Mimi, Giacomo and Derek, who all agreed something divine and unearthly spiritually unparalleled was happening in the universe and destiny played a role. And I was secretly convinced that we weren't meant to end up together any sooner than now; timing was perfect. Not only because he wasn't available before, but because I wasn't in a healthy place before, emotionally or physically. I wasn't truly ready for him, until now.

The rest of the evening flowed miraculously smooth like magic. I finally understood what my happily married friends were talking about when they said: "My soul knew he was the right guy for me."

Derek crashed in the guest bedroom while Mimi and Giacomo slept on the sectional sofa. The next morning when I walked Zeek out the front door, Mimi and Derek's vehicles were gone; everyone had left before we awoke. Zeek had planned to walk home to his house, since it was less than an acre away, but before he did, he kissed me once more, playfully and then fervidly with intensity. And then he indicated that he would call me later on that day. I waved, but didn't watch him walk the entire distance down the driveway. Instead, I sprinted inside and picked up my phone, pressing number five on speed dial.

"Kat, you need to sit. You will never believe what happened to me last night," I chattered, and then went into a long rant, bubbling over with enthusiasm like a fountain struggling to get it all out.

"Okay, slow down, Melody Rae. I'm comin' over, I need to hear about this in person!" she said excitedly.

When Kat arrived she was not surprised to hear that Zeek was my soul mate—she suspected it all along.

Zeek Marcello is my Italian entrée, my **luxurious king salmon: a choice wild fish, top-of-the-line among species with a pronounced, rich flavor which can be enjoyed in a variety of ways.**

Two years later...

Mimi and Giacomo were engaged, the day before Zeek and I married in a quiet ceremony in Tahoe on New Year's Eve, the thirty-first of December, 2012. Zeek allowed Mimi and Giacomo to live in his house since he had moved into mine. With Derek's assistance they managed to remodel the interior of my cabin with expansions, making it much larger and more livable, redesigning it into a stylish chateau.

On the eve of Fourth of July, 2013, we were having an Independence Day celebration and serving an array of creative appetizers that Zeek had finessed together using fresh fruits and vegetables from his garden: melon kabobs, heirloom tomatoes stuffed with summer succotash, watermelon salad with feta and mint served with bruschetta, and crostini. As it turns out, Zeek does most of his shopping at Whole Foods and Trader Joe's and is also an avid gardener, and almost as talented of a chef as his brother. I no longer needed written proof, as my heart was utterly convinced he was written in the stars for me.

It was not intended to be a wedding party but, since our actual wedding ceremony was so private and unceremonious, many who weren't able to celebrate our joining of hearts arrived to congratulate us. I was feeling blessed to see everyone who I hadn't seen in what seemed like an eternity. We invited a variety of our friends as well as our entire families. Zeek's dad, Giovanni, and his older brother, Luca, showed up with his wife, Liberty, and their twin girls. Kat arrived with her daughter, Brooklyn, and her new mate, Steven. Tessa arrived with her loving husband, Sean. My ethereal mother, Katherine Lee, and extraordinary father, Aaron, Sr., (Big Guy) arrived shortly thereafter. And of course, my six older brothers showed up with their wives and kids, too. There were over thirty five people mingling about the patio. Some were sitting on the edge of the pool with their feet dangling in the water, but most were standing about the poolside facing the stage and chatting. In the background, Eric Clapton's *"San Francisco Bay Blues"* song played over the loud speakers. Thanks to Zeek (mister multi-talented) it could be heard in surround-sound now. Substantially massive speakers were arranged all around the pool area. And my outdoor patio never looked so festive with tons of red, white and blue lanterns strewn about the trees. Fourth of July banners and lights decorated the stage area, while the pool was sprinkled with red, white and blue floating candles, and the glasses as well as the appetizers were all adorned with patriotic colors.

Zeek's bongo band were gathering equipment and setting up on the designated stage off to the left of the swimming pool. They had expanded by one auxiliary member, Orrin, and becoming a local hit at the taverns in Mount Shasta and popularly sought after in Redding pubs, as well. They were a heterogeneous bunch. The newest member, a young twenty-something named Orrin, with a strong resemblance to Billy

Idol, was tall and lanky wearing a bright fluorescent yellow tank top, long, baggy, white shorts with excessive pockets and spiked bleached hair, tattoos, and an earring in his nose. Giacomo, with his Italian Ryan Gosling look, was wearing a Giants baseball cap backward, an orange T-shirt, Dockers khaki cargo shorts and was barefooted. Zeek, with his Robert Downey, Jr., features, was wearing his typical attire: sunglasses, royal blue, short-sleeve, button up shirt and untucked khaki slacks with Birkenstocks. Derek, the Dr. Drew clone, was wearing his glasses, typical Levi jean pants, a fitted, tucked in brown T-shirt with the band logo on the front—ZDOG. All the bongos were inscribed with the logo ZDOG: an acronym for Zeek, Derek, Orrin and Giacomo.

"ZDOG's in the house!" I heard Giacomo bellow over the microphone. Zeek took a moment to help me pour glasses of his favorite Bravante Chianti Classico red wine at the outdoor bar, while Mimi delivered appetizers to the tables we'd set up earlier for the performance. When Giacomo wasn't glued to Mimi's side, he was near the stage setting up and chatting with Orrin.

When Giacomo announced the band would begin in a few minutes Zeek walked toward the stage. Then he turned back toward me, winked and blew me a kiss. It still sends shivers up my spine and astounds me that he exists, and that he chose to marry me.

In the microphone, Zeek announced the band members and then paused, turned to face in my direction, and toasted his wine glass in the air. "Our band wouldn't be successful without the support of my lovely, original, funny, witty, gorgeous and supremely sexy wife, Melody Rae. I owe my happiness and success all to you, baby. Because of you, I can see clearly now. Tu sei l'amore della mia vita; mio tutto." Italian translation: you are the love of my life; my everything.

How I adore when Zeek talks in his native Italian tongue. With loving tears welling up in my eyes I blew my king salmon a kiss, which he caught on his cheek. Some applauded loudly, while others whistled at his public bravado of affection for me. Smiling from behind the outdoor wine bar I toasted my glass up in the air toward his, blushing from the inside out, feeling my whole body tremble from the deep connection we share. I am blessed beyond measure, and in a way I never dreamed possible.

Reflecting on my past, I can see clearly now how my eating habits had played a monumental role in who I attracted into my life, and who I craved. I no longer craved Peter. I had craved Peter in the same way I had craved a Hostess Twinkie. And similarly, Peter was an unhealthy, exhilarating rush, providing me with a temporary high and leaving me always wanting more. Even after the man cheated on my repeatedly, I wanted another taste. I can only hope that he has evolved and moved forward on a healthier path, as I have; I sincerely want only the best for him. After divesting myself of all artificial products and processed garbage, I no longer craved foods that were poisonous and no longer attracted unhealthy. Now that I eat healthy, I think healthy, which makes me feel healthy and invariably attract healthy. And healthy doesn't have to be bland, or boring; Zeek is neither. And he is more than good for me, he is my sustenance.

I must say however, I am glad to have met Zeek later in life. Meeting later in life profoundly has its advantages. By the time Zeek and I had met, we were both metaphorically living in the attic and had been through so many major life experiences that we knew what we wanted. Neither of us was living in an illusion as to what the other was about. We weren't apprehensive to ask the deeper questions, or uneasy about hearing the answers. There was no fear on either end. We didn't overreact by jumping to immature conclusions about each other, or discover ways to blame, attack or feel superior. We were able to listen to one another without judgment, showing compassion in a mentally balanced way.

Although I feel enriched and blessed to have found the love of my life, had I not met Zeek I would have remained single and prevailed. I honestly believe that a person can have a healthy, balanced, fully satisfying life without a partner. And who am I to know what my relationship with Zeek will be in the future, but I do know what it is like at this moment. Like, Deepak Chopra said: "Whatever relationships you have attracted in your life at this moment are precisely the ones you need in your life at this moment."

After feeding my body in a healthy way, I was able to evolve into a spiritually and intellectually healthier being. My physical interior-self began to match my soulful interior-self, forming a sense of wholeness. And my wholeness (my balance) attracted Zeek, someone who also feels balance within. It feels good to finally see the results of my inner work paying off. I want to sit right here in this moment of pure bliss and appreciate it for what it is, savoring it like a delicious bite of king salmon with a sip of Chianti red wine.

And feeling blessed, no matter how little you have, is the key. I feel blessed every day to have met Zeek, but also to have experienced all I have. I learned a great deal from all the mistakes I'd made before meeting Zeek; and feel grateful for every man I was fortunate enough to know intimately, as well as every friend, acquaintance and family member who shared my world. All the men and women from my past have helped me to become who I am today.

The unhealthy people provided me with hard experience while the nefarious people provided me with valuable lessons. And the healthy people provided me with immense happiness while the special people provided me with the best memories. By being grateful for all those people I gained the courage to not settle and the wisdom to give up those things which gave me a bad aftertaste. Once I found the self-discipline to let go of all the past garbage in my life—the food and unhealthy relationships—I was able to feel confident to expect more and the willingness to open the door to change, and then it manifested into my life. Most importantly, I learned to keep moving forward and never give up because, believe it or not, unfathomable, remarkable and extraordinary things can happen later in life.

I wholeheartedly believe, deep within my soul, that Zeek is the crème de le crème king salmon for me—my pleasant aftertaste; the love of my life. And what I learned from my own journey is that love is all you need. Therefore, no matter what happens I am guaranteed buoyancy, because I love who

I am. Ergo, no matter what happens in the storyline of my life in the future, I will always be happy.

Since my luxurious king salmon, Zeek, came into my life, infecting me with his strong presence, everything I smell, hear and taste is sweeter. I can no longer smell Kirk's Castile bar soap, or hear the song *"I Can See Clearly Now"* by Johnny Nash, or taste Chianti Classico red wine without melting and becoming physically, spiritually and emotionally undone. He is my dessert, my liqueur and my music, bequeathing me with a sweet, authentic and pleasant aftertaste.

Chianti Classico

May a pleasant aftertaste permeate us all
~Melody Rae~

EAT healthy
THINK healthy
FEEL healthy
ATTRACT healthy

Melody Rae's
Uplift Me
SOUNDTRACK

Red, Red Wine—UB40
My Baby Loves Me (Just the Way That I Am)—Martina McBride
Wild Thing—Tone Loc
Super Freak—Rick James
Runaround Sue—Dion & The Belmonts
Making Our Dreams Come True—Cyndi Grecco
Gimme Some Lovin'—The Blues Brother's
Don't Worry Be Happy—Bobby McFerrin
Joy to the World—Three Dog Night
Louie Louie—The Kingsmen
Three Little Birds—Bob Marley & The Wailers
San Francisco Bay Blues—Eric Clapton
Wonderful Tonight—Eric Clapton
Danny's All-Star Joint—Rickie Lee Jones
I Can See Clearly Now—Johnny Nash
22—Taylor Swift
Little Bit Of Me—Melanie Safka
Baby (You've Got What It Takes)—Brook Benton & Dinah Washington

Melody Rae's
Relationship History
SOUNDTRACK

Lola—The Kinks (Shay)
You Don't Even Know Who I Am—Patty Loveless (Tony)
Why Don't We Get Drunk—Jimmy Buffet (Willie)
Alcohol—Brad Paisley (Peter)
I Can Get Off on You—Waylon Jennings/Willie Nelson (Kyle)

Melody Rae's Collection:
Self-Help, Spiritual, & Astrology Books

A Return to Love—Marianne Williamson
A Year of Miracles—Marianne Williamson
Everyday Grace—Marianne Williamson
A Course of Miracles—Helen Shucman & William Thetford
The Law of Divine Compensation—Marianne Williamson
A Woman's Worth—Marianne Williamson
The Gift of Change—Marianne Williamson
Enchanted Love—Marianne Williamson
The Power of Now—Eckhart Tolle
The Secret—Rhonda Byrne
The Power—Rhonda Byrne
The Magic—Rhonda Byrne
In the Meantime—Iyanla Vanzant
Yesterday I Cried—Iyanla Vanzant
The Tao of Pooh—Benjamin Hoff
The Te of Piglet—Benjamin Hoff
He's Just Not That into You—Greg Behrendt and Liz Tuccillo
Eat, Pray, Love—Elizabeth Gilbert
I'm Okay, You're Okay—Thomas A. Harris
Soul Mates—Thomas Moore
Care of the Soul—Thomas Moore
The Celestine Prophecy—James Redfield
Anatomy of the Spirit—Caroline Myss
The Experiential Guide—James Redfield and Carol Adrienne
The Secret Language of Birthdays—Gary Goldschneider
The Secret Language of Relationships—Gary Goldschneider
The Seven Habits of Highly Effective People—Stephen R. Covey
The Day You Were Born—Linda Joyce
The Personality Compass—Diane Turner & Thelma Greco
Personality Plus—Florence Littauer
Loving Each Other—Leo Buscaglia
Men Are from Mars, Women Are from Venus—John Gray, Ph.D
Choose Your Lover Carefully—Cass & Janie Jackson
Chicken Soup for the Soul—Jack Canfield, Mark Victor Hansen
Chicken Soup for the Soul (Love Stories)—Jack Canfield, Mark Victor Hansen
& Peter Vegso

Lori Jean Phipps

Lori Jean Phipps is an aficionado of comedian memoirs, avid collector of snowmen paraphernalia, rainstorm enthusiast, red wine connoisseur, candle hoarder, water baby, national public radio diehard, ardent music lover, romantic comedy movie junkie, audacious self-published author, as well as an extraordinarily passionate preschool teacher and director, who is college educated with a background in theater, psychology and child development. She received various certificates of notable accomplishments for her commitment to educating children and has self-published various children's books; *Pumpkinpants, Little Turkeys, Tis the Season to be Molly, A Make-up Surprise for My Valentine Eyes, Lizzie the Lazy Leprechaun* and *Eddie the Edible Easter Bunny,* as well as several adult books; *Get it?, Life After Lipstick, Diary of a Preschool Teacher, plentyofpickles.com* and *Aftertaste.*

You can visit the author online on Facebook @ BIG KID Books. www.facebook.com/lorijeanphippsbooks

BIG KID BOOKS

Pumpkin*pants*
Little Turkeys
Tis the Season to be Molly
A Make-up Surprise for My Valentine Eyes
Lizzie the Lazy Leprechaun
Eddie the Edible Easter Bunny
Diary of a Preschool Teacher
Get it?
Life After Lipstick
plentyofpickles.com
Aftertaste

Acknowledgments

A special thanks to my mother, *Colleen Phipps*, for being my biggest supporter and doing the first edit and *Carla Freestep*, owner of Land of Paws Pet Grooming, for offering extensive grooming wisdom in order to supply Melody Rae's character with invaluable canine training and expert knowledge about the dog grooming salon business.

Lori Jean Phipps

*Fish jokes & puns were collected from the following sites:

http://www.jokes4us.com/animaljokes/fishjokes.html
Submissions by: m.deal232, Angienoble_04, denisemedina
http://saintbosco.org/jokes/index.php?jokeid=137
http://www.jokebuddha.com/Clam/recent#ixzz2Wczryct9
http://www.punsandjokes.com/remember-when-you-lost-your-flat-fish-well-i-flounder/
http://www.puncut.com/users/RNHizzoie/
http://www.oum.ox.ac.uk/thezone/funstuff/jokes/fishjoke.htm

*One hundred most beautiful words in the English language assimilated throughout the novel.
deshoda.com/words/100-most-beautiful-words-in-the-english-language/

Ailurophile *A cat-lover.*

Assemblage *A gathering.*

Becoming *Attractive.*

Beleaguer *To exhaust with attacks.*

Brood *To think alone.*

Bucolic *In a lovely rural setting.*

Bungalow *A small, cozy cottage.*

Chatoyant *Like a cat's eye.*

Comely *Attractive.*

Conflate *To blend together.*

Cynosure *A focal point of admiration.*

Dalliance *A brief love affair.*

Demesne *Dominion, territory.*

Demure *Shy and reserved.*

Denouement *The resolution of a mystery.*

Desuetude *Disuse.*

Desultory *Slow, sluggish.*

Diaphanous *Filmy.*

Dissemble *Deceive.*

Dulcet *Sweet, sugary.*

Ebullience *Bubbling enthusiasm.*

Effervescent *Bubbly.*

Efflorescence *Flowering, blooming.*

Elision *Dropping a sound or syllable in a word.*

Elixir *A good potion.*

Eloquence *Beauty and persuasion in speech.*

Embrocation *Rubbing on a lotion.*

Emollient *A softener.*

Ephemeral *Short-lived.*

Epiphany *A sudden revelation.*

Erstwhile *At one time, for a time.*

Ethereal *Gaseous, invisible but detectable; exquisite*

Evanescent *Vanishing quickly, lasting a very short time.*

Evocative *Suggestive.*

Fetching *Pretty.*

Felicity *Pleasantness.*

Forbearance *Withholding response to provocation.*

Fugacious *Fleeting.*

Furtive *Shifty, sneaky.*

Gambol *To skip or leap about joyfully.*

Glamour *Beauty.*

Gossamer *The finest piece of thread, a spider's silk.*

Halcyon *Happy, sunny, care-free.*

Harbinger *Messenger with news of the future.*

Imbrication *Overlapping and forming a regular pattern.*

Imbroglio *An altercation or complicated situation.*

Imbue *To infuse, instill.*

Incipient *Beginning, in an early stage.*

Ineffable *Unutterable, inexpressible.*

Ingénue *A naïve young woman.*

Inglenook *A cozy nook by the hearth.*

Insouciance *Blithe nonchalance.*

Inure *To become jaded.*

Labyrinthine *Twisting and turning.*

Lagniappe *A special kind of gift.*

Lagoon *A small gulf or inlet.*

Languor *Listlessness, inactivity.*

Lassitude *Weariness, listlessness.*

Leisure *Free time.*

Lilt *To move musically or lively.*

Lissome *Slender and graceful.*

Lithe *Slender and flexible.*

Love *Deep affection.*

Mellifluous *Sweet sounding.*

Moiety *One of two equal parts.*

Mondegreen *A slip of the ear.*

Murmurous *Murmuring.*

Nemesis *An unconquerable archenemy.*

Offing *The sea between the horizon and the offshore.*

Onomatopoeia *A word that sounds like its meaning.*

Opulent *Lush, luxuriant.*

Palimpsest *A manuscript written over earlier ones.*

Panacea *A solution for all problems*

Panoply *A complete set.*

Pastiche *An art work combining materials from various sources.*

Penumbra *A half-shadow.*

Petrichor *The smell of earth after rain.*

Plethora *A large quantity.*

Propinquity *Proximity; Nearness*

Pyrrhic *Successful with heavy losses.*

Quintessential *Most essential.*

Ratatouille *A spicy French stew.*

Ravel *To knit or unknit.*

Redolent *Fragrant.*

Riparian *By the bank of a stream.*

Ripple *A very small wave.*

Scintilla *A spark or very small thing.*

Sempiternal *Eternal.*

Seraglio *Rich, luxurious oriental palace or harem.*

Serendipity *Finding something nice while looking for something else.*

Summery *Light, delicate or warm and sunny.*

Sumptuous *Lush, luxurious.*

Surreptitious *Secretive, sneaky.*

Susquehanna *A river in Pennsylvania.*

Susurrus *Whispering, hissing.*

Talisman *A good luck charm.*

Tintinnabulation *Tinkling.*

Umbrella *Protection from sun or rain.*

Untoward *Unseemly, inappropriate.*

Vestigial *In trace amounts.*

Wafture *Waving.*

Wherewithal *The means.*

Woebegone *Sorrowful, downcast.*

AFTERTASTE